THE DEVIL'S GARDEN

THE
DEVIL'S GARDEN

By

W. B. MAXWELL

Author of
IN COTTON WOOL, MRS. THOMPSON, SEYMOUR CHARLTON, ETC.

INDIANAPOLIS
THE BOBBS-MERRILL COMPANY
PUBLISHERS

PRESS OF
BRAUNWORTH & CO.
BOOKBINDERS AND PRINTERS
BROOKLYN, N. Y.

THE DEVIL'S GARDEN

The Devil playeth in a man's mind like a wanton child in a garden, bringing his filth to choke each open path, uprooting the tender plants, and trampling the buds that should have blown for the Master.

THE DEVIL'S GARDEN

THE village postmaster stood staring at an official
envelope that had just been shaken out of a mail-
bag upon the sorting-table. It was addressed to himself;
and for a few moments his heart beat quicker, with sharp,
clean percussions, as if it were trying to imitate the sounds
made by the two clerks as they plied their stampers on
the blocks. Perhaps this envelope contained his fate.

Soon the stamping was finished; the sorting went on
steadily and methodically; before long the letters and
parcels were neatly arranged in compartments near the
postmen's bags. The first delivery of the day was ready
to go forth to the awakening world.

"All through, Mr. Dale."

The postmaster struck a bell, and glanced at the clock.
Five fifty-six. Up to time, as usual.

"Now then, my lads, off with you."

The postmen had come into the sorting-room, and
were packing their bags and slinging their parcels.

"Sharp's the word."

Picking up his unopened letter, the postmaster went
through the public office, stood on the outer threshold,
and looked up and down the street.

To his left the ground sloped downward through a narrowing perspective of house-fronts and roof cornices to faint white mist, in which one could see some cattle moving vaguely, and beyond which, if one knew that it was there, one might just discern a wide space of common land stretching away boldly until the dark barrier of woods stopped it short. To his right the ground lay level, with the road enlarging itself to a dusty bay in front of the Roebuck Inn, turning by the churchyard wall, forking between two gardened houses of gentlefolk, and losing itself suddenly in the same white mist that closed the other vista. Over the veiling whiteness, over the red roofs, and high above the church tower, the sky of a glorious July morning rose unstained to measureless arches of blue.

As always in this early hour of the day, the postmaster thought of his own importance. The village seemed still half asleep—blinds down wherever he looked—lazy, money-greedy tradesmen not yet alive to their selfish enterprises—only the poor laborers of the soil already at work; and nevertheless here was he, William Dale, up and about, carrying on the continuous business of the state.

But how long would he be permitted to feel like this? Could it be possible that the end of his importance was near at hand?

On Her Majesty's Service! He opened the envelope, unfolded the folio sheet of paper that it contained, began to read—and immediately all the blood in his body seemed to rush to his head.

" I am to inform you that you are temporarily suspended." And in the pompous language of headquarters he was further informed that the person appointed to take over control would arrive at Rodchurch Road Station by the eleven o'clock train; that he himself was to come to London on the morrow, and immediately call at the G. P. O.; where, on the afternoon of that day or the morning of a subsequent day, he would be given an opportunity of stating his case in person, "agreeable to his request."

Why had they suspended him? Surely it would have been more usual if they had allowed him to leave the office in charge of his chief clerk, or if they had given charge of it to a competent person from Rodhaven, and not sent a traveler from London? The traveling inspector is the bird of evil presage: he hovers over the houses of doomed men.

William Dale ran his hand round the collarless neck of his shirt, and felt the perspiration that had suddenly moistened his skin.

He was a big man of thirty-five; a type of the strong-limbed, quick-witted peasant, who is by nature active as a squirrel and industrious as a beaver; and who, if once fired with ambition, soon learns to direct all his energies to a chosen end, and infallibly wins his way from the cart-tracks and the muck-wagons to office stools and black coats. Not yet dressed for the day, in his loose serge jacket and unbraced trousers, he looked what was termed locally "a rum customer if you had to tackle un." His dark hair bristled stiffly, his short mustache wanted a lot of combing, a russet stubble covered chin and neck; but the broad forehead and blue eyes gave a suggestion of power and intelligence to an aspect that might otherwise have seemed simply forbidding.

"Good marnin', sir."

One of the helpers at the Roebuck stables had come slouching past.

"Good mornin', Samuel."

It was still music to the ears of the postmaster when people addressed him as "Sir." Especially if, like that fellow, they had known him as a boy. But he thought now that perhaps many who spoke to him thus deferentially in truth desired his downfall.

Quite possible. One never knows. He himself wished them well, in his heart was fond of them all, and craved their regard; although he was too proud to be always seeking it, or even going half-way to meet it.

And he thought, tolerantly, that you can not have everything in this world. Your successful man is rarely a popular man. He had had the success in full measure—if it pleased them, let the envious ones go on envying him his elevated station, his domestic comfort, and his pretty wife.

As he thought of his wife all his reflections grew tender. She was probably still fast asleep; and when, presently, he went up-stairs to the private part of the house, he was careful not to disturb her.

His official clothes lay waiting for him on a chair in the kitchen. They had been brushed and folded by Mary, the servant, who sprang to attention at the appearance of her master, brought him shaving-water, arranged the square of looking-glass conveniently, assisted with the white collar and black tie, and generally proved herself an efficient valet.

She ventured to ask a question when Mr. Dale was about to leave the kitchen.

"Any news, sir?"

"News!" Mr. Dale echoed the word sternly. "What news should there be—anyway, what news that concerns *you?*

"I beg pardon, sir." Buxom, red-cheeked Mary lowered her eyes, and by voice and attitude expressed the confusion proper to a subordinate who has taken a liberty in addressing a superior. "I'm sorry, sir. But I on'y ast."

"All right," said Dale, less sternly. "You just attend to your own job, my girl."

He went down into the office, and did not come up again until an hour and a half later, when breakfast was ready and waiting. He stood near the window for a few moments, meditatively looking about him. The sunlight made the metal cover of the hot dish shine like beautifully polished silver; it flashed on the rims of white teacups, and, playing some prismatic trick with the glass sugar basin, sent a stream of rainbow tints across the two rolls and the two boiled eggs. An appetizing meal—and as comfortable, yes, as luxurious a room as any one could ask for. Through the open door and across the landing, he had a peep into the other room. In that room there were books, a piano, a sofa, hand-painted pictures in gold frames—the things that you expect to see only in the homes of gentlemen.

" Sorry I'm late, Will."

" Don't mention it, Mavis."

Mrs. Dale had come through the doorway, and his whole face brightened, softened, grew more comely. Yes, he thought, a home fit for a gentleman, and a wife fit for a king.

" Any news? "

"They've told me to go up and see them to-mor-row;" and he moved to the table. "Come on. I'm sharp-set."

"Did they write in a satisfactory way?"

"Oh, yes. Sit down, my dear, and give me my tea."

He had said that he felt hungry, but he ate without appetite. The roll was crisp and warm, the bacon had been cooked to a turn, the tea was neither too strong nor too weak; and yet nothing tasted quite right.

"Will," said his wife, toward the end of the meal, "I can see you aren't really satisfied with their answer. Do tell me;" and she stretched her hand across the table with a gesture that expressed prettily enough both appeal and sympathy.

She was a naturally graceful woman, tall and slim, with reddish brown hair, dark eyebrows, and a white skin; and she carried her thirty-two years so easily that, though the searching sunlight bore full upon her, she looked almost a young girl.

Dale took her hand, squeezed it, and then, with an affectation of carelessness, laughed jovially.

"They've appointed a deputy to take charge here during my absence."

"Oh, Will!" Mrs. Dale's dark eyebrows rose, and her brown eyes grew round and big; in a moment all the faint glow of color had left her pale cheeks, and her intonation expressed alarm and regret.

"It riled me a bit at first," said Dale firmly. "How-ever, it's no consequence—really."

"But, Will, that means——" She hesitated, and her lips trembled before she uttered the dreadful word— "That means—suspended!"

"Yes—*pro tem.* Don't fret yourself, Mav. I tell you it's all right."

"But, Will, this does change the look of things. This *is* serious—*now.*" And once more she hesitated. "Will, let me write again to Mr. Barradine."

"No," said Dale, with great determination.

"May I get Auntie to write to him? She said she knows for sure he'd help us."

"Well, he said so himself, didn't he?"

"Yes. Anything in his power!"

Dale reflected for a moment, and when he spoke again his tone was less firm.

"In his power! Of course Mr. Barradine is a powerful gentleman. That stands to reason; but all the same——Let's have a look at his letter."

"I haven't got his letter, Will."

"Haven't got his letter? What did you do with it?"

"I tore it up."

"Tore it up!" Dale stared at his wife in surprise, and spoke rather irritably. "What did you do that for?"

"You seemed angry at my taking on myself to write to him without permission—so I didn't wish the letter lying about to remind you of what I'd done."

"You acted foolish in destroying document'ry evidence," said Dale, sternly and warmly. But then immediately he stifled his irritation. "Don't you see, lassie, I'd 'a' liked to know the precise way he worded it. I'm practised to all the turns of the best sort o' correspondence, and I'd 'a' known in a twinkling whether he meant anything or nothing."

" He said he'd be glad to do what was in his power. Really he said no more."

" Very good. We'll leave it at that. He has done more than enough for us already, and I don't hold with bothering gentlemen in and out of season. Besides, this is a bit in which I don't want his help, nor nobody else's. This is between me and *them*."

He pushed away his uneaten food, stood up, and squared his big shoulders.

" Yes, but, Will dear—you, you won't be hasty when you get before them."

Dale frowned, then laughed. " Mav, trust your old boy, and don't fret." He came round the table, and laid his hand on his wife's shoulder. " My sweetheart, I'm sorry, for your sake, that this little upset should have occurred. But don't you fret. I'm coming out on top. Maybe, this is like touch-and-go. I don't say it isn't. But I know my vaarlue—and I mean to let them know it, if they don't know it already. Look at my record! Who's goin' to pick a hole in it?"

" No, but——"

" There's times when a man's got to show pluck— to stan' to's guns, and assert hisself for what he's worth. And that's what I'm going to do in the General Post Office of all England." As he said this the blood showed redly, and every line of his face deepened and hardened. " You keep a stout heart. This isn't going to shake William Dale off of his perch."

" No?" And she looked up at him with widely-opened eyes.

" No." He gave her shoulder a final pat, and laughed noisily. " No, it'll set me firmer on the road to promotion than what I've ever been. When I get

back here again, I shall be like the monkey—best part
up the palm-tree, and nothing dangerous between him
and the nuts."

All that day Dale was busy installing the deputy.

"You find us fairly in order," he said, with a pride
that did not pretend to conceal itself. "Nothing you
wouldn't call shipshape?"

"Apple-pie order," said Mr. Ridgett. "Absolutely
O. K."

Mr. Ridgett was a small sandy man of fifty, who obviously wished to make himself as agreeable as might
be possible in rather difficult circumstances. During
the afternoon he listened with an air of interested attention while Dale told him at considerable length the
series of events that had led up to this crisis.

"For your proper understanding," said the postmaster, "I'll ask you once more to cast your eye over
the position of the instruments;" and he marched
Mr. Ridgett from the sorting-room to the public office,
and showed him the gross error that had been committed in placing the whole telegraphic apparatus right at
the front, close to the window, merely screened from
the public eye and the public ear by glass partition-
work, instead of placing it all at the back, out of everybody's way. "I told them it was wrong from the first
—when they were refitting the office, at the time of the
extensions. My experience at Portsmouth had taught
me the danger."

It seemed that one evening, about three weeks ago,
a certain soldier on leave had been lounging against
the counter, close to the glass screen. On the other
side of the screen the apparatus was clicking merrily
while Miss Yorke, the telegraph clerk, despatched a

message. And all at once the soldier, who was well versed in the code, began to recite the message aloud. The postmaster peremptorily ordered him to stand away from the counter. An altercation ensued, and the soldier became so impudent that the postmaster threatened to put him outside the door. "Oh," said the soldier, "it'd take a many such as you to put me out."

"Did he say so? Really now!" And Mr. Ridgett looked at Dale critically. "I take it he was a heavy-weight, eh?"

"He gave me my work," said Dale; "and I was all three minutes at it. But *out* he went."

"Really now!" and Mr. Ridgett smiled.

"I had stopped Miss Yorke from operating. And I started her again within four minutes. That was the time, and no more, the message was delayed. That was the time it took me to renew the service with the confidence and secrecy provided by Her Majesty's Regulations. And I ask you, how else could I have acted? Was I to allow a telegram consigned to my care to be blabbed out word for word to all the world?"

"Were there many people in the office just then?"

"Two. But that makes no difference. If it had been only one—or half a one—it couldn't be permitted."

"And was the message itself of a particularly private or important nature?"

"Not as it happens. But the principle was the same."

"Just so."

As it appeared from Dale's narration, the soldier was at first willing to accept his licking in a sports-manlike spirit, was indeed quite ready to admit that he

had been the offending party; but injudicious friends—
secret enemies of Dale perhaps—had egged him on to
take out a summons for assault. When, however, Dale
appeared before the magistrates, the soldier had
changed his mind again—he did not appear, he allowed
the charge to fall to the ground. And there the matter
might have ended, ought to have ended, but for the
fact that the local Member of Parliament suddenly
made a ridiculous fuss—said it was a monstrous and
intolerable state of affairs that soldiers of the Queen
should be knocked about by her civil servants—wrote
letters to other Members of Parliament, to Government secretaries, to newspapers. Then the excitement that had been smoldering burst forth with explosive force, shaking the village, the county, the universe.

Dale, at handy grips with his superior officers, stood
firm, declined to budge an inch from his position; he
was right, and nothing would ever make him say he
was wrong.

"Ah, well," said Mr. Ridgett, "if that's the way
you looked at it. But I don't quite follow how it got
lifted out of their hands at Rodhaven, and brought
before *us*."

"I demanded it," said Dale proudly. "I wasn't
going to be messed about any further by a pack of
funking old women—for that's what they are, at Rodhaven. And I wasn't going to have it hushed over—
nor write any such letter as they asked."

"Oh, they suggested——"

"They suggested," said Dale, swelling with indignation, "that I should write regret that I had perhaps
acted indiscreet but only through over-zeal."

"Oh! And you didn't see your way to——"

"Not *me*. Take a black mark, and let my record go. No, thank you. I sent up my formal request to be heard at headquarters. I appealed to Cæsar."

Mr. Ridgett smiled good-naturedly. "Why, you're quite a classical scholar, Mr. Dale. You have your Latin quotations all pat."

"I'm a self-educated man," said Dale. "I begun at the bottom, and I've been trying to improve myself all the way to where I've risen to."

Once or twice he sought tentatively to obtain from Mr. Ridgett the moral support that even the strongest people derive from being assured that they are entirely in the right. But Mr. Ridgett, who had been sympathetic from the moment of his arrival, and who throughout the hours had been becoming more and more friendly, did not entirely respond to these hinted invitations.

"If you tell me to speak frankly," he said at last, "I should have a doubt that you've made this one false step. You haven't kept everything in proportion."

"How do you mean?"

"Well, I mean it strikes me—quite unbiased, you know—that you've let Number One overshadow the situation. You've drawn it all too personal to yourself."

"I don't see that," said Dale, forcibly, almost hotly. "It's the principle I stand for—pretty near as much as for myself."

"Ah, yes, just so," said Mr. Ridgett. "And now I'm going to ask you to help me find a bedroom somewhere handy, and put me up to knowing where I'd best get my meals;" and he laughed cheerfully. "Don't think I'm *establishing* myself—but one may as well be comfortable, if one can. And I do give you this tip. You're in for what we used to call the devil's dance up there. Cæsar is a slow mover. I mean, it won't be 'Step this way, Mr. Dale. Walk in this minute.' They'll keep you on the dance. I should take all you're likely to want for a week—at the least."

Dale made arrangements for the future comfort of the visitor, and hospitably insisted that he should take his first substantial meal up-stairs.

"It's served at seven sharp," said Dale; "and we make it a meat tea; but you aren't restricted to non-alcolic bev'rages."

"Oh, tea is more than good enough for me, thank you."

"Mavis," said Dale, introducing his guest, "this is Mr. Ridgett, who is so kind as to honor us without ceremony." And, as if to demonstrate the absence of ceremony, he put his arm round his wife's waist and kissed her.

Mr. Ridgett smiled, and opened conversation in a very pleasant easy fashion.

"From the look of things," he said facetiously, "I hazard the guess that you two aren't long home from the honeymoon."

"You're off the line there," said Dale. "We're quite an old Darby and Joan."

"Really!" And Mr. Ridgett's smile, as he regarded Mrs. Dale, expressed admiration and surprise. "Appearances are deceitful. And how long may you have been running in double harness?"

"Eleven years," said Dale.

"Never! Any children?"

"No," said Mrs. Dale.

"No," said her husband. "We haven't been blessed that way—not as yet."

"I note the addition. Not as yet! Very neatly put." Mr. Ridgett laughed, and bowed gallantly to Mrs. Dale. "Plenty of time for any amount of blessings."

Then they all sat down to the table.

During the course of the meal, and again when it was over, they spoke of the business that lay before Dale on the morrow.

"I've ventured to tell your husband that perhaps he has been taking it all too seriously."

"Oh, has he? I'm so glad to hear you say it." And Mavis Dale, with her elbows on the table, leaned forward and watched the deputy's face intently.

"Too much of the personal equation."

"Yes?"

"What I say is, little accidents happen to all of us—but they blow over."

Mavis Dale drew in her breath, and her eyebrows contracted. "Mr. Ridgett! The way you say that, shows you really think it's serious for him."

"Oh, I don't in the least read it up as ruin and all the rest of it. It's just a check. In Mr. Dale's place, I should be philosophical. I should say, 'This is going to put me back a bit, but nothing else.'"

Dale shrugged his shoulders and snorted. Mrs. Dale's eyebrows had drawn so close together that they almost touched; her eyes appeared darker, smaller, more opaque. Mr. Ridgett continued talking in a tone of light facetiousness that seemed to cover a certain deprecating earnestness.

"Yes, that would be *my* point of view—quite general, philosophical. I should say to myself, 'Old chap, if you're in for a jolly good wigging, why, just take it. If you're to be offered a little humble pie to eat—well, eat it.'"

"I won't," cried Dale, loudly; and he struck the table with his clenched fist. "I'm not goin' to crawl on my belly any more. I've done it in my time, when perhaps I felt myself wrong. But I won't do it now when I'm right—no, so help me, God, I won't."

It was as if all restraints had been burst by the notion of such injustice.

"Ah, well," said Ridgett, looking uncomfortable, "then I must withdraw the suggestion."

Mavis Dale was trembling. Her husband's noisy outburst seemed to have shaken her nerves; the downward lines formed themselves at the corners of her mouth; and her eyelids fluttered as if she were on the verge of tears. "Will," she murmured, "you—you ought to listen, if it's good advice. Mr. Ridgett knows the ropes—he, he has experience—and he means you well."

"Indeed I do," said Ridgett cordially.

"And I thank you for it, sir," said Dale. "And now——" He mastered his emotions and was calm and polite again, as became a host. "Now, what about two or three whiffs?"

"If madam permits."

"Mav don't mind. She's smoke-dried."

All three remained sitting at the table. The two men smoked their pipes reflectively, and spoke only at intervals, while Mavis sank into the motionless silence of a deep reverie. The golden sunlight came no more into the room; bright colors of oleograph pictures, hearth-rug, and window-curtains imperceptibly faded; the whole world seemed to be growing quiet and cool and gray. The sounds of voices and the rumble of passing wheels rose so drowsily from the street that they did not disturb one's sense of peace.

All at once Mavis roused herself, or rather, seemed to be roused involuntarily by some inward sensation—perhaps an ugly and unexpected turn that her thoughts had suddenly taken. She gave a little shiver, looked across the table at the visitor as if surprised at his presence, and then began to talk to him volubly.

"Do you know this part of the world? It's a pretty country—especially the forest side. Lots of artists and photographers come here on purpose to take the views."

For a little while she and Mr. Ridgett chatted gaily together; and Dale observed, not without satisfaction, that the deputy patently admired Mavis. "Yes," he thought, "it must be an eye-opener for him or anybody else to come up those stairs and find a postmaster's wife with all the education and manners of a lady, and as pretty as a bunch of primroses into the bargain."

And indeed little Mr. Ridgett was fully susceptible to Mavis' varied charms. He liked her complexion—so unusually white; he liked her hair—such a lot of it; he liked the mobility of her lips, the fineness and straightness of her nose; and he also greatly liked the broad black ribbon that was tied round her slender neck. The simple decoration seemed curiously in harmony with something childlike pertaining to its wearer. He did not attempt to analyze this characteristic, but he felt it plainly—something that drew its components from voice, expression, gesture, and that as a whole carried to one a message of extreme youth.

And how fond of her husband! The anxiety for his welfare that she had shown just now quite touched a soft spot in Mr. Ridgett's dryly official heart.

"You know," said Dale, interrupting the conversation, and speaking as though the subject that occupied his own mind was still under debate, "they can't pretend but what I warned them. I said it's madness to go and put the instruments anywhere but the place I've marked on the plan. If they'd listened to my words *then*——"

"Ah, there you are again," said Mr. Ridgett. "The personal equation!"

"Where's the personality of it?"

"I'll tell you. London isn't Rodchurch. What you said—how many years ago?—isn't going to govern the judgment of people who never heard you say it."

"It ought to have gone on record. It *is* on record over at Rodhaven."

"London isn't Rodhaven either."

Then once again the talk became serious; and once again Ridgett saw in Mrs. Dale's white face, trembling fingers, and narrowed eyes, the deadly anxiety that she was suffering. With that face opposite to one, it would have been monstrously cruel not to offer the wisest and best considered advice that one could anyhow produce.

"Here's *verb. sap*," he said solemnly. "*Ultimatum*, and *ne plus ultra*. I'm giving you Latin for Latin, Mr. Dale. I understand your attitude, and I appreciate its bearing; but I say to you, the best causes sometimes need the best advocates."

"Yes!" Mavis drew in her breath with a little gasp.

"If any of the gentry down here would speak up for you, send you a few testimonials—well, I should get them to do it. You see, from what you tell me of the case, you've your Member of Parliament against you. It would be useful to counteract——"

Then Mavis eagerly explained that the biggest man of the neighborhood had promised to give his support to her husband. This great personage was the Right Honorable Everard Barradine, an ex-Cabinet Minister and a large landed proprietor, who lived over at the Abbey House, on the edge of Manninglea Chase, five miles away. Mr. Barradine had always borne a good heart to her and hers.

"Capital!" said Mr. Ridgett, visibly brightening. "A friend at court—what's the proverb? It's not for me to let fall any remarks about wire-pulling. But naturally there's a freemasonry among the bigwigs. You take my tip, and use Mr. Barradine's interest for all it's worth."

"Well," said Dale, "he has given a promise—of a sort—and I shan't bother him further."

After that the talk became light again. As if the strain of her anxiety was more than Mavis Dale could bear for long at a time, she plunged into frivolous discussion, telling Mr. Ridgett of the splendors and beauties of the Abbey House. It was a show-place. Its gardens surpassed belief; royal persons came hundreds of miles to look at them. And the wild historic woodland of Manninglea Chase was famous, it was said, all over Europe. Talking thus, she seemed as gay and careless as a child of ten.

Mr. Ridgett, puffing his pipe luxuriously, contemplated her animated face with undisguised admiration; and presently Dale felt irritated by the admiring scrutiny.

That was what always happened. At first he felt pleased that people should admire his wife; but if they seemed to admire her the least little shade too much, he became angry. In the lanes, in church, anywhere, he froze too attentive glances of admiring males with a most portentous scowl. It was not that he entertained the faintest doubt of her loyalty and devotion, or of her power to protect herself from improper assiduities; but he loved her so passionately that his blood began to boil at the mere thought of anybody's having the audacity to court her favor. Instinctively, on such occasions, words formed themselves in his mind and clamored for utterance on his lips. "You take care, my fine fellow;" "Hands off, please;" "Let me catch you trying it"—and so on: only thought-counters secretly used by himself, and never issued in the currency of spoken words.

Now the internal warmth was just sufficient to make him push back his chair and break up the party.

"Mavis," he said, rather grimly, "we mustn't detain Mr. Ridgett from his duties." Then he forced a laugh. "I'm nobody; and so it doesn't matter how long I sit over my supper. But we've to remember that Mr. Ridgett is the postmaster of Rodchurch."

II

HE went to bed early; but he knew that he would not sleep until the mail-cart had gone.

His wife was sleeping peacefully. He could feel the warmth of her body close against him; her breath, drawn so lightly and regularly, just touched his face; and he edged away cautiously, seeking space in which to turn without disturbing her. At immeasurably long periods the church clock chimed the quarters. That last chime must have been the quarter after eleven.

Every now and then there came a sound that told him of the things that were happening on the ground floor; and in the intervals of silence he began to suffer from an oppressive sense of unreality. This disruption of the routine of life was so strange as to seem incredible. They were making up the two big bags for the up mail and the down mail; and he was lying here like a state prisoner, of no account for the time being, while below him his realm remained actively working.

As midnight approached, an increasing anxiety possessed him. The horse and cart had been standing under the window for what appeared to be hours, and yet they would not bring out the bags. What in the name of reason were they waiting for now? Then at last he detected the movement of shuffling footsteps; he heard voices—Ridgett's voice among the others; a wheel grated against the curbstone, and the cart rolled away. The sounds of the church clock chiming twelve mingled with the reverberations made by the horse's hoofs as the cart passed between the garden walls. Thank goodness, anyhow, they had got it off to its time.

With a sigh, he turned on his back and stared at the darkness that hid the ceiling. Ah! A profuse perspiration had broken out on his neck and chest. To give himself more air he pulled down the too generous supply of bed clothes, and in imagination he followed the cart.

It was progressing slowly and steadily along the five miles of road to the railway junction. Would Perkins, the driver, break the regulations to-night and pick up somebody for a ride with the sacred bags? Such a gross breach of duty would render Perkins, or his employer, liable to a heavy penalty; and again and again Dale had reminded him of the risks attending misbehavior. But unwatched men grow bold. This would be a night to bring temptation in the way of Perkins. Some villager—workman, field-laborer, wood-cutter— tramping the road would perhaps ask for a lift. "What cheer, mate! I'm for the night-mail. Give us a lift's far as junction, and I'll stan' the price of a pint to you."

A glance up and down the empty road—and then "Jump in. Wunnerful weather we're having, aren't us?" So much for the wise regulation! *Most* wise regulation, if one understand it properly. For when once you begin tampering with the inviolable nature of a mail-cart, where are you to stop? Suppose your chance passenger proves to be not an honest subject, but a malefactor—*one of a gang*. "Take that, ye swab." A clump on the side of his head, and the driver is sent endways from the box-seat; the cart gallops on to where the rest of the gang lurk waiting for it; strong arms, long legs, and the monstrous deed is consummated. Her Majesty's bags have been stolen.

Though so dark in this bedroom, there would be light enough out there. There was no moon; but the summer night, as he knew, would never deepen to real obscurity. It would keep all of a piece till dawn, like a sort of gray dusk, heavy and impenetrable beneath the trees, but quite transparent on the heath and in the glades; and then it would become all silvery and trembling; the wet bracken would glisten faintly, high branches of beech trees would glow startlingly, each needle on top of the lofty firs would change to a tiny sword of fire—just as he had seen happen so often years ago, when as an undisciplined lad he lay out in the woods for his pleasure.

Now! The church clock had struck one. Barring accidents, the cart was at its goal; and in imagination he saw the junction as clearly as if he had been standing at Perkins' elbow. There was the train for London already arrived—steam rising in a straight jet from the engine, guard and porter with lanterns, and a flood of orange light streaming from the open doors of the noble Post Office coach. Perkins hands in his up bag, receives a bag in exchange, and half his task is done. Forty minutes to wait before he can perform the other half of it. Then, having passed over the metals with the cart, he will attend to the down train; hand in his other bag, receive the London bag; and, as soon as the people in the signal-box will release the crossing-gates, he may come home.

Dale knew now that he would not sleep until the cart returned.

When the church clock struck the half-hour after two, he lay straining his ears to catch the sound of the horse's hoofs. Finally it came to him, immensely remote, a rhythmic plod, plod, plod. Then in a few more minutes the cart was at rest under his window again; they were taking in the bags; bolts shot into their fastenings, a key turned in a lock, and the clerk went back to bed at the top of the house. All was over now. Nothing more would happen until the other clerk came down in a couple of hours' time, until the bags were opened, until Ridgett came yawning from his hired bedroom at the saddler's across the street, and the new day's work began. And Dale would be shut out of the work—a director who might not even assist, a master superseded, a general under arrest in the midst of his army.

He gulped and grew hot. "By Jupiter! I'll have to tell them what I think of them up there, and please the pigs!"

Then he remembered the pleadings of his wife. She had implored him to keep a tight hold of himself; and in fairness to her he must exercise discretion. She and he were one. With extraordinary tenderness he mentally framed the words that by custom he employed when speaking of her. "She is the wife of my boosum."

For a little while he calmed himself by thinking only of her. Then, tossing and turning and perspiring again, he began to think of his whole life, seeing it as a pageant full of wonder and pathos. Holy Jupiter! how hard it had been at its opening! Everything against him—just a lout among the woodside louts, an orphan baited and lathered by a boozy stepfather, a tortured animal that ran into the thickets for safety, a thing with scarce a value or promise inside it except the little flame of courage that blows could not extinguish! And yet out of this raw material he had built up the potent, complex, highly-dowered organism known to the world as Mr. Dale of Rodchurch. There was the pride and glory—from such a start to have reached so magnificent a position. But he could not have done it—not all of it—without Mavis.

It would be unkind to wake this dear bedfellow merely because he himself could not sleep. He clasped his hands behind his head, and by a prolonged effort of will remained motionless. But insomnia was exciting every nerve in his body; each memory seemed to light up the entire labyrinth of his brain; each sense-message came inward like a bomb-shell, reaching with its explosion the highest as well as the deepest centers, discharging circuits of swift fire through every area of associated ideas, and so completely shattering the normal congruity between impressions and recognitions that the slight drag of the sheet across his raised toes was sufficient to make him feel again the pressure of thick boots that he had worn years ago when he tramped as new postman on the Manninglea Road.

And each thing that he thought of he saw—hawthorn blossom like snow on the hedgerows, red rhododendrons as vivid as Chinese lanterns in the gloom of the dark copse, the green moss of the rides, the white paint of the gates. The farthest point of his round was Mr. Barradine's mansion, and he used to arrive there just before eight o'clock. With the thought

came the luminous pictures, and he saw again, as clearly as fifteen years ago, the splendor of the Abbey
House—that is, all one can see of it as one approaches
its vast servants' offices. Here, solidly real, were the
archway, the first and the second courtyard, grouped
gables and irregular roof ridges, the belfry tower and
its gilded vane; men washing a carriage, a horse drinking at the fountain trough, a dog lying on a sunlit
patch of cobble-stones and lazily snapping at flies; a
glimpse, through iron scroll work, of terrace balus-
trades, yellow gravel, and lemon-trees in tubs; the oak
doors of laundries, drying-rooms, and so forth.

It was here, outside the laundry, that he saw Mavis
for the first time; and although the sleeves of her print
dress were rolled up and she was carrying a metal
skimming dish, something ineffably refined and superior in her deportment led him to believe that she was
some lesser member of the august Barradine family,
and not one of its hired dependents. He touched his
peaked cap, and did not even venture to say " Good
morning, miss."

Then he found out about her. She was not quite so
grand as all that. You might say she was a young
lady right enough, if you merely counted manners and
education; but she had been born far below the level
of gentility. She belonged to the Petherick lot; and,
living with her aunt at North Ride Cottage, she came
every day to the Abbey to do some light and delicate
work in Mr. Barradine's model dairy. The fact that
she had lost both her parents interested and pleased
Dale: orphanhood seemed to contain the embryonic
germs of a mutual sympathy.

He used to speak to her now whenever he saw her.

One day they stood talking in the copse, and he showed her their distorted reflections on the curves of her shining cream-dish. She laughed; and that day he was late on his round.

Then somehow he got to a heavy sort of chaff about the letters. She said she liked receiving letters, and she never received enough of them. He used to say, "Good morning, miss. My mate started off with a tremendous heavy bag to-day. I expect the most of it was for you. You'll find 'em when you get home this evening—shoals of 'em."

Walking fast on his round he rehearsed such little speeches, and if she made an unanticipated answer he was baffled and confused. He suffered from an extreme shyness when face to face with her.

Then all at once his overwhelming admiration gave him a hot flow of language. Beginning the old cumbrous facetiousness about her correspondence, he blurted out the true thoughts that he had begun to entertain.

"You didn't ought to want for letters, miss, and you wouldn't—not if I was your letter-writer. I'd send you a valentine every day of the year."

As he spoke, he looked at her with burning eyes. He was astonished, almost terrified by his hardiness; and what he detected of its effect on her threw him into an indescribable state of emotion.

Rough and coarse he might be, and yet not truly disagreeable to her fine senses; his freckled face and massive shoulders did not repel her; no instinct of the lovely princess turned sick at these advances of the wild man of the woods. Under his scrutiny she showed a sort of fluttered helplessness, a mingling of beauty

and weakness that sent fiery messages thrilling
through and through him, a pale tremor, a soft glow, a
troubled but not offended frown; and from beneath all
these surface manifestations the undeveloped woman
in her seemed to speak to the matured manhood in him
—seemed to say without words, " Oh, dear me, what is
this? I hope you haven't taken a real fancy to my
whiteness and slenderness and tremulousness; because
if you *have*, you are so big and so strong that I know
you'll get me in the end."

That was the crucial moment of his marvelous life.
After that all his dreams fused and became one. He
felt as if from soft metal he had changed into hard
metal. And, moreover, the stimulus of love seemed to
induce a vast intellectual growth; things that had been
difficult of comprehension became lucidly clear; pre-
judices and ignorances fell away from him of their own
accord. A shut world had suddenly become an open
world.

As a grown man he returned to the benches of evening school. He learned to write his beautiful copper-
plate hand, and knocked the bottom out of arithmetic
and geography. Then came sheer erudition—the nature of chemical elements, stars in their courses, kings
of England with their Magna Chartas and habeas corpuses. Nor content even then, he must needs grapple
with Roman emperors and Greek republics, and master
the fabled lore concerning gods and goddesses, cloven-
footed satyrs, and naked nymphs of the grove.

But he understood that, in spite of all this culture,
in spite, too, of his greater care for costume and his
increased employment of soap and water, Mavis was
still enormously above him. The aunt, a smooth-

tongued little woman whom for a long time he regarded as implacably hostile to his suit, made him measure the height of the dividing space every time that he called at North Ride Cottage. Plainly trying to crush him with the respectability both of herself and of her surroundings, she showed off all the presents from the Abbey—the china and glass ornaments, the piano; the photographs of Mr. Barradine on horseback, of the late Lady Evelyn Barradine in her pony-carriage, of Mr. Barradine's guests with guns waiting to shoot pheasants. And she conducted him into and out of the two choicely upholstered rooms which on certain occasions Mr. Barradine deigned to occupy for a night or a couple of nights—for instance, when the Abbey House was being painted and he fled the smell of paint, when the Abbey House was closed and he came down from London to see his agent on business, when he wanted to make an early start at the cub-hunting and he couldn't trust the servants of the Abbey House to rouse him if he slept there.

"Last time of all," and Mrs. Petherick rubbed her hands together and smiled insinuatingly, "he paid me the pretty compliment of saying that I made him more comfortable than he ever is in his own house. I said, 'If we can't let you feel at home here, it's something new among the Pethericks.'"

It seemed that the bond between the humble family and the great one had existed for several generations. It was a tradition that the Pethericks should serve the Barradines. Mavis' grandfather had been second coachman at the Abbey; her aunt's husband had been valet to Mr. Everard and made the grand tour of Europe with him; aunt herself was of the Petherick blood, and had been a housemaid at the Abbey. It also seemed to be a tradition that the acknowledgment made by the Barradines for this fidelity of the Pethericks should be boundless in its extent.

Aunt spoke of the Right Honorable Everard as though she held him like a purse in her pocket, and Dale at one period had some queer thoughts about this old widow of a dead servant for whom so much had been done and who yet expected so much more. She said Mr. Barradine had charged himself with the musical training of another niece, and he would probably not hesitate to send Mavis to Vienna for the best masters, should she presently display any natural talent. Her cousin Ruby sang like an angel from the age of ten; but Mavis so far exhibited more inclination for instrumental music.

"She'll belie her name, though, if she doesn't pipe up some day, won't she?"

When Dale secured his appointment at Portsmouth, he and Mavis were not engaged. She said, "Auntie simply won't hear of it."

"Not now," he said. "But later, when I've made my way, she'll come round. Mav, will you wait for me?"

"Oh, I don't know," said Mavis. "I can't give any promise. I must do whatever Auntie tells me. I can't go against her wishes."

Yet somehow he felt sure that she would be his. A thousand slimy, humbugging old aunts should not keep them apart. From Portsmouth he wrote a letter to his sweetheart on every day of the year for three years—except on those days of joyous leave when he could get away and talk to her instead of writing to her. At

the end of the three years the postmastership at Rodchurch became vacant, and he boldly applied for the
place.

His life just then was almost too glorious to be true.
All difficulties and dangers seemed to melt away in a
sort of warm haze of rapture. Mrs. Petherick no
longer opposed the marriage; Mr. Barradine, at the
zenith of political power, exerted his influence; the
postmastership was obtained. To top up, Dale made
the not unpleasing discovery that Mavis was an heir-
ess as well as an orphan. She had two hundred
pounds of her very own, " which came in uncommon
handy for the furnishing."

And his education did not cease with wedlock. Mavis
was always improving him, especially in regard to diction. He was pleased to think that he made very few
slips nowadays—an " h " elided here and there; the
vowels still rather broad, more particularly the Hampshire " a "; and one or two unchanged words, such as
" boosum." But these microscopic faults were of no
consequence, and Mav had stopped teasing him about
them. She only warned him of what he knew was
Gospel truth—that the little failures were more frequent under hurry or excitement, and that when deeply moved he had a tendency to lapse badly toward the
ancient peasant lingo.

Nothing to worry about, however. It merely indicated that he must never speak on important matters
without due preparation. He would be all right up
tHere, knowing to a syllable what he wished to say; and
he thought with swelling pride of comparatively recent
public speeches and the praise that he had received
from them. After the Parish meeting last January the

Rodhaven District Courier had said, "With a few happy remarks Mr. Dale adverted again to the fallacy of
plunging the village into the expense of a costly fire-
engine without first ascertaining the reliability of the
water supply." His very words, almost *verbatim*
"Happy remarks!" A magistrate on the bench could
not have been better reported or more handsomely
praised.

The reviewing of these manifold bounties of Providence had produced a sedative effect; but now he grew
restless once more. He felt that twinge of doubt, the
pin-prick of illogical fear which during the last eighteen hours had again and again pierced his armor of
self-confidence. Suppose things went against him!
No, that would be too monstrous; that would mean no
justice left in England, the whole fabric of society
gone rotten and crumbling to dust.

The spaces between the blinds and window-frames
were white instead of gray; the sun had risen; presently the whole room was visible.

Mavis' little face showed pink and warm as a baby's
above the bed clothes. And a sudden longing for caresses took possession of her husband. To wake her,
fold her in his arms, and then, pacified by the embrace,
perhaps obtain a few hours' sound sleep? For some
moments his desire was almost irresistible. But it
would be selfish thus to break her tranquil repose—
poor little tired bird.

He noiselessly slipped from the bed, huddled on
some clothes, washed his face in cold water at the
kitchen sink, and let himself out of the house. The
open air refreshed him almost as much as sleep could
have done. He walked nearly five miles and back on

the Manninglea Road, and would not even glance at the busy sorting-room when he came in again.

Mavis accompanied him to Rodchurch Road Station, and saw him off by the nine o'clock train. He looked very dignified in his newest bowler hat and black frock-coat, with a light overcoat on one arm and his wife's gloved hand on the other; and as he walked up and down the platform he endeavored to ignore the fact that he was an object of universal attention.

When buying his ticket he had let fall a guarded word or two about the nature of his errand, and from the booking-office the news had flown up and down both sides of the station, round the yard, and even into the signal cabins. "See Mr. Dale?" "Mr. Dale!" "There's Mr. Dale, going to London for an interview with the Postmaster-General."

Mr. Melling, the Baptist minister, took off his hat and bowed gravely; Mrs. Norton, the vicar's wife, smilingly stopped Mavis and spoke as if she had been addressing a social equal; then they received greetings from old Mr. Bates, the corn merchant, and from young Richard Bates, his swaggering good-for-nothing son. And then, as passengers gathered more thickly, it became quite like a public reception. "Ma'arnin', sir." "Good day, Mr. Dale." "I hope I see you well, sir."

Mavis got him away from all this company just before the train came in, and made a last appeal to him. Would he recollect what the deputy had said about eating that ugly dish which is commonly known as humble pie?

But at the mention of Mr. Ridgett's advice Dale displayed a slight flare of irascibility.

"Let Mr. Ridgett mind his own business," he said

shortly, "and not bother himself about mine. And look here," he added. " I am not trusting that gentleman any further than I see him."

" I think you're wrong there, Will."

" I know human nature." His face had flushed, and he spoke admonitorily. " I don't need to tell you to be circumspect during my absence—but you may have a little trouble in keeping Mr. R. in his proper place. You'll be quick to twig if he supposes the chance has come to pester you. These London customers—whatever their age—think when they get along with a pretty woman——"

" Oh, Will, don't be absurd; " and she looked at him wistfully, and spoke sadly. " I'm not so attractive as you think me. I may be the same to your eyes—but not to others. It's very doubtful if anybody would want me now—except those who knew me when I was young."

Then after a moment's reflection she said that, if he consented, she proposed to relieve his mind of any silly jealous fancies about Mr. Ridgett by going over to stay with her aunt at North Ride.

" I should be anxious and miserable here, Will, while you were away—whereas with her I could occupy my thoughts."

He immediately consented to the arrangement. An excellent idea. She might go that very afternoon, and safely promise to stay three days. He would write to North Ride and keep her informed as to his movements.

" Good-by, my sweetheart. God bless you."

" Good luck, Will. Good luck, my dear one."

III

THE devil's dance had begun.

They kept him waiting. Days passed; but his hour of crisis postponed itself, and all things combined to enervate him. Above all, the callous immensity of London oppressed his mind. His case, that had been so important down there in the village, was absolutely of no account up here in the city. Not a single sympathizer among these millions of hurrying human beings.

The General Post Office was itself a town within a town—a mighty labyrinth that made the imagination ache. To find one's way through a fractional block of it, to see a thronged corner of any of its yards, to hear even at a distance the stone thunder made by the smallest stampede of its red carts, irresistibly evoked a realization of one's nothingness. Never would he have believed it possible that the local should thus shrink in presence of the central.

He had taken a bedroom on the top floor of a cheap lodging-house near the Euston Road, and every night as he climbed the dimly-lit staircase he knew that he was toiling upward toward a fit of depression. The house was almost empty of lodgers; no one noticed when he went out or came in; at each flight of the stairs his sense of solitude increased.

He had never before lived in a building that contained so many stories, and at first he was troubled by

34

the great height above the ground; but now he could
stand at his open window and look down without gid-
diness. Wonder used to fill his mind as he stared out
toward the southeast at the stupendous field of roofs,
chimneys, and towers; at the sparkling powder of
street-lamps; at the astounding yellow haze that extended across the horizon, illuminating the sky nearly
to the zenith, and seemingly like the onset of a terrific
conflagration which only he of all the thousands who
were threatened had as yet observed. Even this bit
of London, the comparatively small part of the overwhelming whole now visible to his eyes, must be as
big as Manninglea Chase. And beyond his half circle
of vision, behind him, on either hand, the forest of
houses stretched away almost to infinity. The thought
of it was as crushing as that of interstellar distances,
of the pathless void into which God threw a handful
of dust and then quietly ordained that each speck
should be a sun and the pivot of a solar system.

He turned from the window to look at the dark little room, groped his way to the chest of drawers, and
lighted a candle. Its flame sputtered, then settled and
burned unwaveringly. Here in London the nights
seemed as stuffy as the days; there was no life or
freshness, no movement of the air; it was as if the
warm breath of the crowd rose upward and nothing
less than a balloon would allow one to escape from its
taint. But he noticed that even at this slight eleva-
tion he had got free from the noise of the traffic. It
would continue—a crashing roar—for hours, and yet
it was now scarcely perceptible. Listening attentively he heard it—just a crackling murmur, a curious muf-

fled rhythm, as of drums beaten by an army of drum-
mers marching far away.

When he got into bed and blew out his candle, the
rectangle of the window became brighter. After a
little while he fancied that he could distinguish two
or three stars shining very faintly in the patch of sky
above the sashes; and again thinking of remoteness,
immensity, infinity, he experienced a curious physical
sensation of contracting bulk, as though all his body
had grown and was steadily growing smaller. Very
strong this sensation, and, unless one wrestled with it
firmly, translating itself in the mental sphere as a
vaguely distressful notion that one was nothing but
a tiny insect at war with the entire universe.

Day after day he spent his time in the same manner
at the G.P.O.—asking questions of clerks, lounging in
stone corridors, sitting on wooden benches, thinking
that the hour was coming and finding that it did not
come. He was one of a weary regiment of people
waiting for interviews. Clerks behind counters of inquiry offices hunted him up in pigeon-holes, looked for
him in files and on skewers. " Oh, yes, let's see. You
say you're the man from Rodchurch! That's north or
midlands, isn't it? You must ask in Room 45. . . . What
say? Down south, is it? Then you're quite right to
ask here. No, we haven't heard any more about it
since yesterday."

At the end of each fruitless day he emerged from
the vast place of postponement feeling exhausted,
dazed, stupefied. The sunlight made him blink. He
stood holding his hat so as to shade his eyes.

Then after a few minutes, as he plodded along
Queen Victoria Street, his confusion passed away, and

he observed things with a clear understanding. It was a lovely evening really and truly, and these ponderous omnibuses were all carrying people home because the day's work was done. The streets were clean and bright; and there was plenty of gayness and joy—for them as could grab a share of it. He noticed fine private carriages drawn up round corners, waiting for prosperous tradesmen; young men with tennis-bats in their hands, taking prodigiously long strides, eager to get a game of play before dusk; girls who went by twos and threes, chattering, laughing, making funny short quick steps of it, like as if on the dance to reach sweethearts and green lanes. A man selling a mechanical toy—sort of a tin frog that jumped so soon as you put it down—made him smile indulgently.

Outside the Mansion House Station the traffic stopped dead all of a moment, and directly the wheels ceased rattling one heard the cheerful music of a soldiers' band close upon one. It was the Bank Guard—Coldstreams—marching proudly. The officer in charge seemed very proud; with drawn sword, his broad red back bulging above his sash, and the enormous bearskin narrowing to his shoulders and hiding his neck.

The wheels rolled again; the music, floating, fading, died beneath the horses' feet; and Dale stood gaping at a board over the entrance of the railway station. Places served by this District Company had pleasant-sounding suburban names—such as Kew Gardens, Richmond, Wimbledon. Reading the names, he felt a sick nostalgic yearning for the wind that blows through fir-trees, for the dust that falls on highroads, for the village street and the friendly nod—for home.

He ate some food at an eating-house near Black-
friars, and then wandered aimlessly for hours. The
broad river, with its dull brown flood breaking in oily
wavelets against the embankment wall, exercised a
fascination. He admired the Temple, watched some
shadows on a lawn, and wondered if the pigeons by
the cab-rank ever went to bed, or if, changing their natural habits to suit their town-life, they had become
night birds like the owls. The trains passing to and
fro in the iron cage called Hungerford Bridge interested him; and as he approached the Houses of Parliament, he was stirred by memories of his historical
reading.

The stately pile had become almost black against
the western sky by the time that he drew near to it,
and its majestic extent, with the lamplight gleaming
from innumerable windows, gave him a quite personal
satisfaction. It represented all that was grandest in
the tale of his country. The freedom of the subject had
been born on this hallowed spot; here had been thrown
down those cruel barriers by which the rich and powerful penned and confined the poor and humble as cattle
or slaves; by this and because of this, the people's
meeting-place, men like himself had been enabled to
aspire and to achieve. He was aware of a moisture in
his eyes and a lump in his throat while he meditated
thus; and then suddenly his eyes grew hot and dry
again, and his larynx opened. His thought had taken
a rapid turn from the general to the particular. It
was a pity that an interfering ass like their member
should have the right to come in and out here, record
his vote, and spout his nonsense with the best of them.

The metal tongue of Big Ben startled him, a boom-
ing voice that might have been that of Time itself, telling the tardy sunlight and the encroaching dusk that it
was nine o'clock. Under a lamp-post Dale brought
out his silver watch, and carefully set it.

"I suppose they keep Greenwich," he thought,
"same as we do;" and an apprehensive doubt presented itself. Would his clerk have the sense to see to
it, that the clocks down there were duly wound? Ridgett, of course, could not be expected to know that
they were always wound on Thursdays.

St. James' followed Westminster in his tour of inspection, and then, after that amazing street of clubs,
he soon found himself in the white glare, the kaleido-
scopic movement, and the concentrated excitement of
Piccadilly Circus. Then he sauntered through Leicester Square and began to drift northward. The gas
torches outside places of entertainment had arrested
his slow progress. One of the music-halls in the
Square appeared to him as iniquitously gorgeous, and
he gazed through the wide entrance at the vestibule
hall, and staircase. The whole thing was as fine as
one might have expected inside Buckingham Palace
or the Mansion House—crimson curtains, marble
steps, golden balusters, and flunkeys wearing velvet
breeches and silk stockings. It grieved him momentarily to discover that two giant commissionnaires
were both foreigners. He heard them address each
other with a rapid guttural jabber. "Should 'a'
thought there's large-sized men enough in England, if
you troubled to look for 'em."

To this point he had amused himself sufficiently; but

each night as he turned his face toward the Euston Road, his spirits sank and the same queer mixture of bodily and mental discomfort attacked him. It began with the slightly bitter thought of being "out of it." He looked disapprovingly at pallid and puffed young swells gliding past in cabs; at the humbler folk who hurried by without seeming to be aware of his existence, who bumped into him and never said "Pardon!"; at the painted women of the narrower pavements—more foreigners half of them—who leered and murmured.

"Where's the police?" He asked himself the question indignantly and contemptuously. "Can't they see what's going on under their noses? Or don't they *wish* to see it? Or have they been paid *not* to see it? Funny thing if every respectable married man is to be bothered like this—three times in fifty yards!"

These incessant solicitations affected his nerves. So much so, indeed, that he cursed the impudence of one woman and called her a rude name. She did not seem to mind. While he was still in the generous afterglow produced by a bit of plain-speaking, another one had taken her place.

With head high and shoulders squared he marched on, subject for some distance to a purely nervous irritation, together with a disagreeably potent memory of powdered cheeks, reddened lips, and a searching perfume.

Then he thought of his wife, and instantly he had so vivid a presentation of her image that it obliterated all newer visual records. What a lady she looked when bidding him farewell at the station. He had watched her till the train carried him out of sight—a slender graceful figure; pale face and sad eyes; a fluttering handkerchief and a waved parasol; then nothing at all, except a sudden sense of emptiness in his heart.

And once more he mused with gratitude on the things that Mavis had done for him. He thought of how she had saved him from the ugly imaginations of his youth. How marvelously she had purified and elevated him! He used to be afraid of himself, of all the potentialities for evil that one takes with one across the threshold of manhood.

The fantastic dread which recurred to his memory now, as he turned from Dean Street into Oxford Street, had been started when he first heard the legendary tale of Hadleigh Wood. It was said that seventy or a hundred years ago some louts had caught girls bathing in the stream and violated them. The legend declared that one of the offenders was executed and the rest were sent to prison for life. Perhaps it was all a myth, but it helped to give the upper wood a bad name; and out of these fabled materials William had built his fancy—dread and desire combining—a wish that, when he pushed the branches apart, he might see a lass bathing; and a fear that he would not be able to resist an impulse to plunge into the water and carry her off. As he walked through the shade cast by summer foliage, with a hot whisper of nascent virility tormenting his senses, the fancy was almost strong enough to be a hallucination. He could imagine that he saw female garments on the bank, petticoats fallen in a circle, boots and stockings hard by; he could hear the splashing of water on the other side of the holly bushes; he could feel the weight of the nude form slung across his shoulder as he galloped into the gloom with his prey. And later, under the increasing stress of his adolescence, he used to have a dread of realities

—a conviction that he could not trust himself. He
thought at this period not of legends, but of facts—
of things that truly happened; of the brutality of hay-
fields; of a man full of beer dealing roughly with a
woman-laborer who unluckily came in his way alone
and defenceless at nightfall.

From all this kind of vague peril his wife had saved
him. When in the course of his education he read of
nymphs and satyrs, and was startled by what seemed
a highly elaborated version of his own crude imagin-
ings, he had already, through the influence of Mavis,
attained to states of mind that rendered such suggestions powerless to stir his pulses or warm his blood;
and now, as he recognized with proud satisfaction, he
had reached a stage of development wherein the improper
advances of a thousand houris would evoke merely indignation and repugnance. It was not a matter that
one could boast about to anybody except one's self;
but he wondered if Mr. Ridgett, or several other customers who might remain nameless, could say as much.

Thanks to Mav! Yes, he ought always let himself
be guided by her.

And then, by a natural transition of ideas, he
thought of that other great instinct of untutored man
—the fighting instinct. When a person is rising in the
social scale he should learn to govern that also. Although the nobs themselves do it when pushed to it,
scrapping is not respectable. It is common. Nevertheless there must be exceptions to every rule: anger
when justified by its provocation is not, can not be rep-
rehensible.

But dimly he understood that with him cerebral excitement, when it reached a certain pitch, overflowed
too rapidly into action. Whereas the gentry, after

their centuries of repressive training, could always control themselves. They could fight, but they could wait for the appropriate moment. If you stung them with an insult, they resolved to avenge themselves— but not necessarily then and there; and their resolve deepened in every instant of delay, so that when the fighting hour struck, their heads worked with their arms, and they fought *better* than the hasty peasants.

And then he thought of the various advantages still possessed by gentlefolk. How unfairly easy is the struggle of life made for them, in spite of all the talk about equality; how difficult it still is for the humbly-born, in spite of Magna Chartas, habeas corpuses, and Houses of Commons! Finishing his long ramble, he remembered the biggest and grandest gentleman of his acquaintance, and wondered bitterly if the Right Honorable Everard Barradine had done so much as to raise a little finger on his behalf.

Five days had passed, and as yet not a single official at St. Martin's-le-Grand had learnt to know him by sight. Every morning he was forced to repeat the whole process of self-introduction.

"Dale? Rodchurch, Hants. Let's see. What name did you say? Dale! Superseded—eh?"

But on the sixth morning somebody knew all about him. It was quite a superior sort of clerk, who announced that Mr. Dale and all that concerned Mr. Dale had been transferred to other hands, in another part of the building. Dale gathered that something had happened to his case; it was as though, after lying dormant so long, it had unexpectedly come to life; and in less than ten minutes he was given a definite appointment. The interview would take place at noon on the day after to-morrow.

To-day was Saturday. The long quiescent Sunday must be endured—and then he would stand in the presence of supreme authority.

By the end of that Sunday his enervation was complete. The want of exercise, the want of fresh air, the want of Mavis, had been steadily weakening him, and now his anticipations as to the morrow produced a feverish excitement.

Throughout the day he rehearsed his speeches. He was still assuming—had always taken for granted—that the personage addressed would be the Postmaster-General, and he was sure of the correct mode of address. "Your Grace, I desire to respectfully state my position." . . . That was the start all right; but how did it go on? Again and again, before recovering the hang of it, he was confronted with a blank wall of forgetfulness.

And there was the bold flight that he had determined on for wind-up. This had come as an inspiration, down there at Rodchurch over a fortnight ago, and had been cherished ever since. "Your Grace, taking the liberty under this head of speaking as man to man, I ask: If you had been situated as I was, wouldn't you have done as I done?" That was to be the wind-up, and it had rung in his mind like a trumpet call, bold yet irresistible—"Duke you may be, but if also a man, act as a man, and see fair play." Now, however, the prime virtue of it seemed to be lessened: it was all muddled, unstimulating, and flat of tone.

How damnable if some insane nervousness should make him mix things up! Strong as his case was, it might be spoiled by ineffective argument. But was his case strong? Again the cruel twinge of doubt.

IV

THE parquetry all around the square of carpet was so smooth that Dale had slipped a foot and nearly come down when he entered the room and bowed to his judges; and now he moved with extreme caution when they told him to withdraw to the window.

There were three seated at the table, and none of the three was the Postmaster-General. Two of them were obviously bigwigs—so big, at any rate, that his fate lay in their hands; and the other one was a secretary—not the General Secretary—not even a gentleman, if one could draw any inference from his deferential tone and the casual manner in which the others addressed him. He was a sandy person—not unlike Ridgett, but rather older and much fatter.

Once a quiet young gentleman—a real gentleman, although apparently acting just as a clerk—had been in and out of the room. He had given Dale a half smile, and it had been welcome as a ray of sunlight on the darkest day of winter. Instinct told Dale that this nice young man sympathized with him, as certainly as it told him that his judges were unsympathetic.

He stood now in the deep bay window, as far as possible from the table, pretending not to listen while straining every nerve to catch the words that were being spoken over there. His blood was hurrying thickly, his heart beat laboriously, his collar stuck

45

clammily to his perspiring neck. His sense of bodily
fatigue was as great as if he had run a mile race; and
yet one might say that the interview had scarcely begun. What would he be like before it was over? He
summoned all his courage in order to go through with
it gamely.

. . . "You can't have this sort of thing." The words
had reached him distinctly—spoken by the one they
called Sir John; and the one that Sir John called "Colonel" said with equal distinctness, "Certainly not."

Dale's heart beat more easily. As he hoped and
believed, they must be talking of the soldier. Then
the heart-beats came heavy again. Were they talking
of him and not of the soldier? He caught a few other
broken phrases of enigmatic import—such as "storm
in teacup," "trouble caused," "no complaints"—and
then the voices were lowered, and he heard no more
of the conversation at the table.

Presently he saw that the secretary was producing a
fresh file of papers, and at the same moment, quite inexplicably, his attention wandered. He had brought
out a handkerchief, and while with a slow mechanical
movement he rubbed the palms of his hands, he
noticed and thought about the furniture and decoration
of the room. Clock, map, and calendar; some busts on
top of a bookless bookcase; red turkey carpet, the
treacherous parquetry, and these stiff-looking chairs
—really that was all. The emptiness and tidiness
surprised him, and he began to wonder what the
Postmaster-General's room was like. Surely there
would be richer furniture and more litter of business
there. Then, with a little nervous jerk, as of his
internal machinery starting again after a breakdown,

he felt how utterly absurd it was to be thinking about chairs and desks at such a moment. He must pull himself together, or he was going to make an ass of himself.

"Now, if you please." They were calling him to the table. He slowly marched across to them, and stood with folded hands.

"Well now, Mr. Dale." The Colonel was speaking, while Sir John read some letters handed to him by the secretary. "We have gone into this matter very carefully, and I may tell you at once that we have come to certain conclusions."

"Yes, sir." Dale found himself obliged to clear his throat before uttering the two words. His voice had grown husky since he last spoke.

"You have caused us a lot af trouble—really an immense amount of trouble."

Dale looked at the Colonel unflinchingly, and his voice was all right this time. "Trouble, sir, is a thing we can't none of us get away from—not even in private affairs, much less in public affairs."

"No; but there is what is called taking trouble, and there is what is called making trouble."

"And the best public servants, Mr. Dale"—this was Sir John, who had unexpectedly raised his eyes—"are those who take most and make least;" and he lowered his eyes and went on reading the documents.

"First," said the Colonel, "there is your correspondence with the staff at Rodhaven. Here it is. We have gone through it carefully—and there's plenty of it. Well, the plain fact is, it has not impressed us favorably—that is, so far as you are concerned."

"Sorry to hear it, sir."

"No, I must say that the tone of your letters does not appear to be quite what it should be."

" Indeed, sir. I thought I followed the usual forms."

"That may be. It is not the form, but the spirit. There is an arrogance—a determination not to brook censure."

"No censure was offered, sir."

"No, but your tone implied that you would not in any circumstances accept it."

"Only because I knew I hadn't merited it, sir."

"But don't you see that subordination becomes impossible when each officer——"

Sir John interrupted his colleague.

"Mr. Dale, perhaps short words will be more comprehensible to you than long ones."

Dale flushed, and spoke hurriedly.

"I'm not without education, sir—as my record shows. I won the Rowland Hill Fourth Class Annual and the Divisional Prize for English composition."

Sir John and the Colonel exchanged a significant glance; and Dale, making a clumsy bow, went on very submissively. "However you are good enough to word it, sir, I shall endeavor to understand."

"Then," said Sir John, with a sudden crispness and severity, "the opinion I have derived from the correspondence is that you were altogether too uppish. You had got too big for your boots."

"Sorry that should be your opinion, sir."

"It is the opinion of my colleague too," said Sir John sharply. "The impudence of a little Jack in office. I'm the king of the castle."

"I employed no such expression, sir."

"No, but you couldn't keep your temper in writing to your superiors, any more than you could in managing the ordinary business of your office.

"Who makes the allegation?" Unconsciously Dale had raised his voice to a high pitch. "That's what I ask. Let's have facts, not allegations, sir."

"Or," said Sir John, calmly and gravely, "any more than you can keep your temper now;" and he leaned back in his chair and looked at Dale with fixed attention.

Dale's face was red. He opened and shut his mouth as if taking gulps of air.

Sir John smiled, and continued very quietly and courteously. "You must forgive me, Mr. Dale, if by my bruskness and apparent lack of consideration I put you to a little test. But it seemed necessary. You see, as to Rodhaven, the gravamen of their charge against you——"

"Charge!" Dale's voice had dropped to a whisper. "Do they lodge a charge against me, sir—in spite of my record?"

"Their report is of course strictly confidential, and it is not perhaps my duty to inform you as to its details."

"I thought if a person's accused, he should at least know his indictment, sir."

Sir John smiled, and nudged the Colonel's elbow. " Then, Mr. Dale, it merely amounts to this. They say you are unquestionably an efficient servant, but that your efficiency—at any rate, in the position you have held of late—has been marred by what seem to be faults of temperament. They believe—and we believe

—that you honestly try to do your best; but, well, you do not succeed."

"I'd be glad to know where I've failed, sir. Mr. Ridgett, he said he found everything in apple-pie order. That was Mr. Ridgett's very own word."

"Who is Mr. Ridgett?"

"Your inspector, sir—what you sent to take over."

"Ah, yes. But he no doubt referred to the office itself. What I am referring to is a much wider question—the necessity of avoiding friction with the public. We have to remember that we are the servants of the public, and not its masters. Now in country districts —— You were at Portsmouth, weren't you, before you went to Rodchurch?"

"Yes, sir."

"Well, of course, in the poorer parts of big towns like Portsmouth, one has rather a rough crowd to deal with; good manners may not be required; a dictatorial method is not so much resented. But in a country village, in a residential neighborhood, where high and low are accustomed to live in amity—well, I must say candidly, a postmaster who adopts bullying tactics, and is always losing his temper——"

"Sir," said Dale earnestly, "I do assure you I am not a bully, nor one who is always losing his temper."

"Yet you gave me the impression of irascibility just now, when I drew you."

Dale inwardly cursed his stupidity in having allowed himself to be drawn. He had made a mistake that might prove fatal. He felt that the whole point of the affair was being lost sight of; they seemed to have drifted away into a discussion of good and bad manners, while he wanted to get back to the great issue of

right and wrong, justice or injustice. And he understood the ever-increasing danger of being condemned
on the minor count, with the cause itself, the great
fundamental principle, remaining unweighed.

"No one," he said, humbly but firmly, "regrets it
more than I do, gentlemen, if I spoke up too hot. But,
sir," and he bowed to Sir John, "you were wishing to
nettle me, and there's no question that for the moment
I was nettled."

All three judges smiled; and Dale, accepting the
smiles as a happy augury, went on with greater confidence.

"I'm sure I apologize. And I ask you not to turn it
to more than its proper consequence—or to make the
conclusion that I'm that way as a rule. With all respect, I'd ask you to think that this means a great deal
to me—a very great deal; and that it has dragged on
until—naturally—it begins to prey on one's mind. I
am like to that extent shaken and off my balance; but
I beg, as no more than is due, gentlemen, that you
won't take me for quite the man up here, where all's
strange, to what I am down there, where I'm in my
element and on my own ground. And I would further
submit, under the head of all parties at Rodhaven, that
there may be a bit of malice behind their report."

"What malice could there possibly be? They appear
to have shown an inclination to pass over the whole
matter."

"Only if I took a black mark, sir. That's where the
shoe pinched with me, sir—and perhaps with them too.
They mayn't have been best pleased when I asked to
have your decision over theirs."

Then the Colonel spoke instead of Sir John.

"But apart from Rodhaven, we have evidence against you from the village. Your neighbors, Mr. Dale, complain more forcibly than anybody else."

"Is that so?" Dale felt as if he had received a wickedly violent blow in the dark. "Of course," and he moved his hands spasmodically—"Of course I've long expected I'd enemies." Then he snorted. "But I suppose, sir, you're alluding now to a certain Member of Parliament whose name I needn't mention."

"Yes, I allude to him, and to others—to several others."

"If some have spoken against me, there's a many more would have spoken for me."

"But they have not done so," said the Colonel dryly.

For a moment Dale's mental distress was so acute that his ideas seemed to blend in one vast confused whirl. Some answer was imperatively necessary, and no answer could evolve itself. Hesitation would be interpreted as the sign of a guilty conscience. And in this dreadful arrest of his faculties, the sense of bodily fatigue accentuated itself till it seemed that it would absolutely crush him.

"Gentlemen, as I was venturing to say—" Really the pause had been imperceptible: "From the vicar downwards, there's many would have spoke to my credit—if I'd asked them. And I did not ask them—and for why?"

"Well, why?"

"Because," said Dale, with a brave effort, "I relied implicitly on the fair play that would be meted out here. From the hour I knew I was to be heard at headquarters, I said this is now between me and headquarters, and I don't require any one—be it the highest in the land—coming between us."

"Ah, I understand," said the Colonel, with great politeness.

"Such was my confident feeling, sir—my full confidence that, having heard me, you'd bear me out as doing my duty, and no more nor no less than my duty."

Yet, even as he said so, his whole brain seemed as if fumes from some horrid corrosive acid were creeping through and through it. In truth, all his confidence had gone, and only his courage remained. These men were hostile to him; they had prejudged him; their deadly politeness and their airs of suave impartiality could not conceal their abominable intentions. He had trusted them, and they were going to show themselves unworthy of trust.

"Gentlemen," he said the word very loudly, and again there came the check to the sequence of his ideas. In another whirl of thought he remembered those courtyards at the Abbey House, the loyal service of his wife's family, the great personage who might have spoken up for him. Oh, why hadn't he allowed Mavis to write a second time imploring aid? "Gentlemen——" He echoed the word twice, and then was able to go on. "My desire has ever bin to conduct the service smooth and expeditious, and in strict accordance with the regulations—more particularly as set out in the manual, which I can truly ass-ass-assev'rate that I read more constant and careful than what I do the Bible."

He knew that the crisis was close upon.him. Now or never he must speak the words that should convince and prevail; and instinct told him that he would speak in vain. Nevertheless, he succeeded in stimulating himself adequately for the last great effort. He would fight game and he would die game.

"If," he said stoutly, "I am at liberty now to make my plain statement of the facts, I do so. It was seven-thirty-five P. M. Miss Yorke was at the instrument. I was here"—and he moved a step away. "The soldier was there;" and he pointed. "The soldier began his audacity by——"

"But, good gracious," said Sir John, "you are going back to the very beginning."

"For your proper understanding," said Dale, with determination, "I must commence at the commencement. If, as promised, I am to be heard——"

"But you *have* been heard."

"Your pardon, sir. You have examined me, but I have made no statement." .

"Oh, very well." Sir John, as well as the other two, assumed an attitude of patient boredom. "Fire ahead, then, Mr. Dale."

And, bowing, Dale plunged into his long-pondered oration. Their three faces told him that he was failing. Not a single point seemed to score. He was muddled, hopeless, but still brave. He struggled on stanchly. With a throbbing at his temples, a prickly heat on his chest, a clammy coldness in his spine— with his voice sounding harsh and querulous, or dull and faint—with the sense that all the invisible powers of evil had combined to deride, to defeat, and to destroy him—he struggled on toward the bitterly bitter end of his ordeal.

He had nearly got there, was just reaching his man-to-man finale, when the judges cut him short.

"One moment, Mr. Dale."

The nice young man had come in, and was talking both to Sir John and the Colonel.

"Thank you. Just for a moment."

Of his own accord Dale had gone back to the window.

It was all over. Never mind about the end of the speech. Nothing could have been gained by saying it. The tension of his nerves relaxed, and a wave of sick despair came rolling upward from viscera to brain. He knew now with absolute certainty that right was going to count for nothing; no justice existed in the world; these men were about to decide against him.

"Yes,"—and the young man laughed genially—"he said I was to offer his apologies."

Dale listened to the conversation at the table without attempting to understand it. Somebody, as he gathered dully, was demanding an interview. But the interruption could make no difference. It was all over.

"He said he wouldn't take 'No' for an answer."

Then they all laughed; and Sir John said to the young man, "Very well. Ask him in."

The young man went out, leaving the door open; and Dale saw that the secretary had risen and brought another chair to the table. Then footsteps sounded in the corridor, and Sir John and the Colonel smilingly turned their eyes toward the open doorway. Dale, turning his eyes in the same direction, started violently.

The newcomer was Mr. Barradine.

He shook hands with the gentlemen at the table,

who had both got up to receive him; he talked to them
pleasantly and chaffingly, and there was more laughter; then he nodded to Dale; then he said he was much
obliged to the secretary for giving him the chair, and
then he sat down.

Dale's thoughts were like those of a drowning sail-
or, when through the darkness and the storm he hears
the voice of approaching aid. He had been going
down in the deep, cruel waters, with the longed-for
lights of home, the adored face of his wife, the dreaded
gates of hell, all dancing wildly before his eyes—and
now. Breath again, hope again, life again.

He listened, but did not trouble to understand. It
was dreamlike, glorious, sublime. The illustrious visitor had alluded to the fact that Jack, the nice young
man, was a connection of his; and had explained that,
hearing from Jack of to-day's appointment, he determined to go right down there and beard the lions in
their den. He had also spoken of a nephew of Sir
John's, who was coming to have a bang at the Abbey
partridges in September. He further reminded the
Colonel that he did not consider himself a stranger,
because they used to meet often at such and such a
place. He also asked if the Colonel kept up his riding. Now, without any change of tone, he was talking of the case.

And Dale, watching, felt as if his whole heart had
been melted, and as if it was streaming across the
room in a warm vapor of gratitude.

"My interest," said Mr. Barradine, "is simply public spirit; although it is quite true that I know Mr.
Dale personally. Indeed, he and his wife have been
friends with me and my family for more years than
I care to count."

Dale caught his breath and coughed. He was almost overwhelmed by the noble turn of that last phrase. Friends! Nothing more, and nothing less. Not patron and dependents, but friends.

"And, of course," Mr. Barradine was saying, "I want my friend to come out of it all right—as I honestly believe he deserves to come out of it."

Dale felt himself on the verge of breaking down and sobbing. His strength had gone long ago, and now all his courage went too. With his gratitude there mingled a cowardly joy that he had not been left to fight things out alone and be beaten, that succor had come at the supreme moment. Ardently admiring as well as fervently thanking, he watched the friend in need, the splendid ally, the only agent of Providence that could have saved him.

Who would not admire such a prince?

He was old and big, and though rather frail, yet so magnificently grand. His costume was of the plainest character—black satin neck-scarf tied negligently, with a pearl pin stuck through it anyhow, a queer sort of black pea-jacket with braid on its edges, square-toed patent-leather boots with white spats—and, nevertheless, he seemed to be dressed as sumptuously as if he had been wearing all the gold and glitter of his Privy Councilor's uniform. His face seemed to Dale like the mask of a Roman emperor—a high-bridged delicate nose, thin gray hair combed back from a low forehead, a ridge like a straight bar above the tired eyes and a puffiness of flesh below them, a moustache that showed the lose curves of the mouth, and a small pointed beard that perhaps concealed an unbeautiful protrusion of the chin. His voice, so calm, so evenly modulated, had been trained in the senate and the pal·

ace. His attitude, his manner, his freedom from gesture and emphasis, all indicated a born ruler as well
as a born aristocrat. Was it likely that when *he* spoke
he would fail?

Already he had swung the balance. Dale could see
that he would not be resisted. And as the great man
sat talking—chatting, one might almost term it—he
seemed to be taking out of the atmosphere every element of discomfort, all the passionate excitement, the
hot throbs of indignation, the cold tremors of fear.
Dale felt his muscles recovering tone, his legs stiffen-
ing themselves, his blood circulating richly and freely.

"You have here," said Mr. Barradine, "a man of
unblemished reputation, who, acting obviously from
conscientious motives, has in the exercise of his judgment done so and so. Now, admitting for the sake of
argument, that he has done wrong, are you to punish
him for an error of judgment? We do not, however,
admit that it was an error." . . .

Dale looked dogged and stern. He had been on the
point of saying, "I never will admit it;" but the words
would not come out. He must not interrupt. This
was Heaven-sent advocacy.

Mr. Barradine went on quietly and grandly. In
truth what he said now was almost what had been said
by the authorities at Rodhaven—good intentions, over-
zeal, a mistake, if you care to call it so;—but from
these lips it fell on Dale's ear as soothing music. Mr.
Barradine might say whatever he pleased: and the
man he was defending would not object.

"And now if I show the edge of the little private
ax that I myself have to grind!" Mr. Barradine
laughed. They all laughed. "Our member—we agree
in politics; but, well, you know, he and I do not al-

together hit it off. We are both of us getting older than we were—and perhaps we both suffer from swollen head. It's the prevailing malady of the period."

Sir John laughed gaily. "I don't think you show any marked symptoms of it. But I can't answer for what's-his-name."

"Well;" and Mr. Barradine made his first gesture—just a wave of the right hand. "One can't have two kings at Brentford. And honestly I shall feel that you have given me a smack in the face, if——"

"Oh, my dear sir!"

Then they sent Dale out of the room. Really it seemed that they had forgotten his presence, or they might have banished him before. It was the Colonel who suddenly appeared to remember that he was still standing over there by the window.

He waited in a large empty room, and the time passed slowly. It was the luncheon hour, and far and near he heard the footsteps of clerks going to and coming from the midday meal. Bigwigs no doubt would take their luncheon privately, in small groups, here and there, all over the building. He too was getting very hungry.

An hour passed, an hour and a half, two hours; and then he was again summoned to the other room. There was no one in it except the secretary—looking hot and red after a copious repast, speaking jovially and familiarly, and seeming altogether more common and less important than when under the restraining influence of bigwigs.

"Ah, here you are." And he chuckled amicably, and gave Dale a roguish nod. "You've had your wires pulled A1 for you. It's decided to stretch a point in your favor. Not to make a secret, they don't wish to run counter to Mr. B.'s wishes. You have been lucky, Mr. Dale, in having him behind you."

Dale gulped, but did not say anything.

"Very well. I am to inform you that you will be reinstated; but—in order to allow the talk to blow over—you will not resume your duties for a fortnight. You will take a fortnight's holiday—from now—on full pay."

Dale said nothing. He could have said so much. At this moment he felt that his victory had been intrinsically a defeat. But the strength had gone from him; and in its place there was only joy—weak but immense joy in the knowledge that all had ended happily. And the world would say that he had won.

V.

OUTSIDE in the streets his joy increased.
Nothing had mattered. Beneath all surface sensations there was the deep fundamental rapture: as of
a wild animal that has been caught, and is now loose
and free—a squirrel that has escaped from the trap,
and, whisking and bounding through sunlight and
shadow, understands that its four paws are still under
it, and that only a little of its fur is left in those iron
teeth. Security after peril—articulate man or dumb
brute, can one taste a fuller bliss?

But he must share and impart it. Mavis! He
might not go dashing back to Hampshire—the fortnight's exile prevented him from joining her there. A
broad grin spread across his face. What was that
learned saying that his old schoolmaster, Mr. Fenley,
used to be so fond of repeating? "If Mahomet can
not go to the mountain, the mountain must come to
Mahomet."

The memory of this classical quotation tickled him,
and he went chuckling into the Cannon Street post
office and wrote out a telegraph-form.

"Reinstatement. Come at once. Shall expect you
this evening without fail."

Having sent off the telegram, he presently ordered
his dinner in the grill-room of a Ludgate Hill restaurant.

"Yes, let's see your notion of a well-cooked rump-

61

steak. And I'll try some of the famous lager beer.
. . . Oh, bottle or draught's all one to me;" and he
snapped his fingers and laughed. " Now, sharp's the
word, Mister waiter. I'm fairly famished."

The lager beer, served in a glass vase, was delicious
—sunbeams distilled to make a frothing and unheady
nectar. The grilled steak and the fried potatoes could
not have been better done at the Buckingham Palace
kitchens. Never for three weeks had food tasted like
this. All had been dust and ashes in his mouth since
the row began.

Then with appetite satisfied and digestion beginning,
he smoked.

" If you've anything in the shape of a really good
threepenny cigar, I can do with it. But don't fob me
off with any poor trash. For I've my pipe in my
pocket."

The waiter said he had a truly splendid threepenny;
and Dale, enjoying it, talked to the waiter. He could
not help talking; he could not help laughing. After
so much silence it was a treat to hear the sound of his
own loud, jolly voice, and he gave himself the treat
freely.

" You're from the country, sir," said the waiter, politely.

" Yes, bull's eye," said Dale, with boisterous good-
humor. " Hand him out a cokernut. But may I
ask how you guessed my place of origin so pat?"

" Well, sir. I don't know, sir. Haven't had you
here before, I think."

" Oh, you're very clever, you Londoners. I don't
doubt you can all see through a brick wall. Yes, I'm
from the country—but I'm beginning to know my way

about the town too. Ever bin on a steamboat to Rodhaven?"

"Rodhaven? No, sir."

Then Dale told the waiter about the heaths and
downs and woods that lie between Rodhaven and Old
Manninglea.

"Prettiest part of the world that I know of," he
said proudly. "You spend your next holiday there.
Take the four-horse sharrybank from Rodhaven pier
—and when you get to the Roebuck at Rodchurch, you
get off of the vehicle and ask for the Postmaster."

"Yes, sir?"

"He won't eat you," and Dale laughed with intense
enjoyment of his humor. "He's not a bad chap really, though his neighbors say he's a bit of a Tartar. I
give you my word he'll receive you decently, and stand
you dinner into the bargain. I know he will—and for
why? Because I am that gentleman myself."

He could not resist the pleasure of rounding off his
sentence with the grand word "Gentleman," and he
was gratified by the waiter's meekly obsequious reception of the word.

"Thank you, sir. Much obliged, sir."

When leaving, he gave the waiter a generous tip.

To-day his walk through the gaily-crowded streets
was sweet to him as a lazy truant ramble in the woods
during church-time. Everything that he looked at
delighted him—the richness of shop-windows, showing
all the expensive useless goods that no sensible person
ever wants; the liveries worn by pampered servants
standing at carriage wheels; the glossy coats of met-
tlesome, prancing horses; the extravagant dresses of
fine ladies mincingly walking on the common public

pavement; the stolid grandeur of huge policemen, and the infinite audacity of small newspaper boys; the life, the color, the noise. It seemed as if the busy city and the pleasure-loving West-end alike unfolded themselves as a panorama especially arranged for one's amusement; and his satisfaction was so great that it mutely expressed itself in words which he would have been quite willing to shout aloud. Such as: "Bravo, London! You aren't a bad little place when one gets to know you. There's more in you than meets the eye, first view."

And because he was so happy himself, he could sympathize with the happiness of everybody else. He was glad that the rich people were so rich and the poor people so contented; he admired a young swell for buying flowers from a woman with a shawl over her head; he mused on all the honest, well-paid toil that had gone to the raising of the grapes and peaches at a Piccadilly fruiterer's. "Live, and let live"—that's a good motto all the world over. When he saw babies in perambulators, he would have liked to kiss them. When he saw an elderly man with a pretty young woman, he wanted to nudge him and say jocosely, "You're in luck, old chap, aren't you?" When couples of boy and girl lovers went whispering by, he smiled sentimentally. "That's right. You can't begin too soon. Never mind what Ma says. If you like him, stick to him, lassie."

And though still alone, he felt no loneliness. His own dear companion was soon coming to him.

Throughout the walk the only thoughts tinged with solemnity were those which sprang from his always deepening gratitude to Mr. Barradine. He wanted to pay a ceremonious call for the purpose of expressing his thanks, and he felt that he should do this immediately; but for the life of him he could not remember whether the great man's London house was situated in Grosvenor Square or Grosvenor Place. Mavis of could would know. Or he could find out from one of these policemen. He hesitated, and it was the state of his collar that decided him. He would postpone the visit of gratitude, and do it first thing to-morrow morning in a clean collar.

The hall clock at his lodgings announced the hour as close on five, and he mentally noted that the timepiece was inaccurate—three and a half minutes behind Greenwich. As usual, the hall was untenanted, with no servant to answer questions. He searched the dark recesses of a dirty letter-rack, on the chance that he might find a telegram from his wife waiting for him. Then he went gaily up the interminable staircase, making nothing now of its five flights, enjoying their steepness as productive of agreeable exercise.

" Hulloa! " he muttered. " What's this? "

A woman's hat and parasol were lying on a chair, and there was a valise on the floor by the chest of drawers. Turning, he gave a cry of delight. Mavis was stretched on the bed, fast asleep.

She woke at the sound of his voice, scrambled down, and flung herself into his arms.

" Will, oh, Will. My dearest Will! "

" My darling—my little sweetheart. But how have you come to me—have you flown? "

" Don't be silly. "

He was devouring her face with his kisses, straining her to his breast in a paroxysm of pleasure, almost suffocating himself and her in the ardor of the embrace, and jerking out his words as though they were gasps for breath.

"When did you get my wire? Why, it's impossible. I on'y wired two-forty-three. Is it witchcraft or just a dream?"

"Did you wire? I never got it. I was so anxious that I couldn't stay there any longer without news. So I just packed and came. Will—be sensible. Tell me everything."

"Best of news! Reinstated!" He bellowed the glad tidings over her head. She was all warm and palpitating in his arms, her dear body so delicate and fragile and yet so round and firm, her dear face soft and smooth, with lips that trembled and smelled like garden flowers.

"Did you come up by the nine o'clock train? How long have you been waiting here?"

"Oh, don't bother about me. I'm nothing. It's *you* I want to hear about."

Then they sat side by side on the narrow little bed, he with his arm firmly clasped round her waist, and she nestling against him with her face hidden on his breast.

"Mav, my bird, I can't never leave you again. I've bin just a lost dog without you. Did you start before you got my Sunday letter?"

"Yes."

"Every day I wrote—didn't I?—just like the old time. But I've a bone to pick with you, young lady. What d'ye mean by not writing to me more regular? Not even so much as a post-card these last three days!"

"Will—I, I couldn't. I was too anxious while it
all remained in suspense."

"Yes, but you might have sent me a card. I told
you cards would satisfy me. I was thinking of you
off and on all yesterday. I can tell you it was just
about the longest day of my life. Did you and Auntie
go to church?"

"No. Oh, don't ask questions about me—when I'm
dying for a full account of it."

He asked no more questions. After stooping to kiss
the fragrant coil of hair above her forehead, he burst
out into his joyous tale of triumph.

"It was Mr. Barradine that did the trick for me;"
and with enthusiasm he narrated the gloriously oppor-
tune arrival of "the friend at court." Indeed his enthusiasm was so great that he could not keep still
while speaking. He got off the bed, and walked about
the room, brandishing his arms. "He's just a tip-
topper. If you could have been there to hear him, you
wouldn't 'a' left off crying yet. I tell you I was fairly
overcome myself. It was the *way* he did it. 'Of
course,' he said, 'I want my friend to come out of it
as I honestly believe he deserves.' They couldn't
stand up against him half a minute. But, mind
you, Mav;" and Dale stopped moving, and spoke
solemnly, "he's aged surprising these last few
years. He's more feeble like than ever one would
think, seeing him on his horse. I mean, his bodily
frame. The int'lect's more powerful, I should make
the guess, than ever it was. . . . And mind you, here's
another thing, Mav;" and he spoke even more solemnly. "All this is going to be a lesson to me. I've
worn my considering cap most of the time I've been

away from you—and, Mav, I'm going to lay to heart the fruits of my experience. All's well that ends well, old lady. But once bit, twice shy; and in the future I'm going to trim my sails so's to avoid another such an upset." He came back to the bed, and sat beside her again. "I shan't be too proud to say the gray mare's the better horse when it comes to steering through the etiquette book, and I mean to mend my manners by Mav's advice."

"My dear Will—my true husband—I'm so glad to think it's ended as we wished."

Her joy in his joy was beautiful to see. Though her pretty eyes were flooded by sudden tears, her whole face was shining with happiness; and she pressed both her hands against him, and raised her lips to his lips with the rapid movements of a child that craves a caress from its loved and venerated guardian.

"There," he said, after a long hug. "Now use your hanky, and let's be jolly—and begin to enjoy ourselves. You and I are going to have the best treat this evening that London can provide. But I think that, now you've come, I'll do my duty first, and then throw myself into the pleasure without alloy. What's his address?"

"Whose address?"

"Mr. Barradine's."

"How do you mean? His address here, in London?"

"Yes."

"Number 181, Grosvenor Place."

"Ah, I thought it was the Place—and yet I couldn't feel sure it wasn't the Square. Now you shall tie my tie for me."

And, getting out a new collar, he told her that he would go to thank Mr. Barradine there and then. He would be less than no time fulfilling this act of necessary politeness, and while he was away she was to see the people of the house and get a proper married couple's bedroom in lieu of this bachelor's crib.

Mavis, however, thought that Dale was mistaken in supposing the ceremonious call necessary or even advisable, and she gently tried to dissuade him from carrying out his purpose. She considered that a carefully written letter would be a better method of communication to employ in thanking their grand ally. But Dale was obstinate. He said that in this one matter he knew best. It was between him and Mr. Barradine now—a case of man to man.

"He'll look for it, Mav, and would take a very poor opinion of me if I hadn't the manhood to go straight and frank, and say 'I thank you.' Trust your old William for once more, Mav;" and he laughed merrily. "I tell you what I felt I wanted to do at the G. P. O. was a leaf out of the Roman history—that is, to kneel down to him and say, 'Put your hand on William Dale's head, sir, for sign and token, and take his service from this day forward as your bondsman and your slave.' But I shan't say that;" and again he laughed. "I shall simply say, 'Mr. Barradine, sir, I thank you for what you've done for me and for the kind and open way you done it.' So much he will expect, and the rest he will understand."

He was equally determined to despatch a telegram giving the good news to Mrs. Petherick at North Ride Cottage, and he became almost huffy when Mavis again suggested that a letter would meet the case.

" I don't understand you, Mav. You seem now as
if you were for belittling everything. I'm not going
to spare sixpence to keep your aunt on tenterhooks for
course of post."

Mr. Barradine's town mansion stood in a command-
ing corner position, with its front door in the side
street; and from the glimpse that Dale obtained of its
hall, its staircase, and its vast depth, he judged that it
was quite worthy of the owner of that noble country-
seat, the Abbey House.

The servants were at first doubtful as to the pro
priety of admitting him. They said their master was
at home, but they did not know if he could receive
visitors.

"He won't refuse to see me," said Dale confidently.
" Tell him it's Mr. Dale of Rodchurch, and won't detain him two minutes."

"Very good," said the principal servant gravely.
" But I can't disturb him if he's resting."

" Oh, if he's resting," said Dale, " I'll wait. I'll make
my time his time—whether convenient to me or not."

Then they led him down a passage, past a cloak-room
and a lavatory, to a small room right at the back of
the house.

Perhaps the room seemed small only by reason of its
great height. Dale, waiting patiently, examined his
surroundings with curious interest. There were two
old-fashioned writing-tables—one looking as if it was
never used, and the other looking busy and homelike,
with a cabinet full of every conceivable sort of note-
paper, trays full of pens, and little candles to be lighted
when one desired to affix seals. On a roundabout conveniently near there were books of reference that in-

cluded the current volume of the *London Post Office Directory*. The sofas and chairs were upholstered in
dark green leather, the chimney-piece was of carved
marble, a few ancient and rather dismal pictures hung
almost out of sight on the walls; and generally, the
room would have produced an impression of a repel-
lent and ungenial kind of pomp, if it had not been for
the extremely human note struck by the large assort-
ment of photographs.

These were dabbed about everywhere—in panels
above the chair rail, in screens and silver frames, on the
writing-table, and loose and unframed on the mantel-
shelf. They were nearly all portraits of women—and
some nice attractive bits among them, as Dale thought;
young and cheeky ones, too, that he guessed were ac-
tresses and not nieces or cousins. He smiled tolerantly. These photographs brought to his mind a nearly forgotten fancy of his own, together with echoes
of the local gossip. Round Rodchurch the talk ran
that the Right Honorable gentleman was still a rare
one for the ladies. "And why not?" thought Dale.
A childless old widower may keep up that sort of game
as long as he likes, or as long as he can, without
wounding any one's feeling. It wasn't as if her lady-
ship had been still alive.

"Sir, I hope I have not disturbed you; but I couldn't
be easy till I'd cordially and heartily thanked you."

Mr. Barradine had come in, and Dale fired off his
brief set speeches. But instinct almost immediately
told him that once more Mavis had been right and he
wrong. Mr. Barradine was not expecting or desiring
a personal call.

"Not worth mentioning. Nothing at all." He said

these things courteously, but there was a coldness in
his tone that quite froze the visitor. He seemed to be
saying really: "Now look here, I have had quite
enough bother about you; and please don't let me have
any more of it."

"Then, sir, I thank you—and—er—that's all."

"Very glad if——" Mr. Barradine made the same
gesture that Dale had seen a few hours ago: a wave of
the right hand. But to Dale it seemed that it was different now, that it indicated languor and haughtiness;
indeed, it seemed that the whole man was different.
Could this be the advocate who had spoken up so
freely for a friend in trouble? All the majesty and
the force, as well as the generous friendliness, had disappeared. The face, the voice, the whole bearing belonged to another man. The tired eyes had not a
spark of fire in them; those puffy bags of loose flesh,
that hung between the outer corners of the cheekbones
and the thin birdlike nose, were so ugly as to be disfiguring; the mouth, instead of looking soft and kind,
although proud, now appeared to close in the unbending lines of a very obdurate self-esteem.

This new aspect of his patron made Dale stammer
uncomfortably; and he felt something akin to humilia-
tion in lieu of the fine glow of gratitude with which he
had come hurrying from the Euston Road.

"Then my duty—and my thanks—and I'll say good
afternoon, sir."

He had pulled himself together and spoken these last
words ringingly, and now grasping Mr. Barradine's
hand he gave it a mercilessly severe squeeze.

"Damnation!" Under the horny grip, Mr. Barradine emitted a squeal of pain. "Confound it—my good

fellow—why the deuce can't you be careful what you're doing?"

Mr. Barradine, very angry, was ruefully examining his hand; and Dale, apologizing profusely, stared at it too. It was limp in texture, yellowish white of color, with bluish swollen veins, some darkish brown patches here and there, and slight glistening protuberances at the knuckle joints—an old man's hand, so feeble that it could not bear the least pressure, and yet decorated with a young man's fopperies. Dale noticed the three rings on the little finger—one of gold, one of silver, one of black metal, each with tiny colored gems in it —and while heartily ashamed of his rustic violence, he felt a secret contempt for its victim.

"That's all right." Mr. Barradine, although still wincing, had recovered composure, and what he said now appeared to be an implied excuse for the sharpness of his protest. "When you get to my time of life, you'll perhaps know what gout means."

"Sorry you should be afflicted that way, sir," said Dale contritely.

Mr. Barradine had rung a bell, and a servant was standing at the door.

"Good day to you, Mr. Dale. You're going home, I suppose?"

"Not for a fortnight, sir."

"Ah! I hope to return to the Abbey on Thursday morning;" and quite obviously Mr. Barradine now intended to gratify Dale by a few polite sentences of small talk, and thus show him that his offense had been pardoned. "Yes, I soon begin to pine for my garden. Friday, at latest, sees me home again. I always call the Abbey home. No place like home, Dale."

Dale going out, through the long passage to the hall, felt momentarily depressed by a sense of humiliating failure in the midst of his apparent success. If only he could have fought them and beaten them alone, as a strong man fighting unaided, instead of being pulled through the battle by that veinous, blotchy, ringed hand! However, he promptly tried to banish all such vague discomfort from his mind.

All of it was gone when he got back to the lodging-house, and found his wife established in their new room.

VI

"THE Acadia Theater! So be it. They're all one to me."

Mavis had chosen this famous music hall because, as she explained, Chirgwin was performing at it, and her aunt had always said that Chirgwin was the most excruciatingly funny of all music-hall artists.

"So be it. Half a minute, though." Dale counting his money, dolefully discovered that it had run very low indeed. "I begin to think we shall have to cut down our treat a bit."

But Mavis swept away all difficulties. She had brought money—her very own money—her little emergency hoard; and opening her handbag, and tumbling inside it, she produced a five-pound note, and smilingly put it on the dressing-table.

"Hulloa! There's more where that comes from." His quick ear had caught the rustling sound inside the handbag. "There's other notes in there, old lady;" and, laughing, he tried to snatch the bag from her. "How much? Here's a miser, and no mistake."

"Never you mind how much your miser's got." Her lips were smiling, her eyes shining, and with a happy laugh she sprang away from him. "Now, no nonsense. Take me out, and make a fuss of me."

For a moment he stood still, admiring her. She was dressed in her very best Sunday clothes, and, to his eye at least, she looked quite entrancingly nice. Her

straw hat was full of artificial roses that any one
might have sworn were real; her unbuttoned jacket
disclosed the delicate finery of a muslin blouse; her
long skirt, held up so gracefully by the unoccupied
hand, was made of veritable silk. She just looked tip-
top—a picture—to the full as much a lady as the young
dames he had been lately observing; and yet, wonder
of wonders, she was his property.

"By Jupiter, I must have another hug—and then off
we go."

"No," she said archly, and yet decidedly. "No
more kisses till bedtime. I'm all ready to show myself
to company, and I don't wish to be rumpled."

They rode like a gentleman and a lady in a hansom
cab; they dined like a duke and a duchess at the Cri-
terion restaurant; and they were both as happy and
light-hearted as schoolboys on the first day of their
holidays. Like children they made silly little jokes
which would have been jokes to no one but themselves.
He caused immoderate laughter in her by assuming
the airs of a man about town, by affecting a profound
knowledge of the French names for all the dishes on
the table d'hote menu, and by describing how offended
he would now be if any one should detect that he was
not a regular London swell; and she, by whispered
criticism of a stout party at a distant table, sent such
a convulsion of mirth through him that he choked
badly while drinking wine. He had insisted on order-
ing the wine, and in making Mav take her share of it,
although she vowed that the unaccustomed stimulant
would fly to her head.

"Rot, old girl. You dip your beak in it—it's mostly

froth and fizz, and no more strength than the lager beer, as far as I can make out."

"How much does it cost?"

"Shan't tell. Yes, I will," and he roared with laughter, "since it's you that's paying for it. Best part of seven shillings."

"Oh, Will, it's *wicked!*"

"Bosh! This is the time of our lives;" and he chaffed her again about being a secret capitalist. "Blow the expense. Let the money fly. And, Mav, I on'y borrow it. This is all my affair really."

"No, no. You'll spoil half my pleasure if you don't let me pay."

But his money or her money—what did it matter? They two were one, reunited after a cruel, most bitterly cruel separation; her face was flushed with joy more than with wine, and her love poured out of her eyes like a stream of light.

They walked from the restaurant to Leicester Square, arm in arm, proud and joyous, enjoying the lamplight and noise, not minding the airless heat; but when they reached the entrance of the music hall—where he had stood gaping, solitary and sad, a few nights ago—Mavis met with disappointment.

"Oh," she said, "what a shame! They've changed the bill. Chirgwin's name is gone. He was acting here Friday night."

"How d'you know that?"

She followed him into the vestibule, and he asked her again while they waited in the crowd by the ticket office.

"I read it in the paper. Aunt and I were talking of him; and I—I had the curiosity to look at the advertisements—not dreaming that I should come so near seeing him."

"Never mind," cried Dale, in his jovial, far-carrying voice; "there'll be a many as good as him."

"Hush," she whispered. "If you talk like that, they'll know we come from the country;" and she squeezed his arm affectionately. "I don't mind a bit, dear—but there's no one so clever as Chirgwin. Really there isn't."

She at once forgot her trifling disappointment. Placed side by side in extravagantly expensive seats of the stately circle, surrounded by ladies and gentlemen in evening dress, they both gave themselves wholly to the pleasure of this unparalleled treat. All the early items of a long program astounded or charmed him; and her enjoyment was enhanced by recognizing how completely he had thrown off the narrowness or prejudice of village life. Listening to his laughter at almost indecent jokes, his ejaculations of wonder when conjurers showed their skill, his enthusiastic clappings after acrobats had proved their strength, she understood that all his natural sternness was temporarily relaxed; he would not allow himself to be disturbed by any semi-religious notions of propriety or impropriety; he was just a jolly comrade for an evening's sport.

"Brayvo! Brayvo! By Jupiter—wouldn't 'a' credited it without the evidence of my own eyes." The gorgeous curtains had just descended upon a narrow parlor, which a Japanese necromancer had literallly filled to overflowing with colored cardboard boxes produced from the interior of one single top hat. "See! Watch 'em, Mav." Footmen were coming in front of the cur-

tains to remove the plethora of cardboard boxes.
"They're real boxes, Mav."

Sweet music, happy laughter, brilliant light—the
evening glided entrancingly, like a dream in which
neither Greenwich nor any other time is kept.

During the interval before the ballet he took her out
of the circle, strolled with her up and down the prom-
enade, and gave her an American drink in a refreshment saloon. It was appallingly hot, and they were
both longing to quench their thirst with something
big and cold. A magnificent waiter brought them big-
ness and coldness in tall tumblers with straws, and
they sat on a velvet divan and sucked rapturously.

Standing or seated at tables, there were young
bloods with white waistcoats and cigarettes, and young
ladies with rich gowns and made-up faces; through a
gilded doorway one had a vista of the thronged prom-
enade; the air was hot, exhausted, pungent with tobacco smoke; and amid the chatter of voices, the
clink of glasses, the rustle of petticoats, one could only
just hear the great orchestra playing chords of some
fantastic march.

Suddenly Mavis felt a vaguely pleasant confusion of
mind, as though the icily cold liquid, as she slowly absorbed it through the straw, was freezing her intelligence. She could not for a few moments understand
what Dale was whispering at her ear.

"Between you and me and the post, Mav"——And
he told her that, according to his opinion, all these
women parading up and down were no better than
they ought to be. They were of course, socially, much
higher than the common women of the streets, but he
considered them to be, morally, on the same level: al-

though they did not accost strangers, they were all willing to scrape acquaintance with any one who looked as if he had money in his pocket. "Yes, London's a bit of an eye-opener, old girl." Then he laughed behind his hand, and said that she was probably the only respectable woman and virtuous wife in the whole of the theater.

Mavis, although trying to listen, answered at random.

"Will, I do believe there's spirits in this stuff—yes, and strong spirits too."

"Oh, bosh. It's just a refresher. Mostly crushed ice, and a few drops of sirup."

Mavis, however, was quite correct. At the bottom of the glass, and below the light sirupy mixture, there lurked liqueurs of which the potency was only rendered doubtful because of their low temperature. The beginning of the long drink was absolutely delicious, so soothing and so cooling; but at the end of it was as if one had filled one's self with insidious quick-running flame.

Mavis put down her empty tumbler, and looked at it reproachfully.

"Will, it has made me come over all funny. My head's swimming."

When they got back to their seats and were watching the ballet, he too felt the consequences of guileless straw-sucking; but with him the after effects were entirely pleasurable. He felt invigorated, peaceful, massively grand.

He sat placidly enjoying the beauty of the scene, the grace of the dancers, the vibrations of the music. The stage was dark at first, and one could merely make out that it pictured a wildly-imagined grove in the land of dreams; then it grew brighter, and one saw preposterous giant-flowers—foxgloves so big that when they opened there was a human face in each quivering bell. And the flowers came out of the earth and danced; children dressed up as birds, brown boys like beetles, slim girls like butterflies, all came dancing, dancing; with more light every moment, till the dazzle and the blaze seemed to drive away the little people;—and then quite glorious forms appeared, pirouetting, almost flying—pink-limbed houris, fairies, nymphs—"call 'em what you please—a fair knock-out."

"It makes me go round and round," whispered Mavis.

He sat grave and silent—just nodding his head in approval of all he saw, not troubling to applaud any further, impassive as some Eastern sultan for whom slaves and courtiers had made a mask.

Then gradually his mind seemed half to detach itself from the thraldom of external objects. These novel sense impressions, pouring into him, joined themselves to old memories, and, mingling, made up a fuller stream of joy. He seemed to be able to think of five or six things at once; but, as the undercurrent of every thought, there was the same deep-flowing comfort, of which the source lay in his relief at the escape from danger. Those fairies flashing about under the branches of sham trees momentarily evoked the ancient haunting distress of his youth, and out of this thought came the lofty conception of Mavis as his guardian angel. How persistently the first of those fancies lingered—after so many years! Bother the fairies or nymphs, or whatever they were. Household angels

are what a man wants to bring him contentment; and
keep him straight, day by day, and week by week.

Before the ballet was over, he became bored with it.
Too long! Enough is as good as a feast. They were
singing now as well as dancing.

The massive, voluminously quiescent sensation induced by the liqueurs had passed away, and in its place
came increased weariness of the spectacular entertainment. The light, and the music, and the half-naked
women, who still danced and pranced, were affecting
his nerves unpleasantly now. He looked away from
the stage, and stared at the audience. Behind him,
as he knew, there were all those hussies with painted
faces offering themselves for hire. And wherever he
looked, he seemed to see evidences of amorous traffic.
When you examined it attentively, the entire audience
seemed to resolve itself into an endless repetition of
the same small group of two persons of two sexes, each
soliciting the other's favor; a man and a woman sitting
close together, the couple, the factorial two—everywhere, all round the circle, along the three visible rows
of stalls, and again in the private boxes. Those
wealthy men in the boxes were unquestionably accompanied by their mistresses and not by their wives or
sisters. Through the vibrating music and the super-
heated atmosphere, on a river of vivid light, they were
all drifting fast toward the night of love that each pair
had arranged for itself.

And they too would have their night of love. He
looked at his wife, and felt his pulses stirred as much
now as in the far-off days of courtship—more, because
then there was no experience of facts to strengthen his
imagination. He gently pressed her arm, and thrilled

at the mere contact. She was leaning back, fanning
herself with her program, and he observed the round-
ness and whiteness of her neck, the flesh of her shoulder showing through the transparent sleeve of her
blouse, the moistness and warmth of her open lips.

Yet she had told him at Rodchurch Road Station
that she was attractive only to his eyes, and that she
could never again arouse desire in other men. What
utter nonsense! She was simply adorable.

VII

THEY took a cab to drive back in, and he almost carried her up to their bedroom. It was on the same floor as the other room, with the same marvelous bird's-eye view of the starlit sky and the lamplit town. He had got her to himself at last—here, high above the world, half-way to heaven. There seemed to him something poetical, almost sublime in their situation: they two alone, isolated, millions of people surrounding them and no living creature able to interfere with them.

As he knew, they were the only lodgers on this top floor; and so one need not even trouble to avoid making a noise. He gave full voice to his exultation.

"There, old lady." He had opened the window as wide as it would go, and he told her to look out. "The air—what there is of it—will do you good."

"Oh, I couldn't," and she recoiled.

"Giddy?"

"*Giddy* isn't the word. Oh, Will, why did you let me drink that stuff—after drinking the wine?"

"I thought you'd got a better head-piece. Look at *me*. I could 'a' stood two or three more goes at it, and bin none the worse." And he chaffed her merrily. "Here's a tale—if it ever leaks out Rodchurch way. Have you heard how Mrs. Dale behaved up in London? Went to the theater, and drunk more'n was good for

84

her. Came out fair squiffy—so's poor Mr. Dale, he felt quite disgraced."

She was not intoxicated in an ugly way; her speech, her movements were unaffected, and yet the alcohol was troubling her brain. She looked like a child who has been overexercised at a children's party, and who comes home with eyebrows raised, eyes glowing and yet dull, and cheeks very pale.

"Oh, dear, I *am* tired," and she sat down on a chair by the chest of drawers, and slowly took off her hat.

But she got up again and pushed Dale away, when he offered to help her in undressing.

"No, certainly not. What are you thinking of?" and she began to hum one of the pretty airs they had heard at the theater. "But, my word, Will," and she stopped humming, and laughed foolishly, "I shan't be sorry to get out of my things. It *is* hot. This is the hottest night we've had."

"Ah, you feel it. I've got acclim'tized."

He undressed rapidly, and lighting the briar pipe which he had not cared to smoke in the genteel society at the theater, he lay on the outside of the bed.

"Better now, old girl?"

"Yes. I'm all right, Will. Dear old boy—I'm all right."

Lying on the bed and immensely enjoying his delayed pipe, he watched her. She wandered about the room, moved one of the two candles from the mantelshelf to the chest of drawers, put her blouse on the seat of a chair and her skirt across the back of it. Then with slow graceful movements she began to uncoil her hair, and as her smooth white arms went up and down, the candlelight sent gigantic wavering shadows across

the wall-paper to the ceiling. Beneath one of her elbows he could see right out through the open window
into a dark void. From his position on the bed nothing was visible out there, but he could fill it if he cared
to do so—the scattered dust of street lamps below and
the scattered dust of solar systems above.

Soon he puffed lazily, drowsily; then he nodded, and
then the pipe fell from his mouth.

"Hullo!" And muttering, he roused himself. "I
must 'a' dropped off. Might 'a' set the bed on fire."

Mavis, in her chemise and stockings now, with her
hair down, was still at the dressing-table. She did
not turn when he spoke to her. While he dozed she
had fetched the other candle, and in the double light
she was staring intently at the reflection of her face in
the looking-glass.

Dale slipped softly off the bed, moved across to the
dressing-table, and with explosive vigor clasped her in
his arms.

"Oh, how you frightened me!" She had given a
little squeal, and she tried to release herself. "Let me
go—please."

"Rot!" And he lifted her from the ground, and
carried her across to the bed.

"Will—let me go. I—I'm tired;" and she began to
cry. "Be kind to me, Will." The words came in
feeble entreaty, between weak sobs. "Be kind to me—
my husband—not only now—but always."

She sobbed and shivered; and he, holding her in his
arms, soothed her with gentle murmurs. "My pretty
Mav! My poor little bird. Go to sleepy-by, then.
Tuck her up, and send her to sleep, a dear little Mav."
At the touch of her coldly trembling limbs, at the sight

of her tears, all the sensual desire lessened its throb, and the purer side of his love began to subjugate him. That was the greatest of her powers—to tame the beast in him, to lift him from the depths to the heights, to make him feel as though he was her father instead of her lover, because she herself was pure and good as a child. "There—there, don't cry, my pretty Mav."

And she, melting beneath the gentleness and tender-ness of his caresses, wept in pity of herself. "Yes, I'm tired—dead-tired." And the tears flowed un-checked, blotting out emotion, reason, instinct, swamp-ing her in floods of self-pity. "Let me sleep—and let me forget. Oh, let me forget what I've gone through these last two days."

"Anyways, it's over now."

"Yes, it's over. Oh, thank God in Heaven, it's over and done with."

"Just so." And there was a change in the tone of his voice that she might have noticed, but did not. "Just so—but you're talking rather strange, come to think of it."

His arms slowly relaxed, and he let her slide out of his embrace. She sank down wearily upon the pillow, closed her eyes, and for a little while went on talking drowsily and inconsecutively.

"Shut up," he said suddenly. "Hold your tongue. I'm thinking."

Then almost immediately he turned, and, with his hands upon her shoulders, looked down into her face.

"Why didn't you go to church yesterday?"

"What did you say, Will?"

"I said, why didn't you go to church yesterday?"

"Oh—I really didn't care to go."

"That wasn't like you—you so fond of the Abbey Church. Did your Aunt go?"

"Yes."

"You said this afternoon she didn't go."

"She did go. I remember now."

"Ah! Another thing! That actor-feller—what d'yer call 'im—him that you counted on and didn't find—Chugwun!"

"Yes."

"You see the name in the paper?"

"Yes."

"You didn't aarpen t'see it on the boards outside the theater?"

"No."

She was wide awake and quite sober now. But her limbs were trembling again, and her eyes seemed preposterously large as they stared up at him from the white face. "Will!" And she spoke fast and piteously; "don't look at me like this. What's come to you? Why do you ask me such a pack of questions?" And she tried to laugh. "At such a time of night!"

"Bide a bit, my lass. I'm just thinking."

Where had the thoughts come from?—out of blank space?—from nowhere? Yet here they were, filling his head, multiplying, expanding, making his blood rattle like boiling water in a tube as it rushed up to nourish their monstrous growth.

"Will, let go my shoulders. You hurt. Get into the bed—and be sensible. I'll answer all questions in the morning."

"No, I think I'll have the answers now."

He went on questioning her, and his hands growing

heavier crushed her shoulders so that she thought he would break the bones and joints.

"What train did you come up by this morning?"

"The nine o'clock."

"What! D'you mean you went right across from North Ride to Rodchurch Road?"

"Oh, no. I caught it at Manninglea Cross."

"Did you, then? An' s'pose I was to tell you the nine o'clock don't stop at Manninglea Cross!"

"Will! Loosen your hands. It does stop—it did stop there this morning."

"Yes, it did stop—and so it does all mornings. But a fat lot you know about it. And for why? You weren't in it."

"I was—I really was. Will—don't go on so cruel."

"Oh, but I *am* going on." He had lowered his face close to hers, and his hot breath beat upon her cold cheeks. "Now, give me the explanation of what you let slip about going through so much these last two days. What was the precise sense o' *that?*"

"I only meant I've been so anxious."

"Yes, but yer bin anxious best part o' four weeks. What was the mighty difference in yesterday or day before?"

"I didn't mean any difference. I scarce knew what I was saying—or what I'm saying now."

"Oh! Just a remark let fall without a scrap o' sense in it!"

Staring up at him, it was as if she saw the face of a stranger. His eyes were half closed and glittering fiercely; his lips protruded as if grotesquely pouting to express scorn, and on each side of the distended nostrils a deep vertical wrinkle showed like the blackened gash of a knife wound.

"Will, dear, I meant nothing at all."

"You're lying."

Abruptly he took his hands from her shoulders, got off the bed, and went to the chest of drawers. Her handbag was on the drawers; and when she saw him pick it up she sprang after him, clutching at his hands and imploring.

"You'll find nothing there. Nothing that I can't explain;" and she made a desperate gurgling laugh. "Why, Will, old man, it is you that's drunk, yourself, after chaffing me? No, you shan't. No, Will, you shan't."

He gave her a back-hander that sent her reeling. It was the first time he had struck her, and he delivered the blow quite automatically, the thought that she was preventing him from opening the bag and the action that got rid of her interference being all one process. His hand had remained open, but he swung it with un-hesitating force; and now, as he plunged it into the bag, he saw that there was blood on it.

Before he had extracted all the contents of the bag she was back again, once more clinging, clutching, and impeding. He did not strike her again—merely shook her off so violently that she fell to the floor, where she lay for a moment.

In the inner pockets of the bag there were three five-pound notes, together with a tooth-brush and several small articles wrapped up in paper. These he laid on one side, while he carefully examined all the odds and ends that had been packed loose in the bag. Three or four pocket-handkerchiefs, a new piece of scented soap, a pair of nail-scissors—as he looked at each innocent article, he gave a snort.

She had come back, but she had not risen from the ground; while he slowly pursued his investigations she kept quite still, crouching close to his legs, silently waiting.

She could not see what he was doing, but presently she knew that he had begun to unfold the paper from the things she had hidden in the pocket.

"Ah," and he snorted. One of the bits of paper held hairpins; another a side-comb; and another, a bit of trebly folded paper, proved to be an envelope—the envelope of one of the letters that he had sent to her at North Ride Cottage. He looked at the postmark. The postmark told him that the envelope belonged to a letter he had written four days ago.

Then he found what she had put in the envelope before she folded it. It was the return half of a railway ticket, from London to Rodchurch Road—he turned it in his fingers and examined the date on the back of it.

"Last Friday, my lady. Not to-day by any means —and not Manninglea Cross. Issued at Rodchurch Road o' Friday last—the day you come up to London."

"Yes, Will, I won't pretend any more."

She had put her arms round his legs and lifted herself to a kneeling position. "I *did* come Friday. But don't be angry with me. Don't fly out at me, and I— I'll explain everything."

"May I make so bold 's t'a' ask *why* you come, without my permission begged for nor given?"

His voice was terrible to hear, so deep and yet so harsh, and vibrating with such implacable wrath.

"Will, I did it for your sake. I thought if I asked

permission, you'd say no. So I dared to do it myself —feeling certain as life that you were done for if no help came—and I thought it was my duty to bring you the help if I could."

"Go on. I'm listening, an' I'm thinking all the time."

"I thought—Auntie thought so too—she advised it —that Mr. Barradine knowing me so long, ever since I was a girl, if I went direct to him——"

"Ah!" And he made a loud guttural noise, as if on the point of choking. "Ah——so's I supposed. Then I got a bull's-eye with my first thought to-night. So you went to him. Where?"

"At his house."

"Yes, right into his house. By yourself?"

"Yes."

"You didn't think to bring your aunt with you. Two was to be comp'ny at Mr. Barradine's. So in you go— alone—without my leave—behind my back."

"Will—remember yourself, my dear one. You won't blame, you can't blame me. But for him, you were done for. All could see it, except you. I asked for his help, and I got it."

"But your next move! We're talking about Friday, aren't we? Well, after you'd bin to Mr. Barradine, what next?"

"Then I hoped he'd help us."

"Yes, but Friday, Saturday, Sunday? Had yer forgotten my address—or didn' 'aarpen to remember that *I* was in London, too?"

"I was afraid of your being angry. I thought I'd better wait."

"*Where?*"

She looked up at him, but did not answer.

"You've played me false. You've sold yourself to that fornicating old devil. You——"

And with a roar he burst into imprecations, blasphemies and obscenities. It was the string of foul words that, under a sufficient impetus, infallibly comes rolling from the peasant's tongue—an explosion as natural as when a thunderbolt scatters a muck-heap at the roadside.

Then, snarling and growling like an animal, he stooped and cuffed her.

"Will!" "Will!" She repeated his name between the blows. She did not utter a word of complaint, or make an effort to escape. Brave and unflinching, though almost stunned, she raised her white blood-stained face for him to strike again each time that he buffed it from him. "Will!" "Will!"

But her courage and submissiveness were driving him mad, had changed suspicion to certainty. Only guilt could make her take her punishment this way. Nevertheless she must confess the guilt herself. Even in his fury, he remembered to hold his hand open and not clench it—like a cruelly strong animal, tormenting its prey before killing, careful to keep it alive.

"Answer me. Go on with your tale."

"Then stop beating me, and I'll tell you."

He stayed his hand, poised it, and she seized it and clung to it.

"Will—as God sees me—I did it for your sake—only to help you. I couldn't get the help unless I sacrificed myself to save you."

Wrenching his hand away he knocked her to the ground, and she lay face downward. But this blow was nothing, purely automatic, like his first blow, not bringing with it that faint sense of something refreshing, the momentary appeasement of his agony. For in truth the torture that he himself suffered was almost unendurable. Yet up to now his pain, though so tremendous, was unlocalized; it came from a fusion of all his thoughts, and perhaps each separate thought, when it became clear, would bring more pain than all the thoughts together.

The world had tumbled about his ears; his glorious life had shriveled to nothing; his pride was gone, his love was gone, his trust in man and his belief in man's creator; and for a few moments one thought grew a little clearer than the rest. The end of all this must be death—nothing less. He was really dead already, and he would not pretend to go on living. He would finish her, and then finish himself.

Turning his head, he looked at the window; and the open space out there seemed to whisper to him, to beg to him, and to command him. Yes, that way would be as good as another—strangle her, pitch her out, and jump out after her.

"Will!" She had once more scrambled to her knees. "I've loved you faithfully. I've never loved any one but you."

He did not hit her. Grasping the arm that she was stretching toward him, he dragged her upward, seized her round the body, and carried her to the bed.

"Now we'll go to work, you and I." He had thrown her down on her back, and he held her with both his hands about her throat. "Now"—and the sudden pressure of his hands made her gasp and cough—"we'll begin at the beginning."

"Do you mean to murder me?"

"Prob'ly. But not till I've 'ad the truth—and I'll 'aarve it to the last word, if I tear it out o' yer boosum."

"You'll kill me if I tell you."

"See that winder! That's yer road—head first—if you try to lie to me."

Then she told him the whole sickening story of her relations with Mr. Barradine. He had debauched her innocence when she was quite a young girl; she had continued to be one of his many mistresses for several years; then he grew tired of her, and, his attentions gradually ceasing, he had left her quite free to do what she pleased. She had never liked him, had always feared him. The long intermittent thraldom to his power had been an abomination to her, and it was martyrdom to return to him.

"Only to save you, Will. And he wouldn't help unless I done it. It was as much a sacrifice for you as if I'd been hung, drawn, and quartered for your sake."

"And why did you sacrifice yourself in the beginning, before ever you'd seen my face?"

"Auntie made me. It was Auntie's fault, not mine. I told her I was afraid of him."

"Your aunt had been that gait with him herself, in her time?"

"Oh, I don't know."

"Yes, I twigged that—and then the mealy-mouthed, filthy hag came over me. I on'y guessed, but *you* knew. Answer me;" and his grip tightened on her throat, and he shook her. "Answer."

"Oh, I suppose so."

"And that cousin—the one he paid for in foreign parts?"

"I suppose so."

"Those rooms at the Cottage. They were furnished and set out for you and him to take your pleasure."

"He used them for other women—once or twice."

"What other women?"

"Girls from London."

As he questioned her and listened to her answers his passion took a rhythm, upward and downward, from blind wrath to black sorrow; and it seemed that the points reached by the rising curves were becoming less high, while the descending curves went lower and lower, through sorrow into shame, and still down, to fathomless depths of despair. He had heard all that it was necessary to hear. His life that he had thought marvelous and splendid was ridiculous and pitiful; what he had fancied to be success was failure; all that he had been proud of as being gained by his own merit had been brought to him by his wife's disgrace. What more could he learn?

Yet he went on questioning her.

She swore that she had loved him, that she had quite done with the other when she married him, had been true to him in thought and deed ever since their marriage. But she had been tempted two or three times, through her aunt. Mr. Barradine had desired that she should understand with what affection he always regarded her, and he invited her to meet him; and it was the knowledge that he had come to covet her again that made her sure she could get him to do anything for her. At the same time the knowledge terrified her; and when Dale's trouble began, and things with him seemed to be going from bad to worse, she felt as if a sort of waking nightmare was drawing nearer and nearer.

She wrote to Mr. Barradine, simply asking him to exert this influence on behalf of her husband; and the reply—the letter that she tore up—was in these words: "I will do what I can; but why don't you come and ask me yourself?" Of course she knew what that meant.

It was at the railway station, when bidding Dale good-by, that she made up her mind to save him at all costs. When he refused to act on Ridgett's advice, when he showed himself so firm, so unyielding, she knew that he was a man going to his doom, unless she could avert the doom.

"And, Will—believe it or not—no woman ever loved a husband truer than I loved you at that moment. To see you there so brave and strong and good— and yet certain sure to ruin yourself! Well, I couldn't bear it. And if it was to do again, I'd do it."

Slowly he withdrew his hands from her throat, and clasped them together with all his strength. Turning for a moment, he glanced at the open window. The space seemed to have contracted and darkened, so that it looked black and small as a square grave cut out for a child. But if not by the window, what other end to it all would he find? He could not go on like this— with a to-morrow and a day after, and weeks and months to follow.

He turned, and in speaking to her, unconsciously used her name.

"Could you think, Mavis, I cared for my job better'n my honor?"

"I thought you'd never know. And I loved you, Will—only you—no one else."

He scarcely seemed to listen to the answer. He turned from her again; and went on talking, as if to himself or the far-off stars, or the invisible powers that mold men's destinies.

" 'Aardn't I my fingers and brains—to work for you? Would I care—so's you could be what I thought you were—whether I broke my back or burst my heart in working for you? Besides, t'wouldn't 'a' bin that. What was it but the loss of the office—a step back that I'd soon 'a' recovered."

He groaned; then suddenly he unclasped his hands and brandished them. The rhythmic beat of his rage came strong and high, and with savage energy he seized her again.

"It's half lies still. The money? How does that match? He gave it to you. Deny it if you dare."

"Yes, I tried not to take it. He forced it on me."

"Lies! It was the bit for yourself when you drove your bargain—nothing to do with me—you—you. The price of your two or three nights of love."

"No, I swear. He forced the money as a present. The price he paid was his help to you. As God hears me, that's the truth."

Then, answering more and more questions, she resumed her story.

After Dale's departure she went over to North Ride, thinking that Mr. Barradine was at the Abbey, and that he would come to her at the Cottage. She sent a letter inviting him to do so. There was no answer for four days. Then Mr. Barradine wrote to her from London; and she went up on Friday afternoon, and

saw him at Grosvenor Place. "He said he'd engaged
rooms for me at an hotel, and I was to go there; and I
went there."

"What hotel?"

"The Sunderland Hotel—Alderney Street."

"Go on."

"I waited in the rooms."

"Rooms! You mean one room, you slut!"

"No, there were four rooms—a grand suite."

"Go on."

"He said he would come to me next day, or Sunday
at latest. And he didn't come on Saturday—I stopped
indoors all day, afraid to go out for fear of meeting
you—and he didn't come till Sunday, after lunch."

" Ah! How long did he stay? "

"Till early this morning. Will, let me be——I'm
done. You're throttling me."

"Go on. I'll 'aarve it all out of you. Begin at the
beginning. It's Sunday afternoon we're talking of—
ever since lunch time. There's a many hours to amuse
yourselves."

"After dinner he made me dress up."

"What d'you mean?"

"He had brought things in his luggage—fancy
dress."

"What dresses?"

"Oh, boy's things—things he'd bought in Turkey,
on his travels. He made me act that I was his page—
and bring the coffee, and sit cross-legged on the
ground."

"Go on."

"No—what's the use?" She was crying now. "Oh,
God have mercy, what's the use?"

"Go on."

"No. Kill me, if you want to, and be done with it. I don't care—I'm tired out. What I've gone through was worse than death. I'm not afraid of dying."

She would tell him no more; she defied him; and yet he did not kill her. She lay weeping, moaning, at intervals, repeating that desolate phrase, "What's the use? Oh, what's the use?"

Irremediable loss—it sounded in her voice, it crept coldly in his burning veins, it came spreading, flooding, filling the whole earth in the first faint glimmer of dawn. He sat on the edge of the bed, let his hands fall heavy and inert between his knees, and for a long time did not change his attitude.

Just now, looking down at her, he had felt a sickness of loathing. He hated her for the musical note of her voice, the tragic eloquence of her eyes, and above all he hated her for her nakedness. The almost nude sprawling form seemed to symbolize the unspeakable shame of his sex. This was the disgusting female, round and smooth, white and weak, with tumbling hair and lying lips, the lewd parasite that can drag the noble male down into hell-fire. Now he looked at her with comparative indifference, and felt even pity for the broken and soiled thing that he had believed to be clean and sound.

The fusion of his thoughts was over. One thought had split away from all the rest, and every moment was becoming more definite, more logical, more full of excruciating pain. He thought now only of his enemy, of the human fiend who had destroyed Mavis and himself.

At least she had been innocent once. She was clean

and good—really and truly the candid child that she had never ceased to seem to be—when that sliming, crawling reptile first got his coils about her. As he thought of the maddening reality, his imagination made pictures that printed themselves, deep and indelible, on the soft recording surfaces of his brain. Henceforth, so long as blood pumped, nerves worked, and cells and fibers held to their shape, he would see these pictures—must see them each time that chance stirred his memory of the facts for which they stood as emblems.

And with his rage against the man came more and more detestation of the crime itself. At the very beginning it had no possible excuse in honest love. There was nothing belonging to it of nature's grand instinct. It had not the inexorable brutality of primitive passion. Here was an old, or an elderly man, not driven by the force of normal, full-blooded desire, but craftily plotting, treacherously abusing his power, because he was rotten with impure whims—befouling youth and innocence just to obtain a few faint voluptuous thrills.

Then the brain-pictures flashed out with torturing clearness, and Dale saw the criminal renewing the outrage after long years. He was quite old, shaky, infirm, and yet strong enough to consummate the final act of his infinite wickedness. And Dale saw those yellow-white hands, with their nauseating blotches, their glistening blue knobs, and their jeweled rings, as they took possession again of the victim to whom they had once given freedom.

Daylight was coming fast; the flame of the candles had turned so pale that one could scarcely see it. Dale got off the bed heavily and clumsily, blew out one of

the candles and carried the other to the fireplace.
There he lighted the corners of the three bank-notes
and watched them burning in the empty grate till nothing was left of them but black and gray powder. Then
he put on his hat and moved to the door.

"What are you going to do?"

"I don't know."

Blindly raging, he passed through the silent, deserted streets, and presently blundered into Regent's
Park. It was all exquisitely pretty in the pure morning
light, with dew-wet grass, feathery branches of trees,
and the water of a river or lake flashing and sparkling;
and as he stared stupidly about him, he thought for a
moment that he was experiencing an illusion of the
senses. Or was he a boy again safe in his forest? This
sort of thing belonged to the happy past, and could
have no proper place in the abominable present.

He crossed a low rail, walked on a little way toward
the water, and then threw himself face downward on
the grass. He knew where he was now—in the present
time, in a public pleasure-ground. London stretched
about the park, and beyond that there was the vast
round globe; beyond that again there was the universe; and it seemed to him that, big as it all was, it
was not big enough to hold one other man and himself.

When, four or five hours later, he came back to the
lodging-house he found his wife dressed and sitting by
the bedroom table. She had contrived to wash away
nearly all the marks of violence: one noticed only the
swollen aspect of the whole face, an inflamed eyebrow,
and a cut lip. She looked up meekly and fondly as a
thrashed dog.

"Will, have you decided what you will do?"

"No."

Then, while getting together his things and beginning to pack, he told her that he would take his fortnight's leave, as arranged, and carefully consider matters. "And then, at the end of the fortnight, if I'm above ground by that time, I'll let you know what I've decided."

But, on hearing this, she flopped from the chair to her knees, and clung round him just as she had clung when he was first questioning her.

"Will, don't be mad and wicked, and go and take your life."

"Why not? D'you think there's vaarlue in it to me now?"

He spoke quite quietly, but he looked gray, haggard, terrible, his clothes all stained and dirty from his open-air bed.

"Will, for mercy's sake——"

He shook her off, and began to count his money.

" I must keep this," he said. "I'll pay it back later to the right quarter—along with the equivalent of what I burnt."

When he had finished packing he told her that he would settle with the lodging-house keeper, and he gave her a few shillings.

"That's enough to get you home with."

Then he picked up his bag and went out.

VIII

MAVIS had bought a cheap blue veil to protect her
face, and being, moreover, fortunate enough to
find an empty compartment in the through coach to
Rodchurch Road, she did not suffer during the journey
from too curious observation of strangers. She was
going home, exactly as if nothing had happened. Her
husband had said that she was to go, and what else
could she do but obey him?

When the station omnibus pulled up outside the post
office, Mr. Ridgett caught sight of her, and gallantly
came to assist her in alighting. Evidently he noticed
nothing strange about her appearance. She at once
announced the good news that Dale had not only been
reinstated, but given a couple of weeks' holiday; and
Ridgett, genuinely delighted, squeezed both her hands.

"That's something like. Here, let me carry this up-
stairs for you."

"No, thank you, please don't trouble. I can manage."

Mr. Allen, the saddler, had come across from his
shop, and she told him the good news too. Mr. Allen
hurried down the street to tell others. Soon the whole
village knew that Mr. Dale had triumphed, and that
the Postmaster-General was granting him leave of
absence as a special mark of favor.

Mary clapped her hands on hearing the good news,
and was rapturously pleased at seeing her mistress

home again; but she immediately required explanations.

"Oh, lor, mum, whatever have you done to yourself?"

"I have had an accident," said Mrs. Dale. "I fell down—and it has given me a bad headache. I don't want any tea. I shall go to bed early, and try to get a good sleep."

And in truth, she was longing to sleep. After the terrible ordeal of yesterday sleep seemed to be the one good thing left in the world for her. But, notwithstanding supreme fatigue, sleep would not come.

Throughout that first night, and again on succeeding nights, she struggled beneath a suffocating burden of anxiety. In the daylight she had been able to think of herself, but in the darkness she could think only of her husband. She was haunted by the expression of his face, by the tone of his voice, when he had asked her if she supposed that existence was any longer valuable to him, and the sudden instinctive apprehension that she had felt then now grew so strong that she fought against it vainly.

He intended to commit suicide. At first she had thought of all those London bridges, with the dark rivers swirling through their arches and eddying round their piers; then she became sure that he would not drown himself. He was a vigorous swimmer—such a death would be impossible to him. No, he would poison himself, or shoot himself, or hang himself. Perhaps even now it was all over.

In his presence it had seemed impossible to disobey him. Whatever he commanded she must do. But what pitiful weakness! Why, with instinct prompting her, had she not resisted him, refused to let him leave her, stayed with him in spite of blows, and been there to snatch the cup or the rope from his hands, to thrust herself between the pistol and his body?

By day she recognized that her anxiety was unreasoning, based on her own emotions, or at least not logically derived from her knowledge of his character. Of course he had taken the discovery of her secret far worse than she had ever conceived as possible, when timorously thinking of untoward hazards that one day or another might lead to disclosure. But, even then, fully allowing for the effect of his extreme excitement, would he, so brave and self-reliant a creature, be guilty of an act that is in its essence cowardly?

She thought of his courage. He was as brave a man as ever breathed, and yet you could not describe him as reckless or foolhardy. He was wise enough to be chary of exposing himself to useless risks. So much so that he had more than once surprised her by keeping quite calm when she had expected and dreaded perilous energy. Especially she remembered a day out on the Manninglea road when a runaway horse with an empty cart came galloping toward them, and Dale, instead of attempting to stop it, put his arm round her waist and hastily drew her well out of the way. In another hundred yards the runaway went crashing off the road, fell, and smashed the cart into smithereens.

"Tally-ho! Gone to ground," cried Dale cheerily. "There's a nice little bill for Mr. Baker to pay." And then he told her that one of the most dangerous things a pedestrian can do is to interfere with a bolting horse when there's a vehicle behind it. "Mind you," he added, "I'd have had a try at bringing it to anchor if there'd been anybody in the cart. That would have been another pair of shoes. What you're justified in doing for a fellow human being you aren't justified in doing to save a few pounds, shillings and pence."

She clung to this thought of his innate common sense. And there was comfort and hope, too, in another thought. He was a naturally religious man, if not an orthodoxly religious one. The church service bored him; he only attended it from motives of policy; but, nevertheless, when you got him inside the sacred edifice, his behavior was perfect, and you could not watch him on his knees or hear him say "Christ have mercy upon us, O Lord Christ have mercy on us," without being convinced that he did truly believe in an omnipotent God and the punishments or rewards that await us on the other side of the grave. Surely the man who bowed his head like that at the name of Jesus would not, could not, be the man to take his own life merely because it had become an unhappy life.

The hope that lay in such thoughts as these helped her to support the strain of three long waiting days and four long sleepless nights. Then on the fourth day, Saturday, the strain was relieved.

"Mrs. Dale," said Ridgett, speaking to her from the bottom of the stairs, "would you be disposed for a little stroll before tea?"

"No, thank you, Mr. Ridgett."

"Have pity on a lonely stranger, and change your mind," said Mr. Ridgett, smiling up at her.

"No, really not—but thank you for offering it."

"You know, it isn't right the way you shut your-self up this lovely weather."

"I—I have not been feeling quite myself, Mr. Ridgett."

"No, so your maid told me. But, still, I am afraid it's the way to make yourself worse, never going out of doors;" and Mr. Ridgett laughed amiably. "I won't press you—that is, I won't press you to honor me with your company; but I do respectfully press my advice to get out a bit. You know I feel a responsibility to look after you in the absence of your lord and master."

"Thank you."

"By the way, I had a note from him this morning."

"From Mr. Dale?"

"Yes."

"Oh, had you? Where——" Mavis gripped the baluster rail so tightly that the slender wooden uprights rattled. She had nearly asked a question which would have betrayed the fact that she did not know her husband's address. "Did he write from his lodgings?"

"No, he wrote from a public library. Lambeth— yes, the Lambeth Library."

"What did he say?"

"Only confirmed your report that he wouldn't be back till the twenty-eighth." Mr. Ridgett laughed again. "And told me that the clocks ought to be wound up Thursday, and he hoped we hadn't let them run down. We hadn't, you know."

Mavis was inexpressibly relieved; and yet that night she did not sleep any better than on the preceding nights. The worst anxiety had gone, but so much that was distressing in her situation remained. Since Will was alive now, he would continue to live. And that little circumstance of his remembering about the

clocks was full of promise—that is, promise concerning himself. It implied that he meant to go on much
as usual. He would come back, and be postmaster
as in the past. But what would he do with her?

Would he go for a divorce? Publish her shame?
Perhaps, even if he were willing to spare her, he
would not forego the chance of dragging down Mr.
Barradine. Feeling as strongly as he did—and since
the world began, surely no one in such circumstances
had ever felt quite so strongly—he would seize upon
the overthrow of Mr. Barradine's reputation as the
obvious means of obtaining his own revenge. Then
she thought of what such a scandal would mean to a
gentleman of Mr. Barradine's state and status. Mr.
Barradine would move heaven and earth to avert it.
He might even get Will spirited away, never to be
found again! One was always reading in the newspaper of mysterious, inexplicable disappearances. New
fears almost as bad as the old fear began to shake her
again.

Of this there could be no question. Mr. Barradine
would pay a very large sum of money to avoid the
threatened disgrace. And—in the midst of her acute
apprehension and distress—the plain matter-of-fact
idea presented itself: that if Dale were not rendered
irresponsible by jealous ire, one might hope that he
would eventually fall in with Mr. Barradine's views—
that he ought, for everybody's sake, to take his damages, more damages than he would ever get in a court
of law, and then let bygones be bygones.

While dressing of a morning she used to examine
the bruises on her neck, her arms, and her legs. After
passing through the stage of blackness and purpleness,

their discoloration had spread out into faint violet and yellow; now already this was beginning to fade; and it seemed that as the ugly marks of his hands disappeared from her skin, the memory of all the causes that had brought them there began itself to weaken. Certainly the despairing anguish that she had felt, the submission to his unpardoning wrath, the tacit agreement that the discovery gave him license to do anything he liked with her, not only then but throughout the future —all this pertained to a state of mind which could be coldly recollected, but which could not be warmly revived.

How he had knocked her about! Standing before the toilet-glass and looking at her bruises musingly, she tried to remember in what part of the room, and at which period of the long volcanic discussion, each one had been received. All the neck marks could be accounted for on the bed, when he was holding her down and shaking her; that graze above the knee, outside the right thigh had come when she rolled over by the chest of drawers. Raising her eyes in order to see if the lip and eyebrow continued to mend satisfactorily, she was surprised by the general expression of her face. Positively she was smiling. The smile vanished at once, but it had been there—a gentle, melancholy, yet proud little smile. And reflecting, she understood that deep in her thoughts there was truly pride whenever she dwelt upon her husband's violence. It did prove so conclusively how immense was his love.

Jealousy is of course the inevitable accompaniment of love; and while it is active everything else is pushed aside, postponed, or forgotten. And she smiled again, as she thought what queer creatures men are, how ex-

travagantly different from women. She had never
understood them, and possibly never would do so. For
instance, how strange that old Will should not for a
moment have been softened by a recognition of her
success in extricating him from his difficulty! One
might have expected that gratitude would almost coun-
terbalance anger. But, no, not for a fraction of a second could he think that, although what she had done
might be wrong, it had been done with the most unselfish intention and had proved very efficacious.

Then, not in the least expecting that she was about
to cry, she burst into tears.

She had remembered his voice and his look when
he said something about honor and dishonor, and
about working for her till he dropped. Noble and splendid love had spoken in that—such love as few women
are lucky enough to get. Oh, surely if he loved her
like that, he could not leave off loving her altogether,
and never, never, want his Mav again.

Sadness and desolation overcame her. She was
alone in their dear, dear home, disgraced, abandoned,
heart-broken; and her thoughts for a little while were
all prayers. With each one of them she prayed her
husband to go on loving her; to come back and bruise
her limbs, to punish her with fierce glances and cutting
words, to subject her to systematic penitential disci-
pline, if only at the end of it all she might have his love
again.

She sat crying most bitterly; and then, when at last
she dried her eyes, and went down-stairs to gratify
Mary by pretending to eat some breakfast, a supremely
commonplace and yet poignantly sad reflection brought
another flood of tears. What wretched little chances

can produce the most tragically terrific upheavals!
Had she not bought a return railway ticket, the whole
disaster might have been averted. But for that horrible square inch of pink cardboard, all would have
been well, her ordeal would not have been suffered in
vain. The wickedly strong intoxicant had of course begun the mischief by making her blurt out those im-
becile words that first set Will on the rampage; but it
was the knowledge of the telltale ticket, close at hand,
unguarded, certain to be found if looked for, that had
unnerved her so completely. Otherwise, as she now
believed, she could have held her own under his rapid
fire of questions. She could have laughed off his ac-
cusations as absurd—or, at the worst, she could have
gained time to think of plausible explanations. But
the ticket simply paralyzed her.

And she had known that she was running a risk
when she made up her mind to keep it. She bought it
without any thought at all—a stupid thing to do, considering that the cost was the same as two single fares.
Not so stupid, however, as the thrifty idea that if she
and Will traveled home in different trains, she might
after all use her return half. Oh, fatal economy! In
scheming to avoid the loss of five shillings she had
wrecked all her peace and comfort.

On this Sunday she would have liked to go to
church, but a dread of loquacious and inquisitive
neighbors kept her a prisoner in the house.

On Monday morning she almost determined to go
out for a walk but her courage again failed her. Until
noon the village street was dull and lifeless, with only
one or two people visible at a time, and yet she dared
not go down and walk through it. Were she to show

herself, all the idle shopkeepers would issue from their shops, to congratulate her on the postmaster's victory, to inquire where he was spending his holiday and why she hadn't gone for the holiday with him.

Nearly all day she sat by the window of the front room, staring at the trite and familiar scene, and encouraging her thoughts to wander away from her misery whenever they would consent to do so. A butcher's boy leaned his bicycle against the curbstone in so careless a fashion that it immediately fell down; Mr. Bates the corn merchant passed by with an empty wagon; then Mr. Norton the vicar appeared, going from house to house, distributing handbills of special services. And she wondered if he and his wife had ever had a hidden domestic storm in their outwardly tranquil existence. Mrs. Norton must have been quite pretty once, and perhaps at that period she caused Mr. Norton anxieties. But if she had ever needed forgiveness for some indiscretion or other, she had obviously obtained it; and again the thought came strong and clear that people who hold conspicuous positions— such as vicars, tax-collectors, postmasters, and so on— owe a duty to the world as well as to themselves. They must hush things up, and preserve appearances: they can not wash their dirty linen in public.

After twelve o'clock there was much more to look at. The children came shouting out of school, laborers passed to and fro on their way to dinner, and with horns loudly blowing, three heavily-laden chars-a-bancs arrived one after another from Rodhaven. The tourists filled the street, and for about two hours the aspect of things was lively and bustling. Then the horns sounded again, the huge vehicles lumbered away, and the whole village relapsed into drowsiness and inertia. Literally nothing to look at now.

But before tea time that afternoon she saw something in the street that held her breathlessly attentive as long as it remained there. It was Mr. Barradine, riding slowly toward her between the churchyard and the Roebuck stables. She shrank back behind the muslin curtain of her window, and, watching him, passed through an extraordinarily rapid sequence of emotions.

The horse was a chestnut, and it stepped lightly and springily. As she thought of how and when she had last seen its rider, she felt a sensation that was like helplessness, shame, and fear all mingled. It was as though her whole body, muscles, flesh and nerves, quailed and grew weak at the mere sight of him; as though inherited instincts were controlling her, and would always control her whenever she was in his presence; as though she the descendant of serfs must infallibly submit to the descendant of lords—must forever fear the man who had been her master even when he was her lover. Rationally she hated him for the harm that he had done her, but instinctively she feared him for the further harm that he might yet have power to do.

And together with the hatred and the fear, there was a pitiful sneaking admiration. He looked so grand and unruffled—so old, and yet sitting the skittish, high-mettled horse so firmly; so feeble, and yet full of such an absolute confidence in his power to rule and subordinate, accustomed for forty years to the unfailing subjection of such things as servants, horses, and women. Her heart bumped against her stays, and her

face became red and then white, when she thought
that he intended to stop at the post office and ask for
her. But he rode on—gave one glance up toward the
windows from which she shrank still further, and rode
by, right down the street, with the horse swishing its
long tale and seeming to dance in a light amble.

Then, as soon as he disappeared, the spell was
broken.

In all that she had confessed to her husband she
had been sincere; but hers was a simple and easy going
nature, and exaltation could not be long sustained.
After excitement she returned rapidly to a passive and
unimaginative level; and now, quietly brooding, she
could not do otherwise than justify herself for all that
had happened.

At the end of everything she felt a deep-seated conviction that she was in truth blameless. She was not
a bad woman. Therefore it would be wicked to treat
her as a sinner and an outcast. Sinners did wrong because they enjoyed the sin; but she had never been
vicious, or even selfishly anxious for pleasure. Pleasure! She had never cared for that sort of thing. Girls
of her own age used to talk to her about it, and what
they said was almost incomprehensible. She had never
had such feelings, however faintly.

No, her only fault had been in giving way to the
people who had charge of her, and who were too
strong to be resisted. Just at first she had been flattered and pleased when Mr. Barradine had begun to
take notice of her— patting her, and holding her hand,
and saying he admired her hair; but she had not in the
least known where all this was leading. What she told
Will was substantially correct as to the beginning—

but of course her eyes had been opened before anything definite occurred. Then she had told Auntie that she was afraid; and then it was that Auntie ought to have saved her, and didn't. Far from it. Auntie, who in early days had been severe enough, now became all smiles, treating her deferentially, saying: "If you play your cards properly you'll set us all up as large as towers. Don't lose your head. For goodness' sake, don't be wild and foolish, and go offending him so that instead of coming back again he'll look elsewhere."

Then later, when she had, as it were, sacrificed herself on the family altar, she was indignant at finding that he had nevertheless looked elsewhere. There were others—and she said she would never forgive him. Yet she did forgive him. Finally, there came the outrage of his stopping at the Cottage with somebody else. Her aunt had sent her out of the way, but she heard of it; and this time she determined to be done with Mr. Barradine. And yet again she forgave him.

Then she discovered, without any explanations, that *he* had done with her. He was paternal and kind, but she had become just nobody; and her aunt was very angry, saying that she had played her cards badly instead of well. That was about the time that Dale had been two years at Portsmouth. She liked Dale from the first because he was honest and good, and because he seemed to offer her an escape from an extremely difficult position. But if she had been a nasty girl, she would not have made such a marriage; instead of being anxious to secure respectability, however humble, she would have followed Auntie's suggestions and looked out for another protector instead of for a husband. And she had wanted to tell Dale the whole truth; but there again she had been over-ruled. Auntie forbade her to utter a whisper or hint of it; she said that Mr. Barradine would never pardon such a betrayal of his confidence, whereas if a properly discreet silence were preserved he would give the bride a suitable wedding present, as well as push the fortunes of the bridegroom. "'Besides," said Aunt Petherick, " a nice hash you'll make of it if you go and label yourself damaged goods before you're fairly started. Why, it would be just giving Dale the whip-hand over you for the rest of your days." Looking back at it all, Mavis felt that this argument was irre-futable.

After marriage she began to love Will most truly and devotedly—but not for his embraces, which did not even stir her pulses, which only made her tenderly happy that she could make him happy. Now after eleven years her feeling toward him was all unselfish and beautiful, a gentle and deep affection, without a taint of anything that one would not call really *lady-like*. The passion and boisterousness were all on his side.

And thinking of things that she had never told Will, she wondered if this calmness of temperament, or per-haps unusual failure in response, was but another fatal consequence of the Barradine slavery. If so, what cause she had to hate and curse him! The episode with him was simply an irksomeness: it had frozen her in-stead of warming her, checked her expansion, and per-haps, breaking the cycle of normal development, made her imperfect as a woman.

Perhaps this was the real reason why she had re-mained childless. She represented completed womanhood in this respect at least, that she desired to be a mother. The possession of children was the one thing that made her envious of other women. The idea of having a child of her own made her almost faint with longing—a baby to nurse, a little burden to wheel about in a perambulator, a companion to prattle to her all day while Will was busy down-stairs. If the hope of such joy had been taken from her by Mr. Barradine, oh, how immeasureably great was her cause for hatred!

She sat staring at the distant point where he and his horse had just now vanished, and for a little while her thoughts were like curses. Any attributes of grandeur were transitory illusions; he was wholly mean and base: he was the embodied principle of evil that had spoiled the past and that still threatened the future. She wished that he might eventually suffer as much as he had made her suffer. She wished that he might be racked with rheumatism, burned up with gout, tortured with every conceivable painful disease. She wished him dead and crumbling to dust in his coffin.

After tea she came back to the window and stayed there till nightfall.

Little by little the street became dim and vague. Two or three futile oil lamps were lighted, and the shop fronts shone brightly, but all the rest grew dark, like a river or a canal instead of a street. One heard voices, and then people showed themselves momentarily as they passed through the lamplight.

While she watched them passing, her thoughts drifted into generalized sadness.

The shutters went up at the saddler's, and she saw Mr. Allen for a moment—a long, thin man, looking too tall for the frame of the lamplit doorway. Mr. Allen used to have a fine business but he was spoiling it by his folly. It had been his custom to go to neighboring meets of hounds and ask the young gentlemen if the saddles he had made for them were satisfactory, insinuate his fingers between saddle-tree and hunter's withers to see if there was plenty of room, and generally render himself obsequiously agreeable. That was good for trade. But then the hunting gradually fascinated him, and he followed on foot throughout the season, halloaing hounds to wrong foxes, standing on banks and frightening horses, being a nuisance to the gentlemen, and coming home to boast that although he was fifty he had walked twenty-seven miles in the day. And his trade was all going or gone, and he not seeming to care. His wife let lodgings to make up a bit. Very sad.

Candle-light showed in a window of the house next door to the saddler's, and Mavis thought of these neighbors—two sisters, old maids—who had a very, very little money of their own and who endeavored to add to what was barely enough for necessities by selling butterfly nets, children's fishing-rods, stamp albums, and picture post-cards. Two years ago the elder sister tumbled down-stairs and injured her spine; and since then she had been bedridden, lying in the upper room at the back of the house, with nothing to amuse her but a view of the graveyard behind the church. Mavis had been to see her one day this summer, had sat by the bed, and read her a chapter out of the New Testament and then the weekly instalment of a novel in the *Rodhaven District Courier*. Extremely sad.

Then livid-faced, matty-haired Emily Frayne passed by, carrying a brown-paper parcel. This poor overworked girl was the only daughter of Frayne the tailor, who was a confirmed drunkard. All day long she was kept toiling like a slave, cutting out, beginning and finishing gaiters, breeches, and stable-jackets, doing all the work that was ever done at Frayne's; and at night she went round trying to get orders, delivering the goods that she had completed, and being forced to support the impudence and familiarity of coachmen and grooms, who chucked her under the chin and said they'd give her a kiss for her pains because they weren't flush enough to stand her a drink. All painfully sad.

There was a dreadful lot of tippling at Rodchurch: in fact, one might say that drink was the prevailing fault of the village. The vicar publicly touched on the matter in his sermons, and privately he often said that Mr. Cope, the fat landlord of The Gauntlet Inn, was greatly to blame. The tradesmen had a little club at the Gauntlet, where Cope employed a horrid brazen barmaid who sometimes sang comic songs to the club members. Mrs. Cope felt strongly about the barmaid, and quite took the vicar's side in the dispute the day that Cope came out of the tap-room and was so rude and abusive to the reverend gentleman. Mrs. Cope said she'd be glad if Mr. Norton brought her husband to book before the magistrates and got his license taken away.

Dale openly expressed contempt for this boozing Gauntlet club, refused to take up his membership when elected, and had received a complimentary letter from the vicar thanking him for the fine example he had set for others. No, dear old Will, though he liked his glass of beer as well as anybody, would often go a

whole week on tea and coffee; and she thought what a
merit his sobriety had been. Merely considered as
economy, it was a blessing. It is always the drink, and
never the food, that runs away with one's household
money.

Mr. Silcox the tobacconist hurried through the lamplight, unquestionably on his way to the Gauntlet.
Silcox was a chattering foolish creature who had lost
his own and his widowed mother's savings in a ridiculous commercial enterprise—a promptly bankrupt
theater company over at Rodhaven—and it was
thought that the workhouse would be the end for him
and Mrs. Silcox. But early this summer people had
been startled by hearing that the *Courier* had appointed Silcox as their reporter; and local critics were
of opinion that Silcox had taken very kindly to literature, and that he was shaping well, and might perhaps
retrieve the past in making name and fortune. Dale,
who used to chaff Silcox rather heavily, was at present
quite polite to him. It had always been Will's policy
to stand well with the press, and there was no doubt
that during the recent controversy Silcox had endeavored to render aid with his pen.

Lamplight moving now — a cart coming down.
Mavis, peering out, saw that it was old Mr. Bates
again, in a gig this time, going home to his pretty little
farm two miles off on the Hadleigh Road. Fancy his
being still at it so late, only finishing the day's work
long after so many younger men had done. Mr. Bates
was reputed rich—a highly respected person; but the
sorrow of his old age was a bad, bad son. Richard
Bates raced, and habitually ran after women—that is,
when he possessed the use of his legs and was able to

run. But he was a heavy drinker, and it was no unusual thing for the helpers at the Roebuck stables to
have to get out a conveyance at closing time and drive
Richard, speechless, motionless, to Vine-Pits Farm.
He never went to the Gauntlet, but always to the Roebuck—beginning the evening in the hotel billiard-
room, trying to swagger it out at pool with the solicitor and the doctor, then drifting to the stable bar, and
finishing the evening there, or outside in the open yard.
One could imagine the feelings of the old father, waiting up all alone, knowing from experience what the
sound of wheels implied after ten o'clock. Will said
once that he believed Mr. Bates was glad Mrs. Bates
hadn't been spared to see it.

And Mavis, moving at last from the window, thought
that she was not the only sad inhabitant of Rodchurch.
There is a cruel lot of sorrow in most people's lives.

IX

THE second week of the fortnight was passing much quicker than the first week. By a most happy inspiration Mavis had hit upon a means of filling the dull empty time. On Tuesday morning she told Mary that they would turn the master's absence to good account by giving the house an unseasonal but complete spring cleaning, and ever since then they had both been hard at work.

The work gave exercise as well as occupation; it furnished a ready excuse for declining to go over and see. Mrs. Petherick or to allow a visit from her; and, moreover, it had a satisfactory calming effect on one's nerves. While Mavis was reviewing pots and pans, standing on the high step-ladder to unhook muslin curtains, and, most of all, while she was going through her husband's winter underclothes in search of moths, it seemed to her that she was not only retaining but strengthening her hold on all these inanimate friends, and that they themselves were eloquently though dumbly protesting against the mere idea of forcible separation. When she sat down, hot and tired, in the midst of shrouded masses of furniture, to enjoy a picnic meal that Mary had set out on the one unoccupied corner of a crowded table, she was able to eat with hearty appetite; and yet, no matter how tired she might be by the end of the day, she could not sleep properly at night.

If she slept, a dream of trouble woke her. As she lay awake her trouble sometimes seemed greater than ever. It was as though the spring cleaning, which by day proved mentally beneficial, became deleterious during these long night watches. The neater, the cleaner, the brighter she made her home, the more terrible must be a sentence of perpetual banishment.

On Friday afternoon the work was nearly over. Kitchen utensils were like shining mirrors; the flowers of the best carpet were like real blossoms budding after rain; and Mavis on the step-ladder, with a smudged face, untidy hair, and grimy hands, had begun to reinstate the pictures handed to her by Mary, when Miss Yorke came knocking abruptly at the parlor door.

" A telegram, ma'am."

" All right."

Mavis had come down the ladder, and as she opened the yellow envelope she began to tremble.

"Answer paid, ma'am. Shall I wait?"

" No. I—I'll——No, don't wait."

It was from Dale. She had sat down on the lowest step of the ladder, and was trembling violently. " Oh, how dreadful! " She muttered the words mechanically, without any attempt to express her actual thought. " How very dreadful! "

" What is it, ma'am? Bad news? "

" Oh, most dreadful. But perhaps a mistake. I'm to find out;" and she stared stupidly at the paper that was shaking in her fingers. Then, spreading it on her lap, she read the message aloud:—

" Evening paper says fatal accident to Mr.

Barradine. Is this true? Wire Dale, Appledore Temperance Hotel, Stamford Street, S.E."

Then she jumped up, ran into the front room, and looked out of the window. A glance showed her that the village was in possession of some sensational tidings. There was a knot of people standing in front of the saddler's, and another—quite a little crowd—in front of the butcher's; all were talking excitedly, nodding their heads, and gesticulating.

She ran down-stairs and joined the group at the saddler's.

" I never cared for the look of the horse," Allen was saying sententiously. "And I might almost claim to have warned them—no longer ago than last March. The stud-groom was riding him at a meet, and I said, ' Mr. Yeatman, you aren't surely going to let Mr. Barradine risk his neck with hounds on that thing?' 'No,' he said, ' Mr. Barradine has bought him for hacking.' ' Oh,' I said, ' hacking and hunting are two things, of course, but——' "

Then somebody interrupted.

" Chestnut horse, wasn't it?"

"Yes," said Allen, "one of these thoroughbred weeds, without a back that you can fit with to anything bigger than a racing saddle; and I've always maintained the same thing. A bit of blood may do very well for young gentlemen, but to go and put a gentleman of Mr. Barradine's years——"

" Mind you," interposed a Roebuck stableman, " Mr. Barradine liked 'em gay. Mr. Barradine was a horseman!"

Mr. Barradine *liked* gay horses. Mr. Barradine *was*

a horseman. That tremendous sound of the past tense answered the question that Mavis was breathlessly waiting to ask.

"Shocking bad business, isn't it, Mrs. Dale?"

She did not reply; but nobody noticed her silence or agitation. They all went on talking; and she only thought: "He is dead. He is dead. He is dead." She was temporarily tongue-tied, awestricken, full of a strange superstitious horror.

Presently Allen spoke to her again. "There'll never be such another kind gentleman in *our* times, Mrs. Dale; nor one so open-handed. And it's not only the gentry that's going to mourn him. The pore hev lost a good friend."

"Yes," she whispered. "Indeed they have. Indeed they have."

Miss Waddy came out of her absurd little post-card shop and kept saying, "Oh, dear!" She, like almost everybody else in the village except Mavis Dale and Mary, had known the news for hours; but she was greedy for the more and more particularized information that every newcomer brought with him along the road from Manninglea.

"How was the body taken to the Abbey?"

"Sent one of the carriages."

"Oh, dear!"

They continued to talk; and Mavis, listening, for a few moments felt gladness, nothing but gladness. He had gone out of their lives forever. There could be no divorce. Now that he was dead, she would be forgiven. Then again she felt the horror of it. The thing was like an answer to her secret prayer or wish—like the mysterious overwhelming consequence of her curse.

It was as though in cursing him she had doomed him to destruction.

"They caught the horse last night, didn't they?"

"Yes. Some chaps at Abbey Cross Roads see un go gallopin' by, and followed un up Beacon Hill. Catched un in the quag by th' old gravel pits."

"Oh, dear!" said Miss Waddy.

Little by little Mavis pieced the story together. Mr. Barradine had been out riding late yesterday, and the riderless horse had given the alarm some time about nine o'clock in the evening. But, although a widespread search continued all through the night, the body was not found until past noon to-day.

They had found it at Kibworth Rocks. These rocks, situated in Hadleigh Wood, about two miles from the Abbey, were of curious formation—a wide mass of jagged boulders cropping out unexpectedly from the sandy soil, some of them half hidden with bracken, while others, the bigger ones, rose brown and bare and strange. They provided a redoubtable fortress for foxes, and contained what was known as the biggest "earth" of the neighborhood. Not far off, the main ride passed through the wood, making a broad sunlit avenue between the gloomy pines; but no one without local knowledge would have suspected the existence of the rocky gorge or slope, because, although only at a little distance, it was quite invisible from the ride.

The body had been discovered lying in a narrow cleft, the head fearfully battered; and how Mr. Barradine came by his death was obvious. He had been riding through or near the rocks, and the horse, probably stumbling, had thrown him; and then, frightened and struggling away, had dragged him some considerable distance, until the rocks held him fast and tore him free.

What remained doubtful was how or why Mr. Barradine approached the rocks. Of course, his horse might have shied from the ride and taken him there before he could recover control of it; or, as perhaps was more probable, Mr. Barradine might have ridden from the safe and open track in order quietly to examine what was called the main earth, and, if fortunate, gratify himself with a glimpse of two or three lusty fox cubs playing outside the burrows.

However, as Mr. Allen sagely observed, such conjectures were at present idle. These and all other matters would be cleared up at the inquest.

"Oh, dear!" said Miss Waddy. "Will there have to be an inquest?"

"Certainly there will," said Mr. Allen.

"Yes, that's the law always," said somebody else.

"Surely not," said Miss Waddy, "in the case of such a well-known gentleman as Mr. Barradine."

"It would be the same," said Allen, "if it was the Prince of Wales, or the Archbishop of Canterbury. Coroner's Court sits on everybody who doesn't die in his bed certified by his doctor."

"And it rained, too, last night," said Miss Waddy.

"Yes, there was some heavy showers."

"Fancy the poor gentleman lying out in the rain. Oh, dear!"

Mavis Dale left them talking and went back to the post office. In her agitation she had forgotten about the reply telegram to her husband. She got Mr. Ridgett to write the message—her hands were trembling so that she could scarcely hold the pencil.

"Very sorry, I'm sure," said Mr. Ridgett sympathetically. "This was the party you told me of—the gentleman that was giving his support to Mr. Dale?"

"Yes."

"Well, well—very sad. How will you word it?"

"Please say—'Report true. Mr. Barradine killed by fall from his horse yesterday.' And sign it 'Mavis.' No, sign it 'Mav.'"

"Mav!—Ma-v!" Mr. Ridgett looked round, smiling. "That's hubby's pet name for you, isn't it? Upon my word, you two *are* a pair of love-birds. . . . There, off it goes. Good night, Mrs. Dale. I'm truly sorry that you've been deprived of such a friend."

She went up-stairs to her bedroom, and did not come out of it that evening. For a long time she sat on the bed sobbing and shivering. She was glad really, and she knew that she was glad, and yet all the blood in her body seemed to be running coldly because of unreasoning superstitious fear. It was as though she had seen a ghost, and as though the ghost, while imparting to her a piece of surprisingly good news, had at the same time almost frightened her out of her wits. It is so wicked, so impiously wicked to wish for the death of a fellow creature. But what are wishes? Common sense revolts from the supposition that thoughts can kill. Why, if they could, half the population of the world would succumb beneath the impalpable weapons wielded by the other half. It is only toward nightfall, when rooms begin to grow dark, and the deepening shadows give queer shapes to furniture, curtains, and other familiar objects, that one can be foolish enough to entertain such fancies.

She told Mary to bring the candles, and to run out

and buy a night-light. Then Mary helped her to undress and to get to bed; and she slept dreamlessly.
The feeling after all was one of unutterable relief. Mr.
Barradine *was!* Never again would her flesh shrink
at the sight of him; never again could those lascivious
hands touch her.

Next day, between dinner-time and tea-time, while
she was giving final touches to the well-cleaned parlor,
she heard her husband's voice just outside the door.
He had come up-stairs very quietly and was speaking
to Mary on the landing.

"Will, Will!" With a cry of delight, Mavis rushed
out to welcome him. "Oh, thank goodness, you've
come home." She boldly took his arm, drew him into
the parlor and shut the door again. "Will—aren't
you going to kiss me?"

"No." And he disengaged himself and moved away
from her. "No, I can not kiss you."

"Oh, Will. Do try to forget and forgive." She
stood stretching out her hands toward him imploringly,
with eyebrows raised, and lips quavering.

"I can never forget," he said, after a moment's
pause.

Then she tried to make him say that things would
eventually come all right, that if he could not pardon
her and take her to his heart now, he would do so some
time or another. He listened to her pleadings im-
passively, stolidly; his attitude was stiffly dignified, and
it seemed to her that, whatever his real frame of mind
might be, he had determined to hide it by maintaining
an impenetrably solemn tone and manner.

"Will, you've come home, and I'm grateful for it.
But—but I do think you're cruel to me. Especially

considering what's happened, I did hope you'd begin to think kinder to me."

"Mavis," he said solemnly, "it is the finger of God." And he repeated the phrase slowly, with a solemnity that was almost pompous. "It is the finger of God. If that man had not chanced to die in this sudden and startling way, I could never have come home to you. It was the decision I had arrived at before I read of his accident in the paper. Otherwise you'd 'a' never set eyes on me. Now all I can say is, you and I must trust to the future. It will be my endeavor not to look back, and I ask you equally to look forward."

She was certain that this was a set speech prepared beforehand. She knew so well the faintly unnatural note in his voice when he was reciting sentences that he had learned by rote: she who had helped in so many rehearsals before his public utterances could not be mistaken. However, she had to be contented with it. And, stilted and stiff as it was, it certainly seemed to imply that she need not relinquish hope.

He added something, in the same ponderous style, about the probability of its being advisable to put private inclinations on one side and attend the funeral of the deceased in his public capacity of postmaster. This mark of respect would be expected from him, and people would wonder if he did not pay it. Then he left the parlor, and again spoke to Mary.

Mavis, listening, heard him give orders that an unused camp bedstead should be brought down from the clerk's room and made up in the kitchen. He told Mary that he wished to sleep by himself because he felt twinges of rheumatism and was afraid of disturbing the mistress if the pain came on during the night.

And Mavis noticed that all the time that he was talking to Mary his voice sounded perfectly natural.

Then he went down-stairs, speaking again when he was half-way down.

"How goes it, Miss Yorke? Is Mr. Ridgett in the office?"

And this time it was absolutely his old voice—rather loud, rather authoritative, but really quite cheerful.

Thinking of his manner to her and his manner to others, she believed that she could now understand all that he intended. She was to be held in disgrace perhaps for a long time, but appearances were to be kept up. No breath of scandal was to tarnish the reputation of the Rodchurch postmaster; the curious world must not be allowed the very slightest peep behind the scenes of his private life; and she, without explicit instructions, was to assist in preventing any one—even poor humble Mary—from guessing that as husband and wife they were not as heretofore on the best possible terms.

Down below in the sorting-room Dale greeted Mr. Ridgett very heartily.

"Here I am. May I venture to come in a minute? I'm only a visitor till Monday, you know." And he told Ridgett how he had taken a liberty in returning before the stipulated date; but he had written to headquarters explaining the circumstances, and he had no doubt they would approve. "There's the funeral, you know. Though I suppose that won't be till Tuesday or even Wednesday. But there's the inquest. And I felt it like a duty to attend that too."

"Yes, I suppose this is a bit of a blow to you—

knowing him so long. Your good lady was mightily upset."

"So she had cause to be," said Dale gravely.

"He'd always shown himself a real friend?"

"The best friend anybody ever had," said Dale with impressive earnestness. Then, going, he returned to speak in a confidential whisper close to Mr. Ridgett's ear. "It was he who did the trick for me up there. But for *him,* I was to be hoofed out of this, as sure as eggs."

"Really! Well, I'll tell you frankly, I'm not surprised to hear it. Ever since the little Missis came home with the happy tale, I've been wondering what miracle pulled you through so grand with them."

Then Dale went out and down the street, talking to everybody he met.

The village received him with tranquil indifference. No one congratulated him. The greater excitement had obliterated all memory of the less: not a soul seemed to recollect the famous controversy, the postmaster's campaign against detractors, his long absence or his brilliant success. Kibworth Rocks, the drawn blinds of the Abbey House, the decorations of the Abbey Church—these were the only things that Rodchurch could now think of, or talk about.

The inquest, held on Monday in one of the state rooms at the Abbey, brought to light no new facts that were of the least importance. All sorts of people gave evidence, but no one had anything to say that was really worth saying. Mr. Allen, it appeared, had "acted foolish" and been reproved by the Coroner, first for irrelevance and then for impertinence.

Allen had attempted to persuade the Court that the

prime cause of the accident was simply this, that poor
Mr. Barradine's saddle was made by a London firm
instead of by him—Allen. He pooh-poohed the stud-
groom's statement that Mr. Barradine had an ineradicable objection to patent detachable stirrups, and
maintained that he would have been able, in five minutes' quiet conversation, to prevail on the deceased
gentleman to adopt a certain device which was known
to Allen but to nobody else in the trade; and then he
attempted to read a written paper in which he advo-
cated the superiority to the modern plain flap of the
ancient padded knee-roll as a means of rendering the
seat more secure for forehand stumbles.

"It was laughable—but for the occasion—to hear
him spouting out his nonsense, until Doctor Hollis
told him straight he wouldn't put up with it any
longer."

Dale gave this account of the proceedings to Mavis
and to Mr. Ridgett, who had come up to take high tea
on the eve of his departure just as he had done on the
day of his arrival.

"But I admit," said Dale, conscientiously, "there
was one bit of sense in Allen's remarks. He convinced
me against trusting to these blood animals. They're
too *quick,* and they're never *sure.* The grooms an' all
spoke up to Mr. Barradine's knowledge of his ridin'
gen'rally; but it stands to reason, when you're past
sixty your grip on a horse isn't the same thing as what
it once was. Say, your mount gets bounding this way,
that way;" and with his body and hands he indicated
the rapid lateral movements of a horse shying and
plunging. "Well, it's only the grip that can save you.
You aren't going to keep in your saddle by mere bal-

ance—and it's balance that old gentlemen rely on best part of the time."

Mavis listened wonderingly and admiringly. When her husband spoke of the dead man, his voice was grave, calm and kindly. No one on earth could have detected that while the man lived, he had been regarded with anything but affection. She thought of that epithet that people so often echo—Death the Leveler. Could one hope that already, although Will might not know it, might not be willing to know it, death had taken from him all or nearly all of his anger and resentment? If it was only just acting—the stubborn effort to keep up appearances—it was marvelous. Then she sighed. She had remembered that Will never did things by halves.

She felt almost gay, certainly quite light-hearted, when driving out with him to the funeral. It was such a glorious day, not a bit too hot, with a west wind sweeping unseen through the limpid sky; and the whole landscape seeming animated, everywhere the sound of wheels, the roads full of people all going one way. She simulated gravity, even sadness, as they passed the dark pines near Hadleigh Wood; but in truth she was quite undisturbed by her proximity to the fateful spot. It seemed to her that with the murmur of the wheels, the movement of the air, the progressive excitement of every minute, all the tragic or gloomy element of life was rolling far away from her.

The scene presented at the Abbey struck her as magnificent. She had never seen so many private carriages assembled together, and she would not have guessed that the whole county of Hampshire contained so many policemen. There were soldiers also—members of some volunteer or yeomanry corps of which the deceased was honorary colonel. Their brilliant uniforms shone out dazzlingly on a background of black dresses and coats.

Naturally there was not space in the church for all this vast concourse. The nobility, gentry, and other ticket-holders were admitted first, and then there came an unmannerly rush which the constables checked with difficulty. Mavis and Dale were just inside the door; and Mr. Silcox close by, whispering, and pointing out several lords and ladies near the chancel steps. The service was long but very beautiful, with giant candles burning by the draped bier, organ music that seemed to swell and rumble in the pit of one's stomach, and light voices of singing boys that made one vibrate as if one had been turned into glass—all stirring one to a quite meaningless regret, not for the man who lay deaf and dumb and blind beneath the velvet pall, but because of vague thoughts about children who die young and have wings to hover over those they loved down here below. And, oh, the increasing heat of the church, the oppressive crush, the heavy odors of flowers and crape and perspiration! When at last one emerged, and the open air touched one's forehead, it was like coming out of an oven into a cold bath.

Then the remains were consigned to the family vault in the small graveyard behind the church—the crowd filling every vista, the bells tolling, and the soldiers discharging a cannon and making one jump at each regularly timed discharge. Mavis, turning her eyes in all directions, looked at everything with intense interest—at the gentlefolk, now inextricably mixed up with the tenantry and the mob; at her husband, standing so black and solemn, with a face that might have belonged to a marble statue; at the puff of smoke that crept upward when the gun went bang, at the sunlight on the church tower, at the birds flying so high and so joyous above its battlements. And all at once she saw Aunt Petherick—the blackest mourner there, with crape veils trailing to the ground, a red face down which the tears streamed in rivers; sobbing so that the sobs sounded like the most violent hiccoughs; really almost as much noise as the soldiers' gun.

Will had seen her too. Mavis noticed his stony glance at Auntie, when the crowd began to move again.

While he was slowly making his way toward the stables, she got hold of Mrs. Petherick and had a little chat with her. Auntie had now entirely recovered from her recent hysterical storm; the redness of her face was passing off, and its expression was one of anxiety, rather than of grief.

"My dear girl," she said, "I don't yet know what this will mean to me. You know, he promised the house for my life—but he wouldn't give me a lease. I've nothing to show—not so much as a letter. I may be turned out neck and crop."

"Oh, Auntie, I should think his wishes would be respected."

"How'm I to prove his wishes?" said Mrs. Petherick, quite testily. "It'll be wish my foot, for all the lawyers 'll care."

"Oh, Auntie!"

"You know, he faithfully promised to provide for me. And now the talk is he never made a will at all. You can't believe the talk. But, oh, it's awful to me. The suspense! It'll break my heart to give up North Ride."

"Auntie," said Mavis presently; "if you chance upon Will, don't speak to him."

"Why not?"

She whispered the answer. "He found out about *him* and me."

"Oh, did he? How did he take it?"

"Awfully badly."

But Mrs. Petherick did not seem to care twopence about the domestic trouble of Mavis and Will. Her thoughts were engrossed by her own affairs.

"Mavis, I do think this: that if there's a will found, I shall be in it. He wasn't a liar, whatever he was."

That night there seemed to be a tremendous lot of drunkenness in Rodchurch, and when the Gauntlet Inn closed you could hear the shouting as far off as the post office. But next day the village was quietly drowsy as of old: it had got over its excitement.

Weeks passed, and for Mavis time began to glide. All things in the post office itself had resumed their ordinary course, and she felt instinctively that up-stairs, as well as down-stairs, a normal order would rule again before very long. Outwardly she and Dale were just what they used to be. They were not, however, really living as husband and wife. She suffered, but made no complaint. All would come right.

X

MR. BARRADINE had not died intestate. This fact was made known at the post office in a sudden and perturbing manner by a letter to Mavis from Messrs. Cleaver, the Old Manninglea solicitors. Messrs. Cleaver informed her that the London firm who were acting in the matter of Mr. Barradine's will had instructed them to communicate with her, because certain documents—such as attested copies of her birth certificate, marriage certificate, and so on— would presently be required; and it would be convenient to Messrs. Cleaver, if she could pay them a call within the next two or three days.

Mavis gave the letter to Dale when they met at breakfast, and he read it slowly and thoughtfully.

"What do you suppose it means, Will?"

"I suppose it means that you're one of the leg'tees."

"Yes." Mavis drew in her breath. "It came into my mind that it might be that."

"I don't see what else it can be."

His face had become dull and expressionless, and he spoke in a heavy tone.

"I may go over and see Mr. Cleaver, mayn't I?"

"Yes," he said. "But I must go with you."

"When can you get away? I don't think we ought to put it off."

"No. There mustn't be an hour's avoidable delay. I'll take you over this afternoon."

Then, without another word, he finished his break·fast and went down-stairs. Mavis was vibrating with excitement, her eyes large and bright, a spot of poppy color on each cheek; she longed to burst out into all sorts of conjectures, to discuss every possibility, but she did not dare speak to him again just then.

Though the market town of Old Manninglea was only eight miles distant, the roundabout journey thither by rail offered such difficulties that Dale hired a dog-cart from the Roebuck and drove his wife across by road.

Their route for the first four miles was the one they would have followed if they had been going to the Abbey, and as they bowled along behind a strong and active little horse Mavis felt again, but in an intensified degree, those sensations of well-being, of comfort, and hopefulness, that she had experienced when passing through the same scenery on the day of the funeral. All the country looked so warm and rich in its fulness of summer tints—corn ready to cut, fruit waiting to be picked, cows asking to be milked; everywhere plenty and peace; nature giving so freely, and still promising to give more. It seemed to her that as surely as there is a law under which the seasons change, sunshine follows storm, and trees after losing their leaf soon begin to bud again, so surely is it intended that states of mind should succeed one another, that after sorrow should come gladness, and that no one has the right to say " I will keep my heart like a shuttered room, and because it was dark yesterday the light shall not enter it to-day."

About a mile out from Rodchurch they passed the Baptist chapel—a supremely ugly little building that stood isolated and forlorn in a narrow banked enclosure among flat pasture fields—and Mavis, making conversation, called Dale's attention to the tablet that largely advertised its date.

"Eighteen thirty-seven, Will! That's a long time ago."

"Yes," he said, "a many years back—that takes one. Year the Queen came to the throne."

"I wonder why they built it out here—such a way from everybody—such a tramp for the worshipers."

"In those days all non-conformists were a deal more down-trodden than they are now. It was before people began to understan' the meanin' o' liberty o' conscience; and, like enough, that's a bit of evidence."

"How so, Will?"

"Quite likely there wasn't a landlord lib'ral enough to give 'em a patch o' ground within reach o' th' village. Shoved 'em off as far as they could, to please Mr. Parson, and not contam'nate his church with the sight of an honest dissenter."

He said all this sententiously and didactically, as one who enjoys speaking on historical or sociological subjects; but then a cloud seemed to descend upon him, and he relapsed into gloomy silence.

After another mile they came to Vine-Pits Farm, the home of Mr. Bates the corn-merchant. It was one of the few stone houses of the district, a compact snug-looking nucleus from which an irregular wing, rather higher than the main building, advanced to the very edge of the roadway. A much smaller wing, merely an excrescence, on the other side, seemed as if it had gone as far as it could in the direction of making a quadrangle and had then given over the task to a broad low wall. The square piece of garden, though untidy and neglected, derived a great air of dignity from its stone surrounding, and importance was added to the house by the solid range of outbuildings, barns, and stables. A rick yard with haystacks so big that they showed above the tops of fruit trees and yews, three or four wagons and carts, half a dozen busy men, made the whole Bates establishment seem quite like a thriving little town all to itself.

"It's a funny name, Vine-Pits," said Mavis, still making conversation. "I wonder why ever they called it that."

"There was formerly a quantity of old pits 'longside the rick-bargan—same as you see forcing-pits at a market-gardener's—and the tale goes that they were orig'nally placed there for the purpose of growing grapes on the same principle as cucumbers or melons."

"What a funny idea!"

" 'Twas a failure. Sort of a gentleman farmer had the notion he knew better than others, and tried it on year after year till he made a laughing-stock of himself. Anyhow, that's the tale. Mr. Bates has shown me the basis of the pits—built over now by the buildings you were looking at. Ah, here is the old fellow."

Mr. Bates driving toward them in his gig pulled up, and invited Dale to do so also.

"How are you, William?" And he took off his hat to Mrs. Dale. "Your servant, madam. Turn head about, William, and come into my place and take a bit of refreshment."

"No, thank you, Mr. Bates. Not to-day. Some other time."

"No time like the present.   A cup of tea, Mrs. Dale.
I don't care to see those I count as friends pass my
place without stopping."

"I know you mean what you say," said Dale cordially; "but we're for Old Manninglea—business appointment."

"Then I mustn't hinder you.   But look in on your
way back.   Your servant, madam."

Mavis liked the fresh clean complexion and the silvery white hair of Mr. Bates, and there was something
very pleasing in his old-fashioned mode of address,
his courteous way of saluting her, and his gentle
friendly smile as he spoke to her husband.

"Will," she said, as they drove on, "I believe Mr.
Bates is really fond of you."

Dale gave a snort; and then after a long pause
spoke with strong emphasis.

"I'll tell you, Mavis, what Mr. Bates is.   He's a
good man, every bit and crumb of him.   There's no
one between the downs and the sea that I feel the
same respect for that I do for that old gentleman."

"Yes, Will, I know you've always praised him."

"And since you make the remark, I'll admit its
truth.   I do verily believe that Mr. Bates *is* fond of
me."   Then he laughed bitterly.   "I'm not aware of
any one else I could say it of."

"Oh, Will—there's lots are fond of you."

"No—none.   That was one small part of my lesson
last month in London.   I got that tip, straight, at the
G.P.O."

"Will!"

They were driving now through the woods, and
Mavis, glancing from time to time at her husband's

face, saw that it had become fearfully somber. She guessed that this indicated an unfortunate turn of thought, and she talked incessantly in the hope of rendering such thought difficult, if not impossible.

After crossing the bridge over the stream that runs serpentining through the Upper Hadleigh Wood on its way to join the Rod River, they were soon at the Abbey Cross Roads. Here, as they turned into the highroad by the Barradine Arms and the cluster of adjacent cottages, they had a splendid panoramic view of the Abbey estate rolling downward on their left in wide, sylvan beauty as far as the eye could see. From this higher ground, the park showed like an irregular pattern of lighter color on a dark green carpet, and a few of the main rides were visible here and there as truncated straight lines that began and ended capriciously; but all the houses and buildings lay hidden by the undulating woodland. Mavis turned her eyes toward the point where North Ride Cottage shyly concealed itself, and then she glanced back at Dale. He was staring straight in front, not looking to left or right, as if focusing the roadway between the horse's ears.

"It's uphill now, Will, all the way, isn't it? Oh, that's a new cottage. How red the bricks are!"

They had left all the trees behind them now, and, going up the slope through the last strip of fields, they soon emerged on the open heath. For a mile or two the landscape was wildly sad in aspect, just a waste of sand and heather, with naked ridges and boggy hollows, one or two wind-swept hillocks that bore a ragged crest of blackened firs, and in the farthest distance massive contours of grassy down rising

as a barrier to guard the fertile valleys of another
county. It was here that the riderless horse had galloped about and been hunted by the people from the
cross road cottages.

"You *have* driven well. I think it's wonderful,
considering what a little practise you get. . . . Look,
I believe that's a hawk. Must be! Nothing but a
hawk could stand so still in the air. He can see
something down under him, I suppose. Rabbits, perhaps. Though I don't suppose he'd strike at anything
as big as a rabbit, would he?"

Mavis chattered vigorously, to prevent her husband
from brooding on painful things; but, even while talking, she did not obliterate her own real thoughts. Inside her there seemed to be a running chorus of un-
uttered words, and she listened to the inner voice ev-
en when at her busiest with the outward sounding
voice.

"Has he truly left me money? If so, how much?"
These mute questions were perpetually repeated. "A
hundred pounds? Perhaps more than that. He gave
me two hundred when I married. Suppose he has left
me quite a lot of money."

It was not market-day, and the town therefore was
not at its best and brightest. Nevertheless, the appearance of shops, pavements, and nicely dressed young
ladies, had a most exhilarating effect on Mavis when,
after putting up the horse and cart, Dale solemnly
conducted her through the High Street to the solicitor's office in Church Place.

The interview with Mr. Cleaver did not take long,
although such weighty concerns were spoken of.
Dale sat on a chair near the wall, his hat held be-

tween his knees, his eyes lowered; while Mavis sat on a chair close to the solicitor, talking, flushing, throbbing, gradually ascending a scale of excitement so feverishly strong that it seemed as if it must eventually consume her just as fire consumes.

Mr. Barradine had left her two thousand pounds, and this sum was to be paid to her free of all duties. The will had not yet been proved, but everything was in order and probate would be granted any day now; minor legacies would then immediately be cleared off; and, since Mavis would have no difficulty in satisfying the executors as to her identity, she might really consider the money as safe in her pocket. Mr. Cleaver, having made this stimulating communication and described the formalities that she must fulfil, asked a few questions about certain of her relatives.

"Ruby Millicent Petherick. That is a cousin of yours? Yes." And he jotted down a note of any facts that Mavis could supply. "Still a spinster. About your own age, and living abroad. Thank you. That is all you can tell me? There seems to be doubt as to her whereabouts. Your aunt—Mrs. John Edward Petherick—does not know her address. But she will no doubt present herself in due course."

Then Mr. Cleaver indicated that he need not further detain them, and Dale, rising slowly and still looking at the crown of his hat, spoke for the first time and in a very ponderous way.

"This has come as a complete surprise to my wife."

"Yes," and the solicitor smiled, "but not by any means as an unpleasant surprise, Mr. Dale!"

"No, sir, naturally not. My wife having been connected with the family since childhood would be nat-

urally one to be thought of by the head of the family
if wishful to benefit *all* old friends after he was called
away."

"Quite so," said Mr. Cleaver.

"Will," said Mavis, "we mustn't waste Mr. Cleaver's time by telling him our history;" and she gave a
nervous fluttered laugh.

"Mr. Cleaver," said Dale glumly, "will pardon me
for desiring to learn how others stand, as well as yourself."

"Oh, well," said Mr. Cleaver, "I think it might be
premature to go into matters that do not directly concern Mrs. Dale."

"Yes," said Mavis, nervously, "we mustn't ask for
secrets."

"It's just this," said Dale, with stolid insistence.
"I do hope he has done something equally handsome
for those relations of my wife whose names you mentioned—especially for her aunt, Mrs. J. E. Petherick,
who is now past her youth, and to whom it would be
a comfort. Also my wife's cousin Ruby, who is earn-
ing her livelihood on the continent by following the
profession of a muscian. Such a windfall would come
as a blessing to her."

"Mr. Dale," said the solicitor, "I may safely say as
much as this. No one who had the smallest grounds
for expectng anything will find himself left out in the
cold."

"Thank you, sir." Dale had raised his eyes, and,
while speaking now, in the same sententious manner,
he seemed to be observing Mr. Cleaver's face very
closely. "The fact is, my wife and I had no grounds
whatever for expecting to be singled out for special

rewards. On the contrary, it was never in my wife's power to render the long and faithful service rendered by the others; so that if a bequest had fallen to us while others of the Petherick clan—if I may employ that expression—had bin passed over, it might have bin difficult for us to benefit to the detriment of the rest of 'em—at least, without causing fam'ly squabbles."

" Then I'll freely reassure you. Such a contingency will not arise. No," and Mr. Cleaver's tone became heartily enthusiastic. " It is a beautiful will. You'll see all the particulars in the newspapers before a week is over, and you'll say that no critic—however hard to please—could find fault. It is a will that is bound to attract the attention of the press."

" Then thank you again, sir. And good afternoon —with renewed thanks for the courteous way you wrote to my wife, and received the two of us to-day."

" Good afternoon." Mr. Cleaver smiled and shook hands good-humoredly. " My congratulations, Mrs. Dale; and one word of advice, free gratis. Invest your legacy wisely, and don't confound capital with income. You're going to have two thousand pounds all told, not two thousand a year, you know."

" Oh, no, sir—I wouldn't be so foolish as to think so."

They had tea at a pastry-cook's in complete silence, and they were half-way home again before Mavis ventured to rouse her husband from his ominous gloom.

" Will," she said, with an assumption of calmness and confidence, " I didn't at once catch the drift of what you were saying to Mr. Cleaver, and when I tried to stop you it was because I was all on edge from hearing such a tremendous piece of news. Such a lot more than ever I could have *dreamed* of."

He did not answer. Steadily watching the horse's ears, and holding the reins in both hands with the conscientious care of an unpractised coachman, he drove down the slope to the Cross Roads and round the corner into the woods.

"No, but I soon saw what was passing through your mind, Will. You wanted to make quite sure that there would be nothing to cause talk. I don't myself believe people would have really noticed if I had been the only one. But, of course, as I am one of several, it stands to reason nobody can say anything nasty."

Still he did not answer.

"Will, you'll let me take the money, won't you?"

"I don't know. I must think."

"Yes, dear, but you'll think sensibly, won't you? Think of the use—to both of us. If it's mine in name, I count it all as yours every bit as much as mine."

"That's enough now. Don't go on talking about it."

"All right. Are you going to stop at Mr. Bates'?"

"No."

"He was very pressing."

"I've no spirit to tell him—or any one else—what we've heard over there."

"Will," and she drew close to him, nestling against him as much as she could venture to do without causing him difficulty in driving, "you said we were to look forward, not back. Don't get thinking of the past. What's done is done—and it *must* be right to be happy if we can."

"Ah," and he gave a snort, "that's what the heathens used to say. I thought you were a Christian."

"So I am, Will. Christ preached mercy—yes, and happiness too."

"Thought He preached remorse for sins before you reach pardon and peace. But never mind religion—don't let's drag *that* in. And leave me alone. Don't talk. I tell you I want to think."

"Very well, dear. Only this one thing. Keep this before you. Now that he's dead——"

"I've asked you to hold your tongue."

"And I will. But let me finish. However lofty you choose to look at it, it can't be wrong to take the money now he's gone."

"I wish his money had gone with him. Look at it lofty or low—take it or leave it—this cursed legacy reminds me of all I was trying to forget."

XI

FULL particulars of the disposition of Mr. Barradine's fortune had now been published, and the world was admiringly talking about it.

The claims of the entire Petherick family would be once for all satisfied. Mrs. Petherick and that young person who had been sent to learn music at Vienna were each to receive as much as Mavis Dale; three other Pethericks would get five hundred pounds apiece; still more Pethericks would be dowered in a lesser degree. Then came the ordinary servants, with legacies proportionate to terms of service—everybody remembered, nobody left out in the cold. Then, with nice lump sums of increasing magnitude, came a baker's dozen of Barradine nephews, nieces, and second cousins; the Abbey domain was to go to an elderly first cousin; and then, after bequests to various charities, came the grand item that the local solicitor had in his mind when he foretold a salvo of newspaper comment.

The residue of the estate, the larger half of all the dead man's possessions, was to be employed in the establishment of a Home for parentless, unprotected, or destitute female children. The trustees of this institution were to find a suitable site somewhere within five miles of the Abbey House, and if possible on the Barradine property, being guided in their selection of the exact spot by expert advice as to the character of the soil, the qualities of the air, and the facilities for obtaining a supply of pure water. When they had found the site they were immediately to build thereon, and provide accommodation at the earliest date for fifty small inmates, each of whom was to be reared, educated, and finally launched in life with a small dowry. The funds available would be more than sufficient for the number of children named; and Mr. Barradine expressed the wish that the number should not be increased if, as he hoped, the income of the Trust grew bigger with the passage of time. He desired that extension of revenue should be devoted to improving the comfort and amenities of the fifty occupants, to increasing their dowries, and to assisting them after they had gone out into the world.

Not only the *Rodhaven District Courier,* but great London journals also, experienced difficulty in marshaling enough adjectives to convey their sense of admiration for such a perfect scheme. Ever since his death the local praise of Mr. Barradine's amiable qualities had been taking richer colors, and now the will seemed so to sanctify his memory that one felt he must be henceforth classed with the traditional philanthropic heroes of England—those whose names grow brighter through the centuries.

When on Sunday Mr. Norton took for his text those beautiful words, "Suffer little children to come unto Me," all instantaneously guessed what he was getting at, and by the time he finished there was scarcely a dry eye that had not been wet at some point or other of an unusually long sermon. "We have had," he said in conclusion, "a striking instance of that noblest of all the feelings of the human breast, tenderness and care for the weak and helpless; and without abrogating the practise of our church which forbids us to pray for the souls of those who have been summoned away from us, I will ask you all before dispersing today to join with me in a few moments' silent meditation on the lesson to be derived from a kindness that has proved undying—a pity that has the attribute of things eternal, and, speaking to us from the other side of the grave, may in all reverence be described as Angelic."

The talk about the vast sums to be expended in charity produced a curious effect on Mavis Dale. It seemed that her own two thousand pounds was a steadily diminishing quantity; she was still greatly excited whenever she thought about it, but she could not feel again the respectful rapture caused by her first thought of its lavishly generous extent. Perhaps just at first, doing what the solicitor advised her not to do, she had not altogether discriminated between capital and interest. Dazzled by the abstract notion of wealth, she had over-estimated concrete potentialities.

Of course William would allow her to accept the legacy. In the early days after their visit to Old Manninglea she had tormented herself with fears that he would attempt to force a renunciation of benefits from that quarter, and she had determined never to yield to so preposterous an exercise of authority; but now she felt certain that he would not thus drive her to open revolt. He was still somber and silent, but, however long he remained in this gloomy state, he would not interfere with her freedom in regard to the money.

Nevertheless, she felt relieved when he explicitly stated that there would be no further opposition on his part.

"Oh, Will, I can't tell you how glad I am to hear you talk so sensibly about it."

"It is not willingly that I say 'Yes.' Don't you go and think that."

"No. But you do see we couldn't act otherwise?"

"You must accept it—for this reason, and not for any other reason. Our hands are tied. If you refuse it, people would wonder."

"Yes—yes. But, Will, you keep saying *you*, when it's really us. It will be *ours*, not just only mine, you must remember."

"Ah, but I doubt if I could ever take you at your word, there."

After this she sang at her household work. She took as a good sign the fact that he had spoken doubtfully, instead of formally repudiating her suggestion that they were to share alike in all the good things which the money might bring them. She thought it must mean that he was very near to forgiving her. Death had now almost wiped out *everything*. He was feeling more and more every day what she had felt from the beginning, that it was palpably absurd to go on harboring resentment.

Free now from exaggerated estimates, with ideas readjusted to the measure of reality, and her natural common sense at work again, she thought of what the little fortune might truly do for them. It ought to yield a hundred pounds, twice fifty pounds a year— roughly two pounds a week coming in unearned. Why, it *was wealth*. On top of William's annual

emoluments such an income would make them feel
as if they were rolling in money.

Visions immediately arose of all sorts of things that
would now be within the scope of their means—choic-
er meals for William, aprons and caps for Mary, new
curtains and much else new and delightful to beautify
the home. Little excursions too—a regular seaside
holiday during leave-time!

Messrs. Cleaver had intimated that the London solicitors were ready to hand over the money, and Mavis
was talking to her husband about its investment.

"I trust your judgment, Will—and I'd like it put in
both our names."

"Oh, no, I couldn't quite consent to that."

"I do wish you would. If it's invested well, I make
out it ought to bring us a hundred a year."

"Mavis," he said, thoughtfully, "it might be invested to bring more than that, if you were prepared
to take a certain amount of risk."

"Oh, I don't want any risk."

"An' p'raps the risk, after all, would be covered by
the security I'd offer you. That'd be for your lawyers
to decide; it's not for me to urge the safety."

"Will, what is it?"

"I hesitate for this purpose. I want to lead you
up to it, so that you shouldn't turn against the proposal without yourself or your representatives giving
it consideration."

"Will, I wish you'd tell me—I can't bear suspense."

"Then here's the first question. If satisfied of the
security, would you lend out the money on mortgage
with a person who has the chance of setting up himself in an old-established business?"

"What business?"

"I'll tell you in a minute. Take the person first. You haven't asked about *him*. In a sense, his character—honesty and straight ways—is a part of the security. He is somebody you've known for a many years."

"Who is it?"

"Myself."

"Will? What on earth do you mean?"

"Mavis, it's like this—There, bide a bit."

They had been sitting in the dusk after their high tea; and now Mary brought a lighted lamp into the room, and put it on the table between them.

"All right, my girl. Never mind clearing away till I call for you."

He waited until Mary had gone out of the room, and then went on talking. His face with the lamplight full upon it looked very firm and serious, and his manner while he explained all these new ideas was strangely unemotional. He spoke not in the style of a husband to a wife, but of a business man proposing a partnership to another man.

"It seems to me, viewing it all round, a wonderful good chance. An opening that isn't likely to come in one's way twice. Mr. Bates' son has bin and got himself into such a mess over a horse-racing transaction that he's had to make a bolt of it. I can't tell you the facts, because I don't rightly know them; but it's bad —something to do wth checks that'll put him to hidin' for a long day, if he doesn't want to answer for it in a court o' law. Well, then, the old gentleman being worn out with private care, wishful to retire, and seeing a common cheat and waster in the one who ought by nature to succeed him, has offered me to take over the farm, the trade, an' the whole bag of tricks."

"But, surely to goodness, Will, you don't think of giving up the post office?"

"Yes, I do. I think of that, in any case."

"But you love the work."

"Used to, Mavis."

"Don't you now?"

"No. Mavis, it's like this." He had raised a hand to shade his eyes, as if the lamplight hurt them, and she could no longer see the expression of his face. But she observed a sudden change in his manner. He spoke now much in the same confidential tone that he had always employed in the old time when telling her of his most intimate affairs—in the happy time when he brought all his little troubles to her, and flattered her by saying that she never failed to make them easy to bear. "So far's the P.O. is concerned, all the heart has gone out of me. The events through which I've passed have altered my view of the entire affair. Where all seemed leading me on and on, and up and up, I see nothing before me now."

"Promotion!"

"I don't b'lieve I'd ever get it. The best I could hope for 'd be that they'd leave me here to th' end o' my service life. And besides, if promotion comes to-morrow, I don't want it."

"Will, let me say it at once. Take the money. I consent. Whatever you feel's best for you, that's what I want."

He altogether ignored her interruption, and went on in the same tone. "I used to think it grand, and now it all seems nothing. I do assure you when I

was down there handing out a halfpenny stamp or
signing a two-shilling order, I used to feel large
enough to burst with satisfaction. I felt 'I'm the
king o' the castle.'—That was thrown in my teeth as
how I appeared to others. Well, now, I feel like a
brock in a barrel—or not so big as him. Just something small that's got into the wrong box by accident,
and had the lid clapped to on it. I want room for my
elbows, an' scope for my int'lect. I must get the sky
over my head again, and the open roads under my feet.
If I stopped down there much longer, I should go
mad."

"Then, my dear, you mustn't stop."

"These last weeks—fairly determined to chuck it—
I bin thinking o' the Colonies as affording advantages
to any man who's got capacities in him; but now this
chance comes nearer home, and it lies with you to say
if you'll give me the help required for me to take it."

"Yes," said Mavis, earnestly, "and more glad than
words can say to think I'm able to do so."

Indeed she was delighted. She had been deeply
moved by all he told her about his distaste for the
work he used to love, and she recognized that he had
been magnanimous in refraining from reproaches, but
rather implying a purely personal change of ideas as
to the cause of disillusionment and depression. So
that, jumping at the opportunity to prove that she
counted his inclinations as higher than mere money,
she would have accepted any scheme, however un-
promising; but in fact the enterprise appeared to her
judgment as quite gloriously hopeful. Every moment
increased the charms that it presented; above all, its
complete novelty fascinated, and with surprising

quickness she found herself thinking almost exactly what her husband had thought in regard to their present existence. It seemed to her too that she was pining for a larger, freer environment, that this narrow home had become a permanent prison-house, and that she could never really be contented until she got away from it; then she thought of Vine-Pits Farm, the peaceful fields, the lovely woodland, the space, the air, the sunlight that one would enjoy out there; and then in another moment came the fear lest all this should prove too good to be true.

"But, Will, however can Mr. Bates be willing to part with such a splendid business as his for no more than two thousand pounds?"

"Ah, there you show your sense, Mavis." As he said this Dale took his hand from his forehead, and resumed his entirely matter-of-fact tone. "You must understand things aren't always what they seem. The business is not what it was."

"But Mr. Bates is very rich, isn't he?"

"He *ought* to be, but he isn't. That son of his has bin eating him up, slow an' fast, for th' last ten years. The turnover of his trade is big enough, but the whole management of it has gone end-ways. From a man working with capital he's come down to a man financing things from hand to mouth. What's left to him now is strictly speaking his stock, his wagons, his horses, his lease, his household belongings—and whatever should be put down for the good-will."

Then, continuing his purely businesslike exposition, he explained that he would have to make two engagements, one to his wife and one to Mr. Bates. All material property would be charged with Mavis' loan,

and the value of the good-will would be repaid how
and when he could repay it. Mr. Bates was content
to risk that part of the bargain on his faith in Dale's
personal integrity.

"Don't say any more," cried Mavis. "I'm not understanding it, but I know it's all right. Do let's get
it settled before Mr. Bates alters his mind."

"It must be done formally, Mavis, through your
lawyers. Mr. Cleaver is capable and trustworthy.
It's to be a regular mortgage, properly tied up; and
he must approve——"

"I don't care whether he approves or doesn't. I approve."

"Then I thank you," said Dale, gravely, "for the
way you've met me, and I assure you I appreciate it.
As to the trade itself, I b'lieve I shan't go wrong. It's
not so new to me as people might suppose. I'm well
aware of its principles; and, moreover, one trade's
precious like another—and a man's faculties are bound
to tell, no matter how you apply them."

Mavis was overjoyed. When she sang to herself
now while dressing of a morning the notes poured
out loud and full, even when there was scarce a puff
of breath behind them. She felt so proud and happy
to think that fate had given her the power to help
William, and that he had consented to avail himself
of the power. Once more he had begun to lean on
her. As in the past, so in the future, he would derive
support from his poor little misunderstood, but always
well-meaning Mavis.

XII

BY the end of September everything was arranged. Dale had ceased to be postmaster of Rodchurch; the purchase of the business had been completed; and Mr. Bates had moved out of Vine-Pits to a cottage near Otterford Mill, leaving behind him the bulk of his furniture as the property of the incomers. Thus the Dales would have no difficulty in furnishing the comparatively large house that henceforth was to be their home.

For the last two days they had been living chaotically in rooms stripped to a woeful bareness; this morning Mary had gone along the Hadleigh Road with a wagon full of bedsteads, bedding, and household utensils; and now, late in the afternoon, the wagon stood at the post office door again, packed this time with a final load consisting of those treasures which had been held back for transit under their owners' charge.

Mavis had already climbed up, and was settling herself on a high valley of rolled carpets between two mountain ranges formed by the piano and the parlor bookcases. With anxious eyes she looked at minor chains of packing-cases that contained the best china, the mantel ornaments, the hand-painted pictures. Inside a basket on her knees their cat was mewing disconsolately, despite well-buttered paws. The two big horses, one in front of the other, continuously

161

tinkled the metal disks on their forehead bands; Mr. Allen and other neighbors came out of their shops; Miss Yorke and the clerks from the office filled the pavement; children gathered about the wagon staring silently, and Miss Waddy on the opposite pavement waved her handkerchief and said "Oh, dear! oh, dear!"

" Good luck! "

"Thank you, thank you kindly." Dale moved about briskly, shaking hands with every one. Already he had abandoned all trace of his ancient official costume. In cord breeches and leather gaiters, his straw hat on the back of his head, he looked thoroughly farmer-like, and he seemed to have assumed the jovial independent manner as well as the clothes appropriate to the man who has no other master but the winds and the weather.

" So long, Mr. Allen. Put in a good word for me at the Kennels."

" I will so, Mr. Dale."

" Good-by, Mr. Silcox. Hope you'll honor us with a call whenever you're passing. And if you can, give me a lift in the *Courier*. I may say it's my intention to patronize their advertisement columns regular, soon 's ever I begin to feel my feet under me."

" See *Rodchurch Gossip* next issue," said Mr. Silcox significantly.

" Thanks. You're a trump."

"Good-by, Miss Yorke." And he laughed. " 'Pon my soul, I'm surprised it's still *Miss* Yorke; but it'll be *Mrs.* before long, I warrant."

"Oh, Mr. Dale! "

" There, so long," and he shook Miss Yorke's hand

warmly. "And take my excuse if I bin a bit of a slave-driver now and then. I didn't mean it."

"We've no complaints," said one of the clerks. "Good luck, sir!"

Then Dale told his carter to make a start of it, and the wagon creaked, jolted, slowly lumbered away.

Though they moved at a foot pace, it was not easy traveling in the wagon; the china boxes bumped and rattled, the piano swayed so much that all its strings vibrated, and the cat leaped frantically in the basket; but Mavis felt no inconvenience. She was full of hope. For more than a mile Dale walked beside the shaft horse, echoing the "Coom in then" and "Oot thar" of the man with the leader, and the sound of the voices, the plod of the iron shoes, and the bell-like tinkle of the harness were all pleasant to hear. The whole thing seemed to her picturesque and interesting, like a small episode in the Old Testament, and imaginary words offered themselves as suitable to describe it. "Therefore that day her husband gathered all that was theirs, and set her behind his horses and they journeyed into another place."

She smiled at her cleverness in inventing such good Bible language, and then the thought came to her mind that they were going into the promised land. Once she turned her head to get a last glimpse of the church tower, and perhaps be able to pick out the roof of the post office among the other roofs, but the high mass of furniture shut out all the view. Only the sky was visible, with the sun quite low, and so bright that it was almost blinding. And she thought that this chance of the hour being late and the sun being nearly down was a lucky omen. Straight ahead of them the road was sunlit, and the long slanting sunbeams appeared to hurry on before them as if to light up and glorify the land of promise. "If," she said to herself, "we get there before it has dipped and I catch the sunshine on the ricks, I shall know we are going to be happy."

Then all at once she saw Dale's straw hat and face rise above the fore boards of the wagon. He had swung himself on the shaft to see how she was getting on.

"All right, old lady?"

"Yes—lovely."

The tone of his voice had made her heart bound. It was the dear old voice, speaking to her just as he used to speak before their bad time began.

"We'll be there sooner than you know where you are. I think I'll rest my bones a bit."

Then he got into the wagon, and carefully clambering over impediments came toward her. For a moment as he stood over her the sunlight was on his face, and she, looking up at him, thought that he was not only a fine but quite a beautiful man. The light seemed to soften and yet ennoble his features, and his eyes, unblinking in the glare, were blue and clear as water. When he sat down close to her little nest she pushed the basket away from her, and raising her hand laid it on his knees. To her delight he put his hand on hers, and left it there. He was in shadow now, showing a dark profile, and again she admired him—her strong, big, handsome man, her man that she was pining for.

"Will," she said tremulously, "don't move, but just look behind you, and tell me all you see."

"I don't see anything, Mav, unless I heft meself up again."

"No, sit as you are. It just bears out what you said. We're never more to look back. We're only to look forward. Will?"

He had taken his hand away, and turned the back of his head toward her.

"Will," she repeated; but he did not answer. "Will, my dear one, this *is* going to be a fresh start, isn't it? Like a new beginning for us."

"Yes," he said, very seriously, "that's what I build on its being. Take it so. You and I are beginning life again in our new home."

"Bless you for saying it. The one thing I wished to hear."

"Yes, we must help each other. I'll do—I mean to do. But, maybe, it'll be more 'v o' fight than I'm reckoning, and there's a many ways that you can make the fight easier—beyond the one great thing you've done a'ready."

"I will, dear. I will."

Then they were silent. The carter cracked his whip, shouted to his team, and whistled; and the horses, neither frightened by the whip nor excited by the whistling, drew the big wagon at exactly the same steady pace.

And Mavis felt as if her throat had suddenly enlarged itself and become too big for her collar, while her whole breast was swelling and hardening until it seemed so rigidly immense that it would burst all her garments; it was as if her whole being, together with all the thoughts or memories that it contained felt the expansion of some force that had been long gathering and now swiftly was released. In all her life she had experienced no such sensations hitherto. She who had been passive under the desires of others now felt desire active in herself. It was not only that she wanted pardon, kindness, companionship, the things that she had been so systematically deprived of; she wanted the man himself, the partner, and the mate to whom nature had given her a right.

Abruptly she changed her position, scrambling forward close against him, and put up both her hands to his shoulders.

"Will, stoop your head. I want to whisper something."

Then, as soon as he bent toward her, she clasped her hands behind his neck and tried to drag him down in a kiss.

"What yer doin'? Let me be."

"No, I won't. I won't." She was holding him with all her strength, pulling herself up since she could not pull him down. "Be nice to me." And as he recoiled she thrust forward her upturned face, the cheeks hard and white, the eyes burning, the mouth not quite closing even while she spoke. "I won't let you go, till you've kissed me and made it up for good an' all."

She was acting now as instinctively as any wild animal of the woods. What had started in the zone of voluntary impulse had now passed into the ruling power of reflexes; every nerve of her body seemed to be thinking for itself, guiding her, and compelling her to struggle for the desired end. All this nonsense of high-falutin' morality must be swept aside; if he loved her still, he must admit that he loved her; it must be love or hate, but no more sham and pretense, no more of these half measures that made her a wife when people were looking, and an enemy, a culprit in disgrace, or a sexless business associate, when they two were alone behind drawn blinds.

"Mav, you're shaming me. 'A' done. 'Aarve you tekken leave o' yer senses?"

She felt him shiver as he resisted her; then in another moment he gripped her round the waist as brutally and violently as if he intended to pitch her out of the wagon, held her to him so fiercely that he crushed all the breath from her lungs, and gave her a long passionate mouth-to-mouth kiss. And it seemed to her that the strength and brutality of the embrace formed the one supreme gratification that she had been burning to obtain; she wanted to give herself to him as she had never done before, and if he crushed her and broke her and killed her in their joint rapture, she would drink death greedily as something inevitable to all those who empty the deep goblet of love.

"There!" He took his lips away, and she sank back gasping. "You've 'ad yer way wi' me;" and he heaved a sigh that was as loud as a groan. "Oh, Mav, my girl, gi' me yer kisses—kiss me all night and all day—if on'y you make me forget."

Her hat had tumbled off in the struggle, a mesh of brown hair was dangling over her shoulder, and she was still too much out of breath to speak. The wagon rolled heavily forward along the flat road, and the carter cracked his whip continuously to tell the horses they were nearly home. Presently Mavis got up, perched herself beside her husband, and whispered to him jerkily.

"You've nothing to forget, dear. No looking back. But, oh, my darling, I'm going to be more than I ever was to you. I feel it. I *know* it—an' we'll be happy, happy, happy, so long as we live."

She pressed her face against the sleeve of his jacket, and stroked his knee with as much luxurious pleasure as if the rough cord breeches had been made of the softest satin velvet.

"See. Look straight ahead," and she raised her hand and pointed.

Vine-Pits Farm was in sight. The stone house, the barns, the straw ricks, and the fruit trees all seeming to have clustered close together, to form a compact little kingdom of hope and joy.

"Look, dear. How pretty—see the sunlight on the roofs and on the ricks. That's luck. All the straw is changing into gold. My old Will is going to make heaps of golden sovereigns as big as any rick."

"Woo then. A-oo then." The carter stopped the horses outside the garden entrance. "Will the missis get down here at th' front door, or be us to go on into yaard?"

Mrs. Dale got down here, took the cat-basket from her husband, and went gaily up the path to the open front door.

"Don't let th' cat loose," Dale called after her warningly, "or she'll be back to Rodchurch like a streak o' greased lightning. She'll need acclim'tyzing all tomorrow."

Mavis ran through the house to the kitchen, where Mary and a courtesying old woman received her. Then she scampered from room to room, uttering little cries of contentment. Often as she had seen and admired the house during the last few weeks, it had never seemed so perfectly delightful as it did to-day: with its low-ceiled cozy little rooms at the back, its high and imposing rooms in front, its broad staircase and square landing, it would be quite a little palace when all had been set to rights.

Coming hurrying back to the hall, she saw her husband in the porch, a splendid dark figure with the last rays of yellow sunlight behind him. He paused bareheaded on the threshold, obviously not aware of her presence, and she was about to speak to him when he startled her by dropping on his knees and praying aloud.

"O merciful Powers, give me grace and strength to lead a healthy fearless life in this house."

XIII

THE Dales were beginning to prosper now, but their first winter had been an anxious, difficult time.

Dale had made a common mistake in his calculations, and experience soon taught him that what is known as good-will, the most delicate and sensitive of all trade-values, can not by a mere stroke of the pen be transferred from one person to another. Solid customers turned truant; the business went down with terrifying velocity; and old Bates, who loyally came day after day to advise and assist, spoke with sincere regret. "William, I never foretold this. I must see what can be done. I'll leave no stone unturned." And he trotted about, touting for his successor, tramping long miles to beg for a continuance of favors that had unexpectedly ceased, but usually returning sadly to confess that his efforts had again been fruitless. They were gloomy evening hours, when the old and the young man sat together in the office by the roadway; and at night Mavis used to hear her sleeping husband moan and groan so piteously that she sometimes felt compelled to wake him.

"What is it?" Awakened thus, he would spring up with a hoarse cry, and be almost out of the bed before she was able to restrain him.

"It's nothing, dear. Only you were in one of your

170

bad dreams, and I simply couldn't let you go on being tormented."

"That's right," he used to mutter sleepily. "I don't want to dream. I've enough that's real."

"Don't you worry, dear old boy. You're going to pull through grand—in the end. I *know you are.* Besides, if not—then we'll try something else."

She always murmured such consolatory phrases until he fell asleep once more.

The fact was that Bates had been respected by the well-to-do and loved by the humble; and Dale, out here, remained an unknown quantity. Anything of his fame as postmaster that had traveled along these two miles from Rodchurch did not help him. He was not liked. He felt it in the air, a dull inactive hostility, when talking to gentlefolks' coachmen or giving orders to his own servants. The coachmen could take no pleasure in patronizing him, nor the men in working for him. Mr. Bates advised him once or twice to cultivate a gentler and more ingratiating method of dealing with the people in his employ.

"Perhaps, William, I'm to blame for having spoilt 'em a bit;—but it'd be good policy for you to take them as you find them, and get them bound to you before you begin drilling 'em. A soft word now and then, William—you don't know how far it goes sometimes."

"What I complain of is this," said Dale; "they don't show any spirit. Every stroke o' bad luck I've had—every chance where they might step in with common sense, or extra care, or a spark of invention to save a situation for me—it's just as if they were a row o' turnips."

And the strokes of bad luck were so many and so heavy. The elements seemed to be making war against him—such wet days as made it impossible to deliver hay without damage to it, and an accusation from somebody's stables that the last lot was poisoned; then frost, and two horses seriously injured on the ice-clothed roads; then February gales, wrecking the barn roofs, entailing costly repairs; then floods; and last of all *rats*. The unusual amount of land water had driven them to new haunts, and Dale's granaries were suddenly invaded. "Oh, William," said Mr. Bates, horror-stricken, "beware of rats. They are the worst foe. *One* rat will mess up a mountain of grain."

About the time of the vernal equinox there came a tempest in comparison with which all previous wind and rain were but a whispering and a sprinkling. Every door was being rattled as if by giant hands, the glass sang in the latticed windows, and the whole house seemed swaying, when Mary told her mistress that something had gone wrong with the big straw stack and that the master was attempting to climb to the top of it on the long ladder.

Mavis instantly pulled up her skirt in true country fashion to make a cloak, and told Mary to help her open the kitchen door.

"You bide where you be, Mrs. Dale," said the old charwoman. "You ben't goin' to be no use of any kind out there, and you may bring yourself to a misfortune."

But Mavis insisted on struggling through the doorway, into the rude embrace of the weather. Great branches of the walnut tree were waving wildly, while little twigs and buds flew from apple trees like dust; the rain, not in drops but as it seemed in solid packets, struck her face and shoulders with such force that she could scarcely stand against it; a shallow wooden tub came bounding to her along the flagged path and passed like a sheet of brown paper; and just as she got to the corner of the buildings from which she could obtain a view of the rick-yard, thirty feet of pale fencing lay down upon the beehives and the rhubarb bed without a sound that was even faintly audible above the racket of the storm.

But she had no eyes for anything except her husband, and no other thought than of the horrible peril in which he was placing himself. Four men clung to the bottom of the ladder, and yet, with Dale's weight half-way up to help them, could not for a moment keep it steady. On top of the rick one of the tarpaulin sheets had broken loose; the cruel wind was tearing beneath it, wrenching out pegs and cordage, snatching at thatch-hackle, and making the stout ropes that should have held the sheet hiss and dart like serpents.

It seemed to her that the rick was as high as Mont Blanc, and that even on a placid summer day no one but a lunatic would want to scale it. Then she screamed, and went rushing forward.

Dale, in the act of clambering from the top rung of the ladder, had been blown off, and was hanging to a rope over the edge of the stack. With extreme difficulty the men moved the ladder, and he succeeded in getting on it again.

"Gi't up, sir. 'Tis mortally impossible." As well as Mavis, every one of them shouted an entreaty that he would come down.

Probably he did not hear them, and certainly he did not obey them. He went up, not down. Then for half an hour he fought like a madman with the flapping sheet, and finally conquered it.

Mavis, as she stared upward, saw the gray clouds driving so fast over the crest of the stack that they made it seem as if the whole yard was drifting away in the opposite direction; while her man, a poor little black insect painfully crawling here and there, desperately writhed as new billows surged up beneath him, labored at the rope, seemed to use feet, hands, and teeth in his frantic efforts against the overwhelming power that was opposed to him. She felt dazed and giddy, sick with fear, and yet glowing with admiration in the midst of her agonized anxiety.

To the men it was a wonderful and exciting sight that had altogether stirred them from their usual turnip-like lethargy. When the master came down, all shaking and bleeding, they bellowed hearty compliments in his ear.

"Now," said the old charwoman, when Mr. and Mrs. Dale returned to the kitchen, "you've a 'aad a nice skimmle-skammle of it, sir, an' you best back me up to send the missis to her bed, and bide there warm, and never budge. I means it," she added, with authority. "You ben't to put yourself in a caddle, Mrs. Dale, an' I know what I be talkin' of."

After this the men appeared to work better for Dale; perhaps still somewhat sulkily whenever he pressed them, continuing to be more or less afraid of him, but not so keenly regretting the loss of their white-haired old master.

The storm had brought back the floods, and they

were now worse than anything that anybody remembered having ever seen. The feeding sources of the Rod River had broken all bounds; the lower parts of Hadleigh Wood had become a quagmire; and the volume of water passing under the road bridge was so great that many people thought this ancient structure to be in danger of collapsing. Over at Otterford Mill, the stream swept like a torrent through a chain of wide lakes; Mr. Bates' cottage was cut off from the highroad, and the meadows behind the neighboring Foxhound Kennels were deep under water.

In these days Dale took to riding as the easiest means of getting about; and one afternoon when he had gone splashing across to see Mr. Bates, thence to pay a visit of polite canvass at the Kennels, and was now returning homeward by the lanes, he heard a dismal chorus of cries in the Mill meads.

Forcing his clumsy horse through a gap in the hedge, he galloped along the sodden field tracks to the shifting scene of commotion. Three or four idle louts, a couple of children, and a farm-laborer were running by the swollen margin of the mill-stream, yelling forlornly, pointing at an object that showed itself now and again in the swirling center of the current. Plainly, somebody had chosen this most unpropitious season for an accidental bath, and his companions were sympathetically watching him drown, while not daring, not dreaming of, any foolhardy attempt at a rescue.

" 'Tis Veale, sir. A'bram Veale, sir. Theer!" And all the cries came loud and hearty. " Theer he goes ag'in. I see 'un come up and go under. Oo, oo! 'Ain't 'un trav'lin'!"

"Catch th' 'orse!" shouted Dale; and next moment it was a double entertainment that offered itself to hurrying spectators.

The water, charged with sediment from all the rich earth it had scoured over, was thick as soup; its brown wavelets broke in slimy froth, and its deepest swiftest course had a color of darkly shining lead beneath the pale gleams of March sunshine. In this leaden glitter the two men were swept away, seeming to be locked in each other's arms, their heads very rarely out of the water, their backs visible frequently; until at a boundary fence they vanished from the sight of attentive pursuers who could pursue no further; and seemed in the final glimpse as small and black as two otters fiercely fighting.

"Laard's sake," said one of the louts, "I'd 'a' liked to 'a' seen 'em go over the weir and into the wheel—for 'tis to be, and there's nought can stop it now."

The event, however, proved otherwise. Before the submerged weir was reached a kindly branch among the willows, stretching gnarled hands just above the flood level, gave the ready aid that no louts could offer. Here Dale contrived to hang until people came from the mill and fished him and his now unconscious burden out of their hazardous predicament.

This little incident so stimulated Dale's servants that they began to work for him quite enthusiastically. It occurred to them that he was not only a good plucked 'un, but that, however hard his manner, his heart must possess a big soft spot in it, or he could never have so "put himself about for a rammucky pot-swilling feller like Abe Veale."

Veale was truly a feckless, good-for-little creature.

By trade a hurdle-maker, he lived in one of the few remaining mud cottages on the skirts of Hadleigh Upper Wood, and in his hovel he had bred an immense family. His wife had long since died; her mother, a toothless old crone, kept house for him and was supposed to look after the younger children; but generally the Veales and their domestic arrangements were considered as a survival of a barbaric state of society and a disgrace in these highly polished modern times. People said that Veale was half a gipsy, that his boys were growing up as hardy young poachers, and that every time he got drunk at the Barradine Arms he would himself produce wire nooses from his pocket, and offer to go out and snare a pheasant before the morning if anybody would pay for it in advance by another quart of ale.

Drunk or sober now, he widely advertised a sincere sense of obligation to his preserver. He bothered Dale with too profuse acknowledgments; he came to the Vine-Pits kitchen door at all hours; and he would even stop the red-coated young gentlemen as they rode home from hunting, in order to supply them with unimpeachable details of all that had happened. He told the tale with the greatest gusto, and invariably began and ended in the same manner.

"You sin it in th' paper, I make no doubt, but yer can 'aave it from me to its proper purpus. Mr. Dale he plunged without so much as tekking off of his getters and spurs." And then he described how, stupefied by his mortal danger, he treated Dale more like an enemy than a savior. "I gripped 'un, sir, tighter than a lad in his senses 'd clip his sweetheart;" and he would pause and laugh. "Yes, I'd 'a' drowned 'un as well as myself if he'd 'a' let me. I fair tried to scrag 'un. But Mr. Dale he druv at me wi' 's fist, and kep' a bunching me off wi' 's knees, and then when all the wind and the wickedness was gone out o' me, he tuk me behind th' scruff a' the neck and just paddled me along like a dummy."

At this point Veale would pause to laugh, before continuing. "Nor that wasn't all, nether. So soon as Mr. Dale catched his own breath he give me th' artificial respreation—saved my life second time when they'd lugged us on the bank. I was gone for a ghost; but I do hear—as they'll tell 'ee at th' mill—Mr. Dale he knelt acrost me a pump-handling my arms, pulling of my tongue, and bellows-blowing my ribs for a clock hour;" and Veale would laugh again, spit on the ground, and conclude his story. "Quaarts an' quaarts of waater they squeedged out of me afore the wind got back in—an' I don't seem's if I'd ever get free o' the taste o' that waater. Nothing won't settle it, no matter how 'ard I do try."

The gentry who smilingly listened, knowing Veale for a queer rustic character of poor repute, gave him sixpences to assist in his efforts to quench an abnormal thirst. Talking together, they decided that the hero of the tale had done rather a fine thing in a very unostentatious way, and it occurred to several of them that pluck ought to be rewarded. If the chance came they would encourage Dale. The M.F.H. in fact made up his mind to reconsider matters, and see if he could not before long let Dale have an inning at the Kennels.

Throughout this period and well into the hot weather of June Mavis was stanchly toiling, both as clerical

assistant in the office and general servant in the house.
It was she who did most of the cooking, no light task
since meals had to be supplied for the carter and two
of the other men. Mary always worked with a will;
but old Mrs. Goudie, who came for charring twice a
week, used to say that, in spite of being handicapped
by the state of her health, the mistress worked harder
than the maid.

A swept hearth, a trimmed lamp, and the savory
odor of well-cooked food, were what Dale might be
sure of finding at the evening hour; and Mavis tried
to give him something more. He must have peace at
the end of the day, and thus be able to forget the day's
disappointments, no matter how cruel they had been.
She would not let him talk about the business at
night. She said he must just eat, rest, and then sleep;
but she allowed him to read, provided that he read real
books and magazines, not his ledgers or those horrid
trade journals.

So after their supper they used to sit in the pleasant
lamplight very quietly, near together and yet scarcely
speaking to each other, feeling the restful joy of a
companionship that had passed into that deeper zone
where silence can be more eloquent than words. He
was reading political economy for the purpose of opening his mind, " extending the scope of one's int'lect,"
as he said himself, and she watched him as he frowned
at the page or puckered up his lips with a characteristic doggedly questioning doubtfulness. Certainly
no words were needed then to enable her to interpret
his thought. " Look here, my lad "—that was how he
was mentally addressing a famous author—" I'm
ready to go with you a fair distance; but I don't allow

you to take me an inch further than my reasoning faculty tells me you are on the right road." When he frowned like this, she smiled and felt much tenderness. He would always be the same obstinate old dear: ready to set himself against the whole weight of immemorial authority, whether in literature or everyday life.

She did not read, but with a large work-basket on a chair by her knees continued busily sewing until bedtime. And the tenderness that she felt as she stitched and stitched was overwhelmingly more than she could feel even for Will. When her work itself made her smile, all the intellectual expression seemed to go out of her face, and it really expressed nothing but a blankly unthinking ecstasy, whereas her smile at her husband just now had shown shrewd understanding, as well as immense kindness. In fact, at such moments, only the outer case of Mavis Dale remained in the snug little room, while the inward best part of her had gone on a very long journey. She could not now see the man with his book, or the walls of the room; the lamp had begun to shine with ineffable radiance; and she was temporarily a sewing-woman in paradise, stitching the ornamnetal flounces for dreams of glory.

Her baby, a girl, was born at the end of June, exactly three-quarters of a year from the beginning of their new existence. The mother had what is called a bad time, and was slow to recover strength. Nevertheless, she was able to suckle the infant, who did well from its birth and throve rapidly.

It was during the convalescent stage, one evening

when he had come up to sit by her bedside, that Dale told her they had at last turned the corner.

"Yes," he said, "orders are dropping in nicely. We're getting back all the good customers that slipped away from me, and some bettermost ones—such as the Hunt stables—that Mr. Bates himself had lost. You may take it as something to rely on that we're fairly round the corner of our long lane."

Then, holding her hand and softly patting it, he praised her for the way in which she had helped him. "You've been better than your word, Mav; you've supported me something grand."

And he added that henceforth he should insist on her doing less work, at any rate less household work. "There's more valuable things than burning your face over the kitchen fire, and roughing your arms with hot water. I'm going to be done with that messing of the men; I'm arranging their meals on another basis; I mean to keep house and yard as two distinct regions. And as to you, old lady, I intend to turn your dairy knowledge to account. Don't see why we shouldn't keep a cow or two—and poultry—and cultivate the bees a bit. Kitchen garden too. And, look here, I've engaged Mrs. Goudie to come every day instead of twice a week—and we shall want a nurse."

But Mavis flatly refused to have any hired person coming between her and the transcendent joy of her life. She had waited long enough for a baby, and she proposed to keep the baby to herself.

"However successful you come to be," she said to her husband, earnestly, "I shouldn't like you to make a fine lady of me. I want to go on feeling I'm useful to you. That's my pleasure—and if good luck took it from me, I'd almost wish the bad luck back again."

"Hush," he said, gravely. "Don't speak of such a wish, even in joke."

"I only meant I'd wish for the time since we came here. I wasn't thinking of anything before then."

"All right;" and he stooped over her, and kissed her. "You've bin talking more'n enough, I dare say. Take care of yourself, and get well as fast as may be. For I can't do without you."

"That's what I wanted to hear."

"You don't take it for granted yet?"

"No. I want you to say it every time I see you."

"Good night—an' happy dreams."

"Will!" Mavis' voice was full of reproach. "Are you going without kissing the baby?"

Then Dale came back from the doorway, stooped again, and making his lips as light as a butterfly's wings, kissed his first-born.

Before September was over Mavis had not only recovered her ordinary health, but had entered into such stores of new energy that nothing could hinder her from getting back into harness. She herself was astonished by her physical sensations. Languors that had seemed an essential part of her temperament ever since girlhood were now only memories; she felt more alive when passive now than during extreme excitement in the past; her whole body, from the surface to the bones, appeared to be larger and yet more compact. Even the muscles of her back and legs, which ought to have been relaxed and feeble after weeks of bed, had the tone and hardness that only exercise is supposed to induce; so that when standing or walking she experienced a curiously stimulating sense of solidity and power, as if her hold upon the ground was heavier and firmer than it had ever been, although she could move about from place to place with incredibly more lightness and ease.

These new sensations were strong in her one morning when, Dale having risen at dawn, she determined to take a ramble or tour of inspection before the day's work began; and with the mere bodily well-being there was a mental vigorousness that made the notion of all future effort, whether casual or persistent, seem equally pleasurable.

She came out through the front garden, and pausing a moment thought of all the things that ought to be done at the very first opportunity. This neglected garden was a mere tangle of untrimmed shrub and luxuriant weed, with just a few dahlias and hollyhocks fighting through the ruin of what had been pretty flower borders; and she thought how nice it would all look again when sufficient work had been put into it. Some of the broken flagstones of the path wanted replacing by sound ones; the orchard trees were full of dead wood; and the door and casements of the house sadly needed painting. Her thoughts flew about more strenuously than the belated bees that were searching high and low for non-existent pollen. This front of their house would look lovely with its casements and deep eaves painted white instead of gray; and if bright green shutters could at some time or other be added to the windows, one might expect artists to stop and make sketches of the most attractive homestead in Hampshire.

She kissed the tips of her fingers to that rearward

portion of the building where Mary guarded the cradle, and then went through the gate and along the highroad.

It was a misty morning—almost a fog—the sun making at first but feeble attempts to pierce through the white veil. There would come a faint glow, a widening circle of yellow light; then almost immediately the circle contracted, changed from gold to silver, and for a moment one saw the sun itself looking like a bright new sixpence, and then it was altogether gone again. Out of the mist on her right hand floated the song of birds in a field. No rain having fallen during this month of September, the ground was dry and hard as iron, but the roadway lay deep in dust, and a continuous rolling cloud followed her firm footsteps. The air was sweet and fresh, although not light to breathe as it is in spring. One felt something of ripeness, maturity, completion—those harvest perfumes that one gets so strong in Switzerland and Northern Italy, together with the heavier touch of sun-dried earth, decaying fruit, turning fern. When the birds fell silent Mavis took up their song, walked faster; and all things on the earth and in the heaven over the earth seemed to be adding themselves together to increase the sum of her happiness.

She loved, and was loved; she lived, and had given life—bud, blossom, and fruit, all nature and she were now in harmony.

Presently the wood that stretched so dark and so grand on her left tempted her from the highroad. This was her first real walk, and she decided to make it a good one. She would aim for the Hadleigh rides, and, going on beyond Kibworth Rocks to the higher ground, get a view of the new buildings. Will had gone across to the far side of Rodchurch and could not be back to breakfast. It would not therefore matter if she were a little late.

She passed rapidly through open glades, to which the great oaks and beeches still made solid walls. The foliage of the beech trees was merely touched with yellow here and there, while the oaks showed no sign of fading color, and beneath all the lower branches there were splendid deep shadows wherever the undergrowth of holly did not fill up the green wall. This was the true wild woodland, remnant of the ancient forest, the place of virgin timber, dense thickets, and natural openings, that tourists always praised beyond anything else. The stream ran babbling through it, with pretty little pools, cascades, and fords, all owning names that spoke of bygone times—such as White Doe's Leap, Knight's Well, and Monk's Crossing. Locally it was not, of course, so highly esteemed. Cottagers said it was "a lonesome, fearsome bit o' country," and, whether because of the ugly memories that hung about it, or in view of extremely modern stories of disagreements between Chase guardians and poachers, considered it an undesirable short cut after dark from anywhere to anywhere.

To-day it seemed to Mavis friendly and pleasant as well as beautiful. The mist slowly rising was now high overhead, so that one could see to a considerable distance. Some fern-cutters in shirt-sleeves and slouch hats were already at work, cutting with rhythmic precision, calling to one another, and whistling tunefully.

One or two of them greeted her as she passed.

By the time she reached the straight rides and the fir trees the sun came bursting forth bravely, the shadows just danced before vanishing, the mist broke into rainbow streamers, and then there was nothing more between one's head and the milky blue sky. She walked within a stone's-throw of Kibworth Rocks, and did not feel a tremor, scarcely even a recollection. People nowadays came here from Rodchurch and Manninglea on Sunday afternoons, making it the goal for wagonette drives, wandering up and down, and gaping at a scene rendered interesting to them merely because it had once been the background of tragedy; and Mavis was thinking more of these Sunday visitors than of the dead man, as she hurried through the sunlight so near the spot where he had lain staring with glassy eyes throughout the darkness of a July night.

She thought of him a little later, when she stood on the higher ground looking at what live men were constructing in fulfilment of his wish, and her mind did not hold the least tinge of bitterness. At present the Barradine Orphanage was simply an eye-sore to miles and miles of the country-side, but no doubt, as she thought, it would be all very fine when finished. The bad weather of the winter had caused progress to be rather slow; the red brickwork was only about ten feet out of the ground, but a shell of scaffolding enabled one to trace the general plan. It would be a central block with two long, low dependencies, apparently, and, as it seemed, there were to be terraces and leveled lawns all about it; a great deal of clearing work as well as building work would, however, be necessary before the whole thing could take shape and explain itself properly. She stood outside one of its

new ugly fences, and wondered if Mr. Barradine's
trustees had, after all, chosen the site wisely. Poor
old gentleman, it would be unkind if his last fancies
received scant attention. It was rather nice of him
to have this idea of doing good after his death, to plot
it all, and put it down on paper with such painstaking
care.

Truly she was thinking of him now as though he
had been a total stranger, some important person that
she had known well by name but never chanced to
meet. She listened to the faint clinking of brick-
layers' trowels, watched men with hods going slowly
up and down ladders, men carrying poles, men un-
loading half a dozen carts; thought what a quantity of
money was being expended, and how grateful in the
future the little desolate children would be when their
costly home was ready for them; and only as it were
by accident did she remember that she too had cost
the estate money, and perhaps also ought to be grateful. But she had long since ceased to think about the
legacy. What the yokels would call her "small basket
fortune" had served a purpose handsomely, and there
was an end of it. The man from whom it came had
gone as completely as the morning mist went when
the sun began to shine.

The harm he had done her was nothing. If she purposely dragged out its memory, it seemed much less
strong and actual than half one's dreams. Incredible
that little more than a year ago she had been in such
dire and dreadful trouble.

She struck the highroad again a little way short of
the Abbey Cross Roads, and came swinging homeward with long strides, feeling healthy, hungry, happy

And the nearer she drew to home, the deeper grew the happiness. " Oh, what a lucky woman I am," she said to herself.

And with a quite unconscious selfishness that is an essential attribute of joy, and that makes all very successful and contented people think themselves singled out, watched over, and especially guided by fate, she blessed and applauded the beneficently omniscient Providence which had given just enough worry in her youth to enable her to appreciate comfort in mature years, which had delayed motherhood until she could best bear a hearty child, which had wiped out Mr. Barradine and restored her husband's love, which, last of all, had removed Aunt Petherick from North Ride and sent her to live at the seaside.

A small thing, this, perhaps; and yet a Providential boon, a filling of one's lap with bounties. There would have been great awkwardness in having Aunt so near, but forbidden to darken one's door. Will was very firm there: Auntie was not to be admitted at Vine-Pits on any pretext whatever. But it had all worked out so neatly, without the least friction. The new owner of the Abbey wanted North Ride. He had, however, been very kind about the lease or the absence of a lease, and had paid the tenant for life, as she described herself, to surrender possession. Auntie, one might therefore say, was not at all badly treated.

As the master was away and no kind of state necessary, she breakfasted in the kitchen with Mary and Mrs. Goudie. Her baby was asleep in its cradle, which she gently swung with her foot while eating; and the three women all spoke whisperingly. The pots and pans were shining, the hearthstone was white as snow, and through the open doorway one had a pretty little picture of the back pathway, the end of the barn, and a drooping branch of the walnut trees. From the yard beyond came sounds of industrious activity—the rumble of a wagon being pulled from the pent-house, the thump of sacks being let down on the pulleys, and the intermittent buzz of a chaff-cutting machine.

Presently somebody appeared on the pathway, and came slowly and shyly toward the door.

"Oh, bother," said Mary. "If it isn't Mr. Druitt again."

"Good mornin', mum," said the visitor, diffidently. "Would you be doing with an egg or so?"

Mr. Druitt had been introduced by Mrs. Goudie as the higgler, or itinerant poulterer and greengrocer, who served the house in Mr. Bates' time. He was a thin middle-aged man, with light watery eyes, a straggling beard, and an astoundingly dilatory manner. He used to pull his pony and cart into the hedge or bank by the roadside, and leave them there an unconscionable time, while he pottered about the back doors of his customers, offering the articles that he had brought with him, or trying to obtain orders for other articles that he would bring next week; and although apparently so shy himself, no bruskness in others ever seemed to rebuff him. His arrival now broke up the breakfast party, and was accepted as a signal that the day's labors must really be attacked. Mrs. Goudie and Mary pushed back their chairs with a horrid scrooping noise, Mavis got up briskly, the baby awoke and began to cry.

"No, thank you, Mr. Druitt. Nothing this morning."

"I've some sweet-hearted cabbages outside."

"No, thank you."

"It's wonderful late to get 'em with any heart to 'em. I'll fetch 'em."

Thus, as was usual, the higgler went backward and forward between the door and his cart; and Mavis, with the baby on her arm, at intervals inspected various commodities. Eventually she purchased a capon for the Sunday dinner, paid for it, and bade Mr. Druitt good-by.

"Good-by, mum—and much obliged."

But then, quite ten minutes afterward, his shadow once more fell across the kitchen floor. He had not really gone yet. Here he was back again at the kitchen door, staring reflectively at his grubby little pocketbook.

"Beg pardon—but did I mention the side o' bacon I've been promised for Tuesday. It's good bacon."

Mavis Dale with courteous finality dismissed him; but Mary, whose ordinarily red cheeks had become a fiery crimson, spoke hotly and angrily.

"Drat the man. I've no patience with him. He ought to know better, going on so."

"But what harm does he do, poor fellow," said Mavis, indulgently, "except muddling away his own time?"

"He's up to no good," said Mary; and she flounced across to the door, and looked out at the now empty path. "Hanging about like that! Why can't he keep away? I don't want him."

Mrs. Goudie, at the sink, screwed up her wrinkled nut-cracker face, and chuckled.

"No, mum, she don't want un. But he wants she."

And, astonishing as it might seem, this was truly the case. The higgler had fallen in love with Mary; and she, apparently without a single explicit word, had understood the nature of the emotion that stirred his breast. He had somehow surrounded her with an atmosphere of admiration—anyhow he had made her understand.

Mavis laughed gaiiy, and chaffed Mary about her conquest; and henceforth she more or less obliterated herself when this visitor called, and allowed the servant to conduct all transactions with him.

Mary was always very stern, disparaging his gooas, and beating down his prices; while he stood sheepishly grinning, and in no wise protesting against her harshness. He now of course stayed longer than ever, indeed only withdrew when Mary indignantly drove him away.

"Be off, can't you?" cried Mary. "I'm ashamed of you."

"Haw, haw," chuckled Mrs. Goudie. "Don't she peck at un fierce."

"Yes, Mary," and Mrs. Dale laughed, much amused. "I do think you're rather cruel to him."

"'Twill be t'other way roundabout one day, Mary, preaps."

Then Mary tossed her head and bustled at her work. "I ain't afeard o' that day, Mrs. Goudie. He isn't going the right way to win me, I can tell him. I hate his sly ways."

Mavis and the old charwoman thought that Mr. Druitt would win the prize in the end, and with a natural tendency toward match-making tacitly aided and abetted his queer courtship. Except for the disparity of years it seemed a desirable match. It was known that he had a tidy place, almost a farm, eight miles away on the edge of the down; and Mrs. Goudie, who confessed that she had merely encountered him higgling, said the tale ran that he was quite a warm man.

And thus Mary's little romance, announcing itself so abruptly and developing itself so slowly, brought still another new interest to Vine-Pits kitchen. It was something vivid and bright and even fantastic in the midst of solidly useful facts, like the strange flower that blooms on a roadside merely because some high-flying strong-winged bird has carelessly happened to drop a seed.

"What," thought Mavis, "can any of us do without love? And where should we be without the odd chances that bring love to us?"

XIV

FAT easy years came now after the hard and lean
ones; and the Dales in the dual regions of home
and trade were doing really well. Dale had a powerful
decently-bred cob to ride; on Wednesdays, when he
went into Old Manninglea for the Corn Market, he
often wore a silk top-hat and always a black coat; and
at all times he looked exactly what he was, an alert,
industrious, straight-dealing personage who has risen
considerably and who intends to rise still higher in the
social scale.

As to Mavis, she had another baby—a boy this time
—and she was an infinitely proud mother as well as a
very busy woman. She kept cows, poultry and bees;
could and did distil a remarkably choice sloe gin, had
achieved some reputation for her early peas and late
lettuces, and had made the quadrangle in front of the
house a sight that even tourists from London talked
about. It blazed with color from May to November,
and there was one of the Rodhaven drivers who on|
several occasions stopped his char-à-bancs to let the
passengers have a long look at it. Wandering artists,
too, fascinated by the stone walls, the flowers, the
white paint, and the green shutters, would sometimes
ring the bell and ask if Mrs. Dale let lodgings.

Mrs. Dale was rather crushing to masculine intruders of this sort, especially when they adopted an off-
handedly gallant air.

In answering their questions she drawled slightly, and smiled in a manner that, although not contemptuous, might permit them to guess that they had made a tactless mistake.

"Oh, no, we do not let lodgings."

"Don't you really? I think you *ought* to, you know."

"Possibly," said Mavis, drawling and smiling. "But Mr. Dale and I do not think so. Of course if we did, we should put up a board, or notice—and you may observe that there isn't one."

She was, however, always gentle and forbearing with wanderers of her own sex. To two ladies who expressed disappointment at finding no apartments and asked if she did not at least provide afternoon tea, she said at once, "Oh, certainly, I shall be delighted to give you some tea."

They were tired, dusty, not young; and she showed them into the grand front parlor that contained her piano, pictures, well-bound books, and there laid the table and brought the tea with her own hands. Such a tea—the best china, thick cream, three sorts of jam, cakes, and jolly round home-made bannocks! The ladies were so pleased, until they became embarrassed. For of course when they wished to pay, Mavis could not accept payment.

"Oh, indeed no. You're very welcome. I hope that you'll stop and rest as long as you like;" and faintly blushing she shied away from the open purse and hurried out of the room.

"What on earth are we to do?" said one of the ladies.

"I saw a child in the passage," said the other lady.
"Let us offer the child a present."

"Ah. That solves the difficulty. But how much?
I suppose it must be half-a-crown."

"*Nonsense!*" said the other lady, tartly. "That is
more than the price of the whole meal if she had let us
pay for it. A present of a shilling at the *outside*. No,
a shilling is absurd. Sixpence."

"Do you really think so?"

"Yes, sixpence wrapped up in a bit of paper."

"Then *you* must offer it."

And the other lady did. "Is that your little girl?
Oh, what brown eyes—and mamma's pretty complexion. Good afternoon! We are so much obliged. And
this is for *you*, dear—to buy sweeties."

Mavis was not disposed to allow her small princess
to take a tip from a stranger's hand; but natural good-
breeding forced her to acquiesce.

The ladies looked back at her, waved their hands by
the garden gate, and went away talking.

"The child never said 'Thank you.' Badly reared."

"But the mother thanked you. I liked her face. She
must have been distinctly good-looking."

The artists thought her distinctly good-looking even
now, and perhaps, after being repulsed in their quest
for bed and board, drifted off into an idle dream of
how they might have met her a few years ago when
they were less famous but more magnetically attractive. What a sitter she would have been for them, if
she wouldn't be anything else! They admired the extreme delicacy of her nose that seemed so narrow in
the well-rounded face, the loose brown hair that

showed such a red flash in it beneath her sunbonnet, the perfect modeling of full forearms, firm neck, and ample bosom, the whole poise of her graciously solid figure, at once so reposeful and so free. But it was the eyes principally that set them dreaming of vanished youth, abandoned hopes, and lost opportunities. Nowadays Mavis could meet the unduly interested regard of male investigators with a candid unvacillating outlook; there came no hint of feebleness in resistance, too ready submission, or temperamental proneness to surrender; but her eyes, whether she wished it or not, still served as messengers between all that was feminine in her and all that was masculine outside her; and, with no reason not to tell the truth, they told it boldly, seeming to say, " Yes, once I had much to give, and I gave every single bit of it to one man. I have nothing left now for cadgers, sneak-thieves, and other outsiders."

She was a woman steadily completing her cycle. In fact, with her added weight, broadened contours and settled mental equilibrium, she had so changed from the slim, pallid, childish Mrs. Dale of the post office that any old Rodchurch friends might be forgiven for saying that they could scarcely recognize her.

" Really shouldn't have known you," said one of them frankly. " You have furnished like a colt brought in from grass to corn."

This outspoken old friend was Mr. Allen the saddler, who turned up one winter day when Vine-Pits had been thrown into a great state of excitement and confusion by the passage of the hunt right across the meadows behind the orchard. Just after dinner everybody had heard the horn sounding in the woods, with distant holloas and deep music of hounds, and then the pack came streaming out in full cry, and next moment all the horsemen were galloping over the fields and leaping the hedges. The women ran forth from the back of the house; the men abandoned their work. "Oo, oo! Look an' look." There were shouts of rapture each time the horses jumped. "Oo! Crimany! That *were* a beauty!"

Then in another minute Dale himself came galloping to the empty yard, rode his horse along the flags into the garden, and yelled to Mavis that she was to fetch trays of bread and cheese and bannocks as quick as life.

"An' bring the white bob full of beer—an' whisky, an' water—an' some o' the sloe gin; an' devel knows how many glasses."

Mrs. Dale and Mary, before one could look round, carried out into the yard all these light refreshments, and with them Dale regaled the large concourse of unexpected visitors that was pouring through the opened gates. His guests were grooms, second-horsemen, one or two farmers, and several dealers—the people who are rarely in a hurry when out hunting; and after them came pedestrians, a sturdy fellow in a red coat with a terrier in his pocket and a terrier under his arm, a keeper, a wood-cutter, Abraham Veale the hurdle-maker, and just riffraff—the very tail of the hunt, and, as the tail of the tail, that stupid trade-neglecting Mr. Allen. For a while the yard was full of animation, the horses pawing and snorting, Dale bustling hospitably, his wife filling the glasses and handing the food, and everybody talking who was not eating or drinking.

Mr. Allen was exhausted, tottering on his skinny legs, but nevertheless burning with ardor for the chase.

"They've changed foxes," he cried breathlessly. "They've lost the hunted fox, and they've only themselves to thank for it. I told them, and they wouldn't listen. I knew."

"Ah, but you always know," said a second-horseman, grinning.

"If Mr. Maltby," said Allen, "had cast back instead of forward last time I holloa'd, he'd have had the mask on his saddle rings by now."

Then he sank down upon one of the upping-stocks, snatched a hunk of bread, munched hastily.

"Mr. Allen, you've no cheese. Here, let me fill your glass again. How's Rodchurch?" Every time that Mavis passed, she asked a question. "Mr. Allen, how's Miss Waddy's sister?"

"Dead," said Allen, with his mouth full.

"Dead. Oh, that's sad!" Then next time it was: "How's Miss Yorke? Not married yet?"

"No, nor likely to be."

The horse-people soon began to move off again— "Thank you, Mr. Dale. Good night, Mr. Dale. . . You've done us proper, sir. . . . Just what I wanted. . . . Good night, ma'am;"—but the foot-people lingered. The red-coated earth-digger, Veale, and one or two others, had got around Mr. Allen and were chaffing him irreverently.

"There, that'll do," said Dale, joining the group and speaking with firmness. Then he politely offered to have a nag put into the gig and to send Mr. Allen home on wheels.

"Thank you kindly," said Allen. "I'm not going

home; but if your man can rattle me a mile or so up
towards Beacon Hill, it's a hundred to one I shall
drop in with them again. With the wind where it is,
hounds are bound to push anything that's in front of
them up to the high ground."

As soon as Dale went to order his gig the clumsy
facetiousness was renewed.

"'Tes a pity you ben't a hound yersel, Mr. Allen."

"Ah," said Veale, "if the wood pucks cud transform
him on to all fours, what a farder he'd mek to th' next
litter o' pops at the Kennels."

"By gum," said the earth-digger, slapping his leg,
"they pups would have noses. They wuddent never
be at fault, would 'em?"

Old Mrs. Goudie, who had a simple taste in raillery,
was so convulsed by this jesting that she put down
her tray in order to laugh at ease; and chiefly because
she was laughing, Mary laughed also.

"An' you know most o' the tricks o' foxes too, don't
you, Mr. Allen?"

"Now then," said Dale, returning, "that's enough,
my lads. I dropped you the hint by now. You're
welcome to as much more of my beer as you can
carry, but you won't sauce my friends inside my
gates—nor outside, either, if I chance to be there."

"Aw right, sir."

"Take no heed of them," said Allen. "It is only
their ignorance;" and he staggered to his feet.

Dale escorted the honored guest to the gig, then
wiped his perspiring face, lighted a pipe; and then
reproved Mary and Mrs. Goudie for unseemly mirth.

They still had Mary with them, and, although they
did not know it, were to enjoy her faithful service for

some time to come. Now that Mrs. Dale grew her own vegetables, purchases from Mr. Druitt, the higgler, had become rare; only an occasional bit of bacon, or once in a way a couple of rabbits, a hare, a doubtfully obtained pheasant, could ever be required from him; so that the greater part of his frequent visits were admittedly paid to the servant and not to the mistress. But he proved an unconscionably slow courtier. Mary, for her part, when she was teased about him and asked if he did not yet show anxiety to reach the happy day, always tossed her head and said that she was in no hurry, that she doubted if she could ever tear herself away from Vine-Pits, and so on.

Then, at last, a shocking discovery was made. Mary, after an afternoon out, came home with her face all red and blubbered, sat in the kitchen sobbing and rocking herself, and told Mavis how she had heard on unimpeachable authority that the higgler was a married man. He had always been married— and poor Mary confessed that she was very fond of him, although so angry with him for his disgraceful treatment of her.

On the next visit of the higgler Dale was lying in wait for him.

"Come inside, please. I'd like a few words with you, Mr. Druitt;" and the higgler was led through the kitchen, and up the three steps into the adjacent room.

Here, as soon as the door had been shut, Mr. and Mrs. Dale both tackled him. Dale was very fine, like a magistrate, so dignified as well as so severe, accusing the culprit of playing fast and loose with a young woman, of arousing feelings in her bosom which he was not in a position to satisfy.

"A girl," said Mavis, "that we consider under our charge, as much as if she was our daughter."

"Who looks to us," said Dale, "for guardianship and protection."

Mr. Druitt, sitting on the edge of his chair, smiling foolishly, nodded his head in the direction of the kitchen door, and gave a queer sort of wink.

"Meaning *her?*"

"Yes, who else should we mean?"

"I've never said a word of love to her in my life."

"Oh, how," cried Mavis, "can you make such a pretense?"

"Because it's the truth."

"But," said Mavis, indignantly, "you've made her fond of you. You've courted her."

The higgler distinctly preened himself, and smiled archly. "Ah, there's a language of the eyes, which speaks perhaps when the lips are sealed."

Mavis was angry and disgusted. "You, a married man!"

Dale, outraged too, spoke with increasing sternness. "You don't deny you've got a wife?"

The higgler answered very gravely. "Mr. Dale, that's my misfortune, not my fault. But my wife isn't going to last forever, and the day she's gone—that is, the day after I've buried her decently—I shall come here to Mary Parsons and say 'Mary'—mind you, I've never called her Mary yet—I shall say, 'Mary, my lips are unsealed, and I ask you to be my true and lawful second wife.'"

They could make nothing of the higgler.

"It's seven years," he went on, "since Doctor Hollis
said to me, 'I have to warn you Mrs. Druitt isn't
going to make old bones.' However, we find it a long
job. There's a proverb, isn't there? Creaking doors!"

Mavis was inexpressibly shocked. "How can you
talk of your wife so? Have you no feelings for her?"

"Mrs. Dale," said the higgler, solemnly, "I married
my first wife for money, and I've been punished for
my mistake. That's why I made up my mind I'd
marry next time for love—in choosing a wholesome
maiden and not asking what she'd got sewed in her
petticoat or harbored in the bank;" and, nodding, he
again gave his curious self-satisfied wink. "Mr. Dale,
you tell her to wait patiently. I'll be true to her, if
she'll be true to me." Then he rose, and smiling sheepishly, once more addressed Mrs. Dale. "The purpose
of my call this morning was to say I shall have some
good bacon next week."

Mavis refused the bacon, and Dale said a few words
of stern rebuke.

"I can tell you, Mr. Druitt, I take a very poor opinion of your manhood and proper feeling."

Then Mavis interposed to check her husband. The
fact was, she felt baffled by the situation and utterly
at a loss as to what would be the best way of dealing
with it. Whatever one might think of Mr. Druitt
one's self, there was Mary to be considered. What
would ultimately be best for her? The man was
warm; and Mary, who was not growing younger, said
she liked him.

"I'll wish you good morning," said the higgler.

Then, when they thought he had been long gone

and Mavis was talking to Mary, he put in his head at the kitchen doorway.

" Will this make any difference? " he asked shyly. " Should I call again—or do you forbid me the house? "

The three women, Mavis, Mary and Mrs. Goudie, all looked at one another, quite perplexed.

" Er—no," said Mavis, after a pause. " You can call. I may, just possibly, be wanting bacon next week."

" It's a real beautiful side;" and, without a glance at Mary, he disappeared.

Then Mary instantaneously decided that she would wait for him, and not break with him; and she asked Mrs. Dale to run out and tell him that she would wait.

But that Mavis could not do. It would be too undignified. Mary must restrain her emotions till next week, and tell him herself.

XV

THE little girl Rachel at the age of six was able to take interest in everything that happened, and to be a real companion who loved to help her mother at any important task. Thus one winter evening between tea and supper, when Mavis was most importantly engaged, she sat up late by special license and gave her company and aid in the little room behind the kitchen.

"Now, see if you can find the blotting-paper over there on daddy's desk. Quietly, my darling. Very quietly—because we mustn't wake Billy."

Billy, the little boy, was asleep in his cradle, near, but not too near, the cheerful fire; a bluish flicker that reminded one of the frost out of doors showed intermittently among the yellow and red flames; the wick of the lamp on the round table burned clearly; and in the mingling lamplight and firelight the whole room looked delightfully cozy and homelike. Mavis, with a body just pleasantly tired and a mind still comfortably active, paused before starting her labor in order luxuriously to feel the peaceful charm that was being shed forth by all her surroundings.

More and more the very heart of their home life seemed to locate itself in this room, and so every day additional memories and associations wove themselves about the objects it contained. Rachel, young as she was, showed a marked predilection for it, loving it

better than all other rooms. From the dawn of intelligence she had been fascinated by the two guns
and the brass powder-flasks that hung high over the
chimney-place; her first climbings and tumblings
had been performed on the three steps that led to the
kitchen; and she had addled her tender brains, as
well as inflamed the natural greed which is so pardon-
able in infants, by what was to her a sort of differ-
ential calculus before she learned to discriminate
nicely among the various jams kept by Mummy in
the big cupboard.

Nearly all the furniture, as well as the two guns, had
belonged to Mr. Bates. It was solid, and very old—a
tall-boy with a drawer that, opening out, made a writ-
ing-desk; a bureau with a latticed glass front; three
chairs of the Chippendale farmhouse order; and one
vast chair, covered with leather and adorned with
nails, that had probably been dozed in by the hall-
porter of some great mansion more than a century
ago. Here and there Mavis had of course dabbed her
small prettinesses—blue china and a clock on the
mantel-shelf, colored cushions, photographs of the
children, views of Rodchurch High Street, the Chase,
Rodhaven Pier; and the old and the new, the useful
and the ornamental, alike whispered to her of fulfilled desires, gratified fancies, and William Dale.

It was her husband's room. Perhaps that formed
the real source of all its charms, the essence or base
of attraction that lay deep beneath visual presenta-
tions of chairs and fire-gleamings, or associations of
ideas, or memories of past happiness. Those were his
books, behind the latticed glass—the *Elocution Manual*, the *Elements of Rhetoric*, the ten-volumed

People's Encyclopedia, that he had read, and still read so assiduously. It was here that he ate, drank, and mused. Here he did all of his work that wasn't real office work. Here he received such visitors as head coachmen, stud-grooms, and the huntsmen.

In the cupbord with the jam-pots, there were two or three boxes of cigars, the famous sloe gin, and other liqueurs, for the entertainment of such highly esteemed visitors; and so long as one of them occupied the colossal armchair, her husband was quite a different Dale. He was then such a much better listener than usual, so quick to see a joke and so easy to be tickled by it, so debonair that he would swallow almost insulting criticism of his favorite politicians. As she thought of these things her eyelids fluttered and her lips parted mirthfully. She never asked any questions as to Dale's more secret methods of dealing with customers' servants. Obviously he got on well with them; and one might be quite certain that he did not offer any material compliments that were either traditionally illegitimate or open in the smallest degree to a suspicion of corrupt purpose.

And she thought admiringly that her man was really a very wonderful man. Though so candid and straight, he could be grandly silent; he told his womankind all that he considered it good for them to know, and the rest he kept to himself; he had that quality of rulership without which manhood always seems deficient.

"Mummy," said Rachel, "I do believe Mary is reading aloud."

"Is she, darling? Yes, I think she is."

Through the kitchen door one could hear a monoto-
nous murmur.

" D'you think she's reading fairy tales? "

" Perhaps. Would you like to listen to her? "

" Oh, no. I'd sooner stay and help you, Mummy."

" Then so you shall, my angel; and I thank you for
preferring my company."

Mavis, wth the little girl at her knee, got to work.
She had purchased a large scrap-album, and was now
to begin putting in her scraps. For a long time she
had collected interesting extracts from the newspapers,
more especially portions of old numbers of the *Rodhaven Courier* which contained her husband's name.

" Here, Rachel, we'll commence with this;" and she
started the book with a long account of the cere-
monial opening of the Barradine Orphanage. The report of a speech by "Mr. Dale of Vine-Pits Farm "
at a political meeting was the second item, and other
gems followed fast.

Rachel assisted from time to time, by twice upsetting the paste pot, tearing a good many cuttings, and
finally by tilting the heavy album off Mummy's lap
to the floor.

But Mavis thought all these actions rather spirited
and charming than maladroit and annoying. They
proved that Rachel was trying hard to be of use, and
her too rapid and abrupt gestures were a pleasing
evidence that the little creature possessed a vivacious
and not a sluggish disposition. However, the crash
of the album on the floor had awakened Billy, who
was now crying lustily; and Rachel's license having
long since expired, Mavis decided to send both her

treasures to bed. Rachel resisted the edict, and, presently conducted up-stairs by Mary, bellowed more
loudly than her brother; indeed for a little while the
house was filled with the harsh sound of squalling.
Yet this noise, though distressing, was as musical as
harps and lutes to the mother's ears; and while old
Mrs. Goudie in the kitchen was saying: "They children want a smart popping to learn them on'y to
squawk when there's reason for squawking," Mavis
was thinking: "Poor darlings, I'd go up and kiss them
again, if Mary didn't always quiet them down quicker
than I can."

Alone with her newspaper snippets, Mavis did more
reading than pasting. "Heroic Rescue at Otterford
Mill"—that was the description of how Will saved
good-for-nothing Abraham Veale. She knew it almost by heart, but she had to read it again. "Brave
Deed at Manninglea Cross Station"—that was something that made her feel faint every time she thought
of it, and she trembled now as she read in the snippet
of how there had been a frightened dog on the line
between the platforms, and how Will had jumped
down in front of the approaching train and whisked
the dog out of danger just in time.

She folded her hands, puckered her forehead, and
passed into a reverie about him. Combining with her
intense admiration, there was a great horror of all this
reckless courage. He would not have been so foolhardy years ago. It was against the principles that
he had once laid down as limiting the risks that a
brave man may run. It indicated a change in him, a
change that she had never pondered on till now. She
thought of him fighting the wind on top of their rick,

and of several other incidents unchronicled by the
press—of his going with the police at Old Manninglea
when there was the bad riot, of his joining the Crown
keepers when they went out to catch the poachers, of
his wild performance when Mr. Creech's bull got
loose. Goring bulls, bludgeoning men, tempest and
flood—wherever and whatever the danger, he went
straight to it. But it was not fair to her and the babes.
His thrice precious life! And she grew cold as she
thought that an accident—like a curtain descending
when a stage play is over—might some day end all
her joy.

Then she thought once more of that dark period of
their dual existence; and it was the last time that she
was ever capable of thinking of it seriously and with
any real concentration. Had that trouble left any
permanent mark on him? Her own suffering had left
no mark on her. It was gone so entirely that, as well
as seeming incredible, it seemed badly invented, silly,
preposterous. All that remained to her was just this
one firm memory, that, strange or not, there had truly
once been a time when his arms were not her shelter,
and she dared not look into his face.

But he was different from her; with a vastly more
capacious brain, in which there was such ample room
that perhaps the present did not even impinge upon
the past, much less drive it out altogether. She who
in the beginning had tacitly agreed with those who
considered her the obvious superior now felt humbly
pleased in recognizing that he was of grander, finer,
and more delicate stuff than herself. And for the first
and last time she was assailed by a disturbing doubt.
Was he completely happy even now? He loved her,

he loved his children, he loved his successful industry; yet sometimes when she found him alone his face was almost as somber as it had ever been.

And those bad dreams of his still continued. At first, when things were all in jeopardy, it had seemed not unnatural that the troubles of the day should break his rest at night; but why should he dream now, when he was prosperous and without a single anxiety to distress him? Did he in sleep go back to that old storm of anger, jealousy, and grief about which he never thought during his waking hours?

And again Mavis was actuated all unconsciously by the elemental selfishness that mingles with our joy. When we are happy we want others to be happy too, we can not brook their not being so; even transient darkness in those we love seems inimical to the light that is burning so cheerfully in ourselves. Mavis ceased to trouble herself with questions, and forgot that they remained unanswered.

When Dale came in she was, however, more than ordinarily sweet to him, waiting on him, bringing the supper dishes, not sitting down until he was served, and watching him while he ate. She told him that she had been reading about the dog on the railway line, and that he was not to do such things. If he ever again felt such a wild impulse, he was to stifle it immediately by remembering his wife and bairns.

"D'you understand, Will? We won't have it—and we all three think you ought to be ashamed of yourself for not knowing better. You're not a boy."

"No," he said, "I shall be forty-two next year. Look here," and he pointed to his temples. "Look at my gray hair."

" I can't see it."

" But it's there, my dear, all the same. I am beginning to turn toward the sear and yellow leaf, as
Shakespeare puts it."

She admired the easy way in which he quoted
Shakespeare, as if it was the most natural thing in the
world to do. Indeed, all through supper she was admiring him. She thought how beautifully he spoke,
expressing himself so elegantly, and with tones in his
voice that every day seemed to sound a little more
cultivated. At first after their arrival at Vine-Pits,
being plunged again into the midst of purely rustic
talk, he had fallen back in regard to his diction. Instinctively he reverted to the dialect that had been
his own, and that was being used by everybody
about him; but now one might say that he really had
two languages—his rough patter for the yard and the
fields, and his carefully-measured phrasing for the
home, office, and upper circles. She understood that
his constant reading and his unflagging desire for
self-improvement were telling rapidly; and with a
touch of sadness she wondered if, passing on always,
he would finally leave her quite behind.

No, while life lasted, he would hold to her. He
would never shake her off now. Even if she were
old and ugly, useless to him, a dead-weight upon his
ascending progress, he would be true to her now.
Even if his love died, the memory of it would keep
him still hers. And she thought of the pity in him,
as well as the strength. The man who could not resist the appeal of a poor little stray dog would not
break faith with the mother of his children; and she
thought, " Yes, whatever I say to him, I know really

and truly that it was a nobler, better thing to risk all than to allow even a dog to perish. And I love him for not having hesitated then, even when I pray him not to do it again."

Looking at him, she saw the gray hair that she had just now denied; and to her eyes these gray feathers at each side of the forehead not only increased his dignity, but gave him a fresh charm. The gray hair made him somehow more romantic. In her eyes his face was always growing more beautiful, always refining itself, always losing something that had been rather coarsely massive and gaining something that was new, spiritualized, and subtle.

"What are you examining me like that for, Mav? A penny for your thoughts."

"Shall I tell you truly?" and she laughed. "I was thinking if your looks continue to improve at this rate all the girls will get falling in love with you."

"Go along with you."

XVI

IN this manner the full and happy years began to
glide past them. Their prosperity was now firmly
established; the business grew; and money came in
so nicely that Mrs. Dale's mortgage had been paid
off and her two thousand pounds invested in gilt-
edged securities, while Dale hoped very shortly to
discharge the remainder of his obligation to Mr. Bates.
They were, however, as economical as ever in their
own way of life, although they permitted themselves
some license in the generosity they had begun to
practise with regard to their less fortunate neighbors.
But they found, as so many have found before them,
that in personal charity a little money goes a long
way, and that the claims of the very poor, although
sometimes noisy, are rarely excessive. Naturally
they had to be careful for the sake of their children,
the security of whose future must be the first consideration. Dale had promised the baby boy in his
cradle "the advantages of a lib'ral education," and he
intended to act up to this promise largely.

"It is my wish," he said, "that the two of them
shall enjoy all that I was myself deprived of."

New scraps were continually being pasted into the
album, and it seemed to Mavis that she ought to have
bought a bigger one, if indeed any albums were made
of a size sufficiently big to contain all the evidences
of her husband's gratified ambition. Scarce a *Courier*

was published without "a bit" in it that referred to Mr. Dale of Vine-Pits Farm. He was really becoming quite a public character. He had been called to the District Council, on its foundation, as a personage who could not be left out. When the Otterford branch of the Fire Brigade was instituted all agreed in inviting Mr. Dale to be its captain; and four of the once sluggish yard-servants had immediately decided that they must follow their master wherever he led, and had enrolled themselves forthwith under his captaincy. He was a prominent figure at the Old Manninglea corn market, known by sight in its streets, and had recently been chosen as a member of its very select tradesmen's club. This was an affair truly different from that vulgar boozing circle at the Gauntlet Inn which he had denounced so contemptuously in old days. The Manninglea Club was solid and respectable, a pleasant meeting-place where he could take his midday meal after market business in company with men of substance and repute. He was on friendly terms with most of the farmers between the down country and Rodhaven Harbor; and last, but not least, the gentry all passed the time of day when they met him, and many would stop him on the highroads for a chat in the most polite and jolly fashion.

He confessed to Mavis that the sweetest thing in his success was the feeling of being no longer disliked.

"Oh, Will, you never were disliked."

"But that's just what I was. And I begin to get a glimmer of the reason why. I was reading an article in *Answers* last week, and it seemed as if it had been written specially to enlighten me. It was about sympathy. The author, who didn't sign his name, but

was ev'dently a man of powerful int'lect, said that
without understanding you can't sympathize; and he
went on to show that without sympathy the whole
world would come to a standstill."

"Ah," said Mavis, "that's the sort of difficult reading that you like. It's too deep for me."

"It's plain as the nose on one's face, come to think
of it. Sympathy is the key-note. It enables you to
look at things from both sides—to put yourself in another man's place, and ask yourself the question,
What should I be thinking and doing, if I was him?
—I should say if I was he. In the old days I was very
deficient in that. A fool just made me angry. Now
I try to put myself in his place." He paused, and
smiled. "Perhaps you'll say I'm there already—a
fool myself."

"Oh, I wouldn't go so far as to say that;" and
Mavis smiled too. "Not *quite* a fool, Will."

He went on analyzing his characteristics, talking
with great interest in the subject, and after a didactic
style, but not with the heavy egoistic method that he
had often employed years ago.

"No, I never remarked that."

"You know," he said presently, "in spite of all my
bounce, I was a *shy* man.

"It's the fact, Mav. And my shyness came between me and others. I couldn't take them sufficiently free. I wanted all the overtures to come from
them, and I was too ready to draw in my horns if
they didn't seem to accept me straight at what I
judged my own value. For a long while now it has
been my endeavor to sink what was once described
to me as my pers'nal equation. I don't think of my-

self at all, if I can help it; and the consequence is the shyness gets pushed into the background, my manner becomes more free and open, and people begin to treat me in a more friendly spirit."

And he wound up his discourse by returning to the original cause of satisfaction.

"Yes, I do think there are some now that like me for myself—not many, but just one or two, besides dear old Mr. Bates."

"Everybody does. Why, look at that child, Norah. Only been here a month, and worships the ground you tread on."

"Poor little mite. That's her notion of being grateful for what I did for her father. Does she eat just the same?"

"Ravenous."

"Don't stint her," said Dale, impressively. "Feed her *ad lib*. Give her all she'll swallow. It's the leeway she's got to make up;" and he turned his eyes toward the kitchen door. "Is she out there?"

"Yes."

"I spoke loud. You don't think she heard what I said?"

"Oh, no. She's busy with Mrs. Goudie."

"I wouldn't like for her to hear us discussing her victuals as though she was an animal."

"You might have thought she was verily an animal," said Mavis, "if you'd seen her at the first meals we set before her. And even now it brings a lump into my throat to watch her."

"Just so."

"When I told her to undress that night to wash herself, she was a sight to break one's heart. Her poor little ribs were almost sticking through the skin; and, Will, I thought of one of ours ever being treated so."

Dale got up from the table, his face glowing redly, his brows frowning; and he stretched his arms to their full length.

"By Jupiter!" he said thickly, "if only Mrs. Neath had been a man, I'd 'a' given him—well, at the least, I'd 'a' given him a piece of my mind. I'd have told him what I thought of him."

"I promise you," said Mavis, "that I told Mrs. Neath what I thought of *her*."

"An' I'm right glad you did."

This new inmate under their roof was Norah Veale, a twelve-year-old daughter of the Hadleigh Wood hurdle-maker. Mavis, taking a present of tea and sugar to one of the Cross Roads cottages, had found her digging in the garden, and, struck by her pitiful aspect, had questioned her and elicited her history. It was a common enough one in those parts. Not being wanted at home, she had been "lent" to Mrs. Neath, the cottage woman, in exchange for her keep, and was mercilessly used by the borrower. She rose at dawn, worked as the regular household drudge till within an hour of school-time, then walked into Rodchurch for the day's schooling with a piece of dry bread in her pocket as dinner; and on her return from school worked again till late at night. She admitted that she felt always hungry, always tired, always miserable; that she suffered from cold at night in her wretched little bed; and that Mrs. Neath often beat her. She was a bright, intelligent child, black-haired, olive-complexioned, with lively blue eyes which expressed at once the natural trustfulness of youth, a certain boldness and wildness derived from gipsy ancestors, and a questioning wonder that this pleasant-looking world should be systematically ill-treating her.

The horrid, lying, carneying old woman of the cottage received home truths instead of tea and sugar from Mavis Dale, who, with all her maternal feelings aroused, rushed off straightway to hunt for the neglectful father. She found him at the Barradine Arms, and demanded his permission to take away the child. Veale, although sadly bemused, at once said that he could refuse nothing to the wife of his preserver.

"Oh, lor-a-mussy, yes, mum, you may 'aave my little Norrer an' do what you like wi' her. Bless her heart, I look on Norrer and her brothers to be the comfort o' my old age, but I wunt stan' in their light to interfere wi' what's best for any of 'em."

Mavis then took Norah straight home with her to Vine-Pits, bathed her, fed her, clothed her, and made much of her. And Norah proved grateful, docile, amenable, doing all that Mrs. Dale told her to do; and from the first exhibiting an almost superstitious worship of Mr. Dale. For truly, as he himself had surmised, her little starved breast was overflowing with gratitude to the man who had saved her father. It mattered nothing to the children of the mud hovel that their father was not an exemplary character; they did not want him to be drowned; and Norah, hearing in extreme youth of the hero who had interposed between him and such a cruel death, had mentally built a pedestal for the hero and kept him on top of it ever since.

It happened that about the time when Dale was preparing to pay off the last instalment of his debt, Mr. Bates unexpectedly applied for the money. He had never before shown the least anxiety for repayment; it had always been "Take your time, William. I know I'm in safe hands," and so forth; but now he said, " If you can make it convenient to you, William, it would be convenient to me."

" Oh, certainly, Mr. Bates. You shall have it before the end of the week—and I hope you're going to act on the advice I ventured to offer last time; that is, put it in one of these Canadian Government guaranteed stocks."

" I'm sure it was good advice, William—even if I didn't act on it."

" Of course my orig'nal advice was what you ought to have acted on, Mr. Bates. That is to say, bought an annuity with your entire capital."

" Ah, William, I really couldn't do that;" and Mr. Bates turned away his eyes, as if unable to support Dale's friendly regard. " Apart from these annuities for old folk being rather a dog-in-the-manger trick, I —well, one has one's private difficulties, William. One is not always a free agent."

The demand for repayment, and with something of evasiveness or reticence in the old fellow's manner, greatly troubled Dale. Not at all from selfish motives; but because it confirmed a suspicion that he had long entertained. Although invisible locally, disgraced and hiding somewhere at a distance, that blackguardly son was probably still draining the good old man's resources.

So many things pointed to the correctness of this supposition. On the interest of the money that Mavis and Dale had together paid him for the business, he should have been able to live very comfortably; whereas, in fact, his way of life was mean and sorry. His cottage was quite a decent dwelling, separated from the road by a nice long strip of garden, and with a miniature apple orchard behind it; but it showed all those signs of neglect that had been evident at Vine-Pits when the Dales first came there. He had no proper servant, but just pigged it anyhow with the occasional assistance of a woman and her husband. His clothes, though neatly brushed, were too shabby and overworn for a person of his position. And he was not a miser; he was a proud self-respecting man, who naturally would desire to maintain conventionally adequate state, were he able to do so.

These thoughts worried Dale. He really loved Mr. Bates, thoroughly appreciated the great dignity and sweetness of his nature, and felt it to be a monstrous and intolerable thing that the dear old chap at the age of seventy-three, instead of being allowed to end his days in a happy, seemly style, should be as it were bled to death by a conscienceless reprobate. But what could one do? It was like the cruelties of the woods that one regrets, but can not prevent—the rabbits chased by the weasels, the pheasants killed by the foxes, the thrushes destroyed by the hawks.

Any doubt that remained in the mind of Dale was soon dissipated. He told Mavis how he had seen Bates junior—a seedy, wicked-looking wretch now—lurking at dusk in the cottage porch, and how next morning he had ridden over to talk to Mr. Bates about this ill-omened visitor. Mr. Bates said it was true that his son had been there for two or three days, but he was now gone; and he declined to discuss the matter any further. "I can't speak of it, William. I thank you for meaning kindness, but it's a thing I can't speak of."

Dale also told Mrs. Goudie that Richard Bates had shown himself in the neighborhood, and asked her if the fact was generally known. He was aware that Mrs. Goudie had almost as much regard for the old man as he had himself.

"No, sir," said Mrs. Goudie, "I hadn't 'a' heard of it."

"Then that proves how close he kept. No doubt he came and went as surreptitiously as he could. Let it be between ourselves, Mrs. Goudie. Don't spread the tale an inch beyond us three."

"I will not, sir. But, oh, well-a-day, it's a bad bit o' news, sir. I did hope Mr. Bates was cured o' that runnin' sore."

She had been summoned from the kitchen just before leaving for the night; and with her shawl over her head, her wrinkled face working, and her bony hands clasped she stood near the table and waited for Mr. Dale to give the signal for her to withdraw.

"If you should see him, at any time, let me know, Mrs. Goudie."

"I will, sir."

"I might perhaps do good, if I could get hold of him on the quiet and address a few words to him."

"I wish you'd break his neck for him, yes, I do, indeed I do. I could tell you things as 'd make any one say hanging was too good for him."

And, encouraged to talk freely, Mrs. Goudie told Mavis and Dale, what indeed she had often told them before, of the shocking badness of Richard Bates and the ugly scenes that had taken place in this very house; of how he bullied his father to give him money, storming and raving like a lunatic when resisted; and of how the old fellow alone by himself had groaned and wept and prayed. Mrs. Goudie had heard him, after a most dreadful quarrel, praying out loud in his room up-stairs.

"An' believe me, sir, he was a praying for his son all the time—imploring of the Lord to soften his heart like, and save him from the hell-fire that his conduct asked for. You know, sir, he's a very God-fearing man, Mr. Bates."

XVII

THE action of the Dales in regard to Norah Veale
did not pass unnoticed. "They do tell me,"
said humble folk quite far afield, "that Mr. Dale up
to Vine-Pits hev adapted little Norrer Veale same as
if 'twas his own darter; and I sin her myself ridin'
to her schoolin' in Mr. Dale's wagon. I allus held
that Abe Veale was born a lucky one, fer nobody ever
comes adapting my childer; an' how hev he kep' out
o' jail all his days, if 'tisn't the luck?"

Nearer home, so striking an instance of kindness
encouraged the cottagers to do more freely what already they were doing with considerable freedom:
that is, to regard Vine-Pits Farm, and especially the
parts of it presided over by Mrs. Dale, as the proper
place to go in all moments of embarrassment or trib-
ulation. Thus the flagged path by the walnut tree,
the wooden bench beneath the window, and the open
kitchen door, tended to become a sort of court where
Mavis had to listen to an ever-increasing number of
applicants.

It used to be: "Muvver hev sent me to tell you
at once, Mum, she isn't no better but a good deal
worse, and the doctor hev ordered her some strong
soup for to nourish her stren'th;" or "Mr. Scull's
compliments, and might he hev the loan of some but-
ter agin;" or "Mrs. Craddock wishes you, Mum, to
read this letter which she hev written out of her sick-

bed, and every word of it is no more than the truth, as I can vouch for. Mr. Craddock in his cups last night punished her pore face somethin' frightful. She can't go to her work, and there's not so much as a bite of bread or a sip of milk in the house."

Mrs. Goudie declared that Mavis was often imposed upon; and, although Mavis herself wished to give wisely rather than blindly, endeavoring to govern warm impulse with cold reason, certainly very few people went away from the Vine-Pits back door empty-handed.

The gentry, in their turn, learned the commonly accepted fact that Mr. and Mrs. Dale were charitably-minded as well as prosperous, and thought all the better of them, asked for subscriptions, and invited co-operation in various good works. So that their fame was always shining with a steadier brightness, and one might say that nowadays there appeared to be only a single objection occasionally hinted against this fortunate couple. Certain very old-fashioned people refrained from patronizing Dale's business or praising his private life, because of the regrettable and notorious circumstance that he never went to church.

It could not be denied. During a good many years he had been to one funeral and two christenings; and, except for these rare occasions, had entirely abstained from attending any religious ceremonies. And Mavis too had gradually become slack in the performance of her spiritual duties. On Sunday mornings there was the dinner to think about. She still liked to cook the great weekly feast herself. Moreover, after six days of genuine labor, Sunday's fundamental purport as a day of rest is apt to overshadow its symbolic aspects as a day set apart for communion with things impalpable. The Abbey Church was too far off, even if it had not been out of the question for other reasons. It required a walk of two fat miles to get to Rodchurch, and one had to start early if one did not want to arrive there hot and flustered; again there was the risk of rain overtaking one in one's best dress. Every fine Sunday she used to talk at breakfast of intending to go to the morning service; and at dinner of intending to go to the evening service.

If she carried either the first or the second intention into effect, it was Dale's custom to go along the road and meet her returning. And this he now prepared to do, on a warm dry April morning, when obviously there could be no fear of rain and she had set out in her best directly after breakfast.

Dale loved the quiet and the freedom from interruption of these Sunday mornings; he enjoyed the luxury of being able to smoke in the office while he made up his books, and reveled in the lolling ease of the old porter's chair as he read Saturday's *Courier* and the last number of *Answers*. To-day he was peculiarly conscious of the soothing Sunday hush that had fallen widely on the land. All the doors and windows stood open, so that the soft air flowed like water through and through the house, making it an undivided part of the one great generous flooding atmosphere, and giving sensations of vast space and free activities as well as those produced by guarded comfort and motionless repose. The only sounds that reached him were the droning of bees in a border of spring flowers, the pawing of a horse in the stables, the pipe of young voices in the orchard; and all three sounds

were pleasant to his ear. How could they be otherwise; since they spoke of three such pleasant things
as awakening life, rewarded toil, and contented fatherhood?

When presently he went up-stairs to change his
coat, he stood by a window and looked down at the
peaceful little realm that fate had given to him. The
sunlight was glittering on the red tiles of the clustered roofs, the brown thatch of the ricks, and the
white cobblestones of a corner of the yard; and the
blossom of pears and apples was pink and white, as if
a light shower of colored snow had just fallen on the
still leafless trees. Beneath the orchard branches he
could see his children and Norah playing among the
daffodils that grew wild in the grass; the light all
about them was faintly blue and unceasingly tremu-
lous and he stood watching, listening, smiling, thinking.

He observed the gracefulness and slimness of his
daughter's stockinged legs, and thought what a real
little man his son seemed already, so sturdy on his
pins. In his blue overalls he looked like a miniature
ploughman in a smock-frock. Dale laughed when
Billy scampered away resolutely, and Norah had to
run to catch him.

"Le' me go," roared Bill.

"Na, na," said Norah, "you mustn't go brevetin'
about so far. Bide wi' sister and me, an' chain the
daffies."

And Dale noticed the musical note in Norah's voice,
almost like a wild bird singing. It was a pleasure to
him to see the little maid making herself so useful;
and it corroborated what Mavis had told him about

her being splendid in taking care of the chicks, as well as keeping them happy and amused.

He put on his black coat, fetched out a pair of brown dogskin gloves, and then, failing to find the silk hat, came to the top of the staircase and shouted for Mary.

"My hat, Mary. Where in the name of reason is my hat?"

His shouts broke the Sunday silence, filled the house with noise, went rolling through the open windows in swift vibrations. Norah Veale under the blossoming apple tree caught up the cry as though she had been an echo, and ran with the children after her.

"Mary, the master's hat. Mary, Mary! Master wants his hat."

Then she appeared at the foot of the stairs, with an anxious excited face and speaking breathlessly.

"Mary can't leave th' Yorkshire pudden, sir; but she says she saw Mrs. Dale with th' hat in her hand after you wore it on Wednesday to Manninglea."

"Yes, but where is it *now*, Norah?"

"I do think Mrs. Dale must have put it in the cupboard under the stairs to get it safe out of Billy's way."

And sure enough there the hat was. Both children pressed beside Norah to peep in with her when she opened the cupboard door. This hall cupboard was the most sacred and awe-inspiring receptacle in the whole house, because here were kept Dale's fireman's outfit always ready and handy to be snatched out at a moment's notice. Rachel gazed delightedly at the blue coat hanging extended, with the webbed steel on the shoulder-straps, at the helmet above, the great boots beneath, and the shining ax that dangled near an empty sleeve; but the sight was almost too tremendous for Billy. His lively young imagination could too readily inflate this shell of apparel with ogreish flesh and bone waiting to pounce on small intruders, and he clung rather timorously to Norah's skirt.

"Daddy," said Rachel, "I wis' you'd wear your helmet to-day."

"Oh, no, lassie, that wouldn't be seemly. This is more the thing for Sunday. Thank you, Norah." And having taken the silk hat, he laid his hand lightly on Norah's wavy black hair, and spoke to her very kindly. "Nothing like thought, Norah. I believe you've got a good little thinking-box under all this pretty hair, and you can't use it too much, my dear—specially so long as you're thinking about others."

Norah, with her blue eyes fixed on the venerated master's face, seemed to tremble joyously under the caress and the compliment. She and the children came out into the front garden and stood at the gate to watch Dale march away down the white road. He looked grandly stiff, black and large, in his ceremonious costume—a daddy and a master to be proud of.

He went only half-way to Rodchurch, and then sitting on a gate opposite the Baptist chapel indulged himself with another pipe. He made his halt here because several times when he had gone farther he had found Mavis accompanied by old Rodchurch acquaintances who had volunteered to escort her for a portion of the homeward journey, and he felt no inclination for this sort of chance society.

Not a human being, not even the smallest sign of a
man's habitation, was in sight; not a movement of
bird or beast could be perceived in the stretching
expanse of flat fields, across which huge cloud shadows passed slowly; the broad white road on either
hand seemed to lead from nowhere to nowhere, and
Dale, meditatively puffing out his tobacco smoke and
watching it rise and vanish, had that sense of deep and
almost solemn restfulness which comes whenever we
realize that for any reason we are cut off from the possibility of communication with our kind. For a few
moments he felt as a man feels all alone at the summit
of a mountain, in the depths of an untrodden forest, on
the limitless surface of a calm ocean. Yet, as he knew,
there were men quite near to him. Across the road,
not fifty yards away, the brick walls of the Baptist
Chapel were hiding many men and women. Perhaps
it was the complete isolation of this ugly building,
the house of prayer pushed away into the desert far
from all houses of laughter and talk, that had induced
the idea of isolation in himself.

If he listened, he could hear sounds made by men.
Through the chapel windows there came a continuous
murmur, like the buzzing of a monster bee under the
dome of a glass hive—the voice of the pastor preaching his sermon. Then all at once came loud music,
shuffling of seats, scraping of chairs; and a voluminous song poured out and upward in the silent air.
Dale idly thought of this chorus as resembling the
smoke from the pipe—something that went up a little
way and faded long before it reached the sky.

The music ceased. The congregation were leaving
the chapel. Dale got off the gate, put his pipe in his

pocket, and watched the humble worshipers as they came toward him. He knew them nearly all, and gravely returned their grave salutations as they passed by. They were maid-servants and men-servants from Rodchurch, old people and quite young people, a few laborers and cottage-women; and they all walked slowly, not at first talking to one another, but smiling with introspective vagueness. Dale observed their decent costume, their sober deportment, and leisurely gait, observed also a striking similarity in the expression of all the faces. They were like people who unwillingly awake and struggle to recall every detail of the dream they are being forced to relinquish. Observing them thus, one could not fail to understand that, at this moment at least, they all firmly believed that their just-finished song had been heard a very, very long way up.

The road was empty again when the pastor came out and locked the chapel door behind him. He spoke to Dale with a gentle cheerfulness.

" Good day, friend Dale."

Dale, not too well pleased with this easy and familiar mode of address, replied stiffly.

" I wish you good day, Mr. Osborn."

" Good day. God's day. That's what it meant in the beginning, Mr. Dale."

And Dale, resuming his seat on the gate, watched Mr. Osborn go plodding away toward Vine-Pits and the Cross Roads. This pastor, who had succeeded old Melling a few years ago, was a short, bearded man of sixty, and he lived in lodgings on the outskirts of Rodchurch. Evidently he was not going home to dinner. Perhaps he had some sick person to visit, and he

might get a snack at the Barradine Arms or one of
the cottages. It was said that his father had been a
rich linen-draper in some North of England town;
and that he himself would have inherited this flour-
ishing business and its accumulated wealth, if he had
not insisted on joining the ministry. But he threw
up all to preach the Gospel. Dale thought of the nature of the faith that would make a man go and do a
thing like that. It must be unquestioning, undoubt-
ing; a conviction that amounted to certainty.

He did not see Mavis approaching. She called to
him from a distance, and he sprang off the gate and
hurried to meet her. Instinctively, as he drew near,
he looked into her face, searching for the expression
that he had noticed just now in those other faces.
It was not there. She was hot and red after her
walk; her eyes were full of life and gaiety; she seemed
a fine, broad-blown, well-dressed dame who might
have been returning from market instead of from
church, and her first words spoke of practical affairs.

"Holly Lodge is let again, Will, and Mr. Allen says
the new gentleman keeps horses—because he's having
the stables painted. You ought to send a circular at
once, and make a call without delay."

Dale took his pipe out of his pocket, and spoke in
an absent tone.

"I've been thinking what a rum world it is, Mav."

"Yes, but a very nice world, Will;" and she slipped
her arm in his, as they walked on together. "No, not
another pipe. Don't take the edge off your appetite
with any more smoking. There's good roast beef and
Yorkshire pudding waiting for you. That is, if Mary
hasn't made a mess of everything."

XVIII

ON the evening of the next Sunday Dale was quietly going out of the house when Mavis offered to accompany him.

"Off for a stroll, Will? If you can wait ten minutes, I'll come with you."

But he excused himself from waiting, and further confessed that he preferred to be alone. He said he was in a thoughtful rather than a talkative mood tonight.

"You understand, old girl?"

"Yes, dear, I understand. You want to put on your considering cap about something."

"That's just it, Mav. The considering cap. Ta-ta."

Outside in the roadway Mr. Creech, a farmer, hindered him for a few minutes. Between him and Mr. Creech there were certain business arrangements now under negotiation, and it was impossible to avoid speaking of them. Dale, however, cut their chat as short as possible, and directly he had shaken off Mr. Creech he walked away briskly toward Rodchurch.

He had intended to arrive at the Baptist Chapel before the evening service began, but now he was late. The congregation were all on their knees, and the pastor, standing in his desk or pulpit above a raised platform, had begun to pray aloud. Dale paused just inside the door, looking at his strange surroundings, and feeling the awkwardness of a person who enters a place that he has never seen before, and finds himself among a lot of people who have their own customs and usages, all of which are unknown to him. Then he noticed that a man was smiling at him and beckoning, and he bowed gravely and followed the hand. He was led up the little building to some empty chairs on a level with the platform, at right angles to the rows of benches, and close to a harmonium. Mr. Osborn, the pastor, had stopped praying, and he did not go on again until Dale was seated. No one else had looked up or seemed to be aware of the interruption caused by his entrance.

He assumed a duly reverent attitude, not kneeling, but bending his body forward, and observed everything with great interest. There were many differences between the arrangements of this chapel and those of an ordinary church. The absence of an altar struck him as very remarkable. The large platform, with its balustrade and central perch, seemed to be altar, pulpit, and lectern all rolled into one—and choir too, since it was occupied by several men and a dozen girls and young women, who were all now on their knees while Mr. Osborn, looking very odd in purely civilian clothes, prayed loudly over their heads.

He glanced at the high bare walls and narrow windows, and observed that, except for some stenciled texts, there was not the slightest attempt at decoration. Outside, the light was rapidly waning, and inside the building the general tone had a grayness and dimness that obliterated all the bright colors of the girls' dresses and hats. The circumstance that not a single face was visible produced a curious impression

on one's mind. It made Dale feel for a moment as
though he were improperly prying, behind people's
backs, at matters that did not in the least concern him;
and next moment he thought that all the gray stooping forms were exactly like those of ghosts. Then,
in another moment, noticing with what rigid immo-
bility they held themselves, he thought of them as
being dead and waiting for some tremendous signal
that should bring them to life again.

"Now," said Mr. Osborn, "let us praise God by
singing the hundred and twenty-sixth hymn."

Then all the faces showed. It was like a flash of
pallid light running to and fro along the benches as
everybody changed the kneeling to the sitting pos-
ture; and Dale immediately felt that he had been
placed in an uncomfortably conspicuous position. Far
from being situated so that he could pry on the private
affairs of others, he was where everybody could study
him. He was alone, opposite to the entire crowd, instead of being comfortably absorbed in its mass.

"Oh, thank you. Much obliged."

Mr. Osborn, speaking from the pulpit, had said
something to one of his young women, and she was
leaning over the balustrade, smilingly offering Dale
an open hymn-book.

"I am afraid," she said, "that it's very small print;
but I dare say you have good eyes."

She spoke in the most friendly natural manner, exactly as one speaks to a visitor when one is anxious
to make him feel welcome and at home. Dale, startled by this style of address in such a place, made a
dignified bow.

"Give him this," said Mr. Osborn, handing a book
out of the pulpit. "It's a larger character—'long

primer,' as I believe the printers call it. We'll have
the lamps directly; but we are all of us rather partial
to blind man's holiday—not to mention that oil is
oil, and that Brother Spiers doesn't give it away. We
know he couldn't afford to do that. But there it is——
Take care of the pence."

To Dale's astonishment, he heard a distinct chuckle
here and there among the congregation. Then the
same young woman, having found the correct page,
handed him the large-type book. Then the man at
the harmonium struck up, and the whole congregation burst into song.

They sang with a fervent strength that he had never
heard equaled. For a moment the powerful chorus
seemed to shake the walls, to fill every cubic foot of
air that the building contained, and then to go straight
up, splitting the ugly roof, and out into the sky. Otherwise this hymn would have left one no space to
breathe in. Dale felt a sudden rush of blood to the
head, as if the pressure of vocal sound were about to
·produce suffocation; and at the same time he had the
fantastic but almost irresistible idea that the whole
congregation were singing solely at him, that they
and their pastor had together planned to set him alone
in this high place where he must bear the full brunt
of the hymn while they all watched its effect upon
him, and that the hymn itself had been specially and
artfully chosen with a view to him and to nobody else.

> "Hail, sov'reign love, that first began
> The scheme to rescue fallen man!
> Hail, matchless, free, eternal grace,
> That gave my soul a hiding-place."

With his face turned as much as possible from the singers, he stood very stiff and erect, staring at the printed page. Loudly as they had sung the first verse they seemed to sing the second verse more loudly.

> "Against the God that rules the sky,
> I fought with hand uplifted high;
> Despised His rich abounding grace,
> Too proud to seek a hiding-place."

Dale braced himself, squared his shoulders and stood more erect than ever as they struck into the third verse.

They sang louder than before: it seemed to him that they were screaming.

> "But thus th' eternal counsel ran,
> '*Almighty* love, arrest that man!'"

Dale closed the hymn-book, held it behind his back, and stared at the cross-beams of the roof until the hymn was over.

After the hymn Mr. Osborn read a couple of chapters from the Bible, and Dale, seated again, understood how utterly unfounded had been his recent notion that these people were devoting any particular attention to him. He looked at them carefully. Obviously they had not a thought of him. The eyes of those near to him and far from him were alike fixed upon the pastor's face.

But as soon as they sang again he experienced the same sensations again, felt a conviction that the hymn was aimed directly at him.

"Lord, when Thy Spirit deigns to show
    The badness of our hearts,
Astonished at the amazing view,
    The Soul with horror starts.

"Our staggering faith gives way to doubt,
    Our courage yields to fear;
Shocked at the sight, we straight cry out,
    'Can ever God dwell here?'

"None less than God's Almighty Son
    Can move such loads of sin;
The water from his side must run,
    To wash this dungeon clean."

"Now, I think," said Mr. Osborn, "it is fairly light-
ing-up time, and that no one can accuse us of being
extravagant if we call for the match-boxes. Brother
Maghull, please get to work. And, yes, you too,
Brother Hartley, if you will. You're always a dab at
regulating them."

Then the lamps were lighted; two or three men going round to do the work, the congregation generally
assisting as much as they were able, while the pastor,
watching all operations, made genial comments.

"Thank you. Now we begin to see who's who, and
what's what. I say, that's on the smoke, isn't it? I
seem to smell something, or is it imagination? If the
wicks are as badly trimmed as they were three Sundays ago, I shall be tempted to copy the procedure of
the House of Commons, and *name* a member." Then
he smiled. "Yes, I shall name a certain young sister
who must have turned clumsy-fingered because she
was thinking of her fal-lals and her chignon, or her

new hat, when she ought to have been thinking of her duty to our lamps."

A ripple of gentle laughter, like a lightly dancing wave on a deep calm sea, passed from the platform to the outer door; the lamplighters went back to their seats; and the pastor with a change of voice said solemnly: " Friends, let us pray."

Dale observed his manner of holding his hand to his' forehead as if seeking inspiration, the almost spasmodic movements of his mouth, the sort of plaintive groan that started the prayer, and the steadily accumulating earnestness with which it went on.

" O merciful and divine Father, supreme and omnipotent lord of Thy created universe, vouchsafe unto this little knot of Thy lowly creatures . . ."

It was a long prayer; and Dale, surmising it to be an extempore composition, admired Mr. Osborn's flow of language, command of erudite words, and success in bringing some very intricate sentences to an appropriate period.

During the sermon Mr. Osborn several times aroused laughter by little homely jokes coming unexpectedly in the midst of his serious discourse; but Dale no longer felt surprise. He thought that he had caught their point of view, got the hang of the main scheme. These people were genuine believers, and entirely free from any affectation or pretense. They possessed no church-manner: thus, when they spoke to one another here, they did so as naturally as when they were speaking in the fields or on the highroads. Only when they spoke to God, could you hear the vibration and the thrill, the effort and the strain.

And all at once his own self-consciousness vanished.

He felt comfortable, quite at ease, and extraordinarily glad that he had dedicated an hour to the purpose of coming here.

The lamplight enormously improved the appearance of the chapel; the genial yellow glow was surrounded by fine dark shadows that draped the ugly walls as if with soft curtains; there were golden glittering bands on the roof beams, and above them all had become black, impenetrable, mysterious. When one glanced up one might have had the night sky over one's head, for all one could see of the roof. The light shone bright on crooked backs, slightly distorted limbs, the pallor of sickness, the stains of rough weather; on girls meekly folding hands that daily scrub and scour; on laboring men stooping the shoulders that habitually carry weights; on spectacled old women with eyes worn out by incessantly peering at the tiny stitches of their untiring needles; but one would have looked in vain for any types even approximately similar to the stalwart well-balanced youths, the smooth-cheeked game-playing maidens, the prosperously healthful fathers and mothers of the established faith. Dale did not look for them, did not miss them, would not have wished them here.

It might be said that there was not a single person of the whole gathering on whom there was not plainly printed, in one shape or another, the stamp of toil. That fact perhaps formed the root of the difference between this and a Church of England congregation. To Dale's mind, however, there was something else of a saliently differentiating character. Once again he was struck by the expression of all the faces. He thought how calm, how trustful, how quietly joyous these people must be feeling, in order to shine back at the lamps as steadily and clearly as the lamps were shining on them.

" Friends, let us praise God by singing the hundred and tenth hymn before we separate."

They all rose and began to sing their final song; and Dale observed that here and there, as the loud chorus swelled and flowed, singers would sink down upon their knees as though of a sudden impelled to silence and prayer.

> "There is a fountain filled with blood,
>   Drawn from Emmanuel's veins;
> And sinners plunged beneath that flood,
>   Lose all their guilty stains.
>
> "The dying thief rejoiced to see
>   That fountain in his day;
> And there may I, as vile as he,
>   Wash all my sins away."

Dale abruptly sat down, leaned forward, and then knelt upon the boarded floor, hiding his face in his hands. He did not get up until the pastor had given the blessing and the people were moving out.

XIX

As so often happens toward the latter part of April, there had come a spell of unseasonably warm weather; thunder had been threatening for the last week, and now at the end of an oppressive day you could almost smell the electricity in the air.

Mavis warned Dale that he would get a sousing, when he told her that he was obliged to go as far as Rodchurch.

"Won't it do to-morrow, Will?"

"No, I shan't have time to-morrow. Remember I'm not made of barley-sugar. I shouldn't melt, you know, even if I hadn't got my mack."

Norah fetched him his foul weather hat, and ran for his umbrella.

"No," he said, "I don't want that, my dear;" and he smiled at her very kindly. "Besides, if we're going to have a storm, an umbrella is just the article to bring the lightning down on my head."

Norah pulled away the umbrella hastily, as though she would now have fought to the death rather than let him have it.

"Don't wait supper, Mav. I may be latish."

He walked fast, and his mackintosh made him uncomfortably warm. The rain held off, although now and then a few heavy drops fell ominously. It was quite dark—a premature darkness caused by the clouds that hung right across the sky. There seemed

241

to be nobody on the move but himself; the street at Rodchurch was absolutely empty, the tobacconist's shop at the corner being alone awake and feebly busy, the oil lamps flickering in the puffs of a warm spring wind.

He took one glance toward the post office, and then went right down the street and out upon the common. The house that he was seeking stood a little way off the road, and a broad beam of light from an open window proved of assistance as he crossed the broken and uneven ground. While he groped for the bell handle inside the dark porch he could hear, close at hand, a purring and whirring sound of wheels that he recognized as the unmistakable noise made by a carpenter's lathe. As soon as he rang the bell the lathe stopped working, and next moment the Baptist pastor came to the door.

"Mr. Dale—is it not?"

"Yes—good evening, Mr. Osborn."

"Pray come in."

"Thank you. Could you spare time for a chat?"

"Surely. I was expecting you."

Dale drew back, and spoke coldly, almost rudely.

"Indeed? I am not aware of any reason for your doing so."

"I ought to have said, *hoping* to see you."

"Oh. May I ask why?"

Mr. Osborn laughed contentedly. "Since I saw you at our service, you know. Please come into my room."

It was not an attractive or nicely furnished room. All one side of it was occupied by the lathe, bench, and tools; and on this side the boards of the floor, with a carpet rolled back, were covered with wood shavings.

"There, take off your wraps and be seated, Mr. Dale. I'll sort my rubbish. Stuffy night, isn't it?"

Dale noticed that there was no bookcase, and he could not detect more than six books anywhere lying about. Perhaps there were some in the chiffonier. He would have expected to find quite a little library at a house tenanted by this sort of man.

"What do you think of that?" And Mr. Osborn handed him the small round box which he had been turning. "I amuse myself so. It's my hobby."

"You don't feel the want to read of an evening?"

"No, I'm not a book-worm. But one has to do something; so I took up this. If folk chaff me "—and Mr. Osborn smiled and nodded his head—" well, I tell them that infinitely better people than I have done carpentering in their time. Of course they don't always follow the allusion."

Dale himself did not follow it. He understood that this was light and airy conversation provided by Mr. Osborn for the amiable purpose of putting him at his ease. He had taken off the slouch hat and loose coat that had made him look like some rough shepherd or herdsman; and now, as he sat stiffly on a chair, showing his jacket, breeches, and gaiters, he looked like a farmer who had come to buy or to sell stock. His manner was altogether businesslike when, after clearing his throat, he explained the actual reason of the visit. If it would not be troubling Mr. Osborn too much, he desired to obtain information about Baptist tenets, adult baptism, total immersion, and so on. Mr. Osborn, declaring that it was no trouble, and in an

equally businesslike manner, gave him the information.

"Is there anything else I can tell you?"

"I am afraid of putting you out."

"Not in the least."

"Well, then, if you're sure I don't trespass—Mr.
Osborn, the kind way you're receiving me makes me
venturesome. I see an ash-tray over there, proving
you sometimes favor the weed. Would you mind if
I took a whiff of tobacco—a pipe?"

"Why, surely not."

"You won't join me?"

"No, thanks. But I'll tell you what I will do;"
and Mr. Osborn emitted a chuckle. "I'll go on with
my boxes, if you'll allow me."

"I should greatly prefer it."

"You know, I can listen just as well, while I'm fid-
dling away at my nonsense."

"I find," said Dale, as he filled his pipe, "that I rely
on smoking more and more. Seems with me to steady
the nerves and clear the brain. I know there are others that it just fuddles."

"Exactly."

Mr. Osborn had gone back to the lathe, and the
pleasantly soothing whir of the wheels was heard
again, while a fountain of the finest possible shavings
began to spin in the air. For a few moments Dale
watched him at his work. His gray hair flopped
about queerly; he made rapid precise movements; and
he talked as though he still had his eyes on one, although his back was turned.

"There are matches at your elbow, Mr. Dale—on
that shelf—beside the flower-pot."

"Thanks, Mr. Osborn."

He wore a loose blue flannel coat, and Dale wondered if this was a garment that he had bought years
ago to play cricket in. Perhaps he had belonged to
a University. It was quite clear that he must have
had an extremely lib'ral education to start with. And
Dale thought again what he had thought just now in
the porch—that one ought to be precious careful in
dealing with a man of such natural and acquired
powers.

However, the fact that Mr. Osborn was continuing
his work, and yet, as he had promised, at the same
time listening properly, made the interview easier and
Dale more comfortable. He recovered his self-confidence, and after puffing out a sufficient cloud of
smoke, talked weightily and didactically.

"I am desirous not to exaggerate; but I would like
to state that I was well impressed by my experience
of your ritual—if that is the correct term. I seemed
to find what I had not found elsewhere. If I may
speak quite openly, I would say it appeared to me
there wasn't an ounce of humbug in your service."

"Oh, I hope not."

"Now, in the event of a person wishing to become
a member—in short, to embrace the Baptist faith entirely, there are one or two points that I'd like to have
cleared up."

Then Dale asked a lot of questions; and the pastor,
seeming to go on with the work, answered over his
shoulder, or looking round for an instant only.

Dale wished to learn all about the method of receiving adults; he asked also if anything in the nature
of confession or absolute submission to the priest

would be required. And the pastor said, " No, nothing of the sort." Such a person must of course bring a cleansed and purified heart to the ceremony, or it would be the very worst kind of humbug for him to present himself at all. But that was a matter which concerned him and God, who reads all hearts and knows all secrets. Mr. Osborn said it had never been the practise of Baptist ministers to insinuate themselves into the private secrets of their flocks. They left that to the Roman Catholics.

Dale heartily commended the Baptist custom. He said that much of his objection to religion had been caused by what he read of the Roman Catholic faith. As a responsible man he could never bring himself to that abject submission to another man, however you sanctified and tricked out the other man; besides, no one of mature age cares to make a complete confession of his past life. There must always be things that he could not force himself to disclose—follies, indiscretions, perhaps the grievous mistakes which he himself wants to forget, knowing that improvement lies in determination for better conduct, and not in brooding on past failure.

Mr. Osborn looked round, and used a gentle deprecating tone.

"You speak of your objection to religion; but, Mr. Dale, you are a singularly religious man. You are, really."

"I will postpone that part of it, if you please"—and Dale became rather stiff again—"but with the intention of adverting to it later. What I wish first to lay at rest is something in regard to the hymns employed on the occasion of my attendance. The numbers were one hundred and twenty-six, six hundred and fifty-nine, and one hundred and ten. Now I ask you as man to man, feeling sure you'll give me a straight answer: Were those hymns specially selected for the reason that I had chanced to drop in?"

Mr. Osborn stopped work, looked round quickly, and his face was all bright and eager.

"No. But did you feel there was a special message to you in them?"

"I wouldn't put it quite like that," said Dale guardedly.

"Because it so often happens. It has happened again and again—to my own knowledge."

"You'll understand, Mr. Osborn, that I didn't take them as any way personal to myself—certainly not any way offensive; but it occurred to me that it might perhaps be the habit whenever a stranger dropped in to pick out hymns of strength, with a view to shaking him and warming him up, as it were."

The pastor resumed his work. "Those hymns were given out the day before—Saturday. Sister Eldridge had asked for one hundred and twenty-six; number six hundred and fifty-nine was, as far as I remember, also bespoken; and I chose number one hundred and ten myself—because it is a great favorite of mine. So you see, Mr. Dale, at the time we settled on those hymns, we did not know that you were coming—and perhaps you did not know it yourself."

"I did not know it," said Dale.

"Tell me," said Mr. Osborn, "how doubt has assailed you."

"Ah, there you put me a puzzling one;" and Dale puffed at his pipe laboriously.

"You oughtn't to doubt, you know. You have
what men prize—wife, children, and home. You
thrive, and the world smiles on you."

"Yes, I'm more than solvent. I hope to leave Mrs.
Dale and the babes secure."

"But you don't feel secure yourself?"

"I banked a matter of seven hundred last year."

"You know I didn't mean that." Mr. Osborn
worked briskly, and sent the shavings almost to the
ceiling. "But still—lots of men have told me that
material prosperity renders faith easy and doubt difficult. That's the awful danger of trouble—the danger
of thinking that God has deserted us. It's easiest to
recognize His hand when all's going well with us.
That's our poor human nature. And then when our
sorrows come, it's the devil's innings, and he'll whisper: 'Where's God now? He isn't treating you very
kindly, is He, in return for all your praying and kneeling and believing?'"

"Yes, that just hits the nail on the head. It was
what I said—at a period when trouble fell upon me.
It was how the doubt came in and the belief went out.
And nowadays, when, as you mention, things run
smooth and I know I've much to be thankful for, the
doubt holds firm. For one thing prob'bly, I read a
great deal; I've crammed my head with science; can't
ever have enough of it. But, of course, I'm but an
ignorant man compared with you."

"Oh, no."

"Yes. I bow down to education—whenever I meet
it. I needn't apologize—because I hadn't many advantages. I try to make up by application. I read,
and I'm always thinking—and having mastered the

rudiments of science, I can look with some comprehension at the whole scheme of nature. With the result that, viewing my own affairs in the same spirit
that I view the whole bag of tricks, I ask myself that
same old question of *Q. I. Bono.*"

"What's that?"

"That's Latin," said Dale. "*Q. I. Bono.*"

"Oh, yes—exactly."

"Where's the good? Whatever one has, it isn't
enough if this life is all we've got to look to and
there's nothing beyond it."

Mr. Osborn had let the wheels run down. He came
and sat opposite to Dale, and spoke very quietly.

"There is everything beyond it."

"And supposing that's so, one's difficulty begins
bigger than before. It's the life-risk a million times
larger all over again—success or failure, punishment
or peace."

"That's better than what happened to the match
you threw into the fender—extinction."

"I want to believe. Mr. Osborne, I wish to speak
with honesty. I feel the need to believe. If you can
make me believe, you'll do me a great service."

"The service will be done, but it won't be I who
does it."

"I want to be saved. I want the day when you can
tell me I have gained everlasting salvation."

"The day will come; but it will not be my voice
that tells you."

Mr. Osborn got up to fetch one of the six shabby
volumes, and when he had returned to his chair he
went on talking.

"What you should do is to take things quietly. You

are a fine specimen, Mr. Dale, muscularly; but your nerves aren't quite so grand as your muscles." He said this just as doctors talk to patients, and as if Dale had been speaking of his bodily health. "Don't worry —and don't hurry. And I'd like to read you a passage here, to set your thoughts on the right line. . . . Well, well, I fancied I'd put a paper-mark. I shall only garble it if I try to quote from memory. It was Doctor Clifford, speaking about Jesus at our last Autumn Assembly. He says Jesus never put God forward as a severe judge, or hard taskmaster, but as His Father. . . . Ah, here we are. May I read it?"

"Yes, I wish to hear it."

"'God is Father; He is our Father. To Him'— speaking of Jesus—'and to us God is Father, and that means that we are in a deep and real sense His children, and, being children, then brothers to each other; for if God must be interpreted in terms of fatherhood, then man will never be interpreted accurately until he is interpreted in the terms of brotherhood.'" Mr. Osborn closed the book and laid his hand on Dale's knee. "How does that strike you, Brother Dale?"

"It strikes me as beautifully worded—Brother Osborn."

"That's how I want you to think of Him. A Father's love. Nothing strange nor new about it. Just what you used to be thinking as a boy, coming home to Father."

"I can't remember my father," said Dale simply. "He died when I was a baby, and mother married again. I only knew a stepfather."

"Then you'll know the real thing now, if you join us." Mr. Osborn beamed cheerfully. "Understand, I

don't press you. Why should I? The pressure behind you is not of this earth; and if it's there, as I
think it is, you'll no more resist it than the iron bolt
resists the steam-ram. But what's steam and *horse*-
power?" And he beamed all over his face. "This is
ten thousand *angel*-power to the square inch."

The rain began as Dale walked up the village street,
in which no light except that of the public lamps was
now showing. It fell sharply as he emerged into the
open country, and then abruptly ceased. The odor of
dust that has been partially moistened rose from the
roadway; some dead leaves scurried in the ditch with
a sound of small animals running for shelter; and he
felt a heavy, tepid air upon his face, as if some large
invisible person was breathing on him.

Then the heavens opened, and a flood of light came
pouring down. The thunder seemed simultaneous
with the flash. It was a crashing roar that literally
shook the ground. It was as if, without prelude or
warning, every house in England had fallen, every
gun fired, and every powder-magazine blown up.
Dale stood still, trying to steady himself after the
shock, and ascertaining that his eyes had not been
blinded nor the drums of his ears broken.

Then he walked on slowly, watching the storm. The
lightning flooded and forked, the thunder boomed and
banged; and it seemed to Dale that the whole world
had been turned upside down. When one looked up
at the illuminated sky, one seemed to be looking down
at a mountainous landscape. The clouds, rent apart,
torn, and shattered, were like masses of high hills,
inky black on the summits, with copper-colored preci-
pices and glistening purple slopes; and in remote

depths of the valleys, where there should have been lakes of water, there were lakes of fire. In the intervals between the flashes, when suddenly the sky became dark, one had a sensation that the earth had swung right again, and that it was now under one's feet as usual instead of being over one's head.

Dale plodding along thought of all he had read about thunder-storms. It was quite true, what he said to Norah. Lightning strikes the highest object. That was why trees had got such a bad name for themselves; although, as a fact, you were often a jolly sight safer under a tree than out in the open. Salisbury Plain, he had read, was the most dangerous place in England; for the reason that, because of its bareness, it made a six-foot man as conspicuous, upstanding an object as a church tower or a factory chimney would be elsewhere. And he thought that if any cattle had been left out in those wide flat fields near the Baptist Chapel, they were now in great peril. Mav's cows were all safe under cover.

Then, stimulated by a new thought, he began to walk faster. He hurried on until he came to the middle of the flats; then, gropingly through the darkness, and swiftly through the light, he made his way to a gate that he had just seen standing high and solid between the low field banks. He climbed the gate, a leg on each side, to the top bar but one; and there, easily balancing himself, he stood high above every other object.

And he thought: "If I am to be killed, I shall be killed now. I stand here at God's pleasure, to take me or leave me."

He carefully observed the lightning. It fell like a

live shot, a discharge of artillery aimed at a fixed point,
and then bursting seemed to go out in all directions
till it faded with a widespread glare. During this
final glare after each discharge the land to its farthest
horizon leaped into view. Thus he saw all at once the
Baptist Chapel several hundred yards away, but seeming to be close ahead of him, much bigger than it ac-
tually was, looking familiar and yet strange—looking
like the ark waiting to be floated as soon as the deluge
should begin. At the same moment he saw the stones
in the road, blades of grass at the side of the ditch,
and nails on the gate-post near his foot.

He stood calmly surveying the tremendous pageant,
and thought in each roar and crash: "This must be
the climax."

That last flash had crimson streamers, and it
swamped the road with violet waves. The fury and
the splendor of the thing was overwhelming. Was it
brought about by Nature's forces or God's machinery?
Titan . —like a struggle between the divine and the
evil power—some fresh rebellion of Satan just reported up there, and God, rightly indignant, giving the
devil what for—or God angry with *man*! Very magnificent, whatever way you regarded it.

The worst was over, and gradually the storm began
to roll away. Holding his hands high above his head,
he felt the rain-drops beat upon them, saw the lightning soften and grow pale, heard the thunder boom-
ing more gently, grumbling, whispering—as if it had
been the voice of the Maker of heaven and earth, murmuring in sleep.

Such a storm had naturally disturbed everything.
Mavis and Norah were trembling on the lamplit thresh-

old; horses rattled their head-stalls and stamped in the stables; even the bees were frightened in their hives. And a cock, thinking that so much light and noise must mean morning, had begun to crow hours before the proper time.

Dale, listening to the cock's crow while he told Mavis he was safe and sound, thought of Peter, the well-meaning man who wanted to believe but could not always do so.

XX

WHEN the time came for Dale to be baptized Mr. Osborn offered to perform the ceremony at dawn in the stream that runs through Hadleigh Wood; but Dale refused the offer. He said he would much prefer to have it done within four walls, in the evening, at what he supposed to be the usual place, the chapel. He added an expression of the hope that there would not be many people there.

"There would only be a few of ourselves, true-hearted ones, in either event," said Mr. Osborn; "and out of doors is not unusual. I did it that way for George Hitching a year ago. We took him down to Kib Pool, and waited till the sun rose. Then in he went."

And without urging Dale to change his mind, Mr. Osborn in a few words touched off the beauty of this baptismal scene. He described how the dew was like diamonds on the grass, and they stood all among the shadows, and the rising sun seemed to touch George Hitching's head before it touched anything else. "Then we and the birds began to sing together. I promise you it was uncommonly pretty, as well as very moving."

Nevertheless, Dale remained quite firm. That idea of Hadleigh Wood at dawn held no attraction for him.

So far he had said nothing of all this to Mavis, but now one night after supper he broached the subject.

He had laid down his knife and fork, and she had brought him the tobacco jar. He sat filling his pipe slowly, and then instead of lighting it he put it meditatively aside.

"Mavis, something has happened which will probably surprise you. I have found religion again."

" Oh, Will, I am glad."

Mavis was delighted; but when he told her that he was about to join the Baptists she did not feel so well pleased. She scarcely knew what to say. Why should he want to take the creed of dissenters, of quite common people? It was all very well for farm-laborers, sempstresses, and servants; but it did not seem good enough for her Will. Socially it was without doubt a retrograde step; and nowadays, when he got on capitally with the best of the gentlefolk, when they were all jolly and nice to him, it did seem a pity to go and mix himself up with a pack of ignorant underlings. The gentry, who of course all belonged to the Church of England, would not like it any better than she herself.

Moreover, that notion of total immersion was extremely repugnant to her. A grown-up person, an important person, a member of the District Council, splashing about in a tank! She asked him many questions concerning the baptism itself, and he told her all that he knew about it. He did not tell her, however, of Mr. Osborn's proposal that the immersion should occur in the wood-stream.

" What took your fancy, Will dear, with Mr. Osborn's teaching more than anybody else's? "

Then he told her all that Mr. Osborn had said of the fatherly attributes of God, of the fact that men were

veritably His children, and that for communion with
God one must be as a child approaching a father.

"Yes, dear, I'm sure that's true. But Mr. Norton
would say just the same."

"He never *has* said it, Mav. That is, I never heard
him say it."

"Perhaps in those days you didn't note his words.
I'm not arguing, dear. You must do whatever you
judge right, and it will be right for me—if once you've
done it. Only I do assure you what you repeated is
altogether Church of England; and I feel certain Mr.
Norton must have said it times and often."

"Then perhaps he hasn't said it quite in the same
way."

When the evening arrived Mavis asked if she might
come to the chapel, but he said "No." Her presence
would distract his thoughts.

"Very well, dear, I'll stay here. I shall say a prayer
for you. I may do that?"

"Yes, please do that."

Throughout the ceremony, and afterward, he was
very grave and dignified, plainly taking the whole matter with the most profound seriousness. He was silent and solemn throughout the rest of the evening;
but he slept extraordinarily well at night. There were
no dreams, no disturbances of any kind. He lay motionless, sleeping as peacefully as a little child.

Tender thoughts filled the mind of his wife as she
watched him. She thought of the ugly chapel, those
stupid illiterate people, the dark water, the splashing
and the noise; the clumsy absurdness of the whole
rite; and yet, in spite of everything, she now felt the
essential beauty of the idea itself. It seemed to her

most beautiful when applied to this particular case—
the strong brave man who in spirit and heart has made
himself simple and guileless as a child, to be taken
back to the Eternal Father of all children.

XXI

OUTWARDLY his religion sat lightly on him,
but inwardly it was solid and real. He took to
reading aloud one chapter of the Gospel every night,
and soon made a habit of adding a brief extempore
prayer for the benefit of Mary, Norah Veale, and Mrs.
Goudie, who regularly came from the kitchen to hear
him. His reading and praying formed, of course, a
marked innovation; but beyond it there were very few
perceptible changes that could be traced to the fresh
phase of mind into which he had now entered. And
these few changes were traced or perceived by only
one person, his wife.

Mavis saw with satisfaction that the gentlefolk did
not seemed to be huffed. Orders came in from several
of those old-fashioned people who had hitherto held
aloof, but who perhaps were at present generous
enough to think that if you don't go to church, the
next best thing is to go to chapel. The Baptists were
not therefore standing in his way: they had caused
no check to his success.

He bought all the corn and hay which the neighboring farms could spare to sell, so that what others
had grown and cut for miles round was carted straight
into his rick-yard. During the hay harvest he appeared especially grand, riding about the fields on his
horse, grave and watchful, really like a prince with
vassals hard at work for him as far as the eye could

see. On the last day he entertained the farmers to dinner in the best parlor, and afterward they all stood in the front garden, smoking cigars and praising Mrs. Dale's roses and carnations.

Mavis too gave parties; but she as a rule exercised her hospitality at the back of the house, where the little court and the petitioners' bench near the kitchen door were more fully occupied than ever. Here took place the annual summer tea-party for the cottage women, when Mavis was quite like some squire's wife, being courtesied to, receiving votes of thanks, and taking innocent pleasure in the proudness of her position. A far bigger and more difficult affair was when she invited all the children from the Orphanage. Long trestle tables for the girls were set out on the grass paths of the kitchen garden, with a separate and more stately table for the matrons and governesses; urns had been borrowed, seats hired, mountains of food and fruit got ready; and nevertheless the heart of Mavis almost failed her when the two-and-two procession of blue-coated orphans began to arrive. It seemed endless, an army, and she felt that she had attempted something too big for her resources. However, everything went off splendidly. The orphans whooped for joy as they broke their formation and spread out, through the garden, far into the meadows. Out there they looked like large bluebells; and at tea, when their cloaks had been removed and their brown frocks showed, they looked like locusts. Locusts could scarcely have eaten more. After tea Dale's men came from the yard and brought the piano out of the house, and Mrs. Dale played with stiff fingers while Norah Veale, Rachel, and the orphans danced on the flags and up and down the grass paths. The poor little orphans stayed late, and left regretfully. They said it had been the treat of their lives.

But the most interesting party and the one that Mavis enjoyed most came upon her unexpectedly.

One week Mr. Druitt the higgler failed to pay his usual visit, and there was conjecture in the Vine-Pits kitchen as to the reason of his absence. He had never before allowed a week to pass without a call. Mavis asked Mary if he had written to her explaining his absence; and Mary said no, and that she felt very anxious.

But next week he turned up, gay, jovial, looking ten years younger. He stood just inside the kitchen door, smiled at all, and winked most archly at Mary.

" See this, Mary?" And he pointed to the band of black crape on his arm. " Know what that means, Mary? " Then he turned to Mavis. " I call her Mary now, because I can do it with a clear conscience, ma'am. I buried Mrs. Druitt yesterday."

This meant a marriage feast for Mary; nor would the higgler permit of the least delay in its preparation. He was ardent to taste the felicity that had been so long postponed, and refused to listen to any appeals that might be addressed to his sense of propriety, the respect due to the departed, and so forth. Dale, inclined to say he would not put up with Druitt's nonsense, was overborne; chiefly because Mary, having been greatly scared by a facetious remark of her lover, at once took his part in the dispute. He had said, when she pleaded with him for a reasonable breathing-space, that he knew of as many other red-cheeked maids as there were morris-apples at akering-time.

Mary then bustled with her trousseau, of which the cost was defrayed by the Dales.

The charm of that party was its homelike, almost patriarchal character. A Saturday had been chosen to suit everybody's convenience, and the fickle June weather was kind to them. One long table was set out on the flags, in the shade of the house wall, close to the kitchen and the hot dishes; and the meal, which was substantial and lavish, lasted from about half-past three till five o'clock. Dale sat at the head of the table with his wife and the newly married couple; then there were a coachman and his daughter, and the higgler's best man; then Norah Veale and the children, and further off Mrs. Goudie, the dairymaid, and all the men from the yard. Mr. Bates had been asked, but he would not come. Abe Veale came unasked, to Nora's shame and indignation.

"I thought," he said, "as Norrer's true farder, and owing my life to him who is her adapted farder, and so well beknown to Miss Parsons, that I wouldn't be otherwise than welcome."

"You are welcome," said Dale quietly. "Be seated." And Norah felt intensely grateful to Dale and intensely disgusted with her parent.

They ate and drank and laughed; and Norah was sweet with the children, taking them away before they had gorged themselves. Outside the shadow of the wall one had the vivid beauty of flowers, the perfume of fruit, and the lively play of the sunlight; with glimpses through the foliage of smooth meadow, sloped arable, and distant heath; the firm ground beneath them, the open sky above them, and all around them the contented atmosphere of home. All these things together confirmed Mavis in the feeling that she had reached the apotheosis of her party-giving.

At the bottom of the table there was of course slight excess. The fun down there became rather broad. And old Mrs. Goudie made jokes which she reserved solely for weddings, and which she had better have kept to herself even then.

Dale proposed the bride's health, and spoke in the dignified easy style of a man who is accustomed to addressing large audiences, but who is tactfully able to reduce the compass of his voice and the weight of his manner for friendly informal gatherings. He was only heavy—and not a bit too heavy—when he thanked Mary for the kindness she had always shown to him and his. Then he pointed to the gold locket that was his wedding present, and said that when she wore that round her neck, as she was wearing it now, " it reposed on a loyal, faithful heart." This caused Mary to weep.

The opening of the higgler's speech was in deplorable taste—all about widowers making the best husbands. He said, " Widowers know what to expect; so they ain't disappointed. And if they've suffered in their first venture, it's an easy job for Number Two to please 'em;" and he winked to right and left. Mavis and Dale were looking uncomfortable. Fortunately, however, the speech improved toward the end of it. " All I ask of Mary is to look nice—and that she can't help doing, bless her bonny face; to speak nice—and that she can do if she tries, and copies Mrs. Dale; and to act nice—and in that she'll have an example under her eyes, for I mean to act uncommon nice to her."

When, winking and bowing, he resumed his seat by Mary's side, the applause from the bottom of the table was vociferous. "Brayvo. He hev a said it smart. Never 'eard it better worded. Well done, Mr. Druitt."

Half the flowers had lost their color in the extending shadow of the house before Mr. and Mrs. Druitt drove away. The higgler's pony groaned between the shafts of a cart that was much too big for him; rice and old shoes struck the wheels; Mrs. Goudie made her last joke; the men at the yard gate shouted; Norah and the children ran a little way along the road—and then the party was over.

After a few days Mr. Druitt called exactly as usual to offer good bacon. "Mornin', ma'am. Mary sends her love, and the message that she's as happy as the day is long."

"And I hope," said Mavis, "that you are happy too, Mr. Druitt."

"Mrs. Dale," he said, "I don't reco'nize myself. When I think of the past and the present——"

Mavis stopped him. He was of course going to disparage Number One, and she felt that to be so horrid of him.

XXII

THE new housemaid was adequately filling Mary's place, and life at Vine-Pits as of old ran smoothly on. With increasing means the Dales still refrained from frivolous additions to household expenditure. Neither craved for further pomp or luxury; both took pleasure in amassing rather than in squandering.

To get up early, work hard, and go to bed thoroughly tired—all this Mavis took for granted as a correct and undeviating program for one's days. Indeed in her complete satisfaction she tended naturally to a mental attitude that was taking for granted all phenomena, whether objective or subjective. The visible comforts of her home, the love of her husband, the bliss of being the mother of two perfect children, together with her contented thoughts in relation to each and all of these matters, were accepted as so intimately connected with the prime fact of her existence itself that no fear of possible disturbance or cessation ever troubled her. She no more thought of a break in the grand routine of placid joy than she thought of leaving off the process by which she filled and emptied her lungs when breathing.

As perhaps is usual with the majority of successful people, she never considered whether the hour had not come for diminishing the effort that was producing the success. They had fixed no goal which when reached should be a resting-place as well as a winning-post.

265

They were working for the future. The money they earned was for then, and not for now. But she very rarely thought of this remote period; and when she did, it was with absolute vagueness. A lot of money would be required for the children; and eventually she and Will would be old, feeble, unable to go on working, and then a modest amount of money would be required for themselves.

Always in her early dreams of affluence she had pictured holidays, the excitement of traveling, and rapid changes of scene; yet, although since they first came to Vine-Pits they had not been away for a single staying holiday, she had no sense of missing something that might have been enjoyed. It would be absurd to drag Dale away from home while he was so busy. For herself it seemed quite sufficient change and excitement to drive over to Old Manninglea for an afternoon's severe shopping about six times a year.

Now, of a sudden, Dale himself offered to give her a day out at the very first opportunity. Little Rachel had never seen the sea, and expressed a strong desire to look upon the wonders of the deep; so daddy promised to take her and her mother to Rodhaven Pier directly he was free enough to do so. In the end he chose a Sunday for this treat, saying that the better the day the better the deed.

He came out of chapel before the sermon; they dined at noon, and started in good time to catch the train at Rodchurch Road. At the moment of departure, when the horse and wagonette stood ready, and Dale in his silk hat, black coat, and dogskin gloves was about to mount the box-seat, the boy Billy began to howl most pitifully because he was being left behind. Mavis,

whose heartstrings were torn by the sight of her angel's tears and the sound of his yells, looked at Dale
appealingly.

"All right," said Dale. "Will you behave yourself,
Billy, if we take you?"

But this meant taking Norah too, because obviously
Mavis could not manage both children unaided.

"Norah," said Dale, impressively, "I give you two
minutes, and no more, to get yourself and the boy
ready."

Mavis, overjoyed, put Rachel in the back of the wagonette, took her seat by her husband's side, and with
sprightly chat endeavored to make two long minutes
seem two short ones.

"How nice the horse looks! Will, I do feel we are
all in luck. Such a fine day too. Do you think your
top hat is necessary? Wouldn't you be more comfortable in your straw?"

"May be—but I don't think it would be the thing,"
said Dale. "We shall be sure to meet a lot of people
we know."

"I only thought you'd get it so dusty. Is it your
best or the old one?"

He did not answer, because just then Norah and
Billy came rushing down the garden path.

It proved an altogether delightful excursion. There
was so little in it really, and yet long years afterward
Mavis sometimes thought of it as perhaps the happiest
day of her life. They drove through Rodchurch, past
the post office, the church, and other interesting sights;
then along the broader road beneath big trees, to the
railway station. Billy sat between his parents, and
did not behave too well, wriggling, contorting himself,

threatening to jump out, and even grabbing for the reins.

"It's his excitement," said Norah.

"Yes, it's his excitement," said Mavis; and she and Norah talked reassuringly, as if to each other, but really at Dale. "He'll be all right, Norah, when he has had his run about."

"Yes," sad Norah sagely, "children are like that. They must let off steam. As soon as they're tired they remember their manners and behave nicely."

At the Station Inn Dale put up the horse and trap, and the journey was pursued by rail.

The brightness and gaiety of Rodhaven charmed them all. They seemed to get out of the train into another climate, another world. Everything was new and strange—blazing sun with a wind that made you as cool as a cucumber; crowds and crowds of people, Salvation Army band, procession of volunteers; and the pier, the streamers, the sea—and the *sands*.

Rachel scarcely glanced at Ocean's face: the sands were enough for her. They got away from the crowd, and played on the sands. Dale was so jolly with the children, running about, sportively chasing them, hunting for shells, popping the buds of seaweed; while Mavis sat on a dry bit of rock, looking large, red, overblown, and adored her family. The little boy soon became, frankly, a nuisance, wanting his sister's shells, refusing to catch daddy, wishing to paddle in his boots; and Dale, testy at last, very hot and perspiring said: "Ma lad, if you wear out my patience, you'll suffer for your conduct."

Then, almost at the same moment, Dale's top hat blew off; and a mad chase ensued. The hat, like a live thing with the devil in it, bounded and curvetted wildly, doubled away from Dale, dodged Rachel, and sprang right over Norah's head, threatening to make for the open sea. Mavis had scrambled up; and she stood on the rock, a tragic figure, with a finger to her lip, watching the hat chase distractedly. Norah caught the hat in the end, and it was really not much the worse for its gambol.

Mavis' first words were, " Is it your best?"

" No," gasped Dale, very much out of breath; " my second-best."

" Thank goodness," said Mavis.

They made a fine solid meal at tea in a vast refreshment-hall on the sands; Mavis and Norah, with their hats on adjacent chairs and their hair untidy, helping the little ones to top and tail the first shrimps that they had ever encountered; Dale eating heaps of shrimps and drinking cup after cup of tea. The wind blew sand against the glass front of the hall—the smell of the sea mingled with the smell of the shrimps —and they were absolutely happy. But when all felt replete the boy began to cry, and soon howled. " I wis' I lived here always, yes, I do."

" O Billy, you like home best."

" No, I don't. I like this best. I hate home;" and he bellowed.

" He's getting tired," said Norah sagely.

" Yes," said Mavis. " That's all it is. He's getting tired."

He fell asleep directly they got into the lamplit train; and Norah carried him from the station, carried him all the time the horse was being put to and they were getting ready to leave.

" He's too much for you," said Dale kindly. " Give him to me."

" Oh, no, sir."

And Dale whispered approvingly to Mavis, saying that he liked Norah's grit.

Then they drove home; Norah behind with the children, both of them sleeping now; and Dale and Mavis side by side in front, talking quietly as they passed beneath the dark trees and out beneath the bright stars.

XXIII

NORAH was a treasure to them, and she seemed always to be improving. She had done with school now, but she evinced a commendable yearning for further cultivation, buying copy-books with her pocket-money, imitating Dale's clerkly hand; so that already at a pinch she was able to help in the office work. But proud as she felt when permitted to copy out accounts or circular letters, her pride did not spoil her for household labor. In fact she worked, so stanchly at scrubbing, scouring, and so forth, as well as looking after the children, that for a long while Mavis did not detect how poor old Mrs. Goudie was failing, and leaving nearly all her duties to be performed by others. Moreover, in spite of having issued from the untidy hovel of those rammucky Veales, she showed an innate love of cleanliness and order, assiduously brushing her black hair and scrupulously washing her white skin.

Only very rarely she gave a little trouble, and then both Dale and his wife attributed this naughtiness to the Veale origin, finding the explanation of a certain wildness in that strain of gipsy blood which, as was popularly supposed, ran down her pedigree. She disgraced herself when the circus menagerie passed the gates of Vine-Pits. She stood firm with the rest of them watching the great painted vans go by, and the droves of horses, and the tiny ponies; but when the

elephants came she broke away. The size, the weird-
ness, the shuffling footsteps of these beasts made her
beside herself. A lot of ragged children with great
wicked-looking hobbledehoys from the Cross Roads,
were trotting after the elephants; and Norah, joining
this disreputable band, trotted also. She went all the
way to Rodchurch, saw the immense tent set up on
the Common, and probably crept inside to see the entertainment. She did not return for six hours, not till
after dark.

Another thing that made Mavis anxious and angry
was Norah's ineradicable love of the woods. She never deserted work, but, if allowed any time to herself,
she would go stealing off into Hadleigh Wood to pick
flowers or bring back birds' eggs for the children. She
knew perfectly well that she was to keep to the road
or the field tracks, but the sylvan depths seemed to call
her and she could not resist the call.

Once when Norah had been troublesome in this respect, Mavis was so angry that she threatened her with
corporal punishment.

"Look here, my lass," said Mavis, unconsciously
founding herself on the manner of her husband when
administering rebuke, "if you can't obey what I tell
you, I shall ask Mr. Dale to chastise you—yes, my lass,
to give you a lesson you won't forget in a hurry."

Norah hung her head and pouted. Then she looked
up and spoke firmly.

"He wouldn't do it. He's too kind."

"Oh, yes, he would. Don't you make a mistake
about that."

"He *wouldn't.*" Norah's eyes flashed; she stamped
her foot, and turned on Mavis quite fiercely. " He's

so good that he wouldn't hurt a fly, much less beat a
girl. You've no right to say it—behind his back—
what you know isn't true."

"Be off to your work this instant," said Mavis,
stamping also, "or I'll whip you myself." And she
pursued Norah to the kitchen. "You dare to sauce
me like that again as long as you live!"

Before the evening was over, Norah, completely con-
trite, begged to be forgiven for her rudeness; and
Mavis was only too ready both to forgive and to forget. She had felt quite shocked and upset by the
girl's tantrums.

It was almost immediately after this that Norah said
she wished to be a Baptist, and to go to chapel with
Mr. Dale.

"Do you think," asked Dale, when informed of
Norah's petition, "that it is genuine? Or is it just
curiosity?"

"I think it's genuine," said Mavis. "But no doubt
she is influenced by the fact that *you* go there. I do
believe she'd wish to go anywhere—or do anything
that you did."

Dale questioned Norah seriously.

"Why do you wish it? Speak to me with freedom,
my dear."

"I do want to be good, sir." And Norah burst into
tears. "Oh, I do want to be good."

"Then come with me," said Dale.

Henceforth they two went to worship together every Sunday, and Mavis once or twice felt a twinge of
regret that she herself had not been able to abandon
the established church and join the Baptists with her
husband. But that she could not do. The chapel

was too ugly, its eastward wall too bare, its faith too painfully simple and matter-of-fact.

She took great pains with Norah's Sunday costume, dressing her better than before, anxious that the girl should do them credit when seen with Dale in a public place; and Norah, all in her best, following after her master as he made his long strides down the road, trotted like a faithful little dog. She sat beside him in one of the front benches, breathing hard, and following the text with her finger, while Mr. Osborn read the Bible; and she blended her birdlike trills with Dale's strong bass when they both stood up to sing the hymns. Dale liked the note of her voice, took pleasure in observing her piety, and thoroughly enjoyed expounding any difficulties in the sermon while they walked home to dinner or to supper.

If Dale stood outside the chapel talking to elders of the flock, Norah modestly withdrew to a little distance; or if he met people on the road and stopped to chat, she went on ahead, waiting respectfully, and only returning to his side when he walked on again alone. He always kept his eye on her, and saw that she was not being accosted unpleasantly by any undesirable acquaintance.

Once, when Dale had stopped thus to talk to Mr. Maghull, there were two field-laborers leaning against a gate and discussing people as they passed. Neither of them was a Baptist. One was a stupid old man, and his would-be-funny chatter, at which the other kept guffawing, bothered Dale in his serious conversation with Mr. Maghull.

" Be that little Norrer Veale? "

" I dunno."

" I do think that's little Norrer Veale, but I ben't
sure."

" Yes, it is," said Dale, turning and speaking sharply. " What about her? "

" Lord, how she's coming on," said the old man.
" She's an advertisement to your larder, sir; " and he
stared at the girl. " Fillin' out into all a piece o' goods,
ben't un? " Then he laughed, in peasant style. " Give
her another year or two and she'll be a blink to set
some un o' fire pretty quick, if she gets hedge-row
walkin'."

Dale felt annoyed by this rustic criticism, but he
knew that there was substantial truth in it. Norah
was developing rapidly, and showed distinct comeli-
ness. As he walked after her he noticed her figure.
It was still very slender, but it had 'roundnesses that
would soon become rounder, and graceful curves that
would swell with an ampler grace every month till she
reached full growth. He was pleased when he thought
of the good food that she had received in return for
her good work. He thought, too, that he must tell
Mavis to be watchful and careful, a real guardian,
when this childlike bud burst into womanhood.

He felt a glow of indignation at the mere idea of
harm coming to her while she was under their care.
Hands off, there. Any louts who attempted tricks
would have him, William Dale, to reckon with.

For years Dale had been a bad sleeper, but now he
was a good sleeper; and Mavis traced this change directly to the calming effect of his religion. There
could be no question that the improvement dated from
that night on which he was baptized. Since then he
had not once been troubled with bad dreams, and habit-

ually he slept so soundly that he required a lot of rousing in the morning. Another change, among those slight differences that she fancied she observed in him, was his abstraction when reading. Formerly he used to seem particularly alert and vigorous whenever he sat with an open book before him; his whole air was that of lively expectation; the features worked; he was waiting for a passage that he did not agree with. Nowadays he seemed to read in a completely receptive spirit, without questioning, without doubting; and his face reflected the quiet confidence that he was adopting with regard to the author. He never looked up, or stopped to read out anything that struck him; he had withdrawn himself from every-day life and given himself to the world of the book; you had to speak two or three times, and quite loudly, before you could drag him back to material facts.

Still another change, and one that affected them both, Mavis did not altogether attribute to the revival of her husband's religious belief; but she thought that this had accelerated its progress and confirmed its finality. It had begun after the birth of her second child. Then it was that the love between husband and wife purified itself still further; and the refining process had continued; they had passed onward and upward until the beautiful new feelings seemed firmly established, and, without a word spoken, all the old passion had been allowed to fade. It was quite another joy now when they kissed or lay locked in each other's arms: they were a father and a mother, a brother and sister, comrades—but no longer lovers.

She was surprised once or twice to find how calmly and contentedly she thought about all this; without

the least regret for something that was and had ceased
to be; and without a vestige of the confusion of ideas
which makes women in their ripening years cling to
all belonging or seeming to belong to vanished youth,
and to suffer under the loss of anything they possessed
then, even though a better thing has come to them in
its place. She was a woman completing her destined
course; and so that the cycle-curve swept on unbrok-
en, she would be as happy on the downward sweep as
when the sweep was rising.

But in these days, in spite of her mental tranquillity,
she could not sleep well at night; she tossed and
turned, muttered and started, as if the dreams and rest-
lessness that had gone out of Will had found their way
into her. For this reason they generally occupied
different beds, and sometimes different rooms.

Throughout this period while Mrs. Dale's bodily
health was not on its normal level of excellence, Norah
showed magnificent grit and altogether proved worth
her weight in gold.

Dale always remembered the night when she came
to his room, and, after much beating on the door and
calling him by name, at last succeeded in waking him.
Mavis, who had unfortunately caught cold the day before, was now taken with violent colic, and suffering
such pain that she could not restrain her groans and
screams. Ethel, the new maid, was scared out of her
wits by the sight of her afflicted mistress; Dale himself was alarmed; neither of them could do anything.
But Norah did it all. She had sprung out of bed just
as she was, rushed to the scene of disorder, snatched
up the mistress' keys, then had procured and admin-
istered brandy. Then she rushed down-stairs again,

lighted the fire, and began to boil water and to get flannel
for hot compresses.

Dale came down to the kitchen presently, and said
that his wife was feeling easier; the brandy had done
her good. Then, the anxiety having lessened, his attention was held by Norah's scanty attire. She was
in her night-dress and nothing more, and even this
garment was not sufficiently fastened; her black hair
was tumbling loose about her shoulders, and she pat-
tered here and there across the stone floor on her bare
feet.

He began to chide her, rather irritably. "You little
fool, do you want to catch a chill as well—so's to make
two invalids instead of one? Here, put on my jacket."

"Oh, no, Mr. Dale."

"Do as I tell you. Besides, it—well, it isn't seemly
to be running about half naked."

Norah flushed red in the candle-light, and clutched
at her night-dress. Then she hastily put on Dale's
jacket, which swamped her, going far down below her
hips and making her seem a wonderfully strange figure.

Next morning, when she was bringing him his
breakfast, he talked to her of what had "passed a few
hours ago."

"Norah, my dear, I'm sorry I spoke sharply to you
—just when you were doing all that you possibly could
for us. But, you know, I didn't mean it a bit unkind."

"Oh, no, sir," said Norah, shyly.

" It's only that I'm always a stickler for etiquette—
and that sort of thing. I do so like what I call seemly
conduct."

"Yes, sir. I was ashamed the moment you spoke;"
and Norah blushed again. "But truly I hadn't

thought, sir. If I'd given it a thought, I'd never have done it."

"No, you didn't think. And there's nothing on earth for you to be ashamed of. Far be it from me to put thoughts into your innocent little noddle which needn't come there yet a while. You'll understand—and it'll just be instinct to you then—that what's right for children is a bit odd and startling for those who're older. Now don't think any more about it."

"I don't want to, sir—if you say so;" and Norah smiled comfortably once more.

She made and laid his early breakfast for him every morning until Mavis was well enough to come down to do it herself, and Dale had never been better waited on or seen a daintier way of arranging a table. She always gave him a napkin, which was an unusual luxury, and she folded it in fantastic shapes; moreover, undeterred by the notions of economy or caution natural in a proprietor, she brought out pieces of the bettermost china that were rarely used by Mavis; she set one of the smallest and very best afternoon tea-cloths in such a manner that it looked like a diamond instead of a square, and on this, as central decoration, she placed a blue bowl full of flowers. Then, too, she had requisitioned the silver-plated cake basket for the newly-baked bannocks. The silver basket gave a touch of splendor that really made the table seem as if its proper situation was a grand London restaurant or a nobleman's mansion.

"You want to spoil me, Norah," said Dale, watching her. Then he laughed. "But, my dear, all these pretty trickings and ornamentations are fairly wasted on me."

" No, they aren't," said Norah, breathing hard, seeming to purr with pleasure. " They can't be wasted, if you've noticed them, Mr. Dale; " and as she lifted her head, she shook back the dark curling hair from her forehead. " P'raps they'd be wasted if you didn't know they were there."

" Oh, we rough old chaps don't require such prettiness about them."

Norah displayed her small white teeth in a broadening smile; then she looked at the revered master thoughtfully.

" Why do you say you're *old?* You aren't really old, Mr. Dale."

"Oh, aren't I? I wonder what you call old, lassie."

" I call father old, and Mr. Bates—and Mrs. Goudie."

" Well, I mayn't be as old as them—as they; but I think I'm like the walnut tree out there. I still stand up straight, but I fear me I've seen my best days. . . . There! What are you up to now?"

She was lugging and pushing the great porter's chair from its corner.

" I don't want that."

" It's your chair, so why shouldn't you sit in it at breakfast as well as supper?" She brought it to the table, and looked at him over the back of it shyly, yet with a kind of defiance—much as his own children looked at him when they had made up their minds to be cheeky. " It's quite an old man's chair, sir—so it'll suit you nicely."

He sat in the chair, amused by her impudence, but holding up his finger with mock reproof. She had run to the kitchen door, and she stood there for a moment laughing merrily. "Oh, you do look all a gran'father in that chair, Mr. Dale. You do, indeed."

Next moment she was singing at her work outside in the kitchen. Then there came a silence; her shadow passed the window, and he guessed that she was taking a circuitous route to the room up-stairs where the children and Ethel were busily engaged in toilet operations. Rather than risk disturbing him at his breakfast by coming through here, she had gone right round the house and in again at the front door. She was always like that—always thinking of other people's comfort, never sparing her own labor.

Then he heard her voice at a distance somewhere near the cowhouse. She had not gone up-stairs after all; she had gone out there on dairy business. Soon she came singing back—singing, he thought, as blithely as a lark; just as sweetly and tunefully as any bird one could name.

Other people as well as Dale noticed the freshness and unforced music of Norah's singing, and it was not long before she received an invitation to sing among the regularly trained young women at the chapel.

On the morning when she left Dale's side to take her place upon the platform she was woefully nervous. Dale too had been anxious, but directly he heard her voice—and he knew it so well that he at once distinguished it amid all the other voices that made up the platform chorus—he felt perfectly reassured. Her nervousness had not put her out of tune: she was acquitting herself admirably.

They walked home together in a high state of gratification; and he hastened to tell Mavis that the little maid had achieved a success, and that Mr. Osborn had paid her a compliment at the door before everybody. Mavis was delighted. She ran to give kisses of congratulation, and she said that on her very next visit to Old Manninglea she would buy some stuff to make Norah a pretty new dress, which they would set to work on as soon as the evenings began to lengthen again.

A considerable time elapsed before this kind intention became an accomplished fact; but in due course the dress was ready to wear, and Norah looked very nice when wearing it. As to color, it was of so lively a blue that it would permit no shadows even in its deepest folds; it was just a close-fitting brightness that made the girl seem to have shot up in a night to a form of much greater height and increased slenderness. Her hat was made of yellow straw, with a wreath of artificial daisies round the crown. When the tempered sunshine fell upon her as she stood up to sing, she looked like something composed of vivid color, light, and life—like a flower glowing in a garden, a kingfisher hovering over a stream, a rainbow trembling on the crest of a hill. Dale, watching her, thought that in comparison the other maidens on the platform were positively plain.

He told Mavis afterward that he felt certain the dress had been admired, adding that Norah's general appearance did her the utmost credit. And that Sunday they both talked seriously about Norah's future.

"You know," said Dale, "I feel it as a responsibility on us."

"So do I," said Mavis.

"Having taken it up, we must go through with it

to the end. I mean, we must always stand her friends
—and more than that, her guardians."

"Of course."

"In a sense," he went on, didactically, "we may
have made a mistake in bringing her forward to the
extent we've done."

"How so, Will?"

"I mean, if one wished to argue selfish—which of
course I don't wish—well, the selfish view would be
not to have drawn her out but rather keep her down
a bit."

"Oh, she'd be miserable if she didn't feel to be one
of ourselves—and you always said let's treat her that
way."

"I know; and I don't go back on it. I was only
stating the case of selfish policy, for the sake of argument. It's like this. The more useful you teach her
to be, the more we're going to miss her when she
leaves us."

"She'll never leave us."

"Won't she be thinking of taking service in some
gentleman's family when you've perfected her, and rendered her really capable of filling a situation?"

"Oh, no, she'd never want to go away from Vine-
Pits."

"Is that so? Well, of course I regard that as another feather in her cap. I'm glad to think she's
properly devoted to you."

"It isn't me," said Mavis. "It's you she's devoted
to. It's been the same all along. I told you from the
first that child just worshiped you. It's Mr. Dale.
Mr. Dale is the cry with Norah always. She looks on

me as very small potatoes," and Mavis laughed. " I
don't mind. It's how I look on myself."

Dale patted his wife's hand, and smiled. " Rubbish!
But look here, Mav;" and he spoke very thoughtfully.
" I don't wish ever to trade on Norah's gratitude. It
may be, when the time comes, we shall have to decide
for her. It may be that she'll do better for herself in
the long run by going than by staying. If so, we
mustn't be the barrier in her way. We must push her
out into the world, even if she can't see the point of
it. But all that lies far ahead. We needn't worry
about it yet a while. . . . How old is Norah now?"

" Seventeen."

" No? Do you mean to say she has been with us
five years? "

" Yes. Every bit of five years."

" Then how old is Rachel?"

" Eleven."

" And Billy? "

" Five—and more."

" My goodness, Mav," and Dale sighed, " how time
goes." Then he rose from his chair, stretched himself, and sighed again. *"How* time is going!"

XXIV

A NOTHER charwoman had now been engaged; and Mrs. Goudie, retiring on a small pension from the Dales, came to Vine-Pits only to pay her respects or now and then to appear as the least greedy and most deserving petitioner of all those who sat on the bench or stood waiting at the back door. Coming thus for a dole of tea, she asked Norah to inform Mr. Dale that young Bates—as he was still called—had again been seen in the neighborhood. As usual, he had come and gone furtively.

Dale, duly receiving the message, frowned and shook his head ominously. He had never been able to get hold of young Bates, although Mrs. Goudie had reported several of these sinister reappearances, and probably nothing could have been gained by an interview with such a heartless scoundrel. So long as old Bates was weak enough to give, young Bates would be cruel enough to go on taking; and from the aspect of things it appeared that the too generous father would before long be altogether denuded. He was getting shabbier and shabbier in his apparel; his poor old face looked pinched and thin, and the talk was that he lived on starvation rations. It all seemed horrible to Dale —a thing that should not be permitted; and yet what could one do?

He thought about it all next day, and it was more

285

or less occupying his mind at dusk when he sat with
Norah in the office clearing up for the night.

"There, my dear, that'll do. You'll only hurt your
eyes."

"It's all right, Mr. Dale. I can see well enough
just to finish."

Dale was sitting at the table in the window and
Norah stood at his desk beside the high stool, copying
rows of figures out of a huge day-book. He turned
his head and watched her for a minute or so in silence.
Her dusky black hair was like a crown over her stooping face; her left elbow and hand lay on the desk;
and the moving pen in her other hand pointed straight
at the right shoulder, exactly as Dale had taught her
to point it when she first began to imitate his copper-
plate writing. She had been an apt pupil, and there
was no mistake about the help she gave him nowadays.
At the beginning he used to pretend a little, saying
that her aid lightened his labors, merely to encourage
and please her.

"Now stop, lassie. This is what Mr. Osborn terms
blind man's holiday. Shut the book."

"I should have liked to finish," said Norah.

Nevertheless she obeyed him, closing the book and
putting her papers in a drawer.

"Look here, if you *must* be busy to the last moment, come over here nearer the light and address
these envelopes for me—and I'll have a pipe."

Norah came meekly to the window and took the
chair that Dale had vacated for her. Standing close
behind the chair and looking down upon her, he noticed
the deft way in which her hands gathered the loose
envelopes and stacked them; the shapeliness of her

arms and shoulders; and the ivory whiteness of her
cheek. It was the fading light that produced this effect, because she was not by any means a pale girl.
Her skin, although white enough, had warm tones in
it, and under it still warmer tones—a brownish glow,
like a sunburn that had been transmitted by nomad
ancestors who baked themselves under fierce southern
skies centuries ago. The gipsy blood showed to that
extent in her complexion, and to a greater extent in
her hair.

And suddenly he thought of what Mavis had been
as a girl. *She* had a white skin—if you please; much
whiter than Norah's; but she was like this girl in many
respects, was Mavis when he first saw her. She and
Norah were as like as two peas out of one pod in the
matter of looking fragile and yet firm, as gracefully
delicate of form as it is possible to be without arousing any suspicion of debility or unhealthiness. The
back of Mavis' stooping neck used to be exactly like
this girl's—a smooth, round stem, without a crease
or a speck on it, a solid, healthy neck, and yet so slender that his great hand would almost girdle it.

"Aren't I doing right?" Norah looked up quickly.
"I'm copying the addresses off the letters."

"No, you're doing quite right." Dale put his hands
in his pockets and moved away to the high stool.
"What made you think you were doing wrong?"

"Oh, I don't know. I always get nervous when you
watch me and don't say anything."

"Then we'll talk. There, I'll wait till you're
through, and then we'll talk a bit."

"I am through now," said Norah in a minute. "Shall
I put the stamps on?"

"No, don't trouble. I'll do it myself—and post 'em at the pillar."

He had seated himself on the stool and had brought out his pipe. He looked at its bowl reflectively, and then began to talk to Norah about the children.

"Don't you think, Norah, that we ought to be putting Billy out to school?"

Mavis so far had acted as governess, with Norah to assist, and between them they had taught both children to read and write; but this home tuition could not go on indefinitely, and Dale thought that the time had already come when larger and bolder steps must be taken toward achieving that liberal education which he had solemnly promised his son and heir. He was always reading advertisements of attractive seaside schools, where the boy could secure home comforts, the rudiments of sound religious faith, as well as a good grounding in the humanities. Mavis, however, would not yet hear of a separation from her darling. She pleaded that he was such a *little* fellow still; she prayed Will not to hurry.

"Tell me what *you* think about it, Norah—quite candidly."

Norah had hesitated about replying; but she now said that she really thought Dale need not be in a hurry. Billy was so clever that when he did get to school he would learn faster than other boys; and she added that his departure from home would be "a dreadful wrinch for Mrs. Dale."

"But it will be a wrench for her whenever it happens. In life one has to prepare one's self for *wrenches*——That, I fancy, is the better way of pronouncing the word. Yes, wrench after wrench, Norah—that's life;

until the last great wrench comes—and, well, that
isn't life. . . . Who was that passed the window?"
Norah turned her bright young face to the window
and peered out.

"It's Mr. Bates, sir. How funny he looks!"

"What d'you mean—funny?".

"Walking so slow, and leaning on his great stick—
as if he was a pilgrim."

Dale had jumped off his stool; and he ran out to the
road and begged the old man to come in.

"Certainly, William," said Mr. Bates.

He had cut himself a long staff from some woodland
holly-tree, a rough prop that reached shoulder high,
and on this he leaned heavily as soon as he stopped
walking. He looked very old and very shaky.

"Good evening, Miss Veale," he said courteously
as he entered the office.

"Oh, you mustn't call her *Miss* Veale. She's Norah
—one of us, you know." And as he spoke, Dale laid
his hand on the back of Norah's neck to prevent her
from rising. "She's our *multum in parvo*—making
herself so useful to the wife and me that we can't
think what we should ever do without her. Bide
where you are a moment, Norah."

Dale established his visitor on a chair that faced the
rapidly waning light, and addressed him again with
increased deference.

"If you can spare a few minutes, there's a thing I'd
like to speak to you about, Mr. Bates."

"I can spare all the minutes between now and morning," said Mr. Bates cordially, "if I can be of the least
service to you, William."

As much now as in the beginning of the enterprise

Bates held himself at the younger man's disposal, indeed liked nothing better than to give information and counsel whenever his prosperous successor was of a mind to accept either.

"I won't keep you as long as that," said Dale, smiling; "but will you give us the pleasure of your company at supper?"

"You're very kind, William, but I don't think I can."

"Do, Mr. Bates. The wife will be as pleased as me —as I."

The old fellow looked up at Dale hesitatingly; and Dale, looking down at his clean-shaven cheeks, bushy white eyebrows, and the long wisps of white hair brushed across his bald head, felt a great reverence. He would not look at the threadbare shabbiness of the gray cloth suit, or at the queer tints given by time and weather to the black felt hat that was being balanced on two shrunken knees.

"I, ah, don't think I'll present myself before Mrs. Dale—ah, without more preparation than this. Besides, would it not put her out?"

"No, indeed. Quite unceremonious—taking us exactly as you find us—pot-luck."

"Then be it so. You are very good. Thank you, William."

"Thank you, Mr. Bates." Dale seized upon the visitor's hat and stick. "Now you may cut along, Norah, and tell Mrs. Dale that Mr. Bates is kind enough to stay supper—without ceremony."

Norah glided across the office to the inner door, and, going out, asked if she should bring a lamp.

"Yes, bring the lamp in ten minutes—not before,

There's light enough for two such old friends to chat together;" and Dale waited until she had shut the door. "Now, sir, this is kind and friendly. Give me your hand, Mr. Bates. I'd like to hold it in mine, while I say these few prelim'nary words."

"Yes, William?" The old man had immediately offered his hand, and he looked up with a puzzled and anxious expression.

"I merely wish to assure you, Mr. Bates, very sincerely, that if you at this moment could see right into my heart, you'd plainly see my respect, and what is more, my true affection for you, sir."

"I believe it, William,"

"And it has always been a source of comfort to me to think that you, sir, have entertained a most kindly feeling to me, sir."

Mr. Bates had averted his eyes, and he moved his feet restlessly, his demeanor seeming to indicate that he regretted having accepted the supper invitation and was perhaps desirous of withdrawing his acceptance.

"I hope," Dale went on, "I haven't been presumptuous in my estimate of your feeling, sir."

"No." And the old man looked up again. His eyes, his whole face had grown soft, and the tone of his voice was firm, yet rather low and very sweet. "No, William, my feeling for you began in taking note of your sharpness combined with your steady ways, and it has ended in love."

"That's a large word, Mr. Bates."

"It's no larger than the truth."

"Then I say 'Thank you, sir, for the honor you have done me.'" Dale pressed the old chap's hand, dropped it, and returned to the high stool. "And now, after what has passed between us two, man to man, you'll credit me with no disrespectfulness if I make bold to let fall certain remarks."

Bates nodded his white head and stared at the floor.

"There's a thing, sir, that I particularly want to say. It is about yourself, sir——"

"Go on, William," said Mr. Bates, "and get it over. I know what you're after, of course—something about Richard. Well, I'll take it from you. I wouldn't take it from any one else."

"D'you remember all you used to advise me about the danger of rats, telling me to fight 'em as if it was the devil himself, horns and tail, and not just so many stinking little avaricious rodents? You said, one rat was sufficient to mess me up."

Mr. Bates nodded.

"And you knew what you were talking about—no one better. And for why? Because it was your own story you were telling me, in the form of a parable."

"You're wrong there, William."

"Not a bit. You'd had one rat—but, by Jupiter, he was a whooping big 'un, and he'd eaten your grain, and messed you up—he'd ruined your business, and well-nigh broken your heart, and practically done for you."

"Have you finished?" asked Mr. Bates, with dignity.

"Yes, sir—almost;" and Dale in the most earnest manner besought his old friend to resist any further attacks from that wicked son. "I do implore you, sir, not to be weak and fullish. Don't take him to your boosum. He's a rat still—an' he'll gnaw and devour the little that's left to you, so sure as I sit here."

But it was all no use, as he could easily see. Mr. Bates raised his eyes, moved his feet, and then spoke gently but proudly.

"I thank you, William, for your well-meant intentions. I have listened to what you wished to say. Now shall we talk of something else?"

"Yes—but with just this one proviso added. Will you remember that I am your banker, for the full half of what the banker's worth? If the pinch comes, draw on me."

"I thank you again, William. But I shan't need help."

"I think you will."

"Then to speak quite truly, I couldn't take help, William, I really couldn't."

"Why not? Think of all you've done for me. Don't deny me the pleasure of doing something for you."

"I'll consider, William. Please let it rest there."

Dale could say no more and they both sat silent for a little while. Then old Bates spoke again.

"William," he said, "if you'll excuse me, I really won't stay. You have—to tell the truth—agitated me."

"Indeed I'm sorry, sir. But don't punish me by going."

"I am not quite up to merry-making."

Just then Norah arrived, carrying the lamp, and Dale turned to her for aid.

"Norah, speak for me. Mr. Bates says he won't stay. Tell him how disappointed we shall be."

"Oh, do stay, Mr. Bates," said Norah. "It'll be such a disappointment to Mr. Dale."

"Some other evening, Miss—ah, Norah. But you must excuse me this time."

And, having picked up his hat and stick, Mr. Bates bade them good night.

Dale and Norah went out into the road and watched him as he walked away.

"There, Norah;" and Dale, slipping his arm within hers, drew her closer to his side. "Look with all your eyes. You'll never see a better man than that."

They watched him till he disappeared in the gathering darkness; and he seemed just like a pilgrim with his staff, slowly approaching the end of a cruelly long journey.

XXV

IT was perhaps a month after this when Dale heard
news which plainly indicated that the wicked son
had completed his horrible task. He had eaten up all
that there was to eat.

Mr. Osborn said that old Bates had given his landlord notice, and he was leaving his cottage almost immediately. The matter had been brought to the pastor's knowledge because one of the Baptist congregation thought of taking the cottage, and had asked Mr.
Osborn's advice.

Other people, who professed to know more than Mr.
Osborn, said it was true that Bates had given notice,
but it was also true that he owed two quarters' rent
and that the landlord was determined to have his
money. To this end everything the cottage contained
would be seized and sold. And what would happen
to Mr. Bates when not only his house was gone, but
all his sticks of furniture too?

" It do seem a pity he ben't a young orphan female
instead of a wore-out old man, for then he cud move
on into Barradine Home and be fed on the best for
naught."

The cottage and other cottages about Otterford Mill,
although close to the Abbey estate, did not belong to it.
They were the property of various small owners, and
Bates' landlord, as Dale knew, was a tradesman at Old
Manninglea.

Dale, having heard the news on a Sunday evening, put his check-book in his pocket very early next morning and rode over the heath to the market town. There he saw Bates' landlord, readily obtained leave to withdraw the notice, cleared off the arrears, and paid rent for a year in advance. Then he rode straight to Otterford Mill.

"Good morning, William. Pray come in. But will your horse stand quiet there?"

"Oh, yes, sir. He'll stand quiet enough. Only too glad of the chance to stand. I keep him moving, you know."

"Don't he ever get jerking at the rein, and break his bridle?"

"If he did he wouldn't run away. He'd be too ashamed of himself for what he'd done."

"Then step inside, William," said Mr. Bates once more.

He ushered Dale into a bare, sad-looking room; and the whole cottage smelled of nakedness, famine, misery.

"Now, my dear old friend," said Dale cheerily, "what's all this whispering that reaches my ears *in re* you thinking of changing your quarters and leaving us?"

"It's the truth, William. I can't afford these premises any longer."

"Oh, come, we can't have that. We haven't so many friends that we can put up with losing the one we value most of all."

Then he told Mr. Bates what he had done at Manninglea.

The old man frowned, flushed, and began to tremble.

"You shouldn't 'a' done that, William. It was a liberty. I must write and say my notice holds good."

Then there was a brief but most painful conversation, Dale nearly shedding tears while he pleaded to be allowed on this one occasion to act as banker, and Bates resolutely refusing help, refusing even to admit how much help was needed.

"William," he said obdurately, "I recognize your kind intention—but you've made a mistake. You shouldn't have done it, without a word to me. I can only repeat, it was a liberty."

Dale of course apologized, but went on pleading. It was all no use. Obviously Mr. Bates' pride had been wounded to the quick. He was white, shaky, so old, so feeble, and yet firm as a rock. Never till now had he spoken to Dale in such tones of stiff reproof.

"William, we'll say no more. I have paid my way all my days, and at my present age it's a bit too late to start differently."

His last words were: "I shall write next post to confirm the notice."

And he did so.

Then the tale ran round that Mr. Bates was going to the workhouse. People declared that he had ceded all his furniture to the landlord, who could now sell it quietly and advantageously, in a manner which would yield more than enough to wipe out the debt. Perhaps there might even be a trifling balance in the debtor's favor eventually; but meanwhile the homeless and stickless old gentleman would fall as another burden on the rates to which he had so long subscribed.

It was curious, perhaps, but the humble folk spoke of him as the old gentleman, and not as the old man, all at once giving him the title which they only now began to think he had fairly earned as a master and employer, an important personage who used to drive about in gigs, wear a black coat at church, and always have a kind word for you when you touched your cap to him.

"'Tis all a pity but so 'tis, and can't be gainsaid. Th' old gentleman hev come down so low, that 'tis the Union and nought else."

"Is that for sure?"

"Oh, yes, for certain sure. He is a-goin' into workhouse to-morrow maarning."

But he did not go there.

In the morning some one came running into Dale's yard, and shouted what had happened since dark last night.

"Th' old gentleman hev a done fer hisself."

He had been found hanging from the biggest of the apple trees behind his cottage. He had set a ladder against the tree, gone up it, fixed the rope firmly, put the noose round his neck, and stepped off into the air. That was the way they did for themselves in this part of Hampshire.

XXVI

THE suicide of Mr. Bates had a great effect on Dale. The sadness and regret that he felt at the time continued to tinge his thoughts for a long while afterward. He could not shake off the horror of that midnight scene, as he imagined it—the God-fearing man breaking the divine laws, the man full of years who was so near the grave and yet could not wait till it received him naturally, the poor feeble old creature taxing all his remnant of strength to knock out the small spark of life that already had begun to gleam so dimly. How long did he take to drag and raise the ladder, pausing to recover breath, holding his side and coughing, then again toiling?

Another thing that depressed Dale's spirits was the departure of Mr. Osborn, who had gone to the Midlands to take up the ministry of a large church in a large town. And never had Dale more felt the want of priestly support than at this period. The new pastor was a young man who preached eloquently, but Dale would not be able to talk to him as he had talked to Osborn.

Mavis observed again what she had not seen for ages, the gloom on her husband's face when he sat alone, or thought that he was alone. The dull brooding look that spoiled his aspect at such times was like the shadow of a dark cloud on a field; but as in the past the shadow went rapidly, and she fancied she could chase it away as surely as if she had been the sunshine. She would have been startled and pained if she could have seen his face now, as he rode from Manninglea after luncheon at the club.

It was a wet spring day, with dark clouds hanging low over the heath, a cold wind cheeping, soughing, sighing; and Dale's face was darker and sadder than the day. Before mounting his horse in the hotel yard at Manninglea he had gone to the station and bought *The Times* newspaper; now he drew the paper out of his pocket, and sheltering it with his rain cloak, read an advertisement on the front page.

The advertisement told him that a London hospital gratefully acknowledged the receipt of one hundred pounds, being the twenty-first donation from the same hand, and making two thousand and twenty pounds as the total received to date. In accordance with the request of their anonymous benefactor, they inserted this notice, and they offered at the same time their heartfelt thanks.

Dale tore out the advertisement and threw away the rest of the paper.

To his mind, this money was the payment of a very old debt. The amount of his first charitable donation sent nearly fifteen years ago, had been twenty pounds. That, the most urgent part of the debt, represented the four bank-notes given to the wife by Mr. Barradine in London. The other twenty instalments made up the amount of the legacy that came to her at his death. Mavis had lent the money to her husband, had in due course received a similar sum of money from him, and she held it now safely invested; but, as Dale told himself, she did not in truth hold one penny of the dead

man's gifts. All that she had now was the gift of him,
Dale; and the money that soiled her hands in touching
it, the money that had burned his brain, the filthy gold
that had made him half-mad to think of, had gone to
strangers whom neither of them had ever seen. He
had been slow about it; but, thank God, he had done
at last what he wanted to do at the very beginning.

He folded the scrap of paper that was his receipt or
quittance, put it in his breast pocket, and rode on at a
foot-pace. He was absolutely alone, not a soul in sight
wherever he turned his eyes, not a beast, not a bird
moving, the desolate brown heath and the sad gray
sky alike empty of life; straight ahead, about a mile
distant, lay the Cross Roads, the tavern, and the small
hamlet of cottages, but as yet they were hidden by
a rise of the intervening ground; only the fringe of
cultivated land at the point where it met the barren
waste indicated the work or proximity of mankind.
His face grew still darker as he approached these fields
and saw the cluster of houses on their edge.   He
looked at the deep ditch that surrounded the outer-
most field; then turning his head looked again at the
heath, its bleak contours mounting gradually till they
showed an ugly ridge beyond which the downs swelled
up soft and vague against the hanging curtain of
clouds. And he thought of what lay on the far side
of this long grass rampart of down country—the fat-
soiled valley, the other railway line, the trains from
the West of England, full of queer people, running by
night as well as by day.

As he passed the Barradine Arms, he saw three louts
leaning against a dry bit of wall under the eaves of an
outhouse. They stared at him stupidly, not speaking

or touching their caps, just loutishly staring; and he stared at them with black severity. He thought how he himself had been like one of those oafs, living in a cottage not so many miles from this spot. No one now seemed to remember his humble birth, his unhappy youth, his sordid home. Other people forgot everything; while he could forget nothing.

At the Cross Roads he drew rein for a moment, as if undecided as to which way to turn. Before going home he had to pay a business call, and his destination was straight ahead of him, about four miles off as the crow flies. The quickest way to get there, the line nearest to the crow's line, would be to leave the road here and ride through Hadleigh Wood, under the bare beeches, among the somber pines, along the gloomy rides; and the alternative route would be to turn to the right, hold to the open road, and follow its deflected course past the Abbey gates and park, and all round the wild forest. That way would be three miles longer than the other way. He turned his horse's head to the right; and as he went on by the road, he was thinking of the terrible chapter in his life that closed with the death of Mr. Barradine.

Nearly fifteen years ago; yet in all that time, although dwelling so near to the tragic fateful wood, he had been into it only once—and then he had gone there with the hounds and jolly loud-voiced riders, cub-hunting, on a bright September morning. The wood symbolized everything that he wished to forget. And he thought that if he were really a rich man—not a poor little well-to-do trader, but a fabulous millionaire —he'd buy all this woodland, cut down every tree, chase away every shadow, and grow corn in the sun-

light. He would buy woodland and parkland too—he
would burn Aunt Petherick's hidden cottage, the
Abbey with its inner, outer and middle courtyards, yes,
and its church also; he would burn and fell, and grub
and plough, and then plant the seeds of corn that symbolize the resurrection of life; and the sun should
shine on a wide yellow sea, with waves of hope rippling across it as the ripened ears bowed and rose; and
there should be no trace or stain to mark the submerged slime that had held corruption and death.
Then, if he could do that, he would have nothing to
remind him of all he had gone through in the past.

Nothing to remind him?

It made no difference whether the Abbey towers and
the North Ride chimneys were visible or invisible; no
screen of trees, whether leafless as now or carrying the
full weight of foliage, could really screen them from
him; they were inside him, together with all that they
had once signified, a part of himself. If he did not look
at them with introspective eyes, if he ignored their
existence, if he succeeded in not thinking of them,
there was always something else, inside him or outside
him, to carry his thoughts back into the black bad
time.

At this moment it was the Orphanage, with its wet
red roofs and dripping white verandas. His road took
him close in front of it—a lengthy stretch of building
composed of a central block that contained the hall and
schoolrooms, and two lesser and lower blocks connected by cloisters. He glanced at these blocks—long
and low, only a ground floor and an upper story—and
noticed the veranda and broad balconies. The girls
slept here, as Mavis had told him; the younger in one

block and the older in the other block. The whole institution had an air of old-established order and unceasing care; all the paint was new and clean; the gardens and terraces, with hedges and shrubs that had
grown high and thick, were beautifully kept; not a
weed showed in borders or paths; the copper bell in
the belfry turret was so well polished that it seemed
to shine, even though no glint of sunlight touched it.
As he rode by he heard the sound of children's voices,
and, raising himself in his stirrups, looked over the
clipped yew hedge that guarded the lower garden from
the roadway.   A dozen or fifteen small blue-cloaks
were romping joyously under one of the verandas, and
perhaps twenty of the bigger blue-cloaks were soberly
parading two by two in a cloister.

Nothing carried him back so promptly and surely as
the sight of these blue-cloaked girls, and scarcely a day
ever passed without his seeing them. Two by two
they were incessantly tramping the roads for miles
round. He could not walk, ride, or drive without
meeting them. When he heard their footsteps and
knew that they were coming marching by Vine-Pits,
he turned his back to the office window, or went into
the depths of granary or stable. He had hated that
day when Mavis brought them off the road and into
the heart of his home.

With the sound of their shrill cries and merry
laughter lingering in his ears he rode on.

What a hideous and damnable mockery! This was
the monument of that good kind man, the late Mr.
Barradine. Every red tile, every dab of white paint,
every square inch of clean gravel, gave substance and
solidity to the lasting fame of that dear sweet gentle-

THE DEVIL'S GARDEN

305

man. Visitors to the neighborhood always stopped their carriages or motor cars outside the Orphanage gates, questioned and gaped, sent in their cards, begged for permission to go all over it. Inside, no doubt they admired the rows of clean white beds, some of them quite little cots, others big enough for almost full-grown bouncing lasses; they stood with hushed breath before his portrait in the refectory hall or his bust on the stairs; and perhaps they patted the cheeks of some pretty inmate and asked if, when saying her prayers, she always included the name of the patron saint. On high occasions clergymen and bishops came, there to hiccough and weep over his blessed memory. Great lords and ladies praised him, newspaper writers praised him, ignorant fools in cottages praised him; and to high and low the crowning grace of his glorious charity was the selection of the softer, gentler, and too often downtrodden sex as the object of such tender care. That was what set the sentimental rivers flowing. It proved the innate gentleness and sweetness of him who was now an angel in Heaven. When it came to choosing the guests for the lovely home he had built in his mind, he had said: "I will not fill it with a lot of hulking boys. Boys are naturally rough and coarse animals, and can generally fight their way out on top, no matter how stiff the struggle. Give me so many graceful delicate girls; pretty helpless things, dainty little innocent fascinating creatures; not necessarily fatherless girls, but unprotected girls— girls that grievously need protection."

And Dale thought how the man, when he was alive, dealt with any innocent unprotected girl who chanced to fall into his power. In imagination he saw him taking care of Mavis, when she was young and tender, and scarcely knew right from wrong. In imagination he saw it all again—the pattings and pawings, the scheming and devising, the luring and ensnaring—Barradine and Mavis—the man of many years and the girl of few years, the serpent and the dove, the destroyer and the destroyed. Those torturing mental pictures glowed and took form, and were as vivid now as when, in the hour of his grief and despair, he first made them and saw them.

This departed saint, whose memory had become as a fragrance of myrrh, whose name sounded like the clinking of an incense-pot swung by devout hands, whose monument stood firm as a temple built upon the rock, was simply a dirty old beast for whom no excuse could be possible. What worse crime can there be than that of befouling youth? Who is a worse enemy to the commonweal than he who snatches and steals for his transient gratification treasures that are accumulating to make some honest man's life-long joy? Such wanton abuse of society's law and nature's plan is the unpardonable sin; it is sin as monstrous as the enormities that brought down fire upon the dwellers in the cities of the plain.

To Dale the idea of an offense so gross that its perpetrator deserved neither pity nor mercy was if anything stronger now than when it had first entered and filled his mind.

Yet it seemed to him that now, after all the years that had gone by, he could for the first time perfectly understand the dark and shameful tangle of emotions through which the sinner moved onward to his sin. It seemed that with luminous clearness he could look right into the corrupt heart of the dead man. He could understand all, though he could forgive nothing. He could measure the force of every thought and sensation that had pushed the dead man on and on.

After middle-age the blood grows stagnant, habit dulls the edge of appetite, a weariness of the mind and of the body makes one cease to taste well-used delights; a strong new stimulus is required to revive the emotional life that is sinking to decay. Such a stimulus must not only be strong and new, it must be light, delicate, altogether strange. The effect it produces is due to charm and spell as much as to substance and form.

To people who are elderly, youth itself, merely because it is youth, exercises a tremendous fascination. It sheds an atmosphere that is pleasant to breathe. It seems like a fountain of life in which, if we might bathe, we should take some rejuvenating virtue as well as a soothing bliss. There is a common saying that it makes one feel young just to consort with young people.

Then imagine the selfish unprincipled wretch who at the same time feels the new stimulus, experiences the mysterious fascination, and craves for the revivifying delight. Putting himself in the sinner's place, Dale could realize the pressure that drove him to his sin. He could estimate the fearful temptation offered by the mere presence of the fresh young innocent creature that one has begun to think about in this improper manner. She comes and she goes before one's eyes, piercing them with her beauty; she fills one with desire as wine fills a cup; she absorbs one, whether she knows it or not, dominates, overwhelms, makes one her sick and fainting slave. And suppose that while one becomes her slave one remains her master. To what a gigantic growth the temptation must rush up each time that one thinks she is utterly in one's power! How irresistible it must seem if she herself does not aid one to resist it, if through her ignorance or childish faith she invites the disaster one is struggling to avoid, if instead of flying from her danger she draws nearer and nearer to it.

But to yield to such temptation, however tremendous it may be, is abominable, disgusting, and inexpressibly base. No explanation can palliate or apology prevail—the crime remains the same crime, and he who commits it is not fit to live with decent upright men. That was what Dale had felt fifteen years ago, and he felt it with increased conviction now because of the religious faith that had become his guide and comfort. To a believing Baptist there is a peculiar sacredness, in unsullied innocence.

Two hours afterward, when he had transacted his business and drew near to home, he was still thinking of Mr. Barradine and the Orphanage for unguarded innocent girls. He shook himself in the saddle, squared his shoulders, and held up his head as he rode into the yard.

"Here, take my horse," he said sternly, as he swung his foot out of the stirrup.

Then, at the sound of a voice behind him, he felt a little shiver run down his spine, like the cold touch of superstitious fear.

It was only Norah calling to him. She had come out into the rain to tell him that Mavis Dale had gone to Rodchurch and could not be back to tea.

XXVII

A LASSITUDE descended upon him. Things that had always seemed easy began to seem difficult; little bits of extra work that used to be full of pleasure now brought a fatigue that he felt he must evade; interests that he had allowed to widen without limit all at once contracted and shrank to nothing.

He surprised Mavis by telling her that he had resigned his membership of the District Council. During the last winter he had retired from the fire brigade, and Mavis thoroughly approved of this retirement; but she thought it rather a pity that he should cease to be a councilor. She had always liked the sound of his official designation. Councilor Dale sounded so very grand.

The fire brigade had proved a disappointment to him. Since its enrollment he and his men had often been useful at minor conflagrations, of ricks, cottage thatch, and kitchen flues; but they had never been given a chance of really distinguishing themselves. They had saved no lives, nor met with any perilous risks. However, the captain's retirement was made the occasion of showing the regard and respect in which Mr. Dale was held by the whole neighborhood. Secretly subscriptions had been collected for the purpose of giving Mr. Dale a testimonial, and at a very large meeting in the Rodchurch Schoolroom it was presented by one of the most important local gentle-

309

men. "Mr. Dale," said Sir Reginald, "our worthy vicar has mentioned the fact that I have come here to-night at some slight personal inconvenience; but I can assure you that if the inconvenience had been very much greater I should have come all the same." (Considerable cheering.) "And in handing you this inscribed watch and accompanying chain, I desire to assure you on behalf of all here "—and so on. Dale, for his part, said that "had he guessed this testimonial was on foot, he might have been tempted to burk it, because he could not have conscientiously countenanced it. But now accepting it, although he did not desire it, he felt quite overcome by it. Nevertheless he would ever value it." (Loud and prolonged cheers.) The record of all these proceedings, faithfully set forth in the *Rodhaven District Courier*, formed the proudest and finest snippet in Mavis' bulging scrap album; and brought moisture to her eyes each time that she examined it anew.

"I was never more pleased," she said, "than when I knew you wouldn't ever have to wear your fire helmet again; but now I'm wondering if you won't *miss* the Council."

"No, Mav, I shan't miss it."

"One thing I'm sure of—they'll miss *you*."

"They'll get on very well without me, my dear." And then he told her that he was not quite the man he had been. "I'm not so greedy nowadays for every opportunity of spouting out my opinions; and I've come to think one's private work is enough, without putting public work on top of it. You'll understand, I don't mean that I want to fold my hands and sit quiet for the rest of my days. But I do seem to feel the need of taking things a little lighter than I used to do."

This explanation was more than sufficient for Mavis; she sympathetically praised him for his wisdom in dropping the silly old useless Council.

But it was later this evening, or perhaps one evening a little afterward, when something he said set her thoughts moving so fast that they rushed on from sympathy to apprehensive anxiety.

He spoke with unusual kindness about her family, and asked if she had suffered any real discomfort because of his having forbidden intercourse with all the Petherick relations. She said "No." Then he said he had been actuated by the best intentions; and he further added that all his experience of the world led him to believe that one got on a great deal better by one's self than if chocked up with uncles and cousins and aunts. "So I should hope, Mav, that you'd never now feel the wish to mend what I took the decision of breaking. I mean, especially as your people have mostly scattered and gone from these parts, that you'd never, however you were situated, wish to hunt them all out and bring them back to your doors again." Mavis dutifully and honestly said that her own experience had led her to similar conclusions. She thought that relatives were often more trouble than they were worth, and she promised never to attempt a regathering of the scattered Petherick clan.

"You know," he said, "if anything happened to me, you'd be all right. I have made my will long ago. There's a copy of it in there," and he pointed to the lower part of the bureau; "while th' instrument itself lies snug in Mr. Cleaver's safe, over at Manninglea."

"Oh, for goodness' sake, don't speak of it. I can't bear even to hear the word." And then, taking alarm, she said he must be feeling really ill, or such things as wills would never have come into his head. "Tell me the truth, dear. Tell me what you do feel—truly." And she asked him all sorts of questions about his health, begging him to consult a doctor without a day's delay.

"Only a bit tired, Mav—and that's what I never used to feel."

"No, you never did. And I don't at all understand it."

"It's quite natural, my dear."

"Not natural to you."

Then he took her hand, pressed it affectionately, and laughed in his old jolly way. "My dear, it's nothing —just an excuse for slacking off now and then. Remember, Mav, I am not a chicken. I shall be fifty before th' end of this year."

He convinced her that there was no cause for her anxiety; and only too happy not to have to be anxious, she thought no more of this strange thing that her untiring Will now sometimes knew what tiredness meant.

But his lassitude increased. He uttered no further hints about it to anybody; he endeavored to conceal it; he refused to admit its extent even to himself. On certain days to think made him weary, to be active and bustling was an impossibility. Instinct seemed to whisper that he was passing through still another phase, that presently he would be all right again—just as vigorous and energetic as in the past; and that meanwhile he should not flog and spur himself, but just rest patiently until all his force returned to him.

Since to do anything was a severe effort, he had better do nothing. He ceased to bother about Billy's schooling. He postponed making his harvest arrangements; he forgot to answer a letter asking for an estimate, and one Thursday he omitted to wind the clocks. He tried to let his beard grow, in order to escape the trouble of shaving. It grew during three days; but the effect was so disfiguring—a stiff stubble of gray, hiding his fine strong chin, and spreading high on his bronzed cheeks—that Norah and Mavis implored him to desist. Even Ethel the housemaid ventured to say how very glad she felt when he shaved again.

The month of May was hot and enervating; the month of June was wet and depressing. Day after day the rain beat threateningly against the windows, and night after night it dripped with a melancholy patter from the eaves. On three successive Sundays Dale considered the rain an adequate excuse for not going to chapel. He and Norah had a very short informal service within sound and within smell of the roast beef that was being cooked close by in the kitchen, and afterward he meditatively read the Bible to himself while Norah laid the cloth for dinner.

He had said that he did not want to fold his hands and sit quiet for the remainder of his existence; but that was precisely what he desired to do for the moment. He allowed Norah to relieve him of more and more of his office duties, and he idly watched her as she stood bending her neck over the tall desk or sat stooping her back and squaring her elbows at the writing-table. And still sitting himself, he would maintain long desultory conversations with her about nothing in particular when, having completed the tasks that he had entrusted to her, she moved here and there about the office tidying up for the night.

Thus on an evening toward the end of June he talked to her about love and the married state. It had been raining all day long, and though no rain fell at the moment, one felt that more was coming. The air was saturated with moisture; heavy odors of sodden vegetation crept through the open window; and one saw a mist like steam beginning to rise from the fields beyond the roadway. Mr. Furnival, the new pastor, had just passed by; and it was his appearance that started the conversation.

"He is a conscientious talented young man," said Dale; "and with experience he will ripen. At present he seems to me deficient in sympathy."

"Yes, so he does," said Norah, as she opened the desk drawer.

"He hasn't the knack of putting himself in the place of other people. There's something cold and cheerless in his preaching—I don't say as if he didn't feel it all himself, but as if he hadn't yet caught the knack of imparting his feelings to others."

"No more he has," said Norah, putting away her papers.

"Between you and me and the post," said Dale, "I don't like him."

"No more do I."

"What! Don't you like Mr. Furnival either?"

Norah shook her head and said "No" emphatically.

"But he is handsome, Norah. I call him undoubtedly a handsome man. And they tell me that the girls are falling in love with him."

Norah laughed, and said that, if Mr. Dale had been correctly informed, she was sorry for the taste of the girls.

"Then you don't admire his looks, Norah?"

"No."

"It rather surprises me, because I should have thought he was just the sort of person to attract and fascinate the other sex—a bachelor too, without ties, able to take advantage of any success in that line that came his way. I mean, of course, by offering marriage to the party who fancied him."

Norah said again that she thought nothing of Mr. Furnival's alleged handsomeness. She considered him a namby-pamby.

"You are young still. Perhaps I oughtn't to talk like this—putting nonsense in your head. But it'll come there sure enough of its own accord. Your turn will come. You'll fall in love one day, Norah."

Norah, putting the big account-books back on the shelf over the desk, did not answer.

"You've never fallen in love yet, have you?"

Norah would not answer.

"Ah, well." Dale got up from his chair, and stretched himself. "But you'll have to marry some day, you know."

"Oh, no, I shan't."

"Oh, yes, my dear, you will. That's a thing there's no harm for girls to think of, because it's what they've got to prepare themselves for." And Dale delivered a serious little homily on the duties and pleasures of wedlock, and concluded by telling Norah that when she had chosen an honest proper sort of young fellow, neither himself nor Mrs. Dale would stand in the way of her future happiness. "Yes, my dear, you'll leave us then; and we shall miss you greatly—both of us will miss you very greatly, but we shan't either of us consider that. And you mustn't consider it yourself. It's nature—quite proper and correct that under those circumstances you should leave us."

"Never," said Norah. "Never—unless you send me away;" and stooping her head on her arms, she began to cry.

"Oh, my dear, don't cry," said Dale bruskly. "What in the name of reason is there to cry about?"

"Then say you won't send me away," sobbed Norah. "Promise me you won't do that."

"Of course I won't," said Dale, in the same brusk tone. "That is, unless I'm morally certain that——"

"No, no—never."

"Oh, don't be silly. Dry your eyes, and be sensible;" and Dale, plunging his hands in his pockets, hurried out of the office.

He walked as far as the Baptist Chapel, and straight back again; and before he got home he made a solemn resolution to rouse himself from the idle lethargic state into which he felt himself slipping deeper and deeper. Thinking about business and other matters, he decided now that the odd weariness which he had been experiencing must be struggled with, and not submitted to. There was no sense in calmly accepting such a mental and bodily condition. It might be different if there was anything organically wrong with him; but he was really as strong and fit as ever—only a bit tired; but he thought with scorn of the folly of allowing dark days and foul weather to influence one's spirits or one's capacity for effort. That sort of rubbish is well enough for rich old maids who go about the world with a maid, a hot-water bottle, and a poll parrot; but it is degrading and undignified in a successful business man who has a wife and two children to work for, whether the sun shines or the sky is overcast.

At supper he told Mavis that he was going to make a long round of it next day, starting early, and riding far to pay several calls that were overdue. He added that he would not require Norah's assistance in the office, either to-morrow or for some time to come.

"I fear me," he said, "that I've been selfish, and abused the privilege of taking her away to act as secretary, and thereby thrown more on you."

"Not a bit," said Mavis. "Take her just as long as she makes herself useful."

"She has done fine," said Dale, "and lifted a lot off my shoulders. But now I feel I'm all clear, and I restore her to her proper place and duties."

Mavis, if aware of the fact, would have thought it curious that Dale had spoken to Norah of falling in love, because she herself was at this time worried by thoughts of such possibilities with regard to the girl. She noticed various changes in Norah's manner and deportment. Norah, although Dale said she worked well enough for him in the office, showed a perceptible slackness at her household tasks. She seemed to have lost interest, especially in all kitchen work; she was often careless in dusting and cleaning the parlor, and had done one or two very clumsy things—such as breaking tea-cups when washing up—as if her wits had gone wool-gathering instead of being concentrated on the job in hand. Her temper, too, was not so even and agreeable as it ought to have been. She was distinctly irritable once or twice to the children, when they were trying to play with her as of old, and not, as she declared, wilfully teasing her. And once or twice when she was reproved, there had come some nasty little flashes of rebellion.

Mavis, seeking any reason for this slight deterioration of conduct and steadiness, wondered if Norah by chance had a little secret love affair up her sleeve. That would account for everything. But if so, who could it be who was upsetting her? Girls, even at what matrons call the silly age, can not give scope to their silliness without opportunities; and there were no visitors to the house, and certainly none of the men in the yard, who could conceivably be carrying on with her.

Then the suspicions of Mavis were aroused by discovering that Norah was at her old tricks again. If you sent her as messenger of charity to one of the cottages, and more still if you gave her an hour or two for herself, she went stealing off into the forbidden woods. She had been seen doing it twice, and, as Mavis suspected, had done it often without being seen. She knew that she wasn't allowed to do it. There was the plain house-rule that neither she nor Ethel were ever to leave the roads when they were out alone. Yet she broke the rule; and Mavis now suspected that she did not break this rule in order to pick wild flowers and look at green leaves but to meet a sweetheart.

Mavis, thinking about it, was at once angry and apprehensive. A fine thing for all of them, if the little fool came to trouble and disgrace that way. She would not immediately bother Dale about it; but she promptly tackled Norah, roundly accused her of improper behavior, expressed a firm conviction that she was playing the fool with some young man, and threatened to lay the whole matter before the master.

"D'you understand, Norah? We won't put up with it—not for a moment. We're not going to let you make yourself the talk of the place and bring us to shame into the bargain."

Norah, alternately flushing and turning pale, defended herself with vigor. She was indignant not with the threats, but with the suspicion. She swore that she had never for one instant thought of a young man, much less spoken to or made appointments with a young man; and that she had broken the house-rule simply because she found it almost impossible to keep it. She had always loved wandering about under the trees: she used to go there all alone as a baby, and she thought it unreasonable that she might not go there alone as a grown-up person.

Norah's indignant tone suggested complete innocence, and Mavis felt relieved in mind, but yet not quite sure whether the girl was really telling the truth.

She indirectly returned to the charge on the following Sunday, when Norah was about to start for her afternoon out.

"Norah, I want a word with you."

The girl came back along the flagged path to the kitchen door.

"It's just this, Norah. You'll please to remember what I've told you, and act accordingly."

Norah turned her head and answered over her shoulder, rather sullenly, as Mavis thought.

"All right. I remember."

"Don't answer me like that," said Mavis sharply. "And please to remember your manners, and look at people when you speak to them."

"All right," said Norah again, and, as Mavis judged, very sullenly this time.

"Look you here, young lady," she said, with increasing warmth. "I'm not going to stand any of your nonsense—and of that I give you fair warning. Now you just answer me in a seemly manner and tell me exactly where you are going this afternoon, or I'll send you straight back into the house to take off your finery and not go out at all."

Dale, close by in the little sitting-room, heard his wife's voice raised thus angrily, closed the book that was lying open on his knees, and came to the window. "What's wrong, Mav?"

"It's Norah offering me her sauce, and I won't put up with it."

Dale, with the book in his hand, came out through the kitchen, and stood by Mavis on the stone flags.

"Norah," he said seriously, "you must always be good, and do whatever Mrs. Dale tells you."

"Yes, but that's just what she doesn't do;" and Mavis explained that, in spite of repeated orders, Norah had several times gone mooning off into the woods all by herself. "So now I'm reminding her, and asking where she means to go this afternoon."

Norah, with her eyes on the flags, said that she would go to Rodchurch.

"Very good," said Mavis. "Then now you've answered, you may go."

When Norah had disappeared round the corner of

the house, Mavis talked to her husband apologetically
and confidentially.

"Will, dear, I'm sorry I disturbed you when you
were reading;" and glancing at the book in his hand,
she felt ashamed of her recent warmth. "I couldn't
help blowing her up, and I'll tell you why." Then
she spoke of the necessity of keeping a sharp eye and
a firm hand on a girl of Norah's age and attractions;
and she further mentioned her suspicion, now almost
entirely allayed, of some secret carryings-on.

"Oh, I don't think there's anything of that sort,"
said Dale. "No, I may say I'm morally sure Norah
isn't deceiving you there."

"I'm glad you think so. Yes, it's what I think myself. I should have bowled her out if there'd been
anything going on. But, Will, there's other dangers
for her—worse dangers."

"What dangers, Mavis?"

"Well, all the lads naturally are looking at her.
Norah has come on faster than you may have noticed.
I don't want her to mix herself up with any of those
louts that hang about the Cross Roads."

"No."

"And she'll come across them for certain if she gets
trapesing through the trees like she does. There's her
brothers would bring them together. Besides, it isn't
safe—at her age. You know yourself what's always
been said of it."

"Quite so," said Dale. "You are wise, Mavis—very
wise to be watchful and careful."

Then he returned to the sitting-room, settled himself again in the porter's chair, and reopened his book
at the place where he had been interrupted.

It was the New Testament; and just now, while reading the twenty-first chapter of Saint Matthew, he had enjoyed a clear vision of Christ's entry into Jerusalem. Making his picture from materials supplied by an article in the *People's Encyclopedia,* he seemed to be able to see the ancient city and its exotic life as the Redeemer and the disciples must have seen it on that memorable day. Here were the narrow streets and the crowded market-places; the towers and domes; the strangely garbed traders, laden camels, gorgeous Roman soldiers, brown-faced priests, black-bodied slaves; sunlit hills high above one, distant faintly blue mountains far ahead of one—a thronged labyrinth of shadow and light, of noise and confusion, of pomp and squalor.

But the picture was gone, the dream was broken, the hope was darkened. He tried to bring it all back again, and failed utterly. He could not think of Christ riding into Jerusalem; he could only think of Norah walking along the road to Rodchurch.

XXVIII

EXTREME heat came that year with the opening
of July, and the atmosphere at night seemed as
oppressive as in the day.

After an unusually wet June the foliage was rich and
dense, but flowers were few and poor—except the
roses, which had prospered greatly. Throughout the
daylight hours trees close at hand looked solid, as if
composed of some unbending green material; while
those a little way off were rather firm, presenting the
appearance of trees during heavy rain. Indeed that was
the appearance of the whole scene—a country-side being drenched and rendered vague by a heavy down-
pour; but it was sheer heat that was descending, with
never an atom of moisture in it.

The shadows beneath the trees were absolutely
black, impenetrable; a dark cave under each ring of
leaves. Then toward nightfall this shadow grew lighter and lighter, until it was a transparent grayness into
which one could see quite clearly. Thus a girl and a
man sitting under a hedgerow elm five or six hundred
yards away were distinct objects, although perhaps
themselves unaware that they had gradually lost their
shelter and become conspicuous.

Dale, crossing his fields and staring at these two
figures, for a moment fancied that one of them was
Norah. Yet that would have been an impossibility,
because he had just left her behind him at the house;

323

and she could not have swum round in a great half-circle, through the drowsy air, to confront him at a distant point where he did not expect to see her. But the heat made one stupid and slow-witted. This man and woman were farmer Creech's people, and they had come sauntering along the edge of uncut grass to make lazy love to each other. Dale turned aside to avoid disturbing them.

As he returned toward the house presently, he thought of Norah's unwonted pallor. Poor child, the heat seemed to be trying her more than anybody. And he thought of how wan and limp and sad she looked early this morning, when he had again sent her out of his office and flatly refused to let her do any more writing or tidying for him. Even her red lips had gone pale; she dropped her head; her white eyelids and black lashes fluttered as she looked up at him piteously, seeming to ask: "What have I done that you treat me like this, oh, my cruel master?" He had driven his hands deep into his pockets, had shrugged his shoulders, and spoken almost roughly—telling her to go about her business, and not bother. He thought if he gave her time to do it, she might cry again; and he did not want to see any more of her tears.

But off and on throughout the day he had watched her when she did not in the least know that she was being observed. Just after breakfast he had watched her as she scrubbed the kitchen floor, and had noticed the pretty lines of her figure in these sprawling attitudes—her ankles, stockings, and the upturned soles of her buckle-shoes.

He was watching her when she came up from the dairy with the pail that held Mavis' afternoon supply

of milk, and he noticed her stretched arm, bare to the
elbow, and the other arm balancing, the tilted body
helping also to maintain equilibrium. Almost more
than she could manage—why didn't that broad-backed
thick-legged lump of a dairy-maid carry the house-
pail? He would have liked to go out and carry the
pail himself; but that was one of the many things
which he must carefully refrain from doing.

And all day long, though he saw her so often, he
never once heard her sing. She made no song over
her work, as used to be her habit. He wondered if
Mavis was not working her too hard in this terribly
exhausting weather. He wondered also if he would
ever be able to say quite naturally what he had for so
long wished to say and felt he ought to say—that
Norah must be given a holiday, that she must be sent
somewhere at a considerable distance and stay there
in charge of kind and respectable people for an indefinite period. Mavis might consider the suggestion
so strange; and it might be impossible to explain that,
strange as it seemed, it was nevertheless full of wisdom—a suggestion that should be acted upon without
an instant's delay.

The supper table had been brought out into the open
air, and it stood upon the flagged path, where they had
spread their hospitable feast for the higgler's wedding.
Norah was coming in and out of the kitchen, and Dale
sat watching her as she arranged knives, forks, and
glasses. Both the children were to be of the party;
and they might stay up as late as they pleased, because
as it was too hot to sleep in their beds, it did not matter how long the young people remained out of them.
They were now roaming about the orchard with Mavis,

hunting for a coolness that did not exist anywhere except in one's memory, and their voices sounded at intervals languidly.

More and more color was now perceptible; distances were extending; lines of meager flowers, crimson and blue as well as white, showed in a border of the kitchen garden; and the sky, seeming to lift and brighten, was a faint orange above the horizon and a most delicate rose tint toward the zenith—so that till half-past eight, or later, one had the illusion that the night was going to be more brightly lighted than the day.

Nobody had much appetite for supper, but they all sat a long while at the table, glad to rest if they could not eat, hoping that when they moved from their chairs they would find the temperature lower within the house walls than outside them. Mavis gave little op-pressed sighs as she fanned her jolly round face and broad matronly chest with a copy of the *Courier*. Ethel, who to-night seemed an extraordinarily cumbrous awkward creature, flumped the dishes down on the table and shuffled away on her big flat feet. Norah glided to and fro, now here, now there, pouring out milk and water for the children, and ducking prettily when a bat came close to her white face and black hair.

" What, Norah," said Mavis, laughing, " you a coun-try girl, and afraid of a flitter-mouse ! "

" Yes," said Billy, " she's afraid of the flitty-mouse. Isn't she a coward? You are a coward, Norah."   ,

And then the laugh was turned against Billy ; for the bat passing again and lower than before, Billy himself ducked and crouched automatically.

" Who's the coward now, young sir ? "

" I don't mind anything that has wings," said Rachel.

"It's what goes creeping and crawling that I'm afraid of."

"I don't mind ear-wigs," said Billy defiantly.

And Dale, while he talked without interest and ate without appetite, watched Norah. She had changed her gown an hour ago, and obviously when changing had discarded the burden of under-petticoats; this other gown hung close and yet limp about her limbs, modeling itself to each slim length and shapely curve; and he thought it made her look like the statue of a Grecian hand-maiden—such as he had seen many years before in illustrations of learned books. When she stood near him, he noticed nothing but the blackness of her hair or the whiteness of her cheeks; and then he thought she looked somehow wild and fantastic, like a person that one can see only in dreams. But whether she was near him or at a little distance, so long as she remained in sight, he was unintermittently conscious that the essential charm that she shed forth could be traced directly to her youth.

"Good night, daddy."

"Good night, Rachel."

His daughter had kissed him, and she stood between his knees while he patted her and caressed her. She too was young and fresh and sweet-smelling; and yet the touch of her purified one. So long as he was holding her, it seemed to him that a father's love is so great and so pure that there can not be any other love in the world.

But a minute afterward, when his own girl had gone and the other girl was again before his eyes, all the impure unworthy unpermissible desires came rushing back upon him.

They lighted lamps in the kitchen presently, and he sat staring at the open doorway, alone now, after the table had been cleared. The doorway seemed like an empty picture-frame. But each time that Norah came and stood there looking out for a moment, the picture was in its frame. With the light behind her, she was just a thin black figure; and he thought how slight, how weak and small a thing to possess such tremendous, almost irresistible power over him.

Next evening, between tea-time and supper-time, Norah absented herself without leave. Mavis did not miss her at first. Then she thought that very probably the girl was wandering about with the children, or gossiping with the maid at the dairy; but then old Mrs. Goudie, who had come to pay a call at the back door, said she had met Norah and had a chat with her " up th' road." On being further examined, Mrs. Goudie said that Norah, after bidding her good night, had got over the stile at the second footpath into Hadleigh Wood.

Mavis at once became angry and suspicious again, and she went to her husband to report this act of rebellion. The office was empty, but she found him at the yard. He was in his shirt-sleeves, sitting on a corn-bin, and he seemed to be greatly troubled by what she told him that she wished him to do.

She asked him to go into the wood himself and spy out Norah quietly, and see if she was really alone there.

" Oh, I don't much like this job, Mav. Besides, it's to hunt for a needle in a bundle of hay. How do I know which way the lass has gone? "

" I'm telling you she went in at the second path. She

won't have gone far. Probably you'll come upon her this side of the rides—along by the stream, very likely."

But Dale still showed reluctance to undertake the detective mission.

"Then *I* must go," said Mavis. "I can't put up with this sort of thing, and I mean to stop it. She must be made to understand once for all——"

"Very well," said Dale; and he got off the corn-bin and picked up his jacket.

"She'll pay more heed to you than she would to me. But, one word, Will. If you catch her with a young man don't go and lose your temper with *him*. Don't bother about him. Just bring the young minx straight home."

"An' suppose there's no young man."

"Bring her back just the same, and lecture her all the way on her disobedience—and the trouble and annoyance she is giving us. Tell her we're not going to stand any more of it."

"Very well."

He walked along the road at a fairly brisk pace until he came to the second stile, and then he stood hesitatingly. The firs grew thick here, and the shadows that they cast were dark and opaque, encroaching on the pathway, making it a narrow strip of dim light that would lead one into the mysterious and gloomy depths of the wood.

He crossed the stile, and went along the path very slowly, pausing now and then to listen. There was not a sound; the whole wood was as silent as the grave.

Presently the fir-trees on each side of him opened out a little, and here and there beeches and ashes appeared; then the path passed through a glade, the shadows receded, and he had a sensation of being more free and able to breathe better. If he kept on by the path he would soon come to the main ride, that long widely cut avenue which goes close to Kibworth Rocks and gives access to the other straight cuts leading to the Abbey park. He left the path and struck across through the trees, making a line that would take him soon to the wildest part of the ancient Chase, and that, if he pursued it far enough, would eventually bring him out on the big ride near the rocks.

The dark stiff firs gave place to solemnly magnificent beeches; glade succeeded glade; thickets of holly and hawthorn dense as a savage jungle tried to baffle one's approach to lawnlike spaces where the grass grew finely as in a garden, and the white stems of the high trees looked like pillars of a splendid church; the stream ran silently and secretly, not flashing when it swept out under the sky, or murmuring when it slid down tiny cascades beneath the branches.

Dale was following the stream, whether it showed itself or hid itself, and could have found his way blindfold. He knew the wood by night as well as he knew it by day.

He stopped on the edge of the biggest of all the glades, looked about him cautiously, advanced slowly, and stopped again to wipe the perspiration from his forehead. He was very near to the main ride now; straight ahead of him, say two hundred yards away, on the other side of the invisible ride lay the invisible rocks.

One of the beech-trees had fallen, and been left as it fell two months ago. Most of its tender young foliage had shriveled and died, but on branches near its upturned roots a few leaves were bright and green, still drawing life from the ruined trunk. Dale stood by the fallen tree, looking out across the glade. It was all silent and beautiful, with that curious effect of increasing light which made the distances clearer every moment, gave more color to the earth and a more tender glow to the sky.

Then he saw her, a long way off, coming from the direction of the ride through the trees; and he felt the pressure of blood pumping into his head, the weight on his lungs, the laboring pain of his heart, that a man might feel just before he sinks to the ground in an apoplectic fit.

She was all alone, sauntering toward him with her hands full of flowers. She had no hat, and she was wearing the same loose frock that she wore last night.

With the gesture that had become habitual to him, Dale put his hands in his pockets—those wicked hands that no prison could much longer hold, that would defy control, that seemed now to be stretched forth across all the intervening space to touch the face and limbs they hungered for. He moved away from the shadow by the fallen tree, stepped out into the open, went slowly to meet her, and his longing was intolerably acute. He was sick and mad with longing: he wanted her as a man dying of thirst wants the water that will save his life.

"Oh, Mr. Dale, how you hev made me jump!"

At sight of him she dropped the flowers and raised one of her hands to press it against her breast. She had been so startled that she still breathed fast, almost pantingly; but her lips were smiling, and her eyes shone with pleasure.

"Now look here, Norah; this won't do—no, really this won't do." He had taken his hands out of his pockets and clasped them behind his back. He too was breathing fast, though he spoke deliberately and rather thickly. "No, all this sort of thing won't do; it can't be allowed;" and he laid his right hand on her shoulder.

"I'm sorry," she said, watching his face intently.

"You mustn't go and moon about by yourself, like this. You know you mustn't, don't you?"

"Yes, I know. But I couldn't stay indoors."

He had slid his hand downward, and was holding her arm above the elbow. "It is very disobedient. Often and often Mrs. Dale has told you that you mustn't come here."

"I know," she said humbly.

"So now, you see, I am sent to fetch you—and to tell you that you mustn't do it." He was struggling hard to speak in his ordinary tone of voice, but failing. And his imitation of his usual fatherly manner, as he held her arm and led her along, was clumsy and laborious. He stopped moving when they reached the prostrate beech-tree, but continued to talk to her, saying the same things again and again. "Norah, it can not be allowed. You mustn't be disobedient. We can't allow it."

They lingered by the tree, she looking at him all the time, and he scarcely ever looking at her, but glancing about him furtively. Then they sat down side by side on one of the great branches, and as if unconsciously he began to caress her.

"Is Mrs. Dale very angry with me?"

"Yes, Norah, she is angry. You can't be surprised at that."

"Not so angry that she won't never forgive me?"

"Oh, no, she's not so angry as all that."

"But she isn't fond of me, as she used to be."

"Yes, of course she is, Norah." His arm was round her waist, and he lifted her upon his lap, and held her there. "We are both very fond of you."

"*You* are," she whispered. "I know that. . . . . I should die if you ever turned so as not to care for me;" and she nestled against him.

"Norah."

With a last assumption of the fatherly manner he stooped and kissed her forehead. Then she raised her lips to his, and they kissed slowly.

"Norah," he muttered. "Oh, Norah."

He felt as though almost swooning from delight. It was a rapture that he had never known—a voluptuous joy that yet brought with it complete appeasement to nerves and pulses.

"Norah, Norah;" and he continued to kiss her lips and mutter her name.

All thought had gone. It was as though all that was trouble and pain inside him had melted into sweet streams of delight—streams of fire; but a magical flame that soothes and restores, instead of burning and destroying. He went on fondling her, glorying in her freshness, her immature grace, her youthful beauty. And she was silent and passive, yielding to his gentle movements, pressing close if he held her to him, relaxing the pressure and becoming limp if he wished to see her face and held her from him, making him under-

stand by messages through every sense channel that
she was his absolutely.

Then after a while she began to talk in the pretty
birdlike whisper that enchanted and enthralled him.

"Why didn't she want me to come here—really?"

"She—she thought you came to meet some lad."

"Oh, no;" and she gave a little laugh, and pressed
against him. "It's the truth, what I've always answered to her. I came because I couldn't help it.
Shall I tell you all my secrets—secrets I've never told
any one?"

"Yes."

"Ever since I was a child—quite small—I hev always thought something wondersome would happen
to me in Hadleigh Wood."

"Why should you think that?"

He had sat up stiffly, and while she clung whispering at his breast he looked out over her head, glancing
his eyes in all directions. Straight in front of him
across the glade, the great beeches were gray and
ghostly, and beyond them in the strip that concealed
the ride it seemed that the shadows had suddenly
thickened and blackened.

"I'll tell you. But *you* tell me something first.
Does Mrs. Dale think this place is haunted?"

He changed his attitude abruptly, put his hands on
her shoulders and held her away from him, so that
he could see her face.

"What was it you asked me?"

"Does she fancy the wood is haunted?"

"No, why?"

"I believe she does."

"Rubbish. Why should she?"

"They used to say it was. Granny used to say so.
She gave me some dreadful whippings for coming here.
Poor Granny was just like Mrs. Dale about it—always
saying it wasn't right for me to come here."

Dale had settled the girl on his knees so that she sat
now without any support from him. His hands had
dropped to the rough surface of the tree; and he spoke
in his ordinary voice.

"Look here, Norah, never mind for a moment what
your Granny said. Tell me what it was that my wife
said."

"When do you mean? Last time she was angry?"

"I mean, whatever she said—and whenever she said
it—about ghosts or hauntings."

"Oh, a long time ago. It was to Mrs. Goudie."

"I expect you misunderstood her. But I'd like to
know what first put such nonsense into your head—
that Mrs. Dale thought the wood was haunted. Can't
you remember exactly what she did say?"

"She said something about the gentleman's being
killed here, and she wondered at the people coming a
Sundays like they used to."

"Was that all?"

"No, she said something about it would serve them
right for their pains if they saw the gentleman's ghost."

Dale grunted. "That was just her joke. There are
no such things as ghosts."

"Aren't there?" Norah laughed softly and happily,
and snuggled down again with her face against his
jacket. "*You* aren't a ghost—though you made me
jump, yes, you did. But I wasn't afraid of you."

"Hush," he muttered. "Norah, don't go on—
don't." His hands were still on the tree, rigidly fixed

there, and he sat bolt upright, staring out over her head.

"Why not? You said I might tell my secrets. I wasn't afraid. I thought 'Oh, aren't I glad I done what Mrs. Dale told me not to—and come into my wondersome, wondersome wood, and drawn *you* after me!'"

"Norah, stop."

"Why? You're glad too, aren't you? I *know* you are. I knew it when you came walking so tall and so quiet; an' I thought 'This is it—what I always hoped for—wonders to happen to me in Hadleigh Wood.' But I was afraid of the wood once—more afraid than Granny knew. I wouldn't tell her."

"What d'you mean? What wouldn't you tell her?"

"What I'd seen here."

"What had you seen?"

"I kep' it as my great secret—but I'll tell you, because you've found out all my secrets, now, haven't you?"

"Well, let's hear it."

"I saw a man hiding, crawling, ready to spring out on me."

"Oh. When was that?"

"Ages and ages ago, when I was almost a baby."

"Heft yourself, Norah. I want to get up, an' stretch ma legs."

The gentle soothing fire had faded—an invincible coldness crept on slow-moving blood from his heart to his brain. The girl was safe now. He would not injure her to-night. He got up, and stood looking down at her.

"Well," he said quietly, "let's hear some more.
What sort of a man was it?"

"A wild man—with water dripping off him. He
had crept out of the river."

"Do you mean—a sort of ghost or demon?"

"I didn't know."

"Not like an ordinary man—not like any other man
you've ever seen?"

"Oh, no. All wild—fierce and dreadful. Not standing upright—more like an animal in the shape of a
man."

"But surely you told your Granny, or somebody?"

"No. I've never told a soul except you."

"An' you say you were scared, though?"

"Oh, I was, rarely scared."

"Then you must have told your Granny, or one of
'em. You've forgotten, but I expect you told people
at the time."

"I didn't. I didn't dare to at first. I thought he'd
come after me, if I did. I was afraid."

Dale grunted again. "An' d'you mean to say you'd
the grit in you to come back here all the same, after
that?"

"Not for a little while. Then I did. I was all a
twitter, so frightened still, but I was fascinated for to
do it too—just to see."

"But you never saw him again."

"No, and then I began to think it was all a fancy.
D'you think it was a fancy, and not real?"

"My dear girl, no;" and Dale shrugged his shoulders. "You prob'ly saw some poor devil of a tramp
who had slept here, and was getting on the move after

his night's rest." Then he took a step away from the
tree, and spoke curtly. "Come. We must go home."
Norah sprang off the tree, hurried to his side, and,
with her hands linked about his arm, looked up at him
anxiously.

"Yes, but it's all right, isn't it? You're not angry
with me—not turning against me?"

"No, it's all right."

"Then, don't let's go. Let's stay here a little
longer."

"No, we must go—or Mrs. Dale will be coming to
fetch us;" and he began to walk briskly. "And look
here, Norah. I shall inform her I found you here by
yourself, and I have lectured you at full length, and
you've said you'll be good for the future. So don't
answer back if she speaks sharp."

"Oh, I don't mind what she says now;" and Norah
laughed happily as she trotted after him through the
trees.

That evening he sat outside on the bench long after
the supper table had been taken away and the kitchen
door closed. Quite late, when Mavis spoke to him
from an upper window, he said he must have one more
pipe before he turned in.

Norah had been singing in the kitchen while she
washed the plates; then he had heard her humming
softly in the sitting-room; now she had gone up-stairs
and was silent. The thoughts and sensations that had
been suddenly and strangely inhibited a few hours ago
came into play again, warmed his blood once more, re-
possessed his brain. Soon he was impotent to struggle
against them. As he sat huddled and motionless, he
revived each memory and wilfully renewed its delight.

The brick walls, the timber beams, the flooring boards, and plastered partitions could not divide her from him; though hidden at a distance, she shed emanations, fiery atoms, darting sparks, that infallibly reached him: when he closed his eyes in order not to see the empty space before him, she herself was here. He could feel again the light weight of her body upon his knees, her hair brushed against his chin, her face gave itself to his lips.

Then more remote memories came to join the recent memories, deepening the spell that subjugated him. He thought of her crying when he teased her about love and marriage, and when her poor little innocent heart was bursting because of his pretense of not understanding that she craved for no love but his. And he thought of how she had looked in the middle of the night when he covered her with his jacket, and she stood before him trembling and blushing, with her hair all tumbling loose. That had been one of the mental pictures which he could not even make dim, much less obliterate.

He groaned, got up from the bench, and walked very slowly round the kitchen and behind the house. The first breath of air that he had noticed for days was stirring the leaves, and he saw the new moon like a golden sickle poised above the broken summit of a hayrick. It was a serenely beautiful night, with an atmosphere undoubtedly cooler than any they had had of late; he looked at the peaceful fields, and the fruit trees and the barn roof, all so gently, imperceptibly touched by the young and tender moonbeams; and he thought that the thin yellow crescent was being watched by thousands and thousands of eyes, that men were turning their money, and wishing for luck, for fame, or for satisfied love. But he only of all men might not wish for the desire of his heart, and to him only the moon could bring nothing but pain.

He went through the kitchen garden, and stood under an apple tree staring back at the window of her room. And still older memories sprang up and grew strong, so that they might attack and overcome and utterly undo him. The wild bad fancies of his adolescence came thronging upon him. Imagination and fact entangled themselves; the past and the present fused, and became one vast throbbing distress. He thought if he crept beneath the window and called to her, she would answer his call. If he told her to do so, she would come out in her night-dress—she would walk bare-footed through the fields, and plunge with him into the wonderful wood. If he told her to do it, she would go into the stream, and dance and splash—realizing that old dream—the white-bodied nymph of the wood for him to leap at and carry off into the gloom. He wrenched himself round, and made his way rapidly from the garden to the meadow. He could not support his thoughts. The proximity of the girl was driving him mad.

All through the little meadow and again in the wider fields the air had a soft fragrance; the sky was high and quite clear, with a few stars; the whole earth, for as much as he could see of it, seemed to be sleeping in a deep delightful peace. Beyond his fences there were the neighbors' farms, and then there were the heath, the hills; and beyond these, other counties, other countries, the rest of the turning globe, the universe it turned in—and once again he had that feeling of

infinite smallness, the insect unfairly matched against
a solar system, the speck of dust whirled as the biggest
stars are whirled, inexorably.

At the confines of his land he leaned upon a gate,
groaning and praying.

"O Christ Jesus, Redeemer of mankind, why hast
Thou deserted me? O God the Father, Lord and
Judge, why dost Thou torment me so?"

XXIX

VERY early in the morning he told Mavis that he felt sure they ought to send Norah away on a holiday for the good of her health.

"This hot weather has been a severe test for all of us," he said; "and of course what I should consider equally advisable would be to send you and the children along with her, but I suppose——"

"What, me go away just when you're going to cut the grass!"

"Very well," he said, "I won't urge it. But as to Norah, that's a decision I've come to; so please don't question it. She's been working too hard——"

"Did she complain to you yesterday, when you lectured her?"

"No. Not a word. An' she'll prob'ly resist the idea. But she must be overruled, because my mind is made up. So now the only question that remains is— where are you to send her? What about that place for servants resting—at Bournemouth, the place Mrs. Norton collects subscriptions for?"

"Yes, I might ask Mrs. Norton if she could spare us a ticket."

"No, send the girl as a paying guest. I don't grudge any reasonable expense. Or again there's Mrs. Creech's daughter-in-law, over at S'thaampton Water."

"Oh, there's half a dozen people I could think of—"

"All right," he said; "but I want it done now,

342

straight away. And look here, Mav. Take this thing
off my shoulders, and don't let me be bothered. I
shouldn't have decided it, if I didn't know it was right.
I've a long and difficult day before me. You just hop
into the gig, and Tom'll drive you round—to see Mrs.
Norton or anybody else. Only let me hear by dinner-
time that the arrangement is made."

"You shall," said Mavis cheerfully.

"Thank you, Mav. You're always a trump. You
never fail one."

What had seemed an insuperable difficulty was thus
in a moment accomplished. His quietly authoritative
tone had made Mavis accept the thing not only easily
but without a doubt or question, and he thought re-
morsefully that, except for his sneaking, cowardly delay, all this might have occurred a month ago. He felt
a distinct lightening of the trouble as he went back
into his own room, and then the weight of it fell upon
him again. He had succeeded so far as Mavis was
concerned; but how about Norah?

He stood meditating in front of the looking-glass
before he began to shave. When he picked up the
shaving-brush, he noticed that his hand was trembling
—not much, yet quite visibly. It never used to do
that, and he looked at it with disgust. It seemed to
him like an old man's hand.

Then he began to study his face in the glass. No
one would have guessed that this was a man who had
been praying all night. The whole face showed those
signs of fatigue that come after base pleasures, after
riotous waste of energy, after long hours of debauch.
It seemed to him that his gray hair was finer of texture than it ought to be, hanging straight and thin,

with no strength in it; that his eyes were too dim, that
the flesh underneath them had puffed out loosely, and
that his lower lip was drooping slackly—and he shud-
dered in disgust. It seemed to him that his face
changed and grew uglier as he looked at it. It was
becoming like an old man's face he had seen years ago.

In spite of the slight shakiness of his hand he managed to shave himself without a cut, and he was just
about to wash the soap away when he heard a sound
of lamentation on the lower floor. It was Norah
loudly bewailing herself. Mavis had gone down-
stairs and published his sentence of banishment.

Suppose that the girl betrayed their secret. Suppose
that she was even now telling his wife what had happened in the wood. Well, he must go down to them
and flatly deny whatever Norah said. But he tingled
and grew hot with a most miserable shame; his heart
quailed at the mere notion of the sickening, disgraceful
character of such a scene—he, the highly respected Mr.
Dale, the good upright religious man, being accused
by a little servant girl and having to rebut her accusa-
tions in the presence of his wife.

He dipped his head in the basin, and even when under the cold water the tips of his ears seemed as if they
were on fire. He must go down-stairs the moment he
had cooled his face; but he would go as some wretched
schoolboy goes to the headmaster's room when he
guesses that his unforgivable beastliness has been discovered, and that first a thrashing and then expulsion
are awaiting him.

Some of the lying words that he must utter suggested themselves. " Oh, Norah, this is a poor return

you are making for all my kindness. Aren't you
ashamed to stand there and tell such ungrateful false-
hoods. Ma lass, your cheek surprises me. I wonder
you can look me in the face."

But it would be Mavis, and not Norah, who would
look him in the face—and she would read the truth
there. She would see it staring at her in his shifting
eyes, his slack lip, and his weak frown. Her first
glance at him would be loyal and frank, just an eager
flash of love and confidence, seeming to say, " Be
quick, Will, and put your foot on this viper that we've
both of us warmed, and that is trying to bite me; "
then she would turn pale, avert her head, and drop upon
a chair. And for why? Because she had seen the
nauseating truth, and her heart was almost broken.

Then he suddenly understood that there was no real
danger of all this. It was only his own sense of guilt
that unnerved him. Nothing had happened in the
wood. If he behaved quietly and sensibly, he would
be altogether safe, and Mavis would never guess. Truly
all that he had to conceal was that he had been stopped
on the very brink of his sin, that but for a startling interference, an almost miraculous interference, the
wicked thoughts would infallibly have found their outlet in wicked deeds.

If Norah said he took her on his knees and kissed
her, Mavis would think nothing of it—would not even
think it undignified; would merely take as one more
evidence of his kindly nature the fact that, instead of
upbraiding the silly child, he had embraced her. If the
girl howled and said she did not want to go because
she was fond of him, Mavis would think nothing of

that either. Mavis knew it already, and had never thought anything of it.

Therefore if he did not betray himself, the girl could not betray him. All that was required of him was just to maintain an ordinary air of ingenuousness. He had done enough acting in his life to be at home when dissimulating. He must do a little more successful acting now.

After a minute or so he went down-stairs, and was outwardly staid and calm, looking as he had looked on hundreds of mornings: the good kind father of a household, whose only care is the happiness and welfare of those who are dependent on him.

Directly he entered the breakfast-room Norah ran sobbing to him and clung to his hand.

"She is sending me away. Oh, don't let her do it. You promised you wouldn't. Oh, why do you let her do it?"

"This is *my* plan, Norah," he said gently; "not Mrs. Dale's. I wish it—and I ask you not to make a fuss."

"I've told her," said Mavis, "that it's only for her own good; and that she'll be back here in a fortnight or three weeks. But she seems to think we want to be rid of her forever."

"No, no," said Dale. "Nothing of the sort. It's merely for the good of your health—and not in any way as a punishment for your having been rather disobedient."

"Why, I'm sure," said Mavis cheerfully, "most girls would jump for joy at the chance. You'll enjoy yourself, and have all a happy time."

"No, I shan't," Norah cried. "I shall be miser-

able;" and she looked up at Dale despairingly. "Do
you promise I'm really and truly to come back?"

"Of course I do. And it's all on the cards that Mrs.
Dale and Rachel and Bill may follow you before your
holiday is over."

"Oh, I doubt that," said Mavis.

"No," cried Norah, "when I'm gone you'll turn
against me, and forget me. I shall never see you
again, and I shall die. I can't bear it." And she began to sob wildly.

Then Dale, standing big and firm, although each sob
tore at his entrails, pacified and reassured the girl. He
said that she must not be "fullish," she must be "good
and sensible," she must fall in with the views of those
"older and wiser" than herself; finally, after his argu-
ments and admonitions, he laid his hand on her bowed
head as if silently giving a patriarchal blessing; and
Mavis watched and admired, and loved him for his
noble generosity in taking so much trouble about the
poor little waif that had no real claim on him.

"There," she said, "dry your eyes, Norah. Mr.
Dale has told you he wishes it, and that ought to be
enough for you."

And then Norah said she would do what Mr. Dale
wished, even if she died in doing it.

"Oh, stuff, stuff," said Mavis, laughing cheerily. "I
never heard such talk. Now come along with me, and
get the breakfast things;" and she took Norah down
the steps into the kitchen.

Norah came back to lay the cloth presently, and
would have rushed into Dale's arms, if he had not mo-
tioned to her to keep away, and laid a finger on his lips

warningly. But he could not prevent her from whispering to him across the table.

" Will you come and see me, wherever it is? "

" Perhaps."

" Come and see me without *her*. Come all for me, by yourself."

Dale did more work in that one morning than he had done for months. The wet season had naturally postponed the hay-making, but negligence was postponing it still further; now at last he gave all necessary orders. But it was only his own grass that he had to deal with. Letting everything drift, he had not made any of the usual arrangements with his neighbors; this year he would not have to ride grandly round and watch dozens of men and women laboring for him; and there would be no farmers' banquet or speeches or cigar-smoking.

When he came in to dinner he found Mavis all hot and red, but pleased with herself after her bustling activities. The whole business was settled. Norah was to go as a paying guest to that place at Bournemouth, and Mavis would drive her over to Rodchurch Road and put her into the four-fifteen train. At the station they would meet a girl called Nellie Evans, whom by a happy chance Mrs. Norton was despatching to-day; and so the two girls could travel together, and prevent each other from being a fool when they changed trains at the junction; and altogether nothing could have turned out better or nicer.

Mavis, babbling contentedly all through dinner, harped on the niceness both of people and things. Mrs. Norton, and indeed everybody else, had been so nice about it. All Rodchurch had seemed anxious to assist

Mr. and Mrs. Dale in contriving their little maid's holiday. "And it is nice," said Mavis simply, "to be
treated like that." Mrs. Norton had taken her all
round the vicarage garden, and she had never seen it
looking nicer. "Although the flowers aren't anything
to boast of, any more than ours are."

"And what *do* you think? Here's a bit of news
you'll be sorry to hear, though it mayn't surprise you."
Then Mavis related how it had been necessary to procure some sort of trunk to hold Norah's things, because there wasn't a single presentable bit of luggage
in the house, and she had discovered exactly what she
wanted—something that was not immoderate, appear-
ing solid, yet not heavy—at the new shop that had
recently been opened at the bottom of the village near
the Gauntlet Inn. First, however, she had gone to
their old friend the saddler's, wanting to see if she
could buy the box there. But Mr. Allen's shop
was empty, woe-begone, dirty with cobwebs, dead flies,
and mud on the window; and Mr. Allen himself was
ill in bed, being nursed hand and foot, and fed like a
baby, by poor Mrs. Allen. He had been stricken
down by some dreadful form of rheumatism, and three
doctors had said the same thing—that he had brought
this calamity upon himself by his ridiculous, ceaseless
tramping after the hounds.

Dale nodded and smiled, or made his face appro-
priately grave, while Mavis prattled to him; but truly
his mind was occupied only by Norah. She came in
and out of the room, looking pale and limp and resigned; she knew all about the trunk, and that it was
up-stairs and that already the mistress and Ethel had
begun to pack it; she was submitting to destiny, but

out of her soft blue eyes there shot a glance now and then that made him quiver with pain.

He went out of the house the moment dinner was finished, and kept moving about, now in the office, now in the yard, never still. Then, when he was pottering round and round the office for the fiftieth time in two hours, he heard a footstep, and Norah came—to whisper and cling to him, to make him kiss her again; to penetrate him with her ineffable sweetness; to plant the seeds of inextinguishable desire in the last few cells and fibers of his brain that as yet she had not reached.

"I don't ast you to stand in th' road when we drive away. I'd rather not. Say good-by to me now, when there's nobody watchin'."

Then he had to take her in his arms once more; and they stood close to the door, far from the window, pressed heart to heart, mute, throbbing.

"I'm kissing you," she whispered presently, "but you're not kissing me. Kiss me."

And he obeyed her.

"No," she whispered. "Different from that. Kiss me like you did yesterday."

"Very well," he said hoarsely. "This is the good-by kiss. This is good-by." And once again he felt the swift lambent ecstasy of a love that he had never till now guessed at; a joy beyond words, beyond dreams, beyond belief. "Now, you must go;" and he slowly released himself, and held her at arm's length. "That was our good-by. Good-by, my Norah—my darling—good-by." Then he went to the table in front of the window, and sat down.

She came a little way from the door, and spoke to him before going out and along the passage.

"I shan't mind now—however miserable I am—because I know it's all right. An' I promise to be good, an' do all I'm told, an' always be your own Norah."

Then she left him—the gray-haired respected Mr. Dale of Vine-Pits Farm, sitting in his office window for all the world to see; looking livid, shaky, old; and feeling like a Christian missionary in some far-off heathen land, who, having preached to the gang of pirates into whose hands he had fallen, lies now at the roadside with all his inside torn away, and waits for birds with beaks or beasts with claws to come and finish him.

Before the horse was put into the wagonette and the trunk brought down-stairs, Dale had left the house and gone some distance along the road in the direction of the Barradine Arms. Even if Norah had not said that he need not be there at the moment of departure, he would have been unable to remain. He could not stand by and see her piteous face, her slender figure, her forlorn gestures, while they carried her off—the poor little weak thing sent away from hearth and home, cast out among strangers because any spot on the earth, however bare or hard, had become a better shelter for her than the place that should have been sacredly secure.

He walked heavily, with a leaden heart and leaden feet; his eyes downcast, not glancing at the dark trees on one side or the bright fields on the other. But after passing the first of the woodland paths and before coming to the second, he looked up. He had heard the

sound of many footsteps and the murmur of many
voices.   All those blue-cloaked orphans, two and two,
an endless procession, were advancing toward him.

Never had the sight and the sound of them been so
horribly distasteful to him.   They were still a long
way off, and he thought he could dodge them, at any
rate avoid meeting them face to face, if he hurried on
to the second footpath and dived into the wood there.
But then it seemed as if he had stupidly miscalculated
the distance, or that his legs were failing him, or that
the girls came sweeping down the road at an impossi-
bly rapid pace; so that they were right upon him just
as he reached the stile.   He drew aside, and, feeling
that it was too late now to turn his back, watched them
as they passed.

The mistresses must have issued a sudden order of
silence, for they all went by without so much as a
whisper. There were fifty of them, but they seemed to be
thousands.   Dressed in their light blue summer cloaks,
golden-haired, brown-haired, a very few black-haired,
they passed two by two, with the little ones first, and
bigger and bigger girls behind—an ascending scale of
size, so that he had the illusion of seeing a girl grow
up under his eyes, change in a minute instead of in
years from the small sexless imp that is like an amus-
ing toy, to the full-breasted creature that is so nearly
a woman as to be dangerous to herself and to everybody else.

Not one of them spoke, but all of them, little and
big, looked at him—very shyly, and yet with intense
interest.   He stood staring after them, and presently
their tuneful young voices sounded again, filled the air
with virginal music.   He swung his leg over the stile,

and went along the path through the trees where he
had followed Norah yesterday.

He had not intended to leave the highroad, but it
was as if that dead man's girls had driven him into the
wood to get away from their shyly questioning eyes.
He might meet them again if he stayed out there.   In
here he could be alone with his thoughts.

To-day there was plenty of sunlight, and instead of
turning off the path he went straight on to the main
ride.   This too was bright with sunshine, a splendid
broad avenue that was shut close on either side by the
thickly planted firs; the mossy track seeming soft as a
bed, and the sky like an immensely high canopy of
delicate blue gauze.   A heron crossed quickly but
easily, making only three flaps of its powerful wings
before it disappeared; there was an unceasing hum
of insects; and two wood-cutters came by and wished
Dale good afternoon and touched their weather-stained
hats.

"Good afternoon," he said, in a friendly tone.   "A
bit cooler and pleasanter to-day, isn't it?"

"You're right, sir. 'Bout time too."

Then he walked on, alone with his thoughts again,
along the wide sunlit ride toward Kibworth Rocks;
and a phrase kept echoing in his ears, sounding as if
he said it aloud.   "It is the finger of God.   It is the
finger of God."   He was quoting himself really, because he had once used that phrase in a pompously
effective manner.   Could one repeat it as effectively
in regard to what happened near here yesterday?
Could one dare to say that the finger of God interposed, touching his blood with ice, making his muscles
relax, forcing him to loosen his hold on the delicious

morsel that like a beast of prey he was about to devour and enjoy.

He walked with hunched shoulders and lowered head, but there was great resolution, even an odd sort of swaggering defiance in his gait. He stopped short, raised his head, and looked about him at a certain point of the ride. Here he was very near to the open glade where he met Norah; but he was nearer still to the strewn boulders, jagged ridges, and hollow clefts of Kibworth Rocks. If he left the ride, he would see them, brown and gray, glittering in the sunshine.

And he thought again of those fifty orphans or waifs. Why weren't they here to bow and do honor to him who had been the friend of girls in life and who was the guardian angel of girls in death? This was the hallowed spot, the benefactor's resting-place till devout hands raised him and priests sang over him, the rocky shrine of their patron saint.

Dale grunted, shook himself, and went off the ride in the opposite direction—to tread the moss that had been crushed by Norah's footsteps, to push against the branches that had touched her shoulders, to see the dead flowers that had dropped from her hands. He found a shriveled sprig or two of her woodland posy, and carried them to the fallen beech tree.

She was gone now—already a long way from him— at the railway station, with ticket bought, and box labeled, waiting for the train to take her still farther from him. Only a heron could fly fast enough to get to her now before the train possessed her. And he quoted himself again, really saying the words aloud this time. " Good-by—my darling—good-by, good-by."

That was what he meant when he gave her the last kiss. He had said so. He had called it the last kiss. But she—poor lamb—thought it was the last kiss till next time; that it was good-by for three weeks, not good-by forever. He must never see her again. There could be no two ways about *that* decision. He mustn't palter, or trifle, or shilly-shally about that iron certainty. But how without Heaven's unceasing aid would he have strength to keep such a vow?

And sitting on the tree, and thinking for a little while about himself rather than about her, he endeavored to survey his situation in the logical clear-sighted way that had once been customary with him. To what a blank no-thoroughfare he had brought himself. What a damnable mess he had made of his peaceful, happy home.

Of course he had known for a long time what was the matter with him. His disgust with himself at the revelation of his own weakness dated from a long time ago; but the progress of his passing from perfectly pure and normal thoughts about the girl to cravings that he struggled with as morbid impurities was so subtle that it defied anaylsis. At first when he put his hand on her head, or patted her shoulder, every thought behind the fatherly gesture was itself fatherly; and then, without anything to startle one by a recognition of change, the time had come when he felt a slight thrill in touching her, when he was always seeking occasions or excuses for doing it, when the wider the contact the more massive was his satisfaction. Her white neck, her round fore-arms, her thin wrists, irresistibly attracted a caress. He could not keep his hands off her—and it distressed and worried

him whenever he saw anybody else doing quite inno-
cently what he did with an unavowable purpose. Perhaps this was the real cause of his dislike for the new
pastor. After Mr. Furnival's initial appearance at the
chapel, they all three walked a little way together, and
the good-looking young man paid Norah compliments
about her singing, and held her hand and patted it.
Nothing could have been more innoxious, more completely ministerial; and yet Dale had felt that he would
like to take the clerical gentleman by the collar of his
black coat and the seat of his gray trousers, and send
him sprawling over a quick-set hedge into a ploughed
field.

He knew then the nature of the poison that had crept
insidiously into his blood and was beginning to spread
and rage with deadly power. He fought against it
bravely, he fought against it despairingly. He hoped
that chance would cure him, he prayed that heaven
would cleanse him.

He would not believe that his ruin was irretrievable.
That would be too monstrous and absurd. Because,
except for this expanding trouble, everything inside
him, all the main component parts that made up the
vast and still solid thinking organism which had been
labeled for external observers by the name of William
Dale, remained quite unchanged. His religious faith
stood absolutely firm, was strengthened rather than
shaken; he regarded his wife with exactly the same
affection; he loved his children as much as, more than
ever; only this astounding dreadful new thing was
added to him: he worshiped Norah.

In his struggles to free himself from the new mental
growth, he had turned to his children. Instinct seemed

to say that from them and through them should come
an influence sufficiently potent to resist temptation,
however tremendous. He felt so proud of the boy.
Billy was never afraid of him, looked at him so firmly
even when threatened, holding up the pink and white
face, with its soft unformed features and yet a determined set to the chin and mouth already—a real little
man. Dale took his son's hand in his, took Billy with
him into the granary, the hay loft, or across the fields,
cut bits of willow and showed how to make a whistle,
took a hedge sparrow's nest and blew the eggs; and the
boy was proud and happy in such noble society, but he
could not exorcise the evil spell for his grand companion.

Nor could Rachel give freedom. Dale embraced his
daughter with the truest paternal fervor, pumping up
sweet clean love from deep unsullied wells, thinking
honestly and as of old so long as she stood by his side.
At such moments he forced himself to imagine a man
playing the fool with Rachel, and immediately there
came a full normal explosion of parental rage; and he
knew, without the possibility of doubt, that such a
man had better never have been born than encounter
Rachel's father. But these imaginations could not
help him. Thoughts about Rachel and thoughts about
Norah, which once had mingled, were now like two
rivers running side by side but never meeting.

Again, what had rendered the fight hopeless was his
recognition of the overwhelming fact that the spell was
mutual. It was not only that he wanted her, Norah
wanted him. There lay the sweetly venomous throb of
the poison. In her eyes he was *not* old; his gray hair
did not appal her, his rugged frame did not repel her.

All night and all day, during months, yes, during years, she had told him: "You are *not* old; you *need* not be old; *I* can make you young."

He thought, as he had thought again and again, of her artlessness, her ignorance, and her total absence of compunction. It seemed so wonderful. She drifted toward him as the petal of a flower comes on running water, as corn seeds blow through the air, as anything small and light obeying a natural law. She did not in the least understand social conventions. She was not troubled with one thought of right or wrong; she neither meditated nor remembered. How wonderful. The ten commandments and the catechism that she knew by heart, all the hymns she had sung and all the sermons she had heard, did not exert the faintest restraining influence. They had no real meaning for her probably, and she could not therefore bring them into relation with concrete facts. In her innocence, in her virginal simplicity, she would keep the book of life close-sealed until he opened it roughly for her at its ugliest page.

He, or somebody else!

Suddenly he threw away the faded wood-blossoms, sprang up from the tree, and paced to and fro. A wave of revolt came sweeping through and through him. Was he not making mountains out of mole-hills?

If he could trample down all this sentimental fiddle-de-dee, what was the plain English of the case so far as she was concerned? Unbidden, innumerable circumstances stored from local knowledge offered themselves as guides for argument. Take any girl of that class—well, what are her chances? Why, you are lucky if you keep 'em straight until the time comes to

send 'em out into domestic service; their parents
scarcely expect it, barely seem to desire it. But after
that time, when they get among strangers and there's
nobody with an eye on them, they fall as victims—if
you choose to call it so—to the first marauder—to the
young master, the nephew home for his Christmas holidays, or the man who comes to tune the piano. If
not himself, it would be somebody else.

And he thought. "Blast it all, am I a man or a
mouse? Who's to judge me, or stan' in my way, if I
do what I please? Suppose it's found out, well, it must
be smoothed over, covered up, and put behind the fireplace. I shan't be Number One that's bin th' same
road!" and he remembered how lightly other married
men, his neighbors, country farmers, or town tradesmen, amused themselves with their servants, and how
their middle-aged wives just had to grin and bear it.
"An' Mavis," he thought, "can do the same. Heavens
an' earth, I've got an answer ready if she tries to make
a fuss, or wants to take the dinner-bell and go round
as public crier—an answer that ought to flatten her
as if a traction engine had bin over her. 'My lass, who
began it? Bring out your slate and put it alongside
mine, an' we'll see which looks dirtiest, all said and
done.'" While he was thinking in this manner, his
face became very ugly, with hard deep lines in it, and
about the mouth that cruel pouting expression once
seen by Mavis.

He came back to the tree; and sat down, letting his
hands hang loose, his head droop, and his shoulders
contract. The fire had gone cold again.

Now he felt only disgust and horror. Norah's ignorance and disregard of moral precepts, or readiness

to yield to the snares of unlicensed joy, were summed up in the better and truer word innocence. The greater her weakness, the greater his wickedness. If he could not save her from others, he could save her from himself. Then if she fell, it would at least be a natural fall. It would not be a foul betrayal of youth by age; it would not be the sort of degraded crime that makes angels weep, and ordinary people change into judges and executioners.

When a man has reached a certain time of life he must not crave for forbidden delights, he must not permit himself to be eaten up with new desire, he must not risk destroying a girl's soul for the gratification of his own body. If he does, he commits the unpardonable sin. And there is no excuse for him.

The Devil's reasonings to which a few minutes ago he had listened greedily were specious, futile, utterly false. That sort of argument might do for other men —might do for every other man in the wide world— but it would not do for *him*, William Dale. Its acceptance would knock the very ground from under his feet.

For, if there could be any excuse, why had he killed Everard Barradine?

XXX

THEN Dale lived again for the hundred thousandth time in the thoughts and passions of that distant period.

The forest glade grew dim, vanished. He was lying on the grass in a London park, and Mavis' confession rang through the buzzing of his ears, through the chaos of his mind. It seemed that the whole of his small imagined world had gone to pieces, and the immensity of the real world had been left to him in exchange—crushing him with an idea of its unexplored vastness, of its many countries, its myriad races. And yet, big as it all was, it could not provide breathing space for that man and himself.

Soon this became an oppressive certainty. Life under the new conditions had been rendered unendurable. And then there grew up the one solid determination, that he must stand face to face with his enemy and call him to account. It must *at last* be man to man. He must tell the man what he thought of him, call him filthy names, strip him of every shred of dignity—and strike him. A few blows of scorn might suffice—a backhander across the snout, a few swishes with a stick, a kick behind when he turned. He was too rottenly weak a thing to fight with.

His mind refused to go further than this. However deeply and darkly it was working below the surface of consciousness, it gave him no further directions than this.

He got rid of his wife. That was the first move in the game—anyhow. He did not want to think about her now; she would be dealt with again later on. At present he wished to concentrate all his attention on the other one.

He took a bed for himself in a humbler and cheaper house farther west, a little nearer to the house of his enemy; and almost all that day he spent in thinking how and where he should obtain the meeting he longed for. He understood at once that it would be hopeless to attempt such an interview at Grosvenor Place. In imagination he saw himself escorted by servants to that tank-like room at the back of the mansion—the room where the man had treated him as dirt, where his first instinct of distrust had been aroused, where all those photographs of girls had subtly suggested the questioning doubts that led him on to suspicion and discovery. The man would come again to this room, with his tired eyes and baggy cheeks and drooping lip; would stare contemptuously; and at the first words of abuse, he would ring a bell, call for servants, call for the police, and have the visitor ignominiously turned out. " Policeman, this ruffian has been threatening me. He is an ill-conditioned dog that I've been systematically kind to, and he now seems to have taken leave of his senses and accuses me of injuring him. For the sake of his wife, who is a good respectful sort of person, I do not give him in charge. But I ask you to keep an eye on him. And if he dares to return to my door, just cart him off to the police station."

No, that would not do at all. He and Mr. Barradine must meet somewhere quietly and comfortably, out of reach of electric bells, butlers, and police officers.

That first night after the confession he slept sound and long. In the morning when he woke, feeling refreshed and strengthened, his determination to bring about the interview had assumed an iron firmness, as if all night it had been beaten on the anvil of his thoughts while he lay idle. But he was no nearer to devising a scheme that should give effect to the determination.

Mr. Barradine had said that he was going down to the Abbey to-morrow, or next day, Friday, at latest; and in the course of this Wednesday morning Dale decided that the interview must be delayed. It was impossible up here. It would be much easier to arrange down there. He must wait until Mr. Barradine went down to Hampshire, and go down after him. He could call at the Abbey, where the man would be more accessible than up here; and, by restraining himself, by simulating his usual manner, by lulling the man to a false security, he could lure him out of the house—get him out into the open air, away from his servants, perhaps beyond the gardens and as far off as the park copses. Then when they were alone, they two, at a distance from the possibility of interruption, Dale could drop the mask of subservience, turn upon him, and say "Now——"

No, that would not do. It was all childish. For a thousand obscure reasons it would not do at all.

Then, brooding over his wife's confession—the things she had merely hinted at as well as the things she had explicitly stated—he remembered how in the beginning the wood near Long Ride was their meeting-place, how the man had met her there, and led her slowly beneath the trees to the cottage of the procuress. And then an inspiration came. A note to be sent in his wife's name, as soon as Mr. Barradine got home to the Abbey. " Meet me in the West Gate copse. I want to show my gratitude"—or—" I want to thank you again"—something of that sort. " Meet me at the end of North Ride by the Heronry. I will be there if possible four o'clock to-morrow. If not there to-morrow, I will be there next day. Mavis."

He wrote such a letter, in a hand sufficiently like his wife's. Yes, that would fetch him. The old devil would have no suspicions.

Then a cold shiver ran down his spine. It was a thought rising from the depths, warning him, terrifying him. The note would remain *afterward*. If Mr. Barradine did not destroy it—and very likely he would not do so—the note would be found afterward. But after what?

He tore up the note, tore it into tiny pieces. It seemed to him that he had escaped from a danger. His plan had been the idea of a madman. But why? With his skin still cold and clammy, he found himself whispering words which sounded explanatory, but which did not explain: " Suppose a mistake occurred. Yes, suppose a mistake occurred." Then trying to think quietly and sensibly, instead of in this fluttered, erratic way, he forced himself to interpret the real significance of the whisper. Well, suppose he struck too hard, and too often. But again there came the blankness—an abrupt check to thought—the depths refusing to give anything more to the surface.

He decided that he would go down to Hampshire

secretly, letting no one know of his movements; and, stationing himself at some likely spot near the Abbey, he would wait till chance brought them face to face. Yes, that would do. Almost immediately he chose Hadleigh Wood as the place to hide in. Instinct seemed to have suggested the wood rather than any point nearer to the Abbey, and instinct now ordered him to go there and nowhere else. It was a likely road to so many parts; it was full of good hiding-places; and, although it was tricky, with its close thickets suddenly terminating on the edge of unexpected open spaces, he knew it all as well as the back of his right hand. He could lie snug, or range about cautiously, seeing but unseen; and he would not have long to wait before the grand gentleman passed by on his way to or from the Abbey park.

He had got it now. This was right; and he laid all his plans accordingly. First he pawned his silver watch and chain, so obtaining a little money without bothering anybody. The pawnbroker's shop was in Chapel Street, and he went on along the Edgware Road and up a narrow street in search of a shop where he could procure a suit of old clothes. Here again it was as though instinct guided him, because he had no knowledge of London and did not know where to look for a slop-shop; but he pushed on, noticing that the houses were shabby, and feeling sure that he would soon find what he wanted. And this happened. All at once he was among the second-hand clothes; every shop on both sides of the street invited him—the whole street at this sordid end of it was trying to help him. For a very few shillings he bought just the garments that he had imagined—loose and big, made of drab

canvas or drill, the suit of overalls that had been worn
by some kind of mechanic, with two vast inside pockets to the jacket, in which the wearer had carried tools,
food, and his bottle of drink. Dale also bought a common soft felt hat, a thing you could pull down over
your eyes and ears, and make into any shape you
pleased.

When he put on the suit and the hat in his bedroom,
he felt satisfied with their appearance. He said to himself, " After I have slept out a night, and got plenty
of earth stains and muck on this greasy old canvas, I
shall look ·just a tramp wandered from the highroad,
and no one will recognize me if they do chance to see
me—that is, unless I take my hat off. And I don't
do *that,* until I take it off for the purpose of being
recognized by *him.*"

He locked the suit of overalls and the slouch hat
safely in his bag. But next day he brought out the hat,
and wore it while making a very careful tour of inspection in the neighborhood of the Grosvenor Place
mansion. Approaching it from the western side he
spied out the lie of the land, found a mews that had an
entrance in the side street, and judged that this mews
contained Mr. Barradine's horses and carriages. This
proved to be true. Sauntering up and down, and lurking at corners on the side street, Dale waited and
watched. Always seeming to be strolling away from
the house, but glancing back over his shoulder now
and then, he saw Mr. Barradine's brougham come
out of the mews and stand at Mr. Barradine's door. No
luggage was brought down the steps: Mr. Barradine
was merely starting for a drive about town. Dale
came in the evening and observed the house as he

strolled along the main thoroughfare of Grosvenor
Place. There were lights in several rooms, and the
window of the porch showed that the hall was
lighted up. Mr. Barradine had said that he hoped to be
able to get home to-day, but evidently his journey had
been postponed until to-morrow. He had said he
would go on Friday at the latest.

He did not, however, go on Friday. Dale kept the
house under observation off and on all day, and again
in the evening. Mr. Barradine went out driving
twice; but the carriage brought him back each time.
How many more postponements? Would he go to-
morrow? Yes, he would go to-morrow; but this involved more delay. It would be useless to follow him
to-morrow, because he would never pass through the
wood on Sunday. No, he would spend Sunday inside
his park-rails, going to the Abbey church, walking
about the garden, looking at the stables and the dairy.
Moreover, Sunday would be the one dangerous day
in the woods—nobody at work, everybody free to wander; young men with their sweethearts coming off the
rides for privacy; cottagers with squoils hunting the
squirrels all through church time perhaps.

Dale ground his teeth, shook his fist at the lighted
windows, and thought. "If he does not go to-morrow,
I can't wait. My self-control will be exhausted, and I
shall certainly do something fullish."

But Mr. Barradine went home that Saturday. Between ten and eleven in the morning the brougham
stood at the door, a four-wheeled cab was fetched and
loaded with luggage, and the two vehicles drove off
round the corner southward on their way to Waterloo.
And Dale felt his spirits lightening and a fierce gaiety

filling his breast. The time of inaction was nearly over; this hateful sitting down under one's wrongs would not last long now; soon he would be doing something. He took quite a pleasant walk through Chelsea, and over the river to Lambeth, where, after a snack of lunch, he read the newspapers in a Public Library. The Library was a quiet, convenient resort; and yesterday he had written a letter there, to Mr. Ridgett at Rodchurch Post Office—not because he really had anything to communicate, but because it seemed necessary, or at least wise, to send off a letter from London.

He enjoyed a good night's rest, and lay in bed till late on Sunday afternoon. He intended to travel by the mail train—the train that left Waterloo at ten-fifteen, and went through the night dropping post-bags all the way down the line; and it was extremely improbable that he would meet any Rodchurch friends in this train, but he understood that the dangerous part of his proceedings would begin when he got to Waterloo, and he was a little worried, even muddled, as to how and where to change his clothes—or rather to put on that canvas suit over his ordinary clothes. If he made the change here, and any one saw him going out, it might seem a bit odd.

But then his confusion of ideas passed off, and all became clear. He must change at the last possible moment, of course; and he thought, "Why am I so muddled about such simple things? I must pull myself together. Of course I don't mind being seen in London; it is down there that I don't wish to be seen. Anybody is welcome to see me till I'm started, an' perhaps the more people that see me the better."

He therefore shaved, and dressed neatly and carefully; packed his valise with the bowler hat in it,
turned up the brim of the common slouch hat and wore
it jauntily. The overalls were rolled in an unobtrusive
brown-paper parcel to be carried under the arm; and,
having paid for his bedroom, he went out at about
eight o'clock, walking boldly through the streets—
just as Mr. Dale of Rodchurch, dressed in blue serge
and not in his best black coat—Mr. Dale dressed for
the holidays, with a rakish go-as-you-please soft hat
instead of the ceremonious hard-brimmed bowler, and
not too proud to carry his bag and parcel for himself.

All straightforward now. It would be still Mr. Dale
at Waterloo, depositing the bag at the cloak-room,
buying a ticket, and getting into the train with his
brown-paper parcel. Only Mr. Dale would get lost on
the journey, and a queer shabby customer would
emerge at the other end.

But he allowed himself to modify the plan slightly.
It was necessary that he should have a good meal and
also procure food to take with him, and for these purposes he went to an eating-house in the York Road.
This turned out to be just the place he required—a
room with tables where diners could sit as long as they
chose, a counter spread out with edibles to be absorbed
standing, and the company consisting of cabmen from
the station ranks, some railway porters, and a few
humble travelers.

He ordered a large beef-steak; and he ate like a boa-
constrictor, thinking the while: This ought to stick to
my ribs. I can't put away too much now, because it
may come to short commons if the luck's against me."
Then after the meal there came a temptation to hurry

up his program, and get through some of the little difficulties at once. He observed his surroundings. The place was fuller now than when he came in; the atmosphere was thick with tobacco smoke and the steam of hot food; the kitchen was at its busiest; and at the counter the stupid-looking girl in charge was handing over refreshments so fast that it seemed as if soon there would be none left.

He paid a waitress for his supper, and then went into the dark little lavatory behind the room and put on his canvas suit. Coming out into the room again, he intended to say something about having slipped on his overalls for a night job; but nothing of the kind was necessary. Nobody cared, nobody noticed. His difficulty was to make the counter grl attend to him at all. He spoke to her bruskly at last; and then she sold him slices of cold meat, cheese, biscuits, a lot of chocolate and some nuts, with which he filled those two inner pockets of his jacket. They had become his larders now.

There were not more than a dozen passengers in the whole train, and no one on the platform at Waterloo took the faintest notice of him.

No one noticed him three hours later when he left the train at a station short of Manninglea Cross; and soon he was far from other men, striking across the dark country, wth the stars high over his head, and his native air blowing into his lungs. He came down over the heath on the Abbey side of the Cross Roads, and reached Hadleigh Wood just before dawn.

He felt at home now, alone with the wild animals, on ground that he had learned the tricks of when he was like a wild animal himself. He knew his wood as well as any of them. He could make lairs beneath the hollies, glide imperceptibly among the trees, crawl on his belly from tussock to tussock, and startle the very foxes by creeping quite close before they smelled peril. So he hid and glided as the sun climbed the sky, and then waited and watched when the sun was high, now here, now there, but always very near the open rides along which people would be passing. And that day many passed, but not the man he wanted.

He was three days and nights in the wood; and on the morning of the fourth day somebody saw him.

He had moved stealthily to the stream to drink, and while creeping back on hands and knees among some holly bushes by a glade, he paused suddenly. Out there on the grass, so small that she had not shown above the lowest bushes, there was a little girl—a child of about five, in a tattered pinafore, picking daisies and making a daisy chain. Breathless and with a beating heart, he watched her, and he dared not move forward into the sunlight or backward into the shade. She had not seen him yet. She was playing with the chain of flowers—a small wood goblin sprung out of nowhere, a little black-haired devil fired up from hell through the solid earth and out into this empty glade to squat there right in his track. Then she stood upon her feet, and admired the length of the chain as she held it dangling.

Then she dropped the chain, gave a little cry like the note of a frightened bird, and scampered away—never looking back.

Never looking back. But she had seen him. He tried to hope that she had not seen him.

He was hungry now. His provisions were exhausted; he had eaten nothing since last night, and he felt excited and fretful. He said to himself: "If to-day my enemy is not delivered into my hands, I must go out into the open and seek him at all risks, at all costs." It was a dominant idea now. Nothing else mattered.

But that day the man came. When the day was almost over, when the whole wood was fading to the neutral tints of dusk, he came. He was on horseback, sitting easily and proudly, and his chestnut horse paced daintily and noiselessly over the moss.

Dale took off his hat. Then presently he came out of the bracken into the ride, gripped the horse by its bridle, and spoke to the rider.

"Halloa! Dale? But, my good fellow, what the deuce—— Damn you, let go. What are you trying to——"

"I'll show you. Yes, you"—and violent, obscene, incoherent words came pouring from Dale in a high-pitched querulous voice. All his set speeches had been blown to the clouds by the blast of his passion. All his plans exploded in flame at the sight of the man's face—the eyes that had gloated over Mavis' reluctant body, the lips that had fed on her enforced kisses. But what did the words matter? Any words were sufficient. They could understand each other without words now.

He was holding the bridle firmly, pulling the horse's head round; and he grasped Mr. Barradine's foot, got it out of the stirrup, and jerking the whole leg upward, pitched him out of the saddle. The horse, released, sprang away, jumping this way, that way, as it dashed through the brake to the rocks—the clatter of its hoofs sounded on the rocks, and the last glimpse of it showed its empty saddle and the two flying stirrup-irons.

Dale was mad now—the devil loose in him—only conscious of unappeasable rage and hatred, as he struck with his fists, beating the man down every time he tried to get up, and kicking at the man's head when he lay prostrate.

Then there came a brief pause of extraordinary deep quiet, a sudden cessaton of all perceptible sounds and movements. Dale was confused, dazed, breathing hard. That was a dead man sprawling there—what you call a corpse, a bleeding carcass. Dale looked at him. Beneath his last kick, the skull had cracked like a well-tapped egg.

As abruptly as if his legs had been knocked from under him Dale sat down, and endeavored to think.

Then it was as if all his thought and the action resulting from his thought were beyond his control. In all that he did he seemed to be governed by instinct.

At any minute some one might pass by. He must drag the body out of sight. And the instinctive thoughts came rapidly, each one as the necessity for it arose. He must leave no foot-prints, or as few as possible. He unlaced and pulled off his boots, and, noticing the blood on them, made a mental note to wash them as soon as he could find time to do so.

He took the dead man by the heels, and dragged him cautiously toward the rocks—seeking the zigzag line taken by the galloping horse. That was the chance. Instinct directed and explained the task—to make it seem that the horse had dragged him, and battered his life out over the rocks. A good chance. Those stirrups didn't come out. He might truly have been dragged by one of them.

The track of the horse was lost directly the rocks

began. Dale left the body, and cautiously clambered upon the rocks to see if any living thing observed him.

Then he took the corpse by the heels again, and hauled it over the jagged surfaces and through the hollows—conscious all the while of great pain—and finally left it in a cleft, staring stupidly upward. He hurried back to the ride, and sat down by the rank-smelling bracken where he had left his boots. He was startled when he looked at his feet—their soles were covered with blood. He thought it was the dead man's blood, but then discovered it was his own. He had torn his feet to pieces on the rocks. He put on his boots in agony, picked up his hat, and limped away through the hollies into the gloom of the pines. Down in the stream, with the water rippling over his ankles, he stood and listened.

What to do next? They had not yet discovered the dead man; but it seemed to him that they would do so in another minute or two. He tried to think logically, but could not. It seemed now necessary to get clear away before the body was seen—get as far off as possible. Vaguely it occurred to him that he should wait here till night, and it was still only dusk. But then he had a clear vision of the wood at night—lanterns moving in every direction, men's voices, a cordon of men all round the wood. Yes, that would be the state of affairs when they had found the body and were beginning to look for the murderer. This wood was a death-trap. He forgot the pain in his feet, and began to run with the long trotting stride of a hunted stag, careless now of the crash of the bushes and fern as he swung through them.

He paused crouching on the edge of the wood, then came out over the bank, across a road, and into the fields. With arched back he went along the deep ditch of the first field, through a gap, and into the ditch of the next field. To his right lay Vine-Pits Farm; to his left lay the Cross Roads, the Barradine Arms, the clustered cottages. He ran on, in ditch after ditch, under hedges and banks, swinging left-handed in a wide detour till he came to the last of the fields and the highroad to Old Manninglea.

But he had to wait here. He saw laborers on the road, and waited till they were gone. Then he crept through the gap where the ditch went under the road culvert, crossed this second road, and ran stooping on the open heath.

The sky was red, with terrible clouds; and a wind followed him, keeping his spine cold, although all the rest of him was burning. When he looked back he fancied that he saw men moving, and that he heard distant shoutings from Beacon Hill. Rain fell—not much of it, just showers, wetting his hands, and mingling with the perspiration in front, but making him colder behind; and he muttered to cheer himself. "That's luck. That'll wash away the blood. Yes, that's luck. Yes, I must take it for a good sign—bit o' luck."

He walked and ran for miles—over the bare downs, through the fertile valleys, and alongside the other railway line; and late that night he got into a feeding train for Salisbury, where, he was told, he would catch a West of England express for London.

There was delay at Salisbury, and he ate some food and drank some brandy.

Then at last he found himself in the London train, in an empty compartment of a corridor coach. He sat with folded arms, his hat pulled low on his forehead, his eyes peering suspiciously out of the window, or at the door of the corridor. Whenever anybody went by in the corridor, he stooped his head lower and pretended to be asleep.

There were strange people in this train—soldiers and sailors from Devonport; some foreigners too, or people dressed up to look like foreigners; numbers of men also who kept ther heads down as he was doing, as if for some jolly good private reason. Who the hell were they really? Detectives?

The train was going so fast now that it rocked to and fro, and hummed and sang; but it seemed to Dale to be standing still—to be going backward. This illusion was so strong for some moments that he jumped up and went out into the corridor, to look down at the permanent way on that side also. The lamplight from the train showed on both sides that the sleepers, the chairs, the gravel, slipped and slid in the correct direction. The train was flying, simply flying along the inner up-track of the four sets of metals.

" I mustn't be so fullish," he kept saying to himself. " I'm all safe now."

A sudden noise of voices drew him to the corridor; and he stood holding a hand-rail, watching the leather walls and the gangway that led into the next coach leap and dance and bob and sink, while he listened eagerly. The roar of the train was so great here that he could not catch what the hidden men were saying, but he understood that they were sailors making too much noise and a railway guard rebuking them. " It's nothing to do with me," he said to himself. " Why *am* I so fullish?"

He returned to the compartment, sat with his shoulder to the corridor, and brooded dully and heavily. All that fiery trouble about Mavis and her being dishonored had gone out of his mind as if forever; the grievance and the rage and the hatred had gone too; temporarily there was nothing but a most ponderous self-pity.

" What a mess this is," he thought. " What a hash I've made of it. What a cruel thing to happen to me. What an awful hole I've put myself into."

The train swept onward, and he began to doze. Then after a while he slept and dreamed. He dreamed that he was here in this train, not fettered, but spell-bound, unable to move and hide, only able to understand what was happening and to suffer from his perception of the hideous predicament that he was in. Another train, on another of the four tracks, was racing after this train, was overhauling it, was infallibly catching it. Mysteriously he could see into this following, hunting train —it was a train full of policemen, magistrates, wardens, judges, hangmen: all the offended majesty of the law.

He woke shivering, after this first taste of a murderer's dreams. His punishment had begun.

It was daylight at Waterloo, and he slunk in terror; but things had to be done. He washed himself as well as he could, took off his dirty canvas, got his bag from the cloak-room and hurried away. No questions were asked, no bones made about giving him a room at a house in Stamford Street; and he at once went to bed and slept profoundly.

When he woke this time he was quite calm, and able to think clearly again.

He went out late in the afternoon, and saw a message for him on newspaper bills: " Fatal Accident to ex-Cabinet Minister." Then, having bought a paper, he read the very brief report of the accident. He stood gasping, and then drew deep breaths. The *Accident*. Oh, the joy of seeing that word! No suspicion so far. It was working out just as one might hope.

And it seemed that his courage, so lamentably shaken, began to return to him. He felt more himself. He marched off to a post office, and sent his telegram to Mavis: " Evening paper says fatal accident to Mr. Barradine. Is this true? " The main purpose of the telegram was to prove that here he was in London, where he had been last Friday, and where he had remained during all the intervening time; its secondary purpose was to put on record at the earliest possible moment his surprise—surprise so complete that he could scarcely believe the sad news. He gave his utmost care to the wording of the telegram and was satisfied with the result. The turn of words seemed perfectly natural.

Then, having despatched his telegram, he hurried off to call at Mr. Barradine's house in Grosvenor Place— to make some anxious inquiries.

There were people at the door, ladies and gentlemen among them, and the servants looked white and agitated as they answered questions. Dale pushed his way up the steps almost into the hall, acting consternation and grief—the honest, rather rough country fellow, the loyal dependent who forgets his good manners in his sorrow at the death of the chieftain. He would not go

away, when the other callers had departed. He told
the butler of the services rendered to him by Mr. Barradine. " Not more'n ten days ago."

" Don't you remember me? I came here to thank
him for his kindness."

" Ah, yes," said the agitated butler, " he was a kind
gentleman, and no mistake."

" *Kind!* I should think he was. Well, well!" And
Dale stood nodding his head dolefully. Then he went
away slowly and sadly, and he kept on nodding his
head in the same doleful manner long after the door
was shut—just on the chance that the servants might
look out of the hall windows and see it before he vanished round the corner.

He could think now, as well as he had ever done. It
was of prime importance that no outsiders should ever
learn that Everard Barradine had injured him. This
guided him henceforth. It settled the course of his
life there and then. He must return to Mavis; he must
by his demeanor cover the intrigue—or so act that
if people came to know of it, they would suppose either
that he was ignorant of his shame or that he was a
complaisant husband, taking advantage of the situation
and pocketing all gifts from his wife's protector.
No motive for the crime. That was his guide-post.

In the night he got rid of the canvas suit and slouch
hat. Next day he went home to Rodchurch Post
Office, and, speaking to Mavis of Mr. Barradine's
death, uttered that terrific blasphemy. *"It is the finger
of God."*

XXXI

H E acted his part well, and everything worked out easily—more easily than one could have dared to hope for.

Not a soul was thinking about him. He had to assert himself, thrust himself forward, before people in the village would so much as notice that he had come back among them again. The inquest, as he gathered, was going to be a matter of form: it seemed doubtful if the authorities would even make an examination of the ground over there. All was to be as nice as nice for him.

Yet he was afraid. Fear possed him—this sneaking, torturing, emasculating passion that he had never known hitherto was now always with him.

He lay alone in the camp-bedstead sweating and funking. The events of the day made him seem safe, but he felt that he would not be really safe for ages and ages. Throughout the night he was going over the list of his idiotic mistakes, upbraiding himself, cursing himself for a hundred acts of brainless folly. The plan had been sound enough: it was the accomplishment of the plan that had been so damnably rotten.

Why had he changed his addresses in that preposterous fashion? Instead of providing himself with useful materials for an alibi, he had just made a lot of inexplicable movements. Then the pawning of the watch—in a false name. How could he ever explain

that? Anybody short of money may put his ticker
up the spout, but no one has the right to assume an
alias. And the buying of the clothes and hat. Instead
of bargaining, as innocent people do, however small
the price demanded, he just dabbed down the money.
He must have appeared to be in the devil's own hurry
to get the things and cut off with them. The two men
at that shop must have noticed his peculiarities as a
customer. They would be able to pick him out in the
biggest crowd that ever assembled in a magistrate's
court.

But far worse had been his watchings and prowlings
round and about the house in Grosvenor Place. Could
he have blundered upon anything more full of certain
peril? Why, to stand still for ten minutes in London
is to invite the attention of the police. Their very
motto or watchword is " Move on;" and for every policeman in helmet and buttons there are three policemen in plain clothes to make sure that people *are*
moving on. While watching that house he had been
watched himself.

Then, again, the insane episode of the eating-house—
the wild hastening of his program, the untimely change
of appearance in that thronged room—and his rudeness to the woman behind the counter. With anguish
he remembered, or fancied he remembered, that she
had looked at him resentfully seeming to say as she
studied his face. " I'm sizing you up. Yes, I won't forget you—you brute."

His bag too—left by him at Waterloo for a solid
proof that he was *not* in London as he pretended. The
bag was at the cloak-room all right when he came
to fetch it, but perhaps in the meantime it had been

to Scotland Yard and back again. Besides, Waterloo was a station he should never once have showed his nose in; the link between Waterloo and home was too close—his own line—the railway whose staff was replenished by people from his own part of the country. While he was feeling glad that the passengers were strangers, perhaps a porter was saying to a mate: "There goes the postmaster of Rodchurch. He and I were boys together. I should know him anywhere, though it's ten years since I last saw William Dale." He ought to have used Paddington Station—he could have got to Salisbury that way, and gone into the woods the way he came out of them.

Last of all, that child in the glade—a child strayed from one of the cottages, or the child of some woodcutter who had brought her with him, who was perhaps a very little way off, who listened to the tale of what the child had seen five minutes after she had seen it. Of course nothing much would be thought of the child's tale at first; but it would assume importance directly suspicion had been aroused; it would link up with other circumstances, it would suggest new ideas and further researches to the minds of detectives, it might be the clue that eventually hanged him.

It seemed to Dale as he went over things in this quivering, quaking manner that, from the little girl weaving flowers back to the two Jews selling slops, he had recruited an army of witnesses to denounce and destroy him.

Only in one respect had he not bungled. He got rid of the clothes and hat all right. Cut and torn into narrow stripes they had gone comfortably down the drains of the temperance hotel in Stamford Street. That was

a night's wise labor. But the labor and thoughtful
care had come too late, on top of all the previous folly.
And he said to himself, "It's prob'ly all up with me.
This quiet is the usual trick of the p'lice to throw you
off the scent. They're playin' wi' me. They let me sim
to run free, because they know they can 'aarve me
when they want me."

With such thoughts, he went down-stairs of a morning to talk jovially with Ridgett, to chaff Miss Yorke;
and with the thoughts unchanged he came up-stairs
to glower at Mavis across the breakfast-table.

His thoughts in regard to Mavis were extraordinarily complicated. At first he had been horribly afraid of
her—dreading their meeting as a crisis, a turning-
point, an awful bit of touch-and-go work. It seemed
that she of all people would be the one to suspect the
truth. When she heard of the man's death, surely the
idea *must* have flashed into her mind: "This is Will's
doing." But then perhaps, when no facts appeared to
support the idea, she might have abandoned it. Nevertheless it would readily come flashing back again—
and again, and again.

To his delight, however, he saw that she did not suspect now, and there was nothing to show that she ever
had suspected. And he thought in the midst of his
great relief: "How stupid she is really. Any other
woman would have put two and two together. But she
is a stupid woman. Stupidity is the key-note to her
character—and it furnishes the explanation of half her
wrong-doing."

This reflection was comforting, but he still considered her to be a source of terrible danger to him. For
the moment at least, all his resentment about her past

unchasteness and her recent escapade was entirely
obliterated; it was a closed chapter; he did not seem to
care two pence about it—that is, he did not feel any
torment of jealousy. The offense was expiated. But
he must not on any account let her see this—no, because it might lead her, stupid as she was, to trace the
reason. He knew himself that if Mr. Barradine had
died otherwise than by his blows, he would have felt
quite differently toward Mavis. He would have felt then
" The swine has escaped me. We are not quits. That
dirty turn is not paid for." He would have continued
to smart under the affront to his pride as a man, and
association with Mavis would have still been impossible.

Logically, then, he must act out these other feelings;
Mavis must see him as he would have been under those
conditions. But it made it all so difficult—two parts
to render adequately instead of one. In the monstrous
egotism produced by his fear, he thought it uncommonly rough luck that the wife who ought to have
been dutifully assisting him should thus add to his
cares and worries. Sometimes he had to struggle
against insane longings to take her into his confidence, and compel her to do her fair share of the job
—to say, slap out, " It's you, my lady, who've landed
me in this tight place; so the least you can do is to
help pull me into open country."

Moreover, as the days and nights passed, instincts
that were more human and natural made him crave for
re-union. He yearned to be friends with her again. He
felt that if he could safely make it up, cuddle her as
he used to do, hold her hands and arms when he went
to sleep, he would derive fortitude and support against

his fear, even if he obtained no aid from her in dodging the law.

He thought during the inquest that the fear had reached its climax. Nothing that could come in the future would be as bad as this. Yet all the time he was telling himself, " There is no cause for the fear. It is quite baseless. All is going as nice as nice."

Indeed, if he had conducted the proceedings himself, he could not have wished to arrange anything differently. The whole affair was more like a civilian funeral service—a rite supplemental to the church funeral—than a businesslike inquiry into the circumstances and occasion of a person's death. A sergeant and constable were present, but apparently for no reason whatever. Allen talked nonsense, grooms and servants talked nonsense, everybody paid compliments to the deceased—and really that was all. At last Mr. Hollis, the coroner, said the very words that Dale would have liked to put into his mouth—something to the effect that they had done their melancholy duty and that it would be useless to ask any more questions.

But Dale, sitting firmly and staring gloomily, felt an internal paroxysm of terror. Near the lofty doors of the fine state room common folk stood whispering and nudging one another—cottagers, carters, woodcutters; and Dale thought " Now I'm in for it. One of those chaps is going to come forward and tell the coroner that his little girl saw a strange man in the wood." He imagined it all so strongly that it almost seemed to happen. " Beg pardon, your honor, I don't rightly know as it's wuth mentionin', but my lil' young 'un see'd a scarecrow sort of a feller not far from they rocks, the mornin' afore,"

It did not, however, happen. Nothing happened.

And nothing happened when he came to the Abbey again to attend the real burial service—except that he found how wrong he had been in supposing that the fear had reached its highest point. He nearly fainted when he saw all those policemen—the entire park seeming to be full of them, a blue helmet under every tree, a glittering line of buttons that stretched through the courtyards and right round the church. Inside the church he said to himself, " They've got me now. They'll tap me on the shoulder as I come out."

Standing in the open air again he wondered at the respite that had been allowed, and thought, " Yes, but that is always their way. They never show their hand until they have collected all the evidence. The detectives, who've been on my track from the word 'go,' prob'ly advised the relatives to accept the thing as an accident in order to hoodwink the murderer. The tip was given to that coroner not to probe deep, because they weren't ready yet with their case;" and it suddenly occurred to him that he had left deep footsteps in the wood, and that plaster casts had been made of all these impressions.

He looked across a gravestone in the crowded churchyard and saw a strange man who was staring at the ground. A detective? He believed that this man was watching his feet, measuring them, saying to himself, " Yes, those are the feet that will fit my plaster cast."

After the funeral he began to grow calmer, and soon he was able to believe during long periods of each day that the most considerable risks were now over.

Then came news of the legacy to Mavis—the cursed

money that he hated, that threw him back into the earlier distress concerning his wife's shame, that restored vividness to the thoughts which had faded in presence of the one overpowering thought of his own imminent peril.

But here again he was governed by what he had set before himself as his unfailing guide-post—the necessity to conceal any motive for an act of vengeance. What would people think if he refused the money? It was a question not easy to answer, and the guide-post seemed to point in two opposite directions. He was harassed by terrible doubt until he and Mavis went to see the solicitor at Old Manninglea. During the conversation over there he assured himself that the solicitor saw nothing odd in the legacy, and made no guess at there having been an intrigue between Mavis and the benefactor; and further he ascertained that this was only one of several similar legacies. All was clear then: the guide-post pointed one way now: they must take the money.

But this necessity shook Dale badly again. It seemed as if the man so tightly put away in his lead coffin and stone vault was not done with yet. It was as if one could never be free from his influence, as if, dead or alive, he exercised power over one. Dale resisted such superstitious fancies in vain. They upset him; and the fear returned, bigger than before.

It was irrational, bone-crumbling fear—something that defied argument, that nothing could allay. It was like the elemental passion felt by the hunted animal—not fear of death, but the anguish of the live thing which must perforce struggle to escape death, although prolonged flight is worse than that from which it flies.

Dale had no real fear of death—nor even fear of the gallows. If the worst came, he could face death bravely. He was quite sure of that. Then, as he told himself thousands of times, it was absurd to be so shaken by terror. Terror of what? And he thought, " It is because of the uncertainty. But there too, how absurdly fullish I am; for there is no *real* uncertainty. My crime can not and will not be discovered. If I were to go now and accuse myself, people would not credit me."

He thought also, in intervals between the paroxysms, " I suppose what I've been feeling is what all murderers feel. It is this that makes men go and give themselves up to the police after they have got off scot free. They are safe, but they never can believe they're safe; they can't stand the strain, and if they didn't stop it, they'd go mad. So they give themselves up—just go get a bit o' quiet. And that is what I shall do, if this goes on much longer. I'd sooner be turned off short and sharp with a broken neck than die of exhaustion in a padded cell."

Then suddenly chance gave the hateful money an immense value, converted it into a means of escape from the outer life whose monotony and narrowness were assisting the cruelly wide inner life to drive him mad.

He went to Vine-Pits, and the strangeness of his surroundings, the difficulties, the hard work, produced a salutary effect upon him; but most of all he drew strength and courage from the renewal of love between Mavis and himself. That was most wonderful—like a new birth, rather than a reanimation. They loved each other as a freshly married couple, as a boy and girl who have just returned from their honeymoon, and who say, " We shall feel just the same when the time comes to keep our silver wedding."

So he toiled comfortably, almost happily. Mavis was perfectly happy, and he found increasing solace in the knowledge of this fact.

Thence onward his busy days were free from fear, except for the transient panics which, as he surmised, he would be subject to for the remainder of his life. They did not matter, because he could control them to the extent of preventing the slightest outward manifestation. All at once while transacting business he would feel the inward collapse, deadly cold, a sensation that his intestines had been changed from close-knitted substance to water; and he would think " This person " —a farmer, a servant, old Mr. Bates, anybody—" suspects my secret. He guessed it a long while ago. Or he has just discovered the proofs of guilt." Nevertheless he went on talking in exactly the same tone of voice, without a contraction of a single facial muscle, with nothing at all shown unless perhaps a bead of perspiration on his forehead.

" Good morning, sir. Many thanks, sir. . . . Yes, Mr. Envill, the stuff shall be at your stables by one P. M. sharp. I'm making it my pride to obey all orders punctually, whether big or small."

Thus he got on comfortably enough during the daylight waking hours. But the fear that had gone out of the days had made its home in the night. Sleep was now its stronghold.

His dreams were terrible. They were like immense highly-colored fabrics reeling off the vast gray thought-loom—that dreadful thought machine that

worked as well when the workshop was darkened as
when all the lamps were burning. Their pattern displayed infinite variety of detail, but a constant similarity in the main design.

They began by his being happy and light-hearted,
that is, he was *innocent;* and then gradually the horrible fact returned to his memory. Recently, or a long
time ago, he had killed a man. That was always the
end of the dream; his lightness and gaiety of spirits
vanished, and he felt again the load that he was eter-
nally forced to carry on his conscience.

The details of one form in which the dream worked
itself out were repeated hundreds of times. There was
a strange man who at first made himself extremely
agreeable, and yet in spite of all his amiability Dale
did not like him. Nevertheless there was some mysterious necessity to keep friends with him, even to
kow-tow to him. And Dale gradually felt sure that
he and this man had met before, and that the man
knew it, but for some sinister purpose concealed his
knowledge. They went about together in gay and
lively scenes, and the man grew more and more hateful to Dale—becoming insolent, making disparaging
remarks, sneering openly; and laughing when Dale
only tittered in a nervous way and swallowed all in-
sults. And Dale could not do otherwise, because he
was afraid of the man.

And finally this false friend disclosed his true hostile character in some strikingly painful manner.

For instance, the man would make Dale take off
his boots for him in some public place. They were together in a place like the lounge of some grand music-
hall; the electric light shone brilliantly, a band played

at a distance, the gaily dressed crowd gathered round them—young London swells with white waistcoats, pretty painted women, old men and young girls, and all of them watching, all contemptuously amused, all grinning because they understood that, though so big and strong, he was at heart a pitiful sort of poltroon, and that his companion was showing him up publicly. "Yes, you shall take my boots off for me. That's all you're fit for." And in spite of his anguish of resentment, Dale dared not refuse. The man had moved to a divan, he reclined upon his back, lifted his feet; and Dale, pretending to laugh it off as a bit of fun, took him by the heels.

Then he uttered a terrified cry—because he saw it was Barradine, dead, battered, with glassy staring eyes. All the people rushed away screaming, the lights went out, the music ceased: Dale was alone, at dusk, in a rocky wilderness, still dragging the dead man by the heels.

And then he would wake—to find Mavis bending over him, to hear her saying, "My dearest, you are sleeping on your back, and it is making you dream." He clung to her desperately, muttering, "Quite right, Mav. Don't let me dream. It's a fullish trick—dreaming."

Then he would settle himself to sleep again, thinking, "It is all no use. I love my wife; I bless her for the generous way in which she has risked all that money to give me a fresh start; I enjoy the work; I believe I may succeed with the business—but I shall never know real peace of mind. And sooner or later my crime will be brought home to me. It is always so. I've read it in the papers a dozen times. Murderers never get off altogether. Years and years pass; but at last justice overtakes them."

Already, although he did not recognize it, had come remorse for the wickedness of his deed. He had no regret for the fact itself, and not the slightest pity for the victim. Mr. Barradine had got no more than he deserved, the only proper adequate punishment for his offenses; but Dale knew that, according to the tenets of all religions, God does not allow private individuals to mete out punishment, however well deserved—especially not the death penalty.

He resolutely revived his idea of the dead man as a thing unfit to live—just a brute, without a man's healthy instincts—a foul debauchee, ruining sweet and comely innocence whenever he could get at it. Such a wretch would be executed by any sensible community. In new countries they would lynch him as soon as they caught him—" A lot of chaps like myself would ride off their farms, heft him up on the nearest tree, and empty their revolvers into him. And it wouldn't be a murder: it would be a rough and ready execution. Well, I did the job by myself, without sharing the responsibility with my pals; and I consider myself an executioner, not a murderer."

He could now always make the hate and horror return and be as strong as they had ever been, and thus solidify the argument whereby he found his justification; no mercy is possible for such brutes. Subconsciously he was always striving to reinforce it; as if the voice of that logical faculty which he admired as his highest attribute were always whispering advice, reminding him: " This is your strong point. It is the only firm ground you stand on. You can't possibly hope to justify yourself to other people; but if you don't justify yourself to yourself, then you are truly done for."

And he used to think: "I have justified myself to myself all along. I was never one who considered human life so sacred as some try to make out. Why should it be? Aren't we proved to be animals—along with the rest? The parsons own it nowadays themselves, allowing a man's soul to be what God counts most important, but not going so far as to say any animal's soul isn't immortal too. Then where's the sacredness? If it's right to kill a vicious dog or a poisonous snake, how is it so wrong to out a man that won't behave himself?"

Insensibly this consideration had the greatest possible effect on his conduct. Without advancing step by step in a reasoned progress, he understood that any one holding his views on human life generally should not attach an excessive value to his own individual life. He must carry his life lightly, and be ready to lay it down without a lot of fuss. Sauce for the goose is sauce for the gander. He acted on the maxim, risking his life freely, courting dangers that he would have avoided in the days before the day on which he executed Mr. Barradine.

Executed—yes. But God would not have authorized him, although Judge Lynch would. God would say: "It must be left to Me. I will attend to it in My own good time. From My point of view perhaps, keeping the man alive is in truth his punishment, and to kill him is to let him off. You have come blundering with your finite intelligence into the department of omniscient wisdom. Instead of interpreting

My laws, you have set up a law of your own invention."

And Dale sometimes thought: "But there isn't
any God. All that is my eye and my elbow. I believed it once, but I shall never believe it again."

His thoughts about God's laws were curious, and
baffling to himself. They had been always there, always active, but in a manner secondary and faint
when compared with his thoughts about his infringe-
ment of men's laws. Faith in God had seemed to be
quite gone. It used to permeate his entire mind; and
yet it dropped out as though it had been only in one
corner of his mind, and a hole had been made under
that corner for it to fall through. Now he sometimes
had the notion that it went out through many holes,
as if it had been forcibly ejected, and that his whole
mind was left in a shattered and unstable condition.

Then it began to seem that the faith had not truly
been altogether got rid of. Fragments of it remained.

Rapidly then he reached the certainty that he wished
to have the faith back again. His was an orderly
solid mind that could not do with cracks and holes in
it, trimness, neatness, and firmness of outer wall were
necessary to its well-being; openness to windy
doubts ruined it. He felt that an accidental universe
was the wrong box for it. He wanted to believe in
the God who created order out of chaos, the God who
settled cut-and-dried plans for the whole of creation
—yes, the God made in man's image, and yet the
Maker and Ruler of man.

And some days he did believe, and some days he
couldn't. But all at once an idea came, first soothing
then cheering him. He thought: "Whether I believe

or not, I'll take it for granted. I'll act as if God is real."

He did so, acting as if God were believed in as truly by him as by the most stanch believers. He clung to the idea. It seemed to be the way out of all his troubles. He would make peace with God—then there would be no need to bother about men, or offer any confession of his guilt to *them*.

He grew calmer now. Doing things had always suited him better than brooding over things. His new determination illuminated the reason for reckless adventures, and lifted their purpose to a higher plane. He thought now that he held his life at God's will— to be given back to God at a moment's notice.

This thought made him calmer still, made him strong, almost made him happy. A life for a life. He would expiate his offense in God's good time. So no danger was too big for William Dale to face; his courage became a byword; gentlefolk and peasants alike admired and wondered.

Out of the consistent course of action came the consistency of the thought that was governing the action. Assumption of the reality of God as a working hypothesis led to conviction of the existence of God.

Yet strangely and unexpectedly the attempt to formalize his faith almost shook his faith out of him again. Although throughout the episode of his acceptance by the Baptists he seemed so stolid and matter-of-fact, he was truly suffering storms of emotion. He fell a prey to old illusions; that unreasoning fear returned; he was thrown back into the state of terrified egoism which rendered lofty impersonal meditation beyond attainment.

That evening when for the first time he went to the
Baptist Chapel, the illusion was strong upon him
that every man, woman, and child in the congregation
had discovered his secret.   When they all stood up to
sing, it seemed that he was naked, defenseless, utterly
at their mercy. . With every word of their carefully
selected hymn they were telling him that they knew
all about him.   When they began their third verse,
they simply roared a denunciation straight at him:

> " But thus th' eternal counsel ran:
> ' Almighty love, *arrest that man.*' "

And the second and third hymns were just as bad,
shaking him to pieces, tumbling him headlong into
the terror he had felt when his crime was no more
than a week old. The rest of the service entranced and
delighted him, made him think: "These people are
in touch with God, and their God is full of love and
mercy. If He would accept me, I should feel safe."
At the end of the service he knelt, praying for this to
happen. Then he went home and doubted.

The fear was on him again in the beginning of his
interview with Mr. Osborn the pastor. He thought:
"This man has seen through me. He knows. Perhaps his past experiences have taught him to be quick
in spotting criminals. He may have been a prison
chaplain some time or other. Anyhow, he knows;
and he'll try to get a confession out of me, as sure as
I sit here."   But the beauty of the conception of God
as unfolded by Mr. Osborn banished the fear. He
thought: "If I had been told these things before, I
should have never ceased to believe. I feel it through

and through me. This is God; and if I am not too
late, if He will still accept me, I shall be saved. Christ,
the friend, the brother of man—same as described by
Mr. Osborn two minutes ago—can do it for me if He
will. He can take me home to Father." A verse
of one of those hymns echoed in his ears:

> "None less than God's Almighty Son
>   Can move such loads of sin;
> The water from His side must run,
>   To wash this dungeon clean."

And once more he prayed to the God of the Baptists;
and then once more doubted.

While he was walking home, he thought: "It is
too good to be true. Perhaps I'm fullish to pin my trust
to it. Do I believe in it all, or do I not?" He wanted
a sign; and when the storm of thunder and lightning
burst like the most tremendous sign one could ask
for, he seized this opportunity of risking his life, and
said: "Now I stand here for God to take me or
leave me."

He was left, not taken. The fear vanished, the
doubt passed, and he made his way into the Baptist
Church exactly as if, as Mr. Osborn had said, there
was an irresistible pressure behind him, and he could
not make his way anywhere else.

It was all right after his baptism. He knew then
that he would never doubt again. The faith was
permanent now: it would last as long as he himself
lasted. He had no more evil dreams. He slept
soundly, as a man sleeps when he has got home late
after a tiring journey. And in the morning and the

evening of each day he thanked God for having accepted him.

Then came the years of tranquillity, the respite from pain, his golden time. He was prosperous, respected; he had a loved and loving wife, and lovely lovable children; he had grain in his barns, money in his bank, peace in his mind. He felt too all the better part in him growing bigger and bigger; religion, in simplifying his ideas, had increased their value; his intellectual power seemed wider and more comprehensive when exercised with regard to all things that can be learned, now that he had entirely ceased to exercise it with regard to things that must not be questioned.

And then there had happened something that was like the knocking down of a house of cards, the blowing out of a paper lantern, or the obliteration of a picture scratched on sand when the inrushing tide sweeps over it.

His soul turned sick at the thought that God had not accepted, but rejected him. God refused his offer of humble homage, had seen the latent wickedness in him, had kept him alive until he also could see and loathe himself for what he really was—a wretch who in wishes and cravings, if not in accomplished facts, was as vile as the man he had slain.

XXXII

DALE'S meditations had carried him backward and forward through the past years, and left him against the blank wall of the present.

He was sitting on the fallen beech tree in the woodland glade. The sun had set, and the night promised to be darker than recent nights; when he looked at the grand gold watch given to him by his admirers, he could only just see its hands. Nearly nine o'clock. He had been here a long while. It was hours and hours since Norah went away. He sighed wearily, got up, and walked back to his empty home.

Quite empty—that was the impression it made upon his mind both to-night and all next day. He looked at it in the bright morning sunshine, across the meadows, while the scythes laid down the first long swathes of fragrant grass, and it seemed merely the shell of a house. He looked at it in the midday glare, as he came up the field to his dinner, and it seemed cold and black and cheerless. He looked at it in the softer, kinder light of late afternoon, and it seemed to him tragically sad—a monument of woe rather than a house, a fantastic tomb built in the shape of a house in order to symbolize the homely joy that had perished on this spot.

Yet smoke was rising from its chimneys, sound issuing from its windows. All day long it had been full of active cheerful life. It and the fields were happy in the animating harvest toil. Men with harvesters' hats, women with sunbonnets, cracked their rustic jokes, laughed, and sang at their labor; Mavis cooked food, filled the big white bobs with beer, sent out bannocks and tin bottles of tea; Dale's children had rakes and played at hay-making. Only the master, the husband, the father, was unhappy.

No one knew it, of course. To other people he appeared to be just the same as usual, naturally preoccupied with thoughts about the weather as one always is at grass-cutting time, giving his orders firmly, and seeing that they were obeyed promptly, smiling and nodding when you showed yourself handy, frowning and looking rather black if you did anything "okkard or feckless." Who could have guessed, as he looked at his watch and then at the sky, that he was thinking: " It wants five minutes of noon, and she is prob'ly out on what they term an esplanade. There is a nice breeze down there, comin' to her over the waater, blowin' her hair a bit loose, flappin' her skirts, sendin' out her neck ribbon like a little flag behind her. It's all jolly, wi' the mil'tary band, an' the smell o' the waves, an' crowds an' crowds o' people—an' she won't have occasion to think o' me. P'raps they've bid her wear her best—the white frock Mavis gave her, with the stockings to match, and the new buckle-shoes—and likely young lads 'll eye her all over as they pass. Yes, she's seeing now the young uns—the mates for her age—the proper article to make a photograph of a suitable pair; and she'll soon stop thinking anything about me, if she hasn't done it a'ready."

He was in his office still thinking of her, after the

busy day, when the postman brought the last delivery of letters.

"Good evening, sir. Only three to-night."

"Thank you. Good night, George," and Dale had
a friendly smile for this old acquaintance.

Postman George was growing fat and heavy, be-
traying signs of age. He had been a sprightly telegraph boy when Dale was postmaster of Rodchurch.

"Good night, sir. Fine weather for the hay."

"Yes, capital."

When the postman had gone Dale stood trembling.
One of the letters was from her. He felt unnerved by
the mere sight of her handwriting on the envelope—
the hand that was so like his own, the hand that she
had taught herself by laborious study and imitation
of his official copper-plate; and he thought, " If I was
wise I shouldn't open it. If I was strong enough, I
should just burn it, without reading. For, whatever's inside, it's going to make me one bit more des-
p'rate than I am now."

He snatched up his hat, went out of the house, and
walked along the road holding her letter pressed tight
against his heart. There was a gentle air that floated
pleasantly over the fields, and in spite of all the heavy
rain that had fallen such a little while ago, the white
dust rose in high clouds when a motor-car came whiz-
zing by. After the car two timber wagons crept
slowly, and then there were children trailing a broken
perambulator; but directly the road became vacant
again, he leaned against a gate and opened the envelope. He had felt that he must be quite alone when
he read what she said to him, and had intended to go
farther, but he could not wait any more.

" Sir, I beg to say "—That was how he had taught her to begin all letters: she knew no other mode of address. " I beg to say this is a very large place and you can see the sea from the bedrooms." . . .

He read on; and his pleasure was so exquisite and his pain so laceratingly sharp that the sky and the fields swam round and round.

. . . " There's nice girls here, one or two. Nellie Evans do all she can to make me not so miserable. She has a sweetheart at Rodchurch. They all have their boys if you believe their talk.

" And all the marks at the end are the sweet kisses I give my boy. For you are my boy now—my own secret one, and I am your loving girl

" Norah."

She was thinking only of him; she wanted no one younger and handsomer; in her eyes and thoughts he was not old: he was her boy. Those words had a terrible effect upon him. They entered his blood as if they had been an injection of some sweetly narcotic drug; thy lanced deep into his bowels as if they had been a surgeon's knife; they made him like a half-anesthetized patient who at the same time dreams of paradise and feels that he is bleeding to death.

" You are my boy . . . and I am your loving girl."

He moved from the gate, hurried along the dusty road, and entered Hadleigh Wood at the first foot-path. As he got over the stile he was saying to himself, " This letter finishes me. I can't go on with it after this. I'm done for."

Then, as he walked in the cool silence beneath the dark firs, he held her letter to his lips—kissed the inked crosses that she had set as marks to represent her kisses—counted and kissed them and counted them until his hot tears blinded him.

She wanted him; she longed for him; he was her boy.

He could get to her to-night. She was only twenty or twenty-two miles away, as the crow flies—say half an hour's journey if one had the wings of a heron. He could rush home, jump into his gig, and send the horse at a gallop; he could get there by road or rail, somehow; he could telegraph, telling her not to go to bed, telling her to go to the station and wait for him there.

Then he would walk with her in the moonlight by the sea, on the wet sand, close to the breaking waves. When they came back to the Institution no light would be showing from any of the windows, and she might say, "I'm shut out. When they come down to let me in, won't they make a fuss?" But he would say, "You are not going in there again." "What," she would say, "are you taking me back to Vine-Pits after only two days? Don't you think Mrs. Dale will be angry?"

Then he would say, "I'm not taking you back. I'm going to take you half across the world with me. I've tried hard, Norah, but I can't do without you. I own up, I'm beat, I take the consequences. I'm not good, I'm bad. I've done wicked things, and now I'm ripe for the crowning wickedness. I'm going to break my wife's heart, dishonor my children's name, and take you down to hell with me."

Or if he could not say and do all that, he might at least do this. He could pick her up in his arms and wade out to sea with her; he could whisper and kiss and wade until the ribbed sand went from under his feet; and then he would swim, go on whispering, kissing, and swimming until his strength failed him—yes, he could drown himself and her, so that they died locked fast in each other's arms, taking in death the embraces that had been denied them in life.

He was crying now as a child cries, abandoning himself to his tears, not troubling to wipe them away, temporarily overcome by self-pity. But soon he shook off this particular form of weakness, and thought, "What nonsense comes into a man's head, when he's once off his right balance—such wild nonsense, such mad nonsense. Drown *her*, poor innocent. Make her pay *my* bill. Think of it even—when I'd swim the Atlantic to save her life, if it was in danger."

And then the thought that had been the impetus or origin of these fantastic imaginations presented itself again, and more strongly than before. He said to himself, "This letter is my death-warrant. I can't go on. It is my death-warrant."

He had made straight for the main ride, and he walked straight along it in the direction of Kibworth Rocks. As he drew toward them it was as if the spirit of the dead man called him, seeming to say: "Come and keep me company. Our old quarrel is over. You and I understand each other *now*. We are two of a kind, just as like as two hogs from one litter—you the sanctimonious psalm-singer and I the conscienceless profligate—we are brothers at last in our beastliness."

Dale walked with his hands clasped behind his back, thoughtfully looking at the trees, and trying to suppress his wild imaginations. But he could not suppress them. The dead man seemed to say, "Don't be a humbug, don't pretend. You know we are alike. Why, when you looked in the glass the other day, you *saw* the resemblance. You saw my puffy eye-orbits and my pendulous lip in your own face."

Dale shrugged his shoulders, held his head high, and grunted fiercely. But when he was abreast of the rocks, this imagined voice seemed to speak to him again.

"You and I have drawn so near together that there's only one difference now—that you are alive and I am dead. But even that difference will be gone soon."

And Dale, walking on rather slower than before, made an odd gesture of his left hand, a wave of hand and arm together, as of a dignified well-to-do citizen waving off some impudent mendicant: seeming to say, "Be damned to you. Just you lie quiet where I put you, and don't worry. I decline to have anything to do with you, or to allow the slightest communication between us. I simply don't recognize you—nor will I ever admit again that I see the faintest resemblance. If I wished, I could explain why. Only I shan't condescend to do so—certainly not to *you*."

Out of the big ride he went into one of the narrower cuts, and followed it until he came to the woodside boundary of the Barradine Orphanage. This was where Mavis had stood looking at it years ago, when the building was in course of construction. The wooden fence that she had thought so stiff and ugly then was all weak and old, green and moss-covered, completely broken down in many places. Inside, the privet hedge had grown broad and thick; and this barrier, although any one could easily thrust himself through it, was evidently considered sufficient, since no trouble had been taken to repair the outer fence. Indeed, what protective barriers could be needed for such an enclosure? It contained no money or other kind of treasure; and who, however base, would attack or in any way threaten a lot of children?

Dale looked at the top of the belfry tower and the roof of the central block, and thought of it as a temple of youth, a sacred place dedicated to the worship of tender and innocent life. He moved through the trees and found a point where, on higher ground, he could look across into the garden and see a part of the terrace and verandas. None of the girls was visible. They had been gathered into those hospitable walls for the night.

Presently he thought he heard them singing. Yes, that was an evening hymn. The girls were thanking God for the long daylight of a summer's day, before they lay down to rest, to sleep, to forget they were alive till God's sun rose again.

And Dale began once more to think of God. To-night he would not fly from the sound of the girls' voices. All that reluctance and distaste was over and done with; it belonged to the time when he was still struggling against the inevitable drift of his inclinations. Now he had passed to a state of mind that nothing external could really affect.

"The finger of God"—Yes, those were unforgivable words. He stretched himself at full length upon the ground, leaned his head on his elbow, and lay musing.

He taxed his imagination in order to give himself a

concept of what such a tremendous figure of speech should in truth convey. One said finger, of course, because one wished to imply that no effort was used, scarcely any of the divine force drawn upon—just as one says of a man, he did so-and-so with a turn of the wrist, that is, quite easily, without putting his bac.. into it. Yes, he thought, that's about right. Then to make up something for an instance, just to spread the idea as big as it ought properly to be, one might say that once upon a time God gave our sun and all the other suns the slightest push with His finger, *and they haven't done moving yet.*

And it seemed to him that, look where one pleased, one could see the real work of the finger of God. It had been giving him, William Dale, faint imperceptible pushes for fifteen years, and see now at the end where it had pushed him. First it had pushed him upward, higher and higher, to a position of conspicuous pride, to the topmost summit of a fair mountain, where he could look round and say, " I have all that I pined for. This is the world's castle, and I am the king of the castle." Then it had begun to push him down the other side of this mountain, the dark side, the side that was always in shadow, downward and still downward to the miasmic unhealthy plain where all was rankness, downward to the level of corruption and death. Yes, it had brought him, the bold, proud law-maker, down and down till he stood no higher than the victim of his law.

He remembered the common phrase—so often employed by himself—comparing mice with men. Am I a man or a mouse? And it seemed that no cat had ever played with a mouse as the Infinite Ruling Power of the universe had been playing with the man William Dale. He had been allowed to break loose, to frisk and jump, to fancy he was free to run right round the earth if he wished to do so; and all the while he had truly been a prisoner, the helpless prey of his captor, held close to the place of ultimate doom.

If he had been promptly convicted and hanged, it would have been no punishment at all compared with what was happening now. The long delay was the essential part of the punishment, and of the lesson. The fact that no one suspected his crime had given him the period of agonized suspense, with all those dream-torments, the fear of death which was worse than death itself.

He thought of all the things that had appeared to be blind chances but were really stern decrees. The true function of the money that came from the dead man's hand was to keep him always on the rack of memory. And with the aid of the money he had been made to move a little nearer to the site of his crime. He had been made to buy Bates' business so that he might dwell right up against Hadleigh Wood, see it every day from his windows, hear it whispering to him every night when he was not asleep and dreaming of it. But for that apparently lucky chance of Mr. Bates' retirement, he would have gone to some splendid new country, and severing ties of locality, would have shattered associations of ideas, and been *able to forget.* He had made up his mind to go to one of the Australian colonies and make a fresh start there. But that didn't match with God's intentions by any manner of means.

His thoughts returned to Norah, and here again—

here more plainly than anywhere else—he saw the work of God. It was wonderful and awe-inspiring how God had selected the instrument that should destroy him. He felt that he could have resisted the charms of any other girl in the world except this one. In mysterious ways Norah's fascination was potent over him, while it might have been quite feeble in its effects with regard to other men. But for Dale she represented the solid embodiment of imagined seductiveness, allurement, supreme feminine charm; that flicker of wild blood in her was to him an essential attraction, and it linked itself inexplicably with the amorous reveries of far-off days when, young and free and wild himself, he loved the woodland glades instead of hating them.

The selected instrument—Yes, she was the one girl on earth who could have been safely employed to achieve God's double purpose of overwhelming him with base passion and bringing his lesson home to him simultaneously. No other girl that ever was born could have aroused such desire in him, and yet have slipped unscathed out of his arms at the very moment when the consummation of his sin seemed unavoidable. Any other girl must herself have been sacrificed in destroying him; only the child who had frightened him in the wood could instantaneously, by a few unconsidered words, have taken all the fire out of him and changed his heart to a lump of ice. That was a stroke of the Master: most Godlike in its care for the innocent and its confusion of the guilty.

He remembered how grievously he had dreaded this child—the little black-haired elf that had seen him hiding. It had made him shiver to think of her—the small woodland demon, the devil's spy whose lisping treble might be distinct and loud enough to utter his death sentence. A thousand times he had wondered about her—thinking: "She is growing up. She belongs here;" looking in the faces of cottagers' children and asking himself: "Are you she? Or you? Or you?" Then he had left off thinking about her.

She had come into his life again, into his very home, and he had never once asked himself: "Is Norah she?" No, because God would not allow him to do so; it had suited God's purpose to paralyze the outlet of all natural thought in that direction. So she grew tall and strong under his eyes—the dreaded imp of the wood eating his food, squatting at his own fireside; changing into the imagined nymph of the wood that he had seen only in dreams; becoming the very spirit of the wood—yes, the wood's avenging spirit.

He moved from his recumbent position, sat up, and drew out Norah's letter from the breast pocket of his jacket. He read her letter again, and his sadness and despair deepened. There was no revolt now; he felt nothing but black misery. He thought: "I used to fear that she would be the means of my death, and now death is coming from her. This letter is my death-warrant."

There was no other way out of his troubles. Life had become unendurable; he could not go on with it. And this thought became now a fixed determination. He must copy the example of other and better men; he must do for himself, as old Bates and many others had done for themselves when they found their lives too hard for them.

If he didn't—oh, the whole thing was hopeless.

Suppose that he rebelled against this cruel necessity. No, he saw too plainly the torment that would lie before him—disgrace, grief of wife and children, soon all the world wishing him dead. And no joy. The girl would be taken from him. The world—or God —would never allow him to hide and be happy with her.

Suppose he were to carry her off to the Colonies, and attempt to begin the new life that he had planned fifteen years ago. Impossible—he was too old; nearly all his strength had gone from him; the mere idea of fighting his way uphill again filled him with a sick fatigue. And the girl, when she saw him failing, physically and mentally, would desert him. *Her* love could not last—it was too unnatural; and when, contrasting him with other men, she saw that he was feeble, exhausted, utterly worn out, she would shake off the bondage of his companionship. No, there was no possible hope for the future of such a union.

He thought: "Other men at fifty are often hale and hearty, chock-full of vigor. But that's not my case." He felt that, though his frame remained stout enough, he had exhausted his whole supply of nerve-force; and this was due not to length of years, but to the pace at which he had lived them. He thought: "That is what has whacked me out—the rate I've gone. If I'd been some rich swell treating himself to a harem of women, horse-racing, gambling at cards; or if I'd been one of these City gentlemen floating companies, speculating on the Stock Exchange, and so on; or if I'd been a Parliament man spouting all night, going round at elections all day, people would have said: 'Oh, what a mighty pity he doesn't give himself a proper

chance, but lives too fast.' Yet those men would all
be reposing of themselves compared with *me*. It
stands to reason. It could not be otherwise. And
for why? Because a *murderer* lives other men's years
in one of his minutes—and the wear and tear on him
is more than the Derby Race-Course, the Houses of
Parliament, and the Stock Exchange all rolled into
one crowd would ever feel if they went on exciting
themselves from now to the Day of Judgment."

And again he felt self-pity, but of another kind than
that which had stirred him an hour ago. Now it was
clear-sighted, analytical, almost free from weakness.
He thought: "It is a bit rough—it is rather hard, rather
cruel on me, all said and done. For I know that I
might have bin a good man. The good lay in me—
it only wanted drawing out." He remembered the
elevating effect of his love for Mavis, how through
all the time of his belief in her purity he had tried
to purify himself, to purge away all the grossness and
sensualness that, as he vainly fancied, made him unworthy to be the mate of so immaculate a creature;
but he was not allowed to continue the purifying process; her horrible revelation ended it—knocked the
sense out of it, made it preposterously absurd. "If
Mavis had been in the beginning what she has come
to be at last, she would have kept me on the highroad
to Heaven." But all the chances had gone against
him. "My father failed me, my mother failed me,
my wife failed me."

"The worst faults I had in my prime were conceit
and uppishness, but they only came from my ignorance. They'd have been wiped out of me at the start,
if I'd had the true advantages of education; regular

school training, such as gentlemen's sons enjoy, would
have made all the difference. It's all very well to
talk about educating yourself and rising in the world
at the same time, but it can't be done. There's a
season for everything, and the best part of education
must be over before you begin to fight for a position.
Otherwise the handicap is too heavy."

His pity for himself became more poignant; yet
still there was nothing weakening in it, at least nothing that tended to alter his determination. "No,"
he thought, "take me all round, I couldn't originally
have bin meant to turn out a wrong un. I've never
bin mean or sneaking or envious in my dealings with
other people. I've never spared myself to give a
helping hand to those who treated me decently. And
no one will ever guess the kindly sentiments I entertained for many other men, or the pleasure I derived
the few times I could feel: 'This chap is one I respect,
and he seems to like me.' I wanted to be liked, but
the gift o' making myself liked was denied me, Yet,
except for being cast down into sin, I should have got
over *that* difficulty. I was on the right road there
too. By enlarging my mind I'd become more sympathetic. Though always a shy man really and truly,
I was learning to smother the false effects of my shyness."

Thinking thus of his mind, and his long-continued
efforts to improve its powers, he felt: "To go and
extinguish all this is an awful thing to have to do."

Still his determination was not altered. The mystery of that great pageant, the mental life of William
Dale, could not be permitted to unfold itself any further. It must cease with a snap and a jerk, much as

when the electric current becomes too strong for a small incandescent lamp and the bulb bursts, the filaments fuse, and all that the lamp was showing disappears in darkness.

Yes, darkness without a glimmer of hope.

The finger of God—one can't get away from it. If it pushes you toward the light, then rejoice exceedingly and with a loud voice; if it pushes you into the dark, then swallow your tongue and go silently. It seemed to Dale that he comprehended the whole scope and purport of his doom, and that God's tremendous logic made the justice of his doom unanswerable. He understood that the law which he had himself set up was to be binding now. He must execute himself, as he had executed Everard Barradine. It is for this, the hour of hopelessness and despair, that God has been waiting. Now it is God's good time. God has slowly taught him his worthlessness and infamy, so that he may die despairing.

XXXIII

"MAVIS," he said, after supper that evening
"I've noticed a branch at the top of the
walnut tree that doesn't look to me too safe. I must
lop that tree first chance I get—or we shall have an
accident."

Next morning he was up and dressed before the
sun rose, and he came down-stairs very softly, carrying his boots in his hands, and pausing now and then
to listen. The house was quite silent, with no one
stirring yet except himself. He sat on the lowest step
of the stairs and put on his boots, listened again, then
quietly let himself out of the front door.

On the threshold the cool morning air rushed into
his lungs, expanding them widely, making him draw
deep breaths merely for the pleasure of tasting its
freshness and sweetness. The light was still gray
and dim, and the buildings round the yard were vague
and shadowy. In the garden there was a delicious
perfume of roses—those most beautiful of all flowers
pouring out their fragrant charms, although their
glory of color had not yet burst forth from the shadows of night.

Moving like a shadow himself, he hurried noiselessly to his work. One of the shorter ladders would be
long enough to reach the lower branches, and he could
climb from them as high as he wished. He fetched
the ladder from the yard, fixed it in position against

the walnut tree, and then went back to the yard for the other things he wanted.

In the loft where the tools were kept he remained much longer than he had intended. At first there was scarcely any light at all up here, and, having stupidly forgotten to bring a box of matches, he had to grope about fumblingly; but gradually the light improved. He found a saw, and, attaching it to a light cord, slung it round his neck in the approved woodman fashion. The saw would be carried merely for the sake of appearances. Then he hunted for the particular rope that he required for his purposes, and could not find it. He had seen it two days ago, neatly rolled, in the corner with other tackle; but now the corner was all untidy, a confused mass of cordage, and the good new strong rope was concealing itself beneath weak old rubbish. He knew that he could trust this rope, because it was the exact fellow of the one on the pulleys—and with the pulley rope they let down loads that were a good deal heavier than any man.

Then all at once a ray of light shot through a chink in the boarded wall, and came like a straight rainbow across the dusty gray floor and into the corner where he stood stooping. His rope was there right enough, showing itself conspicuously, seeming to rise on its coils like a snake and slip its sinuous neck into his hands, so that he had picked it up and taken it from the corner before he knew what he was doing.

It was necessary to arrange things with care, but he was a strangely long time in making his running noose and satisfying himself that it could not possibly give way or anyhow fail. He was also slow in mak-

ing a stop-knot at the part of the rope that he proposed to attach to the tree, and he felt an extraordinary obtuseness of intelligence while making the
calculations that he had so many times thought out
during the night. " Yes," he said to himself, "twice
the length of my arms. That's quite right. Six feet
is twice the length of my arms—but I'll try it again.
Yes—quite all right. Must be. That's a six foot
drop. That's what I decided—a six foot drop. The
rope'll stand that. But it mightn't stand more. An'
less than six feet mightn't be enough either. Yes,
that's right."

Then he thought: " I am wasting time." He was
conscious of an imperative necessity for speed and a
great danger in acting too hurriedly; and a queer idea
came to him that while in this loft he had been having
a series of cataleptic fits—sudden blanknesses, total ar-
rests of volition if not of consciousness, during which
he had stood still, listening or staring, but not doing
anything to the rope.

He came down from the loft, and in the doorway
below a flood of bright sunlight dazzled him. The
sun had risen. Some of Mavis' pigeons were cooing
gently on the granary roof, a horse in the stables began to whinny, and two of the men came whistling
round the outer barn into the yard.

" Good mornin', sir."

" Good morning."

" Another nice day we are goin' to 'aarve, sir."

" Yes, looks like it."

Seeing his rope and saw, the men asked if there was
a job on hand in which they were to help; but he told
them " No." He was only going to take down a

small branch out of the walnut tree, and he could do it without any assistance.

Then the men went into the stables, and Dale passed through the kitchen garden to the back of the house. Beneath the walnut tree he slung the coiled rope over one shoulder and under the other arm; and then he slowly ascended the ladder, saying to himself: " I am on the steps of my scaffold. The scaffold steps. I am going up the scaffold steps." From the top of the ladder he got upon a branch, and, putting his arms about the stem, began to limb. " Yes," he said to himself, " my gallows tree. I am going up the gallows tree. This is my gallows tree;" and he climbed nimbly and firmly.

The green leaves were all round him, a green tent with pretty loopholes through which he could take peeps at the home that was on the point of vanishing forever from his eyes. He paused on a level with the broad eaves, and looked through between branches at a window on the first floor landing. The casements stood wide open; the square of glass glittered; the muslin curtains just stirred, trembled whitely. Far down below his feet were the flagged pathway, the wooden bench, and three shining milk-pans.

He climbed higher; and it seemed to him that from the moment he left the ground till now he had been like a drowsy man shaking off his sloth, like a drugged man recovering consciousness, like a man who was supposed to be dead rapidly coming to life again. With every inch added to the height from the ground, he felt stronger, more active, fuller of nervous and mus-cular energy. His fingers gripped each branch as firmly as if they had been iron clamps; his feet, en-

cumbered by the stout boots, seemed to catch hold and
cling to the slightest irregularities of the smooth
bark as skilfully and tenaciously as if they had been
the prehensile paws of a cat; not a touch of vertigo
troubled him; he felt as fearless and splendidly alive
as when he climbed tall trees for buzzards' eggs thirty-
three years ago.

Soon he had climbed so high that he knew it would
not be safe to climb higher. He must stop here. At
this point the main stem was still thick enough to
take the shock that in a minute he would give it.
Above this point it might not stand the strain. Besides, this was high enough for appearances. He was
within reach of the branch that had some decayed
wood at the top of it. Sitting astride a branch close
to the stem, he adjusted and fixed his rope, binding
it round and round the stem and over and under the
branch, reefing it, making it taut and trim so that no
strain could loosen it; and all the while he was conscious cf the power in his arms and hands, the volume
of air in his lungs, the flow of blood in his veins, the
nervous force bracing and hardening his muscles. The
rope was fast now. Now he assured himself that its
free length—the part from the tree to the noose—was
absolutely correct as to its amount. Nothing remained to do, nothing but to stand upon the branch,
fix the noose round his neck, and step off into
the air.

Lightly and easily he changed his position, stood
upon the branch, holding the stem with his left hand,
the noose with his right; and the life in him pulsed
and throbbed with furious strength. It tingled
through and through him, filled him as if he had been

a battery overstored with electricity, shot out at his extremities in lightning flashes.

In this final position his head had emerged into a leafless space, so that he could see in all directions; could look down at the house, at that open window, the kitchen door, and the flagged path; could look at the barn roofs, the rick-yard, the beehives; could look at his fields, where the grass lay drying; or could look away at woodland, at heath, at distant hill. He paused purposely to give himself one last look round at all he was leaving.

Yes, here was the world—the bitterly sweet world, smiling once more as it wakes from sleep. Looking down at it he felt an agony of regret. How intolerably cruel his doom. Why should he of all mortals have been made to suffer so? But God's law—his own law. Mentally he was obeying, but physically he was in fierce revolt. Every fiber of him, every drop of blood, every minute nerve-cell was crying out against the execution.

The sunlight flowed across the fields in golden waves, the colors of the flowers sprang out, the soft cool air was like a supremely magnificent wine that could give old nerveless men the strength of young giants; and the very marrow of his bones seemed to shrink and scream for mercy. " Ought to 'a' done it at night," he said to himself. " Mr. Bates didn't wait till daylight. In the dark—that's it. At the prisons they give you a bonnet—extinguishing cap; high walls all round you too; and they do it at the double quick —hoicked out of your cell and pinioned in one movement, bundled through the shed, and begun to dance before you can think. Darkness, the sound of a bell, and the chaplain's whisper, 'Merciful Lord, receive this sinner.' And I've heard say they stupefy 'em first, make 'em so drunk they don't know where they are while they shove 'em into nowhere. . . . Very easy compared with this set-out;" and he groaned. " O God, you've fairly put top weight on me—and no mistake."

But he would have done it if he had not heard his daughter's voice.

Rachel had come to the open window, and she uttered a frightened cry at sight of him perched high in the tree.

" Oh, dads, do take care! "

Next moment her mother came to the window; and they stood side by side, each with a hand to her eyes, watching him in the same attitude of anxiety.

"Don't speak to him," whispered Mavis; and Dale heard the whisper as clearly as if it had been close against his ear.

He could not do it before them. He had been too slow about it; he could not darken their lives with the visible horror of it. And it seemed to him that he had not sufficiently thought of its effect upon them. The whole thing had been clumsily planned. Just at first, when he was found hanging dead with the saw dangling from his neck, it might have been believed that he had slipped and fallen, and hanged himself by accident; but afterward all would have known that it was suicide. The truth would have been betrayed by the running noose, by recollections of Mr. Bates, and by everybody's knowledge of an ancient local custom.

" All right," he said. "Don't alarm yourselves, my

dears. I must give this job up, Mavis. I can't quite reach where I wanted to."

"Mind how you come down," said Mavis. "Do come down carefully."

"Yes, dads," said Rachel, "do *please* come down carefully."

He climbed down slowly, feeling no joy in his respite, saying to himself: "I must think of some other way. I must finish with the hay-making, get the rick complete, and clear up everything in the office—so's at least poor Mav'll find things all shipshape when she has to take over and manage without me. My hurry to get it through was selfishness; for, after all, I've best part of three weeks to do it in. The on'y real necessity is to have it done before Norah comes home."

And again he thought of the finger of God. This clumsy hurried execution had been refused by God. He was being pushed away, so that the last glimpse of his eyes should not see the pleasant picture of home.

He must do it privately, secretly, in a lonely spot; and he must spare no pains, must plot and scheme till he contrived all the convincing details of a likely accident. That was how he had killed Everard Barradine; and he must arrange matters similarly for himself.

XXXIV

TWO or three days passed. The busy yet peaceful life of home and fields was going on; the hay had been carried; the rick was made, and the rick-sheet covered a handsome pile.

Dale worked hard, quite in his old untiring way, and seemed just his natural self; but truly he was mentally detached from the surrounding scene. For the second time in his life, and to a greater extent than the first time, he was subjugated and controlled by one dominant idea. Throughout each day all things around him were dreamlike and unsubstantial, and he performed many actions as automatically as if he had been a somnambulist. He walked and talked or rode on the shaft of a wagon without in the least troubling to think what he was doing, and every time his thought became active it seemed to spring into vigor again merely to obey the prompting of the inner voice that now governed him.

Thus while sitting on the wagon shaft he thought: "If I pitched myself off and let the wheels go over me, that would be *likely*, just the accident that fools are always making, but it wouldn't fulfil the other conditions that have been laid on me. Also it might fail. I might only mess myself up, and not quite kill myself."

Half an hour afterward, as he walked beside the empty wagon back to his hay fields, he was still hammering away at the dominant idea.

A gun and a hedge—no accident can be more common than that. Say you want to shoot some rats that have been showing their ugly whiskers in the field ditches; take your gun, well charged, and blow your brains out among the brambles of an untrimmed hedge.

Or these motor-cars! He thought of the way they came racing down the highroad from Old Manninglea. How would it be to wait for one of these buzzing, crashing, stinking road monsters over there on the edge of the heath, and jump out just in front of it? If one stooped down and took the full shock on one's forehead, it would mean a mess that there would be no patching together again. But one could not attempt that in daylight, because the driver would jam the breaks on, swerve round one, do anything desperate rather than run into one. And if he could not avoid one, he would tell everybody at the inquest that it was a plain suicide and nothing else. There would be passengers in the car too, who would also swear to its being a suicide. And at night these traveling cars have such powerful head-lamps that the roadway is lighted up for a hundred yards in front of them. Even at night, they would recognize it as suicide.

Toward dusk every evening external things became more real, and his hold on life tightening, he suffered more acutely in each hour that passed. Night after night he went back to Hadleigh Wood. It was the wood of despair, the focal point of all his pain, and he was drawn to it irresistibly through the gathering darkness.

On the second evening he found it difficult to get

away. Mavis stopped him, asked him some domestic
question, and then began to talk about a new suit of
clothes for their boy. He was alive again now, emerged
from his somnambulistic state, and he gave full attention to this matter of Billy's new serge suit; nevertheless, all at once she apologized for troubling him,
and inquired if he had anything on his mind.

"No, Mav, of course not."

"Are you sure, Will? Do tell me if you've something worrying you."

"What should I have to worry me?" and he put his
arm round her ample waist, and gave her an affection-
ate squeeze.

"The hay's all right, isn't it?"

"Yes, everything is all right. . . . You can't do
better than you've suggested about Billy. Take him
with you to Manninglea—and, look here, if Mr. Jones
can't fit him properly out of stock, let him make the
suit to measure. Don't consider the extra expense.
We can afford it."

"Thank you, Will." Mavis was delighted. "You've
told me to do the very thing I wanted to do; but of
course I'd never have done it without your authority.
I've been longing to see the little chap in clothes regularly cut out and finished for him, and nobody else."

Going through the yard Dale was stopped by his
men. The foreman wanted directions for to-morrow's
work; the carter asked for three new tires; the stableman regretted to be compelled to report that one of
the horses had broken his manger rack.

As he finally came out on the road, Dale was thinking, "Soon now I shall be gone, but everything here

will be just the same. They will all of them find that
they can do very well without me: the men, the children, Mavis—yes, even Norah. Mavis will be the one
who will grieve for me. Norah will suffer most, but it
will be only for a little while. She'll take another
sweetheart—a real sweetheart this time, and she'll
marry, and give birth to babies; and it will be to her as
if I had died a hundred years ago, as if I had never
lived at all, as if I'd been somebody she'd read of in a
story-book, or somebody she'd dreamed about in one
of those silly nasty sort of dreams which young girls
can't help having, but are ashamed to remember and
always try to forget."

Mavis, however, would wish to remember him, and
be sorry when she found his image fading.   She
would struggle to keep it bright and fresh.   She
would grieve long and sincerely—and then she would
be quite happy. She wouldn't marry again; she
wouldn't do anything foolish. "No," he thought,
"she'll just devote herself to the bairns, working for
them late and early, and managing the business as
well as I have managed it myself. She'll be cheated
a bit here and there, as a woman always is—but, all
said and done, she'll do very well without me. Customers will support her—the word will go round.
'Don't let's turn our backs on the widow of that poor
fellow Dale.'"

And he thought, with a bitterness of heart that almost made him sick, that perhaps after his death many
people might speak well of him; that certainly in the
little world of Vine-Pits Farm and the Cross Road
cottages there would be a natural inclination to exaggerate his few good qualities and be gentle to his

innumerable faults; so that a sort of legend of virtue would weave itself about his memory, making him a humble, insignificant, but local saint—to be placed at a respectful distance and yet not too far from the shrine of that great and illustrious saint the late Mr. Barradine. "Of course," people might say, "one was a grand gentleman, and the other only a common fellow who had raised himself a bit by hard work; but both of 'em were good kind men, and both no doubt have met with the reward of their goodness up there in Heaven."

As soon as he got into the wood he hurried as rapidly as he could toward Kibworth Rocks; and then when he got near them he walked slowly up and down the ride, with his head bowed and his hands clasped behind his back. And each evening the same thing happened. Visions of Norah assailed him; he passed again through the tortures of yearning desire that he had felt when he first read her letter; and he said to himself, "If proof was wanted, here's the proof. This would show me, if I didn't know already, that I must do it."

In imagination he saw her sitting alone on a balk of timber by the sea. Her lands lay loose in her lap; her neck was bent; her whole attitude indicated dejection, loneliness, sadness. She was thinking about him. She was thinking, "How cruel of him not to answer my sad little letter. He can't be so busy but what he could have found time to send me a few lines with his own hand. Just half a sheet of paper would have been enough—with one or two ink crosses at the end, to show me he prized the kisses that I put in my letter to him. It was brutal, yes, and cowardly,

to make Mrs. Dale write instead.   If Mrs. Dale hadn't
written telling me he'd received my letter, I couldn't
have found it in my heart to believe that he'd treat
me so abominably cruel."

And, groaning, he spoke to this mental picture that
he had evoked for his renewed torment.   " Norah, my
sweet one, I can't help myself.   Commands have been
laid upon me.   I'm no longer free to do what I please.
Norah, don't look away from me.   Turn to your boy
—let him see your dear eyes, though the sight of them
makes him bleed."   And the thought-picture obeyed
him.   He saw the entrancing oval of the face instead
of its delicate profile, looked into the profound beauty
of her eyes, felt that her warm red lips were close in
front of him, and that he would go raving mad if they
did not come closer still and let him kiss them.

After such spasms of burning pain he was temporarily exhausted; he felt completely emptied of emotional power, as if his nerves had delivered so fierce
a discharge that they must cease from working until
time and repose had allowed them to replenish themselves.   Then, so long as this state lasted, his love for
the girl was deprived of all material for passion; it
was as though the highest thinking part of him had
been cut off from the sensational mass, and only the
top of his head served to keep alive his memory of
the girl.

Then he thought of her with a fantastic longing that
seemed to him beautiful, immaterial, and innocent.
He said to himself, " I don't shirk my punishment.
I'm going to take it.   But fair's fair—There's no oc-
casion to make myself out worse than I really am.
Norah has taken hold of me a great deal more by my

int'lect than by the low animal kind of feelings that are the mark of the abject sinner. I can't live without her; but if I might live with her, I feel I could be content to let it all remain quite innocent between us. Yes, I feel I could be happy with her just as a companion, provided she and I were alone together, far away from everybody else—yes, I'd take my happiness on those terms, that she was never to be anything else to me but just that."

But soon those treacherous nerves restored themselves, the upper and lower parts of him were all one again, and the diffuse yet darting pain returned. Anger came too. It seemed that the dead man mocked him, went on softly laughing at him.

"What a humbug you are"—he gave the dead man words—"what a colossal humbug. You and your nice Sunday go-to-meeting thoughts. It's so easy, isn't it? to dress up one's rottenness in pretty sentimental twaddle. But you don't deceive anybody. You don't even deceive yourself, not for three minutes at a stretch. You know that underneath all your humbugging pretenses the black sin is unchanged. You are no better and no worse than I was. You are exactly the same as me."

And Dale, breaking his own rule, or forgetting in his anger that he had refused to discuss things with this imaginary voice, answered wrathfully.

"This girl cares for me—that's the difference between us. She offers me love. And that's something you never had."

"How do you know?" said the dead man. "Your Mavis was one of many. And, besides, don't be so sure that Mavis wasn't fond of me. She never ran away from me. She came when I whistled for her."

Dale brandished his arms wildly, turned round, and stared at the pine-trees and the bracken. It seemed to him that some imperishable essence of the man was really here, mingling with the shadows, floating in the dusky air; and that possibly over there among the rocks, if one went to look for it, one might see a simulacrum of the man's bodily shape—perhaps only a gray shadowy outlined form, the odious stranger of dreams. but more vague than in the dreams, stretched on his back, holding up his blood-stained boots, and grinning all over his battered face.

"Yes, perhaps so," said the voice. "But I notice that you don't come in to look for me. You keep to the ride still. Now you've got so very close to me, why do you turn shy of the last little bit? Is it that you wish me to save you trouble by showing myself?"

And Dale made gestures of semi-insane fury, and spoke in a loud, hoarse voice.

"Yes, show yourself if you want to. You 'aarve my leave. Come out an' stan' here before me. I'm not afraid of you—now or hereafter."

"Hereafter—hereafter—hereafter." As Dale moved away slowly, the dead man seemed to mock him, to laugh at him derisively. "Hereafter—yes, that's a big word. Yes, go and talk that out with God."

He went up one of the narrow tracks that led toward the dead man's Orphanage, intending to look at it and perhaps hear again the evening hymn; but before he got to those broken fences he turned and began to wander aimlessly through the trees. All his mind was now full of the awful thought of God, and

of the eternal punishment to which he believed God
had condemned him.

Christ had tried to save him; but the other two persons of the Holy Blessed and Glorious Trinity had
interposed, had prevented Christ from holding any
further communication with him, and together had
issued the fearful decree. That was it. Christ had
not deserted him; he had lost the right ever to approach Christ again. That accounted for everything
—the unutterable desolation, the dark despair, the
overwhelming necessity of death without one ray of
hope.

All that lovely and comforting faith in the endless
loving mercy of God the Son, the Redeemer of mankind, the Friend and sometime Comrade of man, was
to prove useless to him; the gentle creed of the Baptists could not be applied to so vile a case as his; he
was at handygrips with the dread Jehovah, the mighty
Judge, the offended King of creation.

Three Persons and one God—yes, but such different
Persons; and thinking of the triple mystery, he imagined that two of its component parts had probably
seen through him from the very beginning of his religious fervor. Only the other part, the part that he
wished was the whole, had believed in him and gone
on believing in him until it was forbidden to do so
any more.

The awe and reverence that he felt while he thought
in this manner made him bow his head and keep his
eyes humbly downcast, as one not daring to look upward to the heavenly throne; yet, profound and sincere as was his reverential awe, he unhesitatingly
translated all the sublime mystery of the skies into

the simple terms that alone possess plain meaning to man's limited intelligence. Nothing in the naturally courageous bent of his mind prevented him; everything in his experiences of the Baptists, with their constant habit of homely illustration, encouraged him to do so.

He imagined the First and the Third Persons of the Trinity seated royally but vaguely amid the clouds, all about them a splendor of light like that of sunset or dawn, melodious music faintly perceptible, exquisitely beautiful forms of angels rising on white wings, hovering obediently, fading obediently—but they themselves, the Lords of Life and of Death, the Masters of Time and Space, were two tangible concrete old men—two venerable wise old men— the ultimate strained extended conception of two powerful, honored, high-placed old men. And they talked as men would talk—not in the human vocabulary, but conveying to each other, *somehow*, human ideas—about the man William Dale.

It was at the period of his conversion or repentance or baptism, and they were speaking to each other of Their Beloved Son and His newest recruit. And God the Father seemed to say that He would hope for the best—although, as they Both knew, Christ was too easily imposed on. And God the Holy Ghost pursed His lips, and shook His head, and said, "Take it from Me, this fellow Dale will turn out badly"—seeming to add or explain that it was a mere pretense and no true repentance. "He has *never* repented of his crime. But of course he is anxious about his future, and would try any trick to escape the punishment he has richly deserved."

All this was terribly real to him, and he imagined the dread scene more strongly every moment. Those Two went on debating his case—becoming now so solidly presented to his imagination that he could see Them, the purple color of Their robes, the halo of light as in a painted window, Their forms, Their faces. God the Father was not unlike old Mr. Bates, except that He had a long beard and that there mingled with the candid dignity of His expression a consciousness of sovereign power. The Holy Ghost was clean-shaven, very thin, with sharp clearly-cut features as of somebody who does not enjoy robust health, and with a slight but painful suggestion of a Roman Catholic priest who habitually goes deep into private secrets and is never really satisfied until he has extracted the fullest possible confessions. He was the One that Dale had never so much cared about—the *difficult* member of the firm, the sleeping partner who never really slept, who professed to keep himself in the background, but who quietly asserted himself in important moments and proved infinitely the hardest of the Three.

And so it had been in this case. Since time is nothing, and then and now are all one, Dale imagined that while his Judges talked of him in Heaven his whole earthly career had flashed onward to its end; so that he and all that concerned him was disposed of at one continuous sitting. Thus, without a pause, the Holy Ghost was already saying, "You see I was right in my first view of the affair. Dale is disgracing himself again. Now You and I must not allow any further communication between Our dear Son and such an impostor."

Then Christ pleaded for him, prayed for mercy. Christ, although invisible, was certainly there, imploring mercy for the man he had trusted and loved; and, in spite of the fact that He remained unseen, His mere presence glorified and magnified the heavenly scene. The light grew softer and yet more supremely radiant; hosts of angels soared and hovered in vast spaces between the rolling clouds; a vibrating echo of the divine pity swept like music far and near.

But the Holy Ghost brought forward a large strongly-bound volume, opened it, and said very quietly, "Let Me show You what We have against him in the book." And at sight of the book Dale shivered and grew cold to the core of his spine. He knew perfectly well what was entered in the book, and he thought, "It stands to reason They could never get over *that*. I might have known all along *that* would do for me, an' there was no getting round it."

"This is his record," the voice of the implacable Judge continued; "not what I have attributed to him as secret thought, but words taken down as spoken by his own mouth. Having committed his crime, he had the calm audacity—*to lay the blame on US*...... Yes, here is the entry. This is the statement verbatim: 'It is the finger of God.'"

And Christ seemed to plead in an agony of grief still strove to lighten the punishment of the pitiful worm that he had deigned to call His brother man. "Oh, he didn't mean it."

"He *said* it," replied the Holy Ghost, dryly.

"But he didn't think what he was saying—he has been sorry for it ever since."

"Yet, frankly," said the Holy Ghost, "I can not see

that he has made a single effort to put things straight, by removing the blame to the proper quarter—that is, to himself."

Nevertheless, Christ still pleaded, could not be silenced, must go on struggling to save this one man—because He was the Savior of all men, because He was Christ. He was there, certainly, infallibly, although quite invisible—He was there, kneeling at the feet of the other Two, praying, weeping:—He was there, filling Heaven with inconsolable woe because, although His myriad suns shone bright as when He lighted them and His universe swung steady and true in His measureless void, one microscopic speck of dirt only just big enough to hold immortal life was in danger of eternal death.

All these imaginations were absolutely real to Dale, an approximate conception of the truth which he could not doubt; and he thought: "Need I wonder if I have not had the slightest glimpse of His face? It is my doom. Christ is cut off from me. So far as human time counts, the communication was broken that afternoon when I was seeming to see him as he rode into Jerusalem and my hankerings after Norah seemed to snap the thread.

"I was judged at that moment. It was my doom—never more, here or there, to look upon His face."

XXXV

I T was the evening of another day; and Dale stood
motionless in the ride, close to Kibworth Rocks.
The twilight was fading rapidly; clouds that had
crept up from the east filled the sky, and presaged a
dark and probably a stormy night. Every now and
then a gust of angry wind shook the tops of the fir
trees; then the air was still and heavy again, and then
the wind came back a little fiercer than before. Dale
felt sure that there would be rain presently, and he
thought: "If his ghost is really lying in there, it'll
get as wet as that first night when the showers
washed away all the blood."

He stared and listened, but to-night he could not
fancy that he heard the dead man calling to him. He
could not invent any appropriate conversation. It
seemed to him that the ugly phantom was refusing to
talk, that it had become sulky, or that it was pretending not to be there at all in order to effect a most insidious purpose. Yes, that must be the explanation.
It wanted to entice and lure him off the ride—to make
him venture right in there among the rocks, so that he
might be shown the thing that had haunted him in
dreams.

"Very well," said Dale, "so be it. That's the idea.
All right. I agree."

He did not, however, move for another minute or
so. He was thinking hard, and listening eagerly.

But he could hear no sound, could imagine no sound, other than that made by the wind.

Then he moved, and, examining the ground, made his way slowly from the ride to the rocks, thinking the while, "It's impossible to follow my exact footsteps, because things have changed—but this was about the line I took with him."

Forcing himself through a tangle of holly and hawthorn, he came out into the open space and his feet struck against stone. In front of him the rocks rose darkly against the waning light, and he began to clamber about among them, over smooth round surfaces, along narrow gullies, and by cruel jagged ridges, seeking to find the exact spot where he had left the dead body. "It was about here," he said, after a time. "It was close by here. Prob'bly down there, where the foxgloves and the blackberries have taken root. Anyhow, that's near enough. I've come as near as I can;" and he sat down upon the ledge just above this hollow, and looked about him, attentively, in all directions.

The wind had ceased to blow; not a leaf stirred; silence reigned over the strewn boulders. Downward, where the ground fell away to a deep chasm, everything was indistinct; to the west, beneath banked masses of cloud, the last glow of the sunset showed in blood-red bands, and on this side all the intervening trees were black as ink; all about him the shadows filled every hollow, and the rocks were like shoals or reefs above the surface of a stagnant sea.

The place was a wilderness, a solitude, the dead and barren landscape of dreams—quite empty, unoccupied, a place that even ghosts would shun. He sat thinking, and listening; and soon it occurred to him that, though all seemed so dead and so silent, this place was really full of life. He heard the faint buzz of belated bees questing in tufts of heather or foxglove bells, a bat flitted over his head, some small furred thing scuttled past his feet; and in the air there were thousands of winged insects, whose tiny voices one could hear by straining one's ears. Listening intently for such murmurs, he thought: "Perhaps really and truly one has not any right to kill the smallest of these gnats. All that stuff about self-protection, an' struggle for existence, is just fiddle-de-dee in so far's God's concerned. He never meant it, an' never will approve of it. It's just nature's hatefulness and cruelty—not permitted or intended, an' to be put right some day."

It grew darker and darker, and the shadows rose all round him till he was like a man who had climbed out of the gray sea upon the only rock that was not yet submerged. When he got up presently and looked down at the hollow where he believed the corpse had lain, he could no longer see it. It was gone, lost in shadow.

Then he knelt upon his rock, and prayed—offered up the last agonized prayer of a despairing human soul. "O God—have mercy on me just so far's this. Don't let me die hopeless. I've submitted myself into Your hands. I don't complain. I don't question. I'm going to do it. But don't send me out in total darkness. Give me a blink of light—just one blink o' light before I go."

Was it this that had been wanted, this that had been waited for—the true acknowledgment, the true

submission, the cry for mercy of the repentant creature who has already tasted more than the bitterness
of death?

He rose from his knees, and without once looking
back left the rocks and came through the thicket to
the ride. It grew darker, the clouds dropped still
lower, and the wind again blew fierce and strong. He
left the broad ride and sauntered along one of the
narrow tracks. He could hear the wind as it tore
through slender branches high above his head, but
down here it did not touch him; and he strolled on
slowly, feeling extraordinarily calm, full of a great
reverence and wonder, not noticing external things
because he wished to maintain this strange inward
peace.

Then soon the voluminous but indefinite sensations
of mental tranquillity concentrated their soothing messages to make the comfort of one definite thought, and
Dale said to himself: " Christ has returned to me."

And then he saw Him—not for an instant believing
that he really saw Him, that he had passed from the
order of common facts into the realm of miracles,
that the usual laws of heaven had been broken by a
special material manifestation, or anything of that
sort; but that he saw Him with the beautifully clear
visualization for which he had longed and prayed.
And it seemed to him that the power of his thoughts
took a splendid leap, and that he could now understand everything that hitherto had been unintelligible
and inexplicable. Very God, and very man. Yes,
this was the man—a man after his own heart—the
comrade with whom one could work shoulder to
shoulder and never know fatigue—the unfailing friend

whom one dared not flatter or slobber over, but the grip of whose hand gave self-respect and the glance of whose eyes swept the evil out of one's breast. And this was God too—the only God that men can worship without fear; Whose power is so great that it makes one's head split to think of, and Whose love is greater than His power.

And the voice of Christ seemed to speak to him, not by the channel of crudely imagined words, but in a transcendent joy that was sent thrilling through and through him.

"Then I need not despair," he said to himself. "That was the voice of Christ telling me to hope."

He strolled on with bowed head, and remembered the night when he sat in Mr. Osborn's little room, staring at the carpenter's bench, and struggling between belief and doubt. He had said: " I want to be saved. I want the day when you can tell me I have gained everlasting salvation." And Mr. Osborn had answered him: " The day will come; but it will not be my voice that tells you."

It was dark, but he did not mind the darkness. He walked on, not knowing where he was going, and time passed without his thinking of the lateness of the hour. He had forgotten his wife and his home; he had forgotten Norah; he had forgotten all his pain.

Then the odd and unexpected character of an external object made an impression sufficiently strong to rouse him from his reverie. and he thought dreamily: " What is that? Why, yes, it is what I was asking for—a blink of light."

Suddenly, straight in front of him, he saw the gleam again. What could it be? Then again—something right ahead, in the darkness of the trees, a bright flicker—as might be made by a man waving a lantern. There it was again, but brighter than before, quite a long way off. And he walked on faster.

Then, looking up, he saw a red glow in the sky, and he thought: "The heath is on fire." He walked faster, saw a column of crimson smoke and a great tongue of flame above the pine trees, and thought: "It is much nearer than the heath. It must be right on the edge of the wood."

He ran now, and soon the track was brightly lighted and confused sounds grew plain—shouting of voices, the galloping of a horse, the clamorous ringing of a bell. The trees opened out and he was running along the high ground above those broken fences, looking down at the Orphanage gardens, at men clustered like black ants, at solid buildings that seemed to send forth sheets, lakes, and seas of flame.

He rushed down the slope, burst through wooden barriers and leafy screens, shouting as he came. In the glare on the upper terraces there were many people—men, women, children; some of the men vainly endeavoring to fix and work unused hose-pipes; others dragging away furniture, curtains, carpets that lay in heaps near the central hall; the greatest number of them struggling with ladders, advancing and recoiling in front of the low block at the further end of the building.

"Are they all out?" shouted Dale. "Have they all been got out?"

Terror-stricken voices answered as he passed. "There's seven they can't get at. . . . Seven have been left. . . . They're the little ones."

And running in the fiery glare, he thought: "Yes, mercy has been vouchsafed me. This is my chance."

All things were plain to him; there was nothing that he could not understand. This fire must have broken out in the low block he had passed, and at first it seemed insignificant; as a precautionary measure the girls were fetched out of that block; the bell had been rung, and a messenger was sent galloping to summon the engine and brigade which would not arrive for an hour; and the stupid guardians of the place had wasted precious minutes in what they considered another precaution only, carrying furniture from the big hall. Nothing was done at the further block, because that appeared to be in no danger. They hadn't reckoned with the wind. The wind had sent the fire licking up the woodwork, dancing over slates and tiles, springing at the roof of the hall; and all at once the far block was involved. A furnace blast of flame leaped at it, billowing waves of smoke rolled through it; and it crackled and screamed and blazed. The bigger girls had just time to escape; but the children, seven of the smallest, were left on the upper floor.

"It's Mr. Dale. Oh, Mr. Dale, 'tis pitiful. You can hear 'em squealin' up theer. Oh, Mr. Dale, sir, what can us do?"

The heat was tremendous, and as the men came staggering back they pushed him away. Then they clustered round him, each face like a fiery mask, and yelled to make themselves heard above the noise of the wind and the flames, the clatter of falling stone, and the cries of hysterical women.

He broke free from them, stood alone near the burning shell of the veranda, and hoarsely shouted

from there. " Come on, ma lads, Give me the ladder.
Don't shrink or skulk. Come on. If I can stan' it—
so can you. Fetch those floor-rugs."

He was almost breathless, but joy seemed to give
force to his laboring lungs. He was thinking:
" Mercy has been shown. I have been reserved for
this. Instead of destroying that one child, I am to
save these other children."

He had no doubt; he knew that he would do it.
Nothing could stop the man who was doing his appointed work.

To all others the thing seemed impossible. He had
taken off his jacket and put it over his head, and the
women became silent when they saw him climb high
on the ladder and spring blindfold through the flames.
The ladder fell with half its length on fire and then
smoldered like a shattered torch. Then they saw
clouds of smoke pouring outward from a window; and
the flames on the balcony lessened and grew dim, as
if choked by the smoke. Then there came a shout,
and the men with the stretched rug moved stanchly
to his call.

He was out again on the balcony, with a child in
his arms.

" That's one," he shouted, as he dropped her to the
men below. " I b'lieve they're all alive."

So he came and went, rapid and sure, carrying his
burdens. " That's two. . . . That's three. . . .
That's four. They're well-nigh suffocated—but
they're alive." He crawled on the floor to find them,
snatched the blankets and sheets off the beds,
wrapped them from head to foot. " That's five. . . .
That's six. She has fainted—but she's alive."

On the balcony the red-hot metal had burned his feet nearly to the bone, his blistered hands were big and soft as boxing gloves, even the air in his lungs was on fire. While he crawled and groped between the beds for the last of the children, the floor began to bulge and sag, and fragments of the plaster ceiling rained upon his head and back.

"That's seven. Fainted. Wants air. . . . Still alive."

They all shouted to him. "Don't go back, sir. There's no more. You've got 'em all out now. Oh, sir, don't go back."

But he went, gasping for breath, and muttering, "May be another. P'raps there's another. Better see."

He had got to the middle of the room when the floor gave way under him; and almost at the same moment there was a crash and the whole roof fell in. He went down amid the sudden wreck, down to a narrow couch of wood and stone, where he lay and still could think. He was pinned with an iron beam across his chest, in darkness, with the roar of the flames just above his head; smashed, mangled, roasting; but still full of a joy and hope that obliterated pain. He whispered faintly: "O God the Father and God the Holy Ghost, accept this my expiation."

And he whispered again.

"This fire has cleansed me. O Christ, take me to Thy bosom, white and spotless as the driven snow."

That was his last thought. There came another crash, a rending pang, and peace.

THE END

English Reviews of The Devil's Garden

London Times

It is good in these days of scamped art and hectic sentimentality to come across so strong, so carefully wrought, so artistically complete a story as that Mr. W. B. Maxwell offers us in his latest novel. Here is a book fit to take its place beside that earlier and masterly work of his, *In Cotton Wool*. Once more he adopts methods which are not without their great moments of surprise but are leisurely and deliberate. If Mr. Maxwell sets out to accomplish a task he carries it through. And readers of his new tale will, I am sure, agree with me that the result is worthy of the labor he has expended and that the impression conveyed by the finished design is of something not merely satisfying but curiously impressive. Mr. Maxwell's story may be described as the biography of a self-made man who is shown in the most striking and dramatic way succumbing to the elemental side of his nature at every crisis of his career. Fortunately a local disaster permits him to make atonement and redeem his sin with a singularly gallant and appropriate end. The history is recorded with unflagging vigor. Mr. Maxwell has had a fine theme and he has handled it finely. *The Devil's Garden* should extend its author's already high reputation.

London Morning Post

W. B. Maxwell's new book seems to us to be incapable of comparison with anything he has yet done and to elude the reviewer's ordinary terms of classification. It has the air that one or two books in a thousand have of having written itself, or, in other words, Mr. Maxwell appears to have been sure of himself and of his subject from begin-

ning to end of it. It has that appearance of completeness
and finality that suggests a book that had to get written.
The minor persons of the drama seem to belong, like Mr.
and Mrs. Dale, to a real world of flesh and blood. Dis-
inclined as we are for prophecies, we venture to think it
will stand the test of time.

London World

Mr. W. B. Maxwell is perhaps the most powerful and
the most arresting of the novelists of the day. His analy-
sis is masterly. He follows his man into the fog of religious faith, the crude materialism of which has probably
never been more definitely and unsparingly set forth. His
situations are dramatic, and they are treated with that
instinct for the right word, that subtle knowledge of what
to leave to the imagination, which is the dramatist's best
gift. The book abounds in clever sketches of men, all
touched with that insight which finds its complete expression in William Dale—one of the most elaborate and most
finished portraits in all Mr. Maxwell's fine gallery.

London Daily Citizen

Since the appearance of his first novel, Mr. W. B. Maxwell has been regarded as one of the most promising of
the younger generation of novelists. The individuality of
his style, the maturity of his thought, his grip of life, his
craftsmanship, made him stand out with glaring promi-
nence from the general ruck of fiction writers. But one
always felt that there was better to come, that the writer
had in him fuller, richer matter than he had yet given out.
There was an extraordinary sense of reserve power in his
work. And in his new book Mr. Maxwell has fulfilled the
promise of his earlier books. *The Devil's Garden* is a fine
novel; in some respects it is a great novel. It is undoubtedly the best thing he has done, the strongest, the firmest,

the most convincing. It places Mr. Maxwell absolutely in the front rank of modern novelists, among the few who can be numbered on the fingers of one's hands, of those who really count. Mr. Maxwell has, in fact, "arrived." His book has in it something of the inevitableness of a Greek drama. It is told with extraordinary power.

London Daily Chronicle

After the bosh and bathos, the howling sentimentality, the sickening gush, the nightdress stupidities so often offered to us as English fiction, it is a joy, a relief and a strengthening to read the full, fine novel which Mr. Maxwell has produced. It touches the primal passions, the ultimate, intimate realities, with restraint, sincerity and conviction. His patient synthesis of William Dale's personality can only be fitly described by the much-trampled adjective—masterly. The conception of Dale's way and methods of redemption is touched with genius. Mr. Maxwell has added to his laurels.

The London Globe

It is not until we stand well away from Mr. Maxwell's novel, and view it in retrospection, that we realize its amazing cleverness or appreciate its masterly craftsmanship. If Mr. Maxwell had not already made a reputation as a novelist, *The Devil's Garden* would have made it for him. By its power and impressiveness, *The Devil's Garden* easily stands out as one of the books of the year.

London Daily News

The book is something of a tour de force. It succeeds. It is a most impressive achievement. A novel of great power and a fine technical performance as well.

Pall Mall Gazette

The hesitating stigma which the Libraries Associations

have placed upon Mr. W. B. Maxwell's new novel must have surprised, not only the readers of *The Devil's Garden*, but all who have had occasion to enjoy and admire its author's brilliant gifts as a writer of fiction. The quality of Mr. Maxwell's work and the sincerity of his method are too well known for this disparagement to affect his reputation. He is a fearless and faithful student of life and too genuine an artist to cater to the merely prurient. It is gratifying to think that this present action will probably call renewed attention to the very fine work that Mr. Maxwell has been producing for the past half-dozen years. Some of his books are masterpieces of delicate anaylsis, and as a moralist there is no writer of fiction to-day who conveys a sterner or more bracing message.

London Daily Telegraph
Mr. W. B. Maxwell has contrived, in the form of fiction, a very powerful and impressive homily. Its glowing and vigorous sincerity carries conviction along with it. Mr. Maxwell is not afraid to paint life in its full colors. The tragedy has the air of being inevitable, and the plain language in which it is told seems thoroughly in harmony with the plain and honest study of life in the rough.

Aberdeen Free Press
Mr. Maxwell's novels are among the outstanding works of fiction of the year; they are always thoughtful and contain a definitely planned situation which is worked out with care and elaboration into smooth and flowing narrative which produces a deep and definite impression. He possesses a wonderful psychological insight which enables him to lay bare the inmost motives of his characters, and his figures are not types but realities. In his new novel the central figure is Mr. Dale, the village postman. The story is one of extraordinary power, told with sincerity and conviction which grip the reader to the end.

www.ingramcontent.com/pod-product-compliance
Lightning Source LLC
Chambersburg PA
CBHW020828030726
47496CB00001B/136